DEEP TRAUMA

A RILEY BRIGHTON THRILLER BOOK 1

KAT EDWARDS

sugar pine
PUBLISHING

Editing, design, and distribution by Bublish
Published by Sugar Pine Publishing

ISBN: 978-1-64704-968-3 (paperback)
ISBN: 978-1-64704-961-4 (eBook)

DEDICATION

This story is dedicated to my father, who still haunts me.
You were right, Dad. It had to be told.

CHAPTER ONE

"Get the hell out of the goddamned road," the enormous bald man growled.

Riley Brighton squinted up at the giant towering over her in the middle of the 101 Freeway. Blinded by the glaring headlights of the gridlocked pre-dawn traffic, she hadn't seen him emerging from the darkness. "Unless you have some kind of death wish," he added, brushing past her in her full leathers to get a better look at the body lying in lane three.

"Your timing's slightly off," she snapped back sarcastically, thinking she could have used someone his size only moments ago to help with traffic control. The man gave her a double take, locking his eyes on her when she pried her full-face helmet off and her long dark braid swung loose.

She scanned the scene again, wondering how many cars had run over the body, and how many had just narrowly missed hitting her. The pounding in her chest hadn't subsided yet, even though all five lanes of the southbound commute into the city were now at a dead standstill. And in LA, that meant the freeway would probably be tied up for hours. So, the man's tone seemed unnecessarily hostile now, in her view. If it wasn't for that, he might have found her a little chattier.

She might have explained how she'd come across the accident. That she'd been exceeding the speed limit, quite excessively no less, when the sight of the twisted, motionless body in lane three had come rapidly into the beam of her headlight. And that once she'd realized the form was human, she'd immediately pulled off the freeway and launched into action using a flair from her motorcycle's toolbox to get traffic stopped before anyone else got hurt.

Her knees were still quivering, and she wasn't entirely sure she could keep her breakfast down as she tried to process the horrific sight at her feet. As an ER physician, she was no stranger to trauma, but stumbling across such a grizzly scene on her morning commute had totally blindsided her. Especially as the victim was a fellow motorcyclist—an urban warrior, of sorts—in the battle against LA's notoriously distracted motorists.

Her throat seemed to pinch itself closed as she stared down at the man sprawled on the asphalt in front of them. His limbs were a jumble of incongruous angles, with open wounds, bloodless and gaping, like holes in worn leather. *No blood flow*, she noted. His heart had probably ruptured on impact. *Jesus,* she thought, the poor guy hadn't had a chance.

She glanced up again at the giant now breathing heavily at her side. His shoulders seemed to swell like a cobra's hood as he stared her down. Clearly, he wanted her out of the way. She considered that perhaps he was an off-duty police officer, or maybe a first responder on his way into the city for an early shift. When she broke from his gaze, the man extended a beefy arm, as if to restrain her, while he leaned in to get a closer look at the body. His verbal skills needed work, she decided. Riley stepped casually around him, determined to do what her training called for.

Slipping the reinforced glove off her right hand, she tucked it under her left arm, and knelt down on the pavement to check the body for a pulse she knew she wouldn't find. The victim was still warm, but just as she'd suspected, there were no signs of life. In fact, his head and neck were so contorted that for a moment she almost thought his helmet was on backward. She leaned forward, reaching for one of his hands—the one that wasn't pinned under his chest—and closed her fingers around it gently. It was small for a man, almost delicate, clearly the hand of someone quite young.

"Sorry, buddy," she murmured looking down at him. "Hope it was quick."

The giant stepped back as she got to her feet, he seemed now suddenly appeased. Riley shot him a dismissive glance as she headed toward the emergency lane where she'd left her bike. "Your turn now, big guy," she called over her shoulder. With all the witnesses in the southbound lanes presently staring at the spectacle from behind their windshields, she was confident that the oversized man would keep traffic in check until the CHP arrived.

As she reached her motorcycle idling on the side of the road, Riley turned to survey the scene one last time. *Where was the victim's bike?* she wondered. The large black pickup truck on the shoulder probably belonged to the giant, but there was no sign of the dead man's ride.

She pulled the cuff of her reinforced jacket back, checking her wristwatch—6:15 a.m.

Her eyes swept methodically over the scene. Maybe the motorcycle had been launched over the concrete divider into the northbound lanes. But she hadn't noticed traffic on that side of the barrier swerving or breaking to avoid anything.

And now, she heard the distant wail of the CHP and paramedics approaching. *Finally!*

She grasped the end of her braid and wrapped it around her neck before pulling on her full-face helmet again.

The deep, resonant blare of a fire truck's horn punctuated the din of sirens as it neared the scene, its red lights splintering the darkness in eye-piercing shards.

Riley straddled her Kawasaki Ninja 300 cc sportbike. She depressed the clutch, revved the throttle a little and kicked the stand up. Then she threw it into gear and pulled her wheels back onto the tarmac.

Ahead of her, all five lanes of the southbound 101 Freeway into the city were now wide open—a stretch of deserted asphalt replacing the typical congested snarl of metal and motion she usually dueled with each morning. She was on the right side of a backup for once, and that meant, despite the delay, she'd still make it to work on time.

A moment later she was leaning into the wind created by her rapid acceleration. She wrapped herself around the low, sleek black torpedo as closely as the designer's signature adorning the fuel tank under her chest. Then her left foot clicked smoothly through the range of gears until she was nothing but a streak of light in the darkness.

CHAPTER TWO

Only minutes later, Riley was making her way across the pedestrian bridge that united the four-level parking garage and LA City General Hospital. Within the throng of foot traffic, now thick in both directions, she recognized the determined stride of Astrid Wolf, one of her physician colleagues from the emergency department, approaching from the opposite direction.

Riley checked her watch again. No, she wasn't late. She hadn't thought so; the sun was just coming up, its muted golden glow splintering through the fencing of the pedestrian bridge.

Astrid was probably just on a mission for an early breakfast after a long night shift. That was her habit. But even at a distance, something seemed off. Riley read her colleague in the way one read an old friend—though, admittedly, they didn't seem to talk much anymore.

"Jackass Jackson's looking for you," Astrid snapped as she passed by without even making eye contact. "Better arm yourself with a tranquilizer dart and a straitjacket."

Riley stopped in her tracks as if she'd just been caught in a snare. "Wait. Why?"

Wolf spun around, raising an eyebrow and smirking, in the way that always made the bite of her wit just a little sharper. "Hell if I know, Brighton. That man's always got someone's nuts in a sling. Don't take it personally."

Riley felt the sting when Astrid turned then, disappearing down the stairwell—headed, no doubt, to the breakfast burrito truck parked below on Spencer Street. She missed the old Astrid, the one who had always been on her side during residency, the one who would have taken the time to show a little more concern. Wolf had changed it seemed. Ever since she'd been passed over for promotion two years earlier by the department's chairman, Dr. Jackson.

Riley caught Wolf's warning again as she heard the pneumatic hiss of the ER's glass doors as they opened to admit her, this time from one of the night nurses. "Dr. Jackson's looking for you, Rye," she announced, tilting her head apologetically as she wheeled a legless old man with a bloody nose toward the triage desk.

"What the hell is he doing here so early?" Riley muttered to herself scanning the corridors on her way through the department. As she passed the already congested ambulance entrance on her way to change into a pair of scrubs, she saw Dr. Rudolph Jackson striding toward her, full tilt, his brow furrowed under his graying temples. The tails of his long white lab coat fanned out like the ventral fins of a great white shark behind him; his eyes fixed on her from halfway down the hallway.

She immediately dropped her gaze and darted into the women's locker room, letting the door swing closed behind her.

Four years at Northwestern's prestigious Feinberg School of Medicine in Chicago, three years of residency in emergency medicine at LA City—the number one program in the country—and now her faculty position in that same level one trauma center had taught her more than just how to manage the sick and injured. Like most warriors in her field, Dr. Riley Brighton knew the importance of placing focus over feelings. Afterall, it was the most basic of skills in her line of work. Jackson had done his best to drill that into her during her first year of residency.

"Feelings are personal, Brighton; do us all a favor dear, keep them to yourself."

And at that very moment—feelings barely in check after the ordeal she'd faced on her morning commute—she opted to keep very much to herself by taking the back hallway out of Jackson's path.

It was halfway through the morning when Rudolph "Jackass" Jackson finally caught up with her. Riley was suturing one of the ER's regulars: Leonard Robinson, a fifty-five-year-old man known on the streets as Shorty. It seemed Shorty had had another unfortunate run-in with his wife, Paula.

"That woman! Sheesh! She got her a mighty fine right hook, Doc," Shorty lisped through the gap previously occupied by his front teeth.

"I'll need you to stop talking for just a moment," Riley said again, dabbing the man's lip with a gauze sponge to stem a steady trickle of blood. "You'll want me to fix this as best as possible, sir, and that means no more talking or moving for just a few more minutes please."

"You got it, Doc," he said before realizing his mistake. "Sorry, sorry! Okay, I'll hush up now. But I just wanted to tell you, Doc, only reason this happened, see, is 'cause Paula ain't been taking her meds. I don't want nothin' bad to happen to my woman. You feel me?"

"Got it," Riley said softly through her mask, realizing that the woman Shorty still affectionately referred to as Taller Paula was no doubt downtown, being booked for spousal battery at that very moment.

Riley knew all too well that Paula—as dangerous as she was when unmedicated—likely meant the world to him. She also knew the woman's lack of access to appropriate resources was an unfortunate reality in the constellation of problems faced by those down on their luck and living on the streets. She still grappled with the order of things. Which came first: being homeless in LA or a decline in mental health?

"That's much better," Riley said, pausing to load the last thread of suture onto her needle holder. "Now let's finish up here, shall we? Just one more stitch and you'll be as good as new."

"Mm-hmm," Shorty muttered, doing his best to comply for another few seconds.

As Riley pushed the tray of used instruments away from her and straightened her back to stretch out the cramp she'd earned leaning forward to sew, she caught sight of Jackson over her shoulder. He was propped against the doorway, one leg crossing the other, in his spotless Brunello Cucinelli Italian oxfords and his long white lab coat. He seemed to be watching her every move.

"I'll finish up here, Dr. Brighton," the nurse who had been assisting Riley said, nodding his head in the direction of Jackson. "You go ahead if you need to."

"Thanks, Ben, I appreciate it." Riley ripped off her latex gloves and shot them into the open trash can before moving to the corner sink to wash her hands.

"My office, Brighton. Five minutes," Jackson commanded before striding off.

"Sounds like you in hot water, Doc," Shorty lisped, lifting himself up on one elbow. "Want me to sic Taller Paula on that pompous ass? I owe you one."

"That's quite all right, thank you, Mr. Robinson. I think I can handle this on my own. See what you can do to make sure Paula takes her meds, though. There's a free mental health clinic on Maple Avenue. I'll leave their business card at the checkout desk with your discharge instructions. Make an appointment to see a counselor there named Jenna. She'll take good care of Paula." Turning toward the nurse, Riley added, "Ben, make sure Mr. Robinson gets a tetanus booster before he's discharged and see if someone from social work can come and chat with him, would you?"

Placing a hand on Shorty's shoulder, Riley bent down, making eye contact. "Mr. Robinson, domestic violence is no light matter, sir. I want you and Paula both to be safe."

"Right on, Doc." The man's voice was heavy with gratitude. "She don't feel safe—that's the problem, see. Ever since what they done to her li'l sister, she ain't been the same."

"I'm sorry to hear that. I hope Jenna at the clinic can help."

"You seen it on the news, Doc? How they left poor Celia and her boy to die? Set them both on fire and all. Like they was nothin' but trash."

"That sounds just awful." Riley said, shaking her head. She knew that in that moment, her own facial expression couldn't have been a source of comfort for Shorty. Afterall, as a kid, she'd lost her father in a fire. "That kind of tragedy will really scar someone," she almost whispered, eager to move on.

"I've got this, Dr. Brighton. You go ahead to your meeting," Ben assured, assisting Shorty to his feet.

Riley nodded in appreciation on her way out. Then she paused in the doorway and turned to the nurse. "It's Riley. Ben, it's just plain *Riley*. I'm not *your* doctor or your professor. I'm your colleague, your peer."

"Oh right." He chuckled with a wink. "True that, Riley—it's just that Dr. Jackson gets a little riled when the nurses don't use titles."

"Remind me when I get back from his office to share some of the titles we have for *him* with you," Riley said, grinning playfully.

Rudolph Jackson's spacious office and adjacent conference room were four floors above the emergency department in an administrative block of the hospital—far from the busy trenches, where there was little chance his Italian leathers and silk ties would ever encounter the hazards of blood and the other bodily fluids his staff waded through daily.

"Come" was all he barked when Riley knocked on his office door.

Before stepping in, she took a second to straighten the collar of the oversize lab coat she'd snatched from a row of hooks outside the operating rooms on her way up. Three sizes too large, the jacket hung awkwardly over her slight form like an unfurled mainsail. Rules were rules, though, and Riley knew never to visit Jackson's office without covering up her bloodstained scrubs. She looked down at the name embroidered on the top pocket: *Dr. Hudson, Intern*. The pockets were stuffed with dozens of handwritten clinical notes on three-by-five cards. Whoever the coat belonged to was evidently very tall and quite attuned to detail. She'd be sure to return it to the exact hook she'd lifted it from.

"Good morn—" Riley had started as she entered, but she was immediately taken aback when she saw two hospital administrators sitting at Jackson's conference table. Their conversation came to a sudden halt as all eyes turned to her.

Riley recognized the bigwigs at the table as Dr. Hilary Stephens, the current chief of medical staff—a woman in her fifties, notorious for her stony demeanor—and Roger Harrison, the puffy-faced director of hospital personnel.

"Sit" was all Dr. Jackson said, motioning to the head of the conference table from his chair behind his desk under the expansive windows.

"Don't mind if I do," Riley said casually, though, admittedly, she felt her heart skip a beat at the sight of the administrators. This wasn't an ordinary meeting. Even Jackson's tone was edgier than usual, and that was saying something.

As she pulled out a padded armchair and eased into it, Jackson got up from his desk and took a seat directly behind her. This maneuver left Riley staring at the two administrators facing her from across the conference table. Jackson was completely out of sight now yet uncomfortably present—and *literally* breathing down her neck. Riley recognized the move as one intended to intimidate, but she neither flinched nor offered any objection to the odd seating arrangements.

Stephens was the one to break the silence as she consulted the legal pad sitting on the table in front of her.

"Good morning, Dr. Brighton." The woman's angular face contorted into a gesture intended to pass for a smile, though Riley wasn't buying it. "We would like to ask you a few questions about the Williams case. We have concerns."

Riley forced a neutral expression. *The Williams case, shit*, she thought, she should have guessed.

Harrison from personnel—a bit of a mouth breather, Riley noted—placed a large sweaty palm on the tabletop between them. Leaning forward, he softened his tone in the way one might when talking to a child. "You see, Dr. Brighton," he chimed in, "we'll need to know *exactly* what happened in the ER that night."

"From your perspective, that is," Stephens quickly added. She seemed to be implying that Riley's assessment might be in a class all its own.

Ah. The ol' good cop, bad cop routine.

Riley eyed the pair. Her mind drifted to Jackson behind her. And what was his role? Not to referee, she was certain of that. Riley could feel his eyes burning into her back, though the man remained conspicuously silent.

"We know you have a stellar reputation in the department, Dr. Brighton." Now Harrison was openly fawning. Apparently, he was the good cop. Riley found herself intrigued by his bloodshot eyes. They sank into his doughlike face in the way two hot coals might. *Hypothyroidism?* she wondered. *Sleep apnea, maybe?* The sight was so distracting, she missed the first part of his sentence. ". . . and that your judgement is regarded as excellent. It's just that we are getting some conflicting stories about who was in charge."

Riley leaned her elbows on the conference table casually, suppressing the urge to crack her knuckles. "I'm happy to shed any light that I can on the events of that evening, of course. To be honest, I'm a little shocked no one has raised questions before today." Riley kept her tone neutral, though she knew her words must have been like a wrecking ball to Jackson's plan of intimidation. Why hadn't he asked her about that night himself? Wasn't that his responsibility? Why the ambush with administration?

She put two and two together. Jackson wasn't going to be happy with the details of the Williams case. That was clear. Especially if what Riley suspected was true about Tobias Bach, the residency director working that night, whom Jackson had inexplicably appointed instead of Astrid Wolf two years earlier.

The room fell silent in the wake of Riley's accusation. Harrison's eyes shifted to Jackson sitting behind her, and then to Hilary Stephens. Riley sighed in satisfaction, knowing Jackson was likely squirming in his seat after the hardball she'd just pitched. She focused on the midmorning sun streaming through the office windows, highlighting tiny particles of dust suspended in midair as the silence persisted.

"The unexpected death of a child in the ER is, of course, a huge concern for us," Stephens finally said, deflecting Riley's accusation.

Riley felt her face flush. She locked her eyes on the woman.

"That child's name was Leroy Williams, Dr. Stephens." Riley paused, checking her tone before continuing. "He was a sweet, innocent little six-year-old who had suffered an unbelievably cruel life."

Stephens sat back in her chair, pale faced, crossing her arms over her chest and dropping her gaze. Riley wasn't moved by the woman's retreat. Was it the tragic death of a child or the inevitable malpractice suit that had Stephens so concerned?

"Our records show the little guy had been in the foster care system ever since the death of his mother last year in a fire that left him badly burned," Harrison from personnel interjected without looking up.

"He never talked about the fire." Riley's gaze drifted to the window. "I'd always hoped it was something he didn't remember.

Most of his visits to the ER were for his asthma attacks. No doubt a result of the injury his lungs had sustained in the weeks he'd spent on a ventilator in the ICU." She felt her throat threatening to cinch itself closed, but she managed to squeeze the words out. "He was the bravest little kid I've ever met."

She took a breath and refocused, realizing her quarrel wasn't with Stephens or with any potential plaintiff attorneys, but with Jackson himself. If what she suspected was right—that his ally, Bach, was the one actually responsible for the child's death—Jackson would do everything in his power to hide the facts. Riley had seen how he operated on that front on so many occasions. For one, there was the time he covered for Bach after a teen had accused him of inappropriate conduct when her mother had left the ER briefly to park her car. The girl's allegation had conveniently been chalked up to the effects of the pain medications she'd just received for a broken arm. As far as Riley could tell, no formal complaint had ever been filed about the incident. And then there was the time a streetwalker had said Bach told her she got exactly what she deserved after her pimp had almost beaten her to death. Bach didn't even deny that one. He'd simply doubled down, saying the woman needed an education, and he saw that as his role. There were so many other stories that had circulated in the department about Bach's misconduct over the years, it was inexplicable to Riley that the man still held a medical license.

He'd always made her skin crawl. She thought back to the first time she'd ever heard about Bach. It was during her residency when she'd been a first-year. He was just finishing his third and final year of training in those days. They'd both been working on the night shift when one of the nurses had come to Riley for help.

"Dr. Bach is out of control; someone needs to do something." The nurse had been shaking as she burst into the room where Riley was caring for a heart attack victim. "He's cruel in a way I've never seen before."

"What are you talking about?" Riley pulled her aside, keeping her eyes locked on her patient's heart monitor.

"Dr. Bach is sewing his patient's lacerations using a local anesthetic I've explained to him is expired, so the poor woman is in agony. Every time she complains or moves, he cusses her out. I don't know what's wrong with that man."

"I can't leave this patient right now," Riley had pleaded, looking over her shoulder at the woman. "Can you get someone else in there to help you?"

"I've already tried. No one wants to confront him."

Riley's patient had been unstable—she couldn't step away, not even for a moment—but she'd felt her blood boil on hearing the nurse's account.

The next morning at the end of her shift, she and the nurse waited outside Jackson's office for him to arrive. She'd been shocked at his response, totally blindsided.

"You're not much of a team player, are you, Brighton?" Jackson said, towering over her, his hands tucked deeply into his lab coat pockets. "Dr. Bach has a bright future in this department. We're lucky to have him. I have it on good authority that his family is responsible for the anonymous funding our residency program has been receiving the last few years. So, you see, in essence, Brighton, you owe him one."

After that, Riley found herself scheduled to work every weekend for the entire summer. Retribution that had seemed clearly unfair, but the worst part was hearing that the nurse who had reached out to her for help that night had been fired for reportedly not checking the expiration date on the local anesthetic Tobias Bach had used. All Riley could make of it was that Jackson really believed Bach's family was the source of the department's anonymous funding. And Tobias had never dispelled those rumors; why would he? Riley knew they were false, but she wasn't at liberty to disclose the truth, not in those days, not while she was still in her residency. Even as a first-year, she wondered how Jackson could be so naïve.

But that was a question for another time. She had more pressing matters to contend with now—like what kind of department head didn't perform his own investigation into the tragic and unexpected death of a child before orchestrating an ambush of his staff by administration.

One who's not interested in the facts, she decided.

The picture was coming slowly into focus, and she didn't like the way it was shaping up. Someone was going to have to take the fall again for Jackson's golden boy, Bach. And it was beginning to look like this time, that someone would be Riley Brighton herself.

CHAPTER THREE

Riley sat in the staff lounge, sipping old coffee from a paper cup and reflecting on her meeting hours earlier with Jackson and the two administrators. She had done her best to keep her composure, but she still felt the heat rising in her chest. The problem was she didn't have the proof she needed. Not yet anyway. But in her bones, Riley knew Bach was to blame for whatever had gone wrong that night in the Williams case—and there now seemed to be a concerted effort by Jackson and the administration to cover it up.

She *hated* Bach. That's what had Riley doubting herself. She *wanted* it to be him. She wanted him to go down for whatever had happened to the kid. Everyone knew little Leroy Williams had been through absolute hell. What six-year-old deserved a death sentence after having survived third-degree burns over 80 percent of his body in the fire that left him *orphaned?* Not to mention the dozens of painful surgeries he'd endured in the following months.

Bach was inept at best, in her opinion. And if the night-shift nurses were right, he was a sociopath.

Riley checked her watch. It was time to get back to the trenches. Her colleagues were probably already in over their heads; the ER was always bustling by that time in the afternoon, and she had heard at least one ambulance arrive in the last few minutes. Just as she stood to get back to work, two LA City paramedics entered the break room, chatting.

". . . and no motorcycle anywhere to be found!" a tall brunette was saying.

"Totally bizarre. Hit-and-run, of course?" the chunky blonde asked.

"Looks like it."

"But what? They stole his motorcycle after they ran him down? Makes no sense."

"Nope. Here's the crazy part: CHP says he didn't even have a motorcycle, just the motorcycle helmet. And get this—the helmet was on *backward*, so he was essentially blindfolded."

"That's nuts. What the hell?"

Riley tried to keep her voice from rising. "On the 101 this morning?"

The paramedics exchanged a quick glance, then the brunette nodded at her. "Yeah. You hear about it too, Doc?"

"Yeah. Crazy, right?" she said, nodding slowly. But just like her gut instinct regarding Bach's culpability in the Williams case, Riley's internal alarm bells were going off. It was beginning to look like what she'd come across on the freeway that morning was more than just a bizarre motorcycle accident. Was it a case of suicide? A murder?

✳ ✳ ✳

It was dark when Riley got home that evening. That was the thing she disliked most about twelve-hour shifts in the fall and winter—it was almost as if she were living in a world without the benefits of sunlight for half the year.

Indio met her at the front door of her bungalow, his tail wagging wildly, his wet jowls quivering with joy as he huffed a greeting. Riley dropped to her knees and hugged the dog's neck before sitting on the floor to pull off her long boots. A pile of mail sat on the entryway tiles where it had landed when the postal worker popped it through the slot in the front door earlier.

"We'll go out for a run after dinner, Indy" she said, rubbing the dog's ears. "Easy boy, easy." And with her words, Indio melted into a groaning puddle at her side, just as he had four years earlier when she'd rescued him from the shoulder of the highway.

Later, after a dinner of leftover pasta puttanesca, Riley sat on her couch with her three-legged cat, Artemis, and Indy at her feet as she sifted through the day's mail. The local news was on TV, the volume low.

A large decorative envelope, obviously a formal invitation, caught her eye among the usual litany of junk mail and coupons she'd retrieved from the entryway. It was a weighty, overstuffed letter. Riley smiled at the name of the sender: The Shira Altman Foundation. She tore the package open and examined the contents. Just as she reached for her phone to call her mother, a TV news broadcast caught her attention.

"In a second baffling incident this month, a pedestrian was struck and killed on the 101 Freeway in predawn rush-hour traffic. LAPD is withholding further information until the victim is identified, but similarities between this case and that of a blindfolded young woman killed two weeks ago on the same stretch of freeway are undeniable." The newscaster paused briefly with a solemn expression. "Anyone with information about the incident is urged to contact the Los Angeles City Police Department." A phone number with a local area code flashed on the chyron at the bottom of the newsfeed. Riley immediately raised her smartphone, quickly snapping a picture of the number.

"Crazy," she muttered, absently rubbing her forehead. She reached for the control to turn the volume up, but the reporter had moved on to the next story without skipping a beat.

She sat on the edge of the couch, phone on speaker mode and balanced on her knee. The number rang at least ten times before it was picked up. After Riley had relayed a brief description of what she'd witnessed that morning at the accident scene on the freeway and provided her contact information, she was informed that one of the officers assigned to the case would reach out to her soon.

She tossed her dinner dishes into the sink, pulled on a sweatshirt, and grabbed Indio's leash.

As Riley's running shoes hit the sidewalk, the dog hesitated. He tugged on his lead, turning back in the direction of the house and sitting defiantly.

"What is it, boy?" Riley's eyes took him in curiously.

When the dog refused to budge, she scanned her surroundings, glancing over her shoulder back toward the hedges that bordered her front yard. It occurred to her suddenly how quiet the street was. There was an unusual stillness in the air. She found herself holding her breath. Indio cast his eyes up toward her and stopped his panting, as if he too were listening intently. Riley felt the hairs on the back of her neck rise, almost as if someone were watching her. Her eyes swept along the sidewalk in both directions. Nothing seemed out of order. She shrugged it off. *A bad day will do that,* she mused, wondering if the dog was perhaps picking up on her angst.

"Let's go, Indy." She nudged the dog again with a quick tug on his leash and broke into a run. A minute later, they had settled into a comfortable pace on their normal route around the neighborhood, the hazy light of the streetlamps overhead spotlighting their way.

By the time they returned home, it was pushing ten-thirty. Riley showered, pulled on her robe, cracked open a cold India Pale Ale and tackled the dishes in the kitchen sink. She planned to surf in the morning; it was her day off, so she wanted to get to bed by eleven.

As she finished up in the kitchen, she found herself rehashing the events of the day: finding the downed motorcyclist—scratch that— finding the *dead pedestrian with a motorcycle helmet on backward,* getting all that freeway traffic at the scene to stop without getting herself killed, the encounter with the belligerent giant who'd ordered her out of the road, the run-in with Jackson and the administrators over the Williams case, and now the latest unsettling detail: the dead man she had come across on the 101 might be connected to a similar incident on the same stretch of road earlier that month.

Suddenly, the idea of going surfing the next morning felt irresponsible, dwarfed by her growing suspicion that what she'd witnessed as the first person on the scene might have more importance to the case than she'd imagined. Maybe she should cancel her beach plans and just head down to LAPD to make sure someone got her statement.

Through the dimly lit archway between the kitchen and the living room, Riley saw Indio suddenly fly off the couch and park himself, ears perked, at the front door.

Someone was outside. At this hour, that was odd.

Riley flipped off the living room light and crouched down next to Indy, peering through the mail slot in the front door, the dog's low, soft growl reverberating in her ear.

A marked LAPD patrol car was parked across from her driveway and two figures were approaching.

CHAPTER FOUR

The uniformed police officer sitting on the couch across from Riley turned his squawking shoulder radio down to a soft chatter and pulled out a small notepad from the Velcro pocket on his jacket with his name embroidered on it: Garcia.

Riley rested a hand on Indy's head, keeping him calm and within reach as she perched on the edge of a stool she had dragged in from the kitchen. The second officer remained standing, leaning against the archway of the small entry hall, chewing relentlessly on a wad of gum and twirling a set of keys around his middle finger.

"Go on, ma'am; what happened next? Was the victim conscious when you arrived? Was she moving at all?"

"She?" Riley said suddenly, wondering if they were talking about the same accident.

"They," the gum chewer corrected. "Did *they* have a pulse?" He pushed himself off the wall briefly, shifting his sizable weight as he shot a furtive glance at his partner. "Seriously, Garcia, didn't you just take the department's sensitivity training?"

The officer's sarcastic tone caught Riley off guard.

"Right, did *they* have a pulse?" Garcia repeated, a slight flush rising in his cheeks.

"No . . . no signs of life at all."

Riley heard her own words tumble out of her mouth like clods of dirt tossed carelessly into an open grave. She was struck by how cold she sounded. Cold and clinical. Not at all how she had felt at the scene that morning. Not how she felt right now.

But surely sensitivity wasn't a requisite for the current conversation. All this was just a matter of routine for them, wasn't it? For all of them. For police officers, first responders, and people like herself. People who operated on the dark edges of life in LA, in that hazy band between civility and the brutal reality that occasionally shattered the peace of normal people's lives.

"And the man you've described," Garcia went on. "The individual who directed you out of the road—did he give a name?"

The officer leaning against the wall cut in. "More importantly, did you give him *your* name?"

"No, I pretty much left as soon as he took over. It looked like he knew what he was doing. I had to get to work, anyway, and it was apparent my services weren't needed there. Besides, he was right," Riley admitted reluctantly, thinking back on how the scene had unfolded. "It was dangerous for me, standing out there in the middle of that freeway. I've treated so many people in the ER who were foolish enough to stray into traffic on a busy road after an accident. They don't often survive . . ." And now, hearing her own words, it struck her, just how careless she had been with her own life that morning. She hadn't been herself lately, she realized. Not since she'd lost little Leroy Williams a week earlier. Nothing had been the same since that night.

"Here's my card." Garcia tucked his notepad away, dug into his breast pocket, and extracted a card with bent edges. Handing it to Riley, he added, "If you think of anything else, you can contact me any time. You don't have plans to travel in the next few days, do you?"

"Ah no." Riley hesitated, glancing back and forth between the two officers. "Is there a problem if I do?"

"No problem," the gum chewer conceded, standing just a little straighter. "But there may be more questions from our detectives as things develop."

"Of course. You'll know where to find me . . . Officer Hahn," she said, her eyes settling on his name tag. "If I'm not here at home, I'm in the ER at City General most days."

Hahn merely dipped his cap politely before he and his partner walked out to their vehicle.

Riley locked the door behind them. Indy let out a soft groan and cocked his head, ears perked, until he heard the squad car pulling away.

"Come on, boy. It's bedtime. They're gone now. Let it go, buddy."

A moment later, the soft clicking of Indy's claws on the hardwood floor trailed behind her, down the hallway and into her room.

CHAPTER FIVE

The water was frigid at Zuma Beach the next morning as Riley hit the surf. She was glad she had worn her full-length wetsuit and not her shortie.

She paddled through the ice-cold spray of the surf and out past the breakers, greeting her fellow surfers from afar with the usual cheers and hoots and the universal surfer's hand gesture: the *shaka*. There were Paul, Brian, and Dave, and a little farther up, Charlie and the older guys. And out past the break was that tall gal, the one who drove the Sprinter van that looked like it could hold a dozen surfboards. *What's her name? Holly? Yeah, right, Holly.*

Riley waved in the woman's direction and swung her board wide so she could catch the next swell unobstructed and without getting in anyone's way.

An hour later, when she was thoroughly exhausted and numb from the cold, Riley sat on the beach watching the swarm of early-morning surfers thin out as folks headed back to the grind of their normal lives. Only the die-hards, like the persistent gulls squawking above, remained. Most of them—the older, retired guys like Charlie and company—still hung in there, playing like kids in the surf.

Riley had forgotten to pack her thermos of hot coffee for the morning. Perhaps her late-night visit from the LAPD had thrown off her customary beach-day preparations. After loading her board into her hatchback and hitting the changing room to rinse down, she peeled her wetsuit off with white, trembling hands, tugged on her fleecy sweats, and headed for the little coffee house across the street.

She found Holly from the beach in line at the coffee shop in front of her. She was easy to spot at almost six feet tall, with her wet shoulder-length hair leaving a ring around the collar of her pink sweatshirt. Riley had been wanting to ask the woman how she liked her van and if it was outfitted with racks for her surfboards.

"Hey, there," Riley said when she caught Holly's eye. "Beautiful morning, isn't it?"

"They're all beautiful when I can make it to the beach." Holly smiled. The woman was a striking sight up close, Riley thought, strong and beautiful, *the perfect athletic form*. And then a realization struck her. And in that split second, Riley knew she hadn't succeeded in hiding her surprise that she suspected Holly had not always been a Holly. That perhaps, at one time, she might have gone by the name Steve or Ryan, or Jim.

And now Riley could see Holly's shoulders tighten. The smile that had come so easily only a moment earlier was replaced by something less certain. Holly broke eye contact then as she scanned the almost packed coffee shop for an open seat.

"Want to share a table?" Riley offered almost too eagerly, motioning to a high-top next to the window as she picked up her order from the counter.

"Sure," Holly agreed, though she seemed to hesitate for just a moment as she gathered up a fistful of napkins, which she carefully wrapped around the giant bear claw pastry she'd just ordered.

"That's humongous." Riley laughed, nodding toward the pastry as Holly approached. "You can't possibly eat all that by yourself. I foresee sharing in your future."

"Really?" Holly softened, breaking into a wide smile as she took her seat. "Seriously, I usually order two of these," she said, tearing the bear claw in half and pushing a section across the red lacquered tabletop on a napkin toward Riley.

"I was just kidding, but truth be told, I *am* starving." Riley snatched up the pastry and sank her teeth into the offering before there could be any reneging. Holly's smile widened. And when Riley started to chuckle with her mouth full, Holly broke into a laugh that turned heads and had Riley feeling as if she was with an old friend.

"Cute ink," Holly said, pointing a well-manicured fingernail at the tiny blue butterfly tattoo on Riley's wrist. "You lost a loved one?"

"Yeah . . ." The smile left Riley's face. She set what was left of the pastry back on the napkin and tucked her hands under her thighs. "It's for my dad. He passed when I was just a little kid."

"Sorry, I didn't mean to pry. Anyway, it's pretty."

"Thanks." Riley tried to let it drop.

"My grandmother thought the same about butterflies after my grandfather passed. She said they were the spirits of the dead coming back to visit." Holly snorted ironically. "And she told me *I* was the one with an overactive imagination."

By the time Riley finished her coffee, half an hour had passed. She was just about to politely excuse herself from her chat with Holly and head home when, out of the corner of her eye, she caught sight of a few of the older surfers entering the coffee shop.

They were dressed in their baggy sweats and flip-flops, towels draped around their necks like scarves; Charlie was wearing his wraparound sunglasses—the type folks who have just had cataract surgery sometimes wear.

She couldn't hear what they were saying, but Riley could clearly read the body language of the older men, and it didn't bode well. They stared at the back of Holly's head as though watching a cockroach scurry through a restaurant.

Riley took a deep breath, set her expression neutrally, and did her best to focus on Holly, who was explaining that the reason she and her husband had invested in the Sprinter van was not for their surfboards but because of their five dogs.

Just then Charlie began making his way over. Riley felt every muscle in her body tense. When he reached their table, he placed a cold hand on the small of Riley's back, leaning his head between the two of them with a smirk on his face.

"Riley, does your boyfriend know you're out with another man?" Charlie sneered.

Riley saw red. Before she could think, she was on her feet. "Touch me again, old man, and see what happens."

Charlie took a step backward; clearly shocked at her response, he almost stumbled. The color drained out of Holly's face as she did her best to shrink, though the scene had clearly drawn the attention of everyone in the cafe.

"Apologize immediately to my lovely friend for that totally asinine remark," Riley demanded in a low growl.

Charlie looked as if he was about to pee himself. He pulled off his sunglasses, revealing an age-spotted, wizened face incapable of reconciling Riley's response.

"Fuck's sake, it was just a joke . . ." Charlie swallowed hard but refused to look in Holly's direction. Riley felt the rush of anger leaving her body as reason seeped slowly back to take its place.

"Very poor judgement on your part, sir," she said, keeping her voice low enough to encourage onlookers to mind their own business. "Now go on, Charlie. Get your coffee and move along. You were obviously out in that cold water for far too long this morning."

Charlie and the gang of older guys were out of the shop in minutes. Eager to save face, they lingered defiantly, huddling outside in the parking lot, coffee cups in hand, talking among themselves. Riley kept an eye on them through the coffee shop's window, occasionally catching them glancing up to where she and Holly were seated. She relaxed a little, seeing that the smirks had left their faces. After a while, they split up and went their separate ways, Charlie casting one last look over his shoulder at the window where Holly sat staring silently at him.

"I should be used to it by now, but it doesn't get any easier," Holly said, standing to gather her belongings and leave now that the coast had cleared.

Riley was at her side in a second. "I'm sorry that happened. Really, Holly. Some people—"

"Seriously, Riley, it's all good. I get it. That generation feels threatened by everything besides their patriarchy. Folks like Charlie just don't have the bandwidth for anything they can't predict or control." She sounded composed, but Riley could see the tears gathering in Holly's eyes before she pulled her sunglasses on. They headed for the exit, and Riley could feel the stares of the other coffee shop patrons trained on her back.

"I'll be okay. Thanks for walking me out," Holly said, looking down at Riley. "Trust me, it's worse when you get it from your own family. I can shake off clowns like Charlie."

"I can't imagine," Riley said, placing a hand on Holly's arm as they paused briefly in the parking lot.

Holly pressed her lips tightly together, a tear slipping from under her glasses. She brushed it away with the pad of her thumb. "I think he got to me because I just have so much shit going on right now at work. We've been dealing with a senseless tragedy. The last few weeks have been an absolute nightmare, and I suppose my threshold is a little lower than usual."

"Sorry" was all Riley could offer.

"Anyway, catch you next time," Holly said, pulling her towel around her neck and heading back toward the beach parking lot.

Riley watched her go, head bowed, shoulders slack.

On the drive home from the beach, Riley thought about how difficult things must have been for Holly that morning. How difficult they might have been every day of her life, and how many times she had endured such insults, such inhumanity. And for what? What difference did it make to someone like Charlie what Holly's gender identity was? How was that any of his business?

Riley was almost home when suddenly she recalled something one of the officers had said the night before about the fatality on the freeway. He had called the victim *her* only to be corrected by his partner, who had said *they*. Riley thought she now understood what the confusion about pronouns might have been. The deceased individual had probably been a transgender person like Holly.

Riley hadn't been able to stop thinking about the scene—specifically, the victim's hand, which, in retrospect, had been far too delicate for a cisgender man. And, of course, the troubling thought that what she had come across was not an accident at all. Who could have done such a thing? And in the wake of what she'd just seen happen to Holly, she wasn't about to let it go. Not until she knew more about who that unfortunate soul had been and how *they* had come to be in the middle of the freeway on foot, with a motorcycle helmet on backward.

CHAPTER SIX

After a quick run with Indy and a hot shower, Riley picked up the business card Officer Garcia had left on her coffee table the night before and examined the address listed at the bottom in royal-blue ink. She had no intention of waiting for the detectives to contact her. She had questions that needed answers.

Riley pulled into the West Valley LAPD parking lot at around noon, surprised to see that it was almost empty. *Lunchtime*, she deduced. She parked right up front, slipped off her helmet, secured it to the back of her road rocket, and jogged up the granite staircase toward the entry.

"What can I do for you, miss?" The desk sergeant blinked, taking in the look of her—the bikers' jacket, the long black boots, the thick, dark braid that hung down to her waist. Riley leaned her elbows on the counter, peering in through the slot in the bulletproof window.

"Hi, there," she said smoothly, trying to sound as relaxed as she could, knowing what she was about to ask was entirely unorthodox. "I was interviewed last night by . . ." She paused to reach into the top pocket of her jacket and pull out the business card. "Officer Garcia,

I guess it was," she said, pressing the card against the window for the sergeant to examine. "He and his partner came to my home to interview me about an accident that happened on the 101 yesterday morning. I was expecting to hear from the detectives by now."

The sergeant stared back at her, seemingly not following her line.

"You see, I'm an emergency physician at LA City, and I'd stopped at the scene of an accident to help. But unfortunately, the victim had already passed. I just wanted to know if there was anyone I might chat with about the latest on this incident." Riley waited, but the sergeant made no attempt to reply, so she added, "There was no update on the local news this morning, and I haven't been able to stop thinking about the patient. I was wondering if you had made an ID yet?"

"Speaking of ID," the sergeant managed, "do you happen to have your work badge on you, Doctor?"

"Of course. Sorry. Silly of me not to have started with that." Riley smiled as she pulled her official hospital ID on its colorful lanyard from a zippered pocket on her jacket. That seemed to do the trick.

"Let me see if Detective Roberts is available." The sergeant's eyes never left her as he picked up the phone on the counter.

*　　*　　*

Detective Roberts sat at her desk across from Riley. The woman slipped her reading glasses off and rubbed the bridge of her nose between her bloodshot eyes with her thumb and forefinger. Judging from the number of crumpled coffee cups in the trash can at her side, Riley guessed she had probably pulled an all-nighter.

"Thank you for stopping by, Dr. Brighton. Believe it or not, you just saved us a trip. I was about to call and see if my partner or I could come by to ask a few questions."

"Just plain Riley is fine, Detective. And of course, I'm happy to help in any way. I'm not sure what I can add, though. I told the officers everything last night. But I haven't been able to stop thinking about the victim. I was curious to know if family had been contacted." Riley's eyes swept over the detective's desk, taking in the scattered folders, the large tabletop calendar with its multi-colored ink scribbles, a pile of Sharpie markers, and the framed portrait of a small African American boy with a bow tie and a gap in his bright, innocent smile. He had the same inquisitive eyes and deep dimples as the detective.

"We're still in the early phases of this case, as you can imagine." The detective rested her head in her interlaced hands and leaned back in her chair. "To be honest, judging from the state of the body, I'd say our victim had probably been living on the streets for a while. We're still waiting for the autopsy results, and as of now, we don't have an ID. Unfortunately, we often don't make one on the unhoused . . ." She gave Riley a pointed look. "They're seldom missed, if you know what I mean."

It wasn't a question. Riley knew exactly what the detective meant. In a city of ten million, there were thousands of nameless, throwaway people, and hundreds of unidentified dead piling up in the morgue each year.

"Right," was all Riley could manage, the word barely a whisper.

"What is of most concern to me at this point is the man you described to officers Garcia and Hahn. The individual who dismissed you from the scene. Do you think you could identify him if you saw him again?"

"I think so, he was quite distinctive." Riley paused, conjuring the sight of the man, and with that, the hostile vibe he'd given off. "It was still dark. But he was quite large. A giant of a man, really."

"Did you see how he arrived at the scene? His vehicle?"

"There was a pickup truck parked on the side of the road near my motorcycle when I left. I already shared that fact with Officers Garcia and Hahn."

"Right. But anything unusual about it? . . . Like maybe front-end damage?"

Riley's mouth felt suddenly dry. "Jesus, I didn't look that closely," she said, feeling blindsided that she'd not even considered the possibility the giant had somehow been involved in the accident.

The detective seemed to be processing Riley's response carefully before she went on. "Did you happen to notice the color, or make of the vehicle? Or if there was anyone inside?"

"There may have been someone in the passenger seat. I can't be sure, though." Riley paused and then added, "It was an oversize pickup. You know the type—big wheels, high bumper. Dark color. Black, I think."

"Any stickers, flags, or distinctive markings?"

"Yes, actually, now that I think about it. There was a white sticker in the rear window. I've seen one just like it before, but I don't know what it symbolizes. It was, uh . . ." She tried to find the right words. "I don't know . . . a creepy-looking skull, I guess, with triangular eyes and pointed teeth. Do you know what it means?"

To her surprise, Detective Roberts nodded, opened her laptop, and typed something into the search bar of her browser.

"You mean like this?" she said, turning the screen toward Riley.

"Yes, that's it. What is it?"

The detective closed her laptop and leaned her elbow on her desk. Her fingers resting across her lips perhaps signaling a reluctance to respond. All Riley got out of her was a deep sigh.

"I'm guessing whatever it is, it isn't good," Riley surmised, attempting to prompt the detective to elaborate, but the woman's mind was evidently elsewhere.

"Thank you for saving us a trip today by coming in, Dr. Brighton. That's all. We'll be in touch if need be. I'll have the sergeant see you out."

"That won't be necessary, Detective, thank you." She stood and retrieved her jacket from the back of her seat. The woman answered only with a tight smile.

As she neared the exit at the end of a long corridor, Riley heard the rapid-fire clicking of the detective's low heels gaining on her.

"Dr. Brighton . . . Riley," she called out breathlessly. "One more thing, just an added precaution . . ." She lowered her voice as she closed the gap between them and said, "You might want to change your morning route to work for a few days. Or switch to commuting by car until we know more." Riley froze, taking in the detective's meaning. "We feel certain this was a violent crime, Dr. Brighton, not an accident. And right now, you're the only witness we've had come forward."

"Really?"

"Yes, other than a commuter in the traffic backup who told the CHP that the man you've described left the scene only a moment after you pulled away on your motorcycle."

"Got it," Riley said, doing her best to keep her tone neutral as she processed the detective's words.

A few minutes later, as she pulled out of the parking lot, she paused. Her moto idled in the driveway as she scanned the parked cars and pickups on either side of the boulevard. Instead of turning left to head back to the freeway, she took an immediate right and wound her way slowly toward home, on the Valley's surface streets, checking her rearview mirrors frequently.

CHAPTER SEVEN

Riley sat on the couch with dinner in her lap, surfing local TV news stations in search of updates on the freeway incident from the day before. Artemis lay next to her, purring loudly while Indio waited patiently at her feet, wondering if he would score any leftovers.

"Sorry, you're out of luck, Indy. It's all gone, bro," Riley said, wiping her mouth with a crumpled napkin and sliding her empty plate onto the coffee table. The dog gave her an incredulous double take. "You know where your chow is, boy."

Artemis stopped purring then, seemingly annoyed at the unnecessary chatter. She opened her big green eyes and gave Indy her customary scowl. The dog whined a soft rebuke before setting off for the kitchen, his head lowered.

Surprisingly, there were no news updates on the case Detective Roberts had referred to as a "violent crime." This unsettled Riley almost as much as the warning she'd been given about altering her route to work for the next couple of weeks. Was the man she had encountered at the scene really the killer? Why else would he chase her off? And why had he left the scene just before the CHP arrived? Bigger questions loomed now—like if he'd noted the license plate on her motorcycle and could possibly find her if he wanted to.

As soon as she'd come home from the police station, Riley had pulled out her laptop and looked up the symbol she'd seen on the pickup's back window—the skull insignia that Detective Roberts hadn't elaborated on or explained. The emblem was known as Jaded Justice, and while it was meant to represent a ruthless vigilante, some violent fringe groups embraced the symbol as an icon of their white supremacist beliefs.

Riley sat quietly, piecing the events together. She had surmised the freeway victim's identity was probably transgender from the interaction she'd had with the officers at her home the night before, and that, coupled with what she'd just learned about the skull emblem in the window of the pickup truck at the scene, sent a chill down her spine.

She flipped off the TV, rose from the couch, and headed to the kitchen to clean up. The last thing she wanted to do was dwell on the horrors of inhumanity and the murderous intentions of bigots.

After finishing in the kitchen, Riley took care of something she'd meant to do since the previous evening when she'd opened her mail. She picked up the overstuffed envelope with the return address of the Shira Altman Foundation and called her mother.

"Hiya, sweets. What's happening on your end?" her mother crooned, using the same upbeat tone she'd used ever since Riley was a kid. It always lifted her spirits.

"Hey, Mum, I've been meaning to call. I got the invitation yesterday. I'm so excited for you. I can't wait to attend."

"It isn't going to be a problem, is it, Rye? You won't ruffle any feathers at work, will you?"

"Oh, I imagine there will be a few confused looks, but I'm cool with it." Riley smiled, imagining Jackson's surprise when he finally learned of her family connections to the department's anonymous source of funding. "The timing might be perfect, in fact," she added without elaborating.

"Your cousins will be there too, I hope, and Aunt Naomi is coming from New York with her new husband."

"Oh . . . Wait, what number is he? Number three or number four?"

"He's actually a very nice man. I was quite surprised. You will be too."

"I'm sure you're right. I only hope she's happy this time." A silence hung between them before Riley added, "And that she has a good prenuptial agreement."

They both laughed then. "If there's one thing I know about my sister, Rye, it's that she's pretty savvy when it comes to the family trust. Her husbands are always more loaded than she is."

∗   ∗   ∗

Indio was at Riley's side the second he heard her lift his leash off the counter near the back door. It was well into the evening, and she grabbed her weighty new flashlight—the fancy one she'd bought from the Home Shopping Network—from the hallway closet. She zipped up her hooded sweatshirt and headed out for an evening walk.

For some reason, she had decided to leave home via the back entry across a small stretch of mowed lawn and out through the tall wooden gate into the alleyway. Perhaps she'd chosen the route out of an abundance of caution. It made sense, after all. If she needed to be vigilant on her commute because someone with nefarious intent might be looking for her on the freeway, then surely it made sense that someone might already have found her. It wouldn't have been hard to locate an address linked to her bike's license plate number.

The sweet perfume of the jasmine growing along the wooden fence in the alleyway hung heavily in the cool night air. The far-off hum of traffic on the freeway was somehow reassuring in its testimony to life as usual.

They walked side by side through the dimly lit alley. Riley's flashlight, on the lowest setting, swept over the gravel ahead in a soft glow. The patter of Indio's paws halted every now and again while he sniffed out some novelty or paused to listen to the distant barking of neighborhood dogs.

Several blocks later, Riley, feeling somewhat more relaxed, turned out of the alleyway and headed back home via the frontage road. She flipped the flashlight off—it was less necessary now with the occasional streetlamp—but that didn't mean she'd let her guard down. She scanned the vehicles parked along the curb in both directions on her street, looking for anything out of the ordinary. Traffic in the neighborhood was predictably light, given the hour. Most commuters would be home by now, perhaps finishing dinner or getting their children ready for bed.

Half a block from home, Indio suddenly froze, emitting a low, soft growl. Riley followed the dog's gaze to a vehicle cruising slowly down the road toward them, coming to a brief halt directly in front of her bungalow. She quickly stepped into the shadow of one of the many large pepper trees lining the street.

Crouching in the darkness next to Indio, Riley watched the car advance in her direction and then continue by, seemingly oblivious to her presence, despite the fact that whoever was driving was obviously in search of something or someone.

As she watched the vehicle depart, confusion began to replace her fear. There were no telltale emblems of hate plastered on the rear window. On the contrary, what sort of violent extremist would drive a Honda wagon with a rainbow bumper sticker?

A minute later, the street was quiet again, but Indio refused to budge from his position in the shadows. Just as Riley was about to insist they continue—they were almost home—she saw the giant.

He was sitting in his big black truck parked across the street from her bungalow, with a pair of field glasses pressed to his face.

And he was looking right at her.

CHAPTER EIGHT

Riley's heart pounded ferociously against her ribs. Before she could think, her hands were already in motion. She raised her flashlight, lodged it between two branches of the pepper tree, pointing right at the man's field glasses, and turned it on. Just as advertised on the Home Shopping Network, all one thousand lumens of it went straight into what she assumed were his night vision goggles.

Then she was running back toward the corner, half a block away. Indy was ahead of her, pulling wildly on the leash. Her feet flew over the darkened sidewalk like stray missiles. The dog rounded the bank of hedges near the intersection at full speed, almost pulling Riley out of her shoes. He took off toward the alleyway, fast as a racehorse with her in pursuit, gasping for breath.

By the time they reached the back gate to her bungalow, Riley realized they had made a terrible mistake in returning home.

Someone was in her backyard, sweeping the beam of a flashlight toward the alleyway. In her panic, Riley yanked Indio's leash, intending to bolt for a neighbor's house, but the dog was having none of it. He sat down, right where he was, and let out a sharp yelp of protest.

"Dr. Brighton is that you?" a voice called from the other side of the fence. It sounded vaguely familiar, but, more importantly, it seemed not to upset Indio, who lurched ahead, pulling Riley toward the intruder without hesitation.

"Who's there? Who is it?" Riley could barely get the words out.

"It's LAPD, ma'am. Officers Garcia and Hahn. Are you all right, ma'am?"

"Holy shit," Riley exclaimed, throwing herself through the gate.

*　　*　　*

Thirty minutes later, Riley was sitting on the couch in her living room, trying not to spill the cup of hot tea she held between trembling hands.

"As my partner said, Dr. Brighton, we just happened to be in the area. This is our usual beat—"

"It's Riley, Officer Garcia. Just plain Riley, please," she interrupted, doing her best to keep the sharpness out of her voice this time. "I'm telling you, there was a man sitting in a parked truck across the street, just two doors down, watching my house. I don't care if there's no one there now. He *was* there, and I feel certain it was the man I described to you and Detective Roberts. The same man I saw at the accident scene yesterday."

"Very well, ma'am . . . Riley," Garcia said. "There is no one there now. That's the good news." He paused, offering her the flashlight Officer Hahn had retrieved for her from the pepper tree half a block away. "As I was saying, we were just on our routine beat when dispatch received an anonymous call that there was a disturbance at this address. And, of course, since we had been here only last night, we recognized the house number immediately."

Riley sat there silently, not really hearing his words. Who could have called the LAPD? And why? What for? What had the disturbance been? The officers had already checked the house thoroughly. Nothing was out of place; there were no signs of a break-in. And Artemis seemed unfazed. That alone was proof that nothing untoward had occurred in the house in Riley's absence. None of it made sense.

"Detective Roberts informed us that she'd asked you to keep an eye out for anything suspicious—" Garcia started, but Riley cut him off mid-sentence.

"You mean like a giant psychopath stalking me?"

"Of course," he continued, casting his partner a look Riley couldn't quite interpret. "We'll keep watch on your place tonight, don't worry. The word is already out for the midnight shift to maintain a presence in the neighborhood. Unless you would feel more comfortable staying with a friend tonight," he added. "Any family in the area?"

"No, no. It's fine." Riley sipped her tea, settling herself. "I have Indy with me, and besides, I wouldn't want to alarm anyone," she said, processing how she might explain the current situation to her mother. "I'll call if there are any problems." She glanced at her watch, realizing how late it was already.

After the police left, Riley sat on her bed, surfing the internet for news on the freeway incident again, Indy at her side and Artemis curled up on one of her pillows. There was nothing posted that she hadn't already seen. No new insights to be gained.

She typed a second search into her browser—*blindfolded woman, fatality, 101 Freeway, September 2023*—hoping to find news on the other case that purportedly had similarities to the incident she had been involved in. In a few minutes, she hit pay dirt with a banner dated September 6, 2023.

TRANSGENDER WOMAN BRUTALLY MURDERED ON 101 FREEWAY

Post–Labor Day traffic was severely affected Tuesday after a pedestrian was struck and killed on the 101 in the predawn hours just north of Van Nuys Boulevard. The victim, identified as Lexi Drake of Santa Monica, is described as a twenty-four-year-old transgender woman, reported missing by her work colleagues a day earlier. Witnesses allege two men fled the scene in a pickup truck after the blindfolded victim was pushed into traffic lanes. Detectives from the West Valley division of the LAPD are investigating the incident as a potential hate crime. Anyone with information regarding this case is urged to contact the LAPD.

The story ended there. A growing sense of unease shadowed Riley as she sat in the soft orange glow of her bedside lamp listening to Indio's snoring. She couldn't determine if she was more upset about the horrific details of the incident or the cold, indifferent reporting that seemed to give equal weight to a brutal murder and the morning traffic report. She read the news clip again, this time trying to dispel the sense of injustice she'd felt bubbling up in her chest over the victim's outing. Perhaps that had been necessary to peg the incident for what it appeared to be. A hate crime.

Riley scrolled through the online posts of news stories from that week in September until all she could find was duplicate information. It was time to shift gears. She then checked the usual social media platforms using the same search terms. She followed each post down the ensuing rabbit holes until she had thoroughly exhausted all avenues without learning anything of substance. She'd have to get to sleep soon. The morning required the customary predawn start to her workday, and her commute always took a little longer when she wasn't on her motorcycle.

Just as she was about to give up, she came across the website of a citizen sleuth group with a rainbow trademark calling themselves the Avenging Allies. The post was made by the group's leader, identified simply as Themis. The organization specialized in solving hate crimes against the LGBTQ community and was pursuing information from the public on the Lexi Drake murder.

Riley clicked on the Contact Us link and put in her personal email address and a brief message asking to be contacted about a "possibly related matter."

Then she pulled the covers up, turned off her bedside lamp, and curled up next to Artemis with her hand wrapped tightly around the only weapon she had in the house: her weighty new flashlight.

CHAPTER NINE

Riley darted into the break room at work to take a few bites of her sandwich and down a cup of sludge that had once passed for coffee on the previous night's shift. The ER had been overrun all morning with casualties following the derailment of an early commuter train on its way into the city.

By the time Riley and her colleagues got the last critical patients off to surgery and the minor injuries triaged, the waiting room was thoroughly backed up with the usual cases. There would be no reprieve in the foreseeable future, but she realized suddenly that she was grateful for the distraction the morning's events had provided from the things that would otherwise have been on her mind. Until now, she hadn't thought about the terrifying incident with the man outside her house last night or the issues surrounding the Williams case, which she'd narrowly forgotten about. She was also thankful she hadn't seen Dr. Jackson, but that was no surprise, given his aversion to rolling up his sleeves during a disaster.

She wouldn't be able to avoid him for long, though. No doubt hospital administration would be demanding more answers about the unexpected death of a child on her shift. It was a foregone conclusion; there would be a lawsuit. Of course, that meant there would need to be a convenient scapegoat, and *that* was worrying her.

"Ambulance in trauma bay five, GSW," Sonya, one of the nurses, called breathlessly, poking her head into the break room as she flew down the hallway, pulling on a plastic apron over her scrubs.

"On it," Riley replied, taking one last swig of coffee and darting for the door, though she was anything but enthusiastic to handle another gunshot wound. She *hated* guns and the careless, callous way they could end lives with just the slightest tug on the trigger and how, with so little effort, a firearm could destroy families and the tranquility of entire communities. She had recently told a medical student that she'd seen enough bloodshed from gun violence over the last few years to float a boat. And perhaps that was the reason GSWs were now her specialty.

Three minutes later, she was up to her elbows in it. "Where the hell are the trauma surgeons?" she exclaimed, holding pressure on the large-caliber exit wound between the gang tattoos on a dying teenager's chest. The pungent metallic odor of an uncontrolled hemorrhage permeated the air as she packed the wound with sterile gauze to staunch the flow. The shrill tone of the patient's monitor alarms issued an ominous warning that drowned out even the overhead calls for "all hands on deck in trauma bay five."

"They're still tied up in surgery. The operating rooms have been overwhelmed all day with injuries from the train," Sonya replied, shouting above the racket. She snatched the intercom off the wall and alerted the blood bank to initiate the massive transfusion protocol stat.

"Good thing he's already intubated. I'm glad you're here, Burt," Riley said, turning to the respiratory therapist at the bedside. He'd just taken over from the paramedics and was ventilating the patient with a bag device. "Keep his tidal volume low, will you?" Riley grabbed a surgical chest tray from under the counter and a sterile gown and gloves and threw them all onto a bedside stand. She scanned the monitors and the patient's physical presentation for a few seconds before saying, "Looks like a tension pneumo. What do you think, Burt? Does that trachea look deviated to you?"

"As bad as I've ever seen, Doc." He cringed, reducing the pressure he was applying to the resuscitation bag and increasing the rate of ventilation. Riley listened to the teen's chest with her stethoscope. Then, just in case the unconscious patient could still hear her, she bent down next to his ear, and in a soft but deliberate voice, she did her best to prepare him for what was to come.

"We'll take good care of you, son." Riley never knew the names of patients in the ER who were victims of violence. Calling the young man John Doe number 869 didn't seem likely to build trust. She tried to sound confident, "I'm going to place a tube between your ribs to help reinflate a collapsed lung. That's going to hurt a bit, and you'll need surgery soon to get this bleeding under control. But you're going to make it. Hang in there, buddy."

At that moment, a breathless intern from the trauma surgery service—who, in Riley's estimation, looked like the tallest fifteen-year-old she'd ever seen—dashed into the room, ripping off his lab coat and tossing it into the corner as if he were a lifeguard about to spring into the kiddy pool.

"Where's your senior?" Riley barked, eyes sweeping over his lanky form incredulously. She turned then to the nurse. "Sonya, grab a twenty-four-gauge chest tube ASAP."

"Dr. Lim sends her apologies," the intern announced, his long legs striding toward Riley with surprising confidence, given her obvious skepticism. "Our team is just finishing in the OR. They'll be here soon. I'm pretty sure they'll want an X-ray before anyone puts in a chest tube, though." He pushed his way past the nurse to get a better look at the patient and inadvertently contaminated the sterile area she had just set up at the bedside.

"There's a hook in the hallway for superhero capes," Riley said, barely keeping her tone in check. The intern hesitated, his eyes finding the discarded garment on the floor. "When you've picked up after yourself, you can gown up if you want to help. But hurry, we don't have much time." Riley caught the sudden flush in his cheeks when he bent to pick up his discarded coat, and a deck of three-by-five cards tumbled out of his top pocket, scattering onto the floor.

"But . . . but you need to wait for Dr. Lim," the intern insisted, visibly doubting Riley's lead as he stuffed his pockets again. "We haven't seen a chest X-ray, so what makes you think he needs a chest tube?"

At this, Riley lost her cool. "How long do you think this patient can tolerate a heart rate of a hundred and ninety and a blood pressure that low?" she snapped, tilting her head toward the monitors beeping wildly beside them. "The only thing we have time for now is action. Not X-rays and *not* discussion." She grabbed a disinfectant swab and painted the intended tube insertion site between the dying teen's ribs.

"Lung compliance is really decreasing, Doc," Burt reported from the head of the bed, eyes wide.

"Sonya, I'm ready for that tube," Riley announced as she extended her gloved hand. The nurse slipped the device, a small spear-like instrument, out of its protective sleeve and into Riley's hand. A second later, Riley punched the tip of the chest tube between two of the patient's ribs. She withdrew the inner core and set it aside, leaving a small rigid hose in place. A sudden woosh of air escaped from the youth's chest, relieving the deadly airlock that had been crushing his heart and lungs from within. Then she handed the other end of the tube to Sonya, who attached it to a suction device that would help keep the lung properly inflated. Riley turned to Burt again. "Compliance improve any?"

"Like night 'n' day." He puffed out his cheeks in relief. Seconds later, the patient's vital signs began to move in the right direction, though they were still unacceptable in Riley's view. There had been just too much blood loss, she told herself as she began to secure the chest tube with a few heavy-duty stitches.

"What did you say your name was?" She glanced at the intern then, doing her best to improve her tone now that they had overcome the most immediate danger.

"Doug . . . I mean, it's Dr. Hudson, ma'am."

"Well, Dr. Hudson, put on the gown and gloves Sonya has been kind enough to set out for you. Then you can help her put on a dressing over this tube insertion site. Just watch that you're cautious around the sterile field this time," Riley added, giving Sonya a nod of gratitude and a look to counter the one she was getting in return—one that said, *What am I, a babysitter?*

Riley ripped off her bloody gloves and crossed the room to call the surgical suites again. She and her team had done what they could, including starting the massive transfusion protocol. But without surgical intervention to control bleeding, all that newly transfused blood would ultimately just end up on the floor.

As if on cue, the senior trauma surgeon and her team strode in; she breathed a sigh of relief as she laid eyes on Riley.

"God, I was hoping you were here today, Rye. I knew you would handle whatever it was—thank you, thank you," she said, pulling on a pair of gloves to examine the patient's wound, which Riley had packed with gauze.

"Thanks, Krista. It was touch and go there for a minute with a tension pneumo on the left, but I had good help from Burt and, of course, Sonya, who's always a rock star in the worst cases. Every pair of hands helped." The lanky intern glanced over his shoulder then from the bedside, where he was doing his best to appear useful while Sonya secured a large dressing around the chest tube site. Riley couldn't help but draw a parallel between the look in his eyes and the one she so often saw in Indio's when Artemis had just reminded him of his position in the pecking order.

Within minutes, the trauma team was whisking the patient off to the operating room, crimson transfusion bags swinging from the IV poles on the gurney and an entourage of support staff and medical trainees in tow.

Riley stood in the middle of the vacant trauma bay looking down at the pools of congealing blood at her feet, the victim's shredded clothing—cut off to allow for thorough examination—and a myriad of surgical supply wrappers littering the floor.

She felt numb, as if somehow the world was a little slower and duller in the wake of all the commotion. She thought about all the resources being poured into saving the young man's life and how long and difficult his recovery might be—and whether or not he would make it through surgery. And then there were the bigger questions, the ones she seldom deliberated because they could be so crushing. If the patient survived, would he just return to the same environment where he was bound to be a victim again? Would he, next time, perhaps be the shooter?

She headed for the break room, her head buzzing, hoping someone had had time to brew a fresh pot of coffee. Trauma cases were always such a paradox—emotionally draining but somehow also energizing. There was an indescribable peace, a flow of clarity best described as a singularity that came from navigating multiple streams of dynamic data in the middle of a disaster.

Today, she could honestly say her team had done well in their management of the patient's injuries. There was no question they had all played a part in executing a lifesaving intervention. And for those things, she should have been grateful. But that's not what she felt. What she felt was lucky, and that was cold comfort to anyone in her profession. Because no one was lucky all the time.

*　　*　　*

Later that evening, as Riley was on her way to the locker room to change out of her scrubs and head home, she ran into Hudson. The intern had come back to the ER from the operating rooms, he told her, to give an update on their GSW patient.

She remembered the long, tedious days of internship and felt a pang of empathy for him. The dark circles under his eyes told a story of their own, and when he reported that the patient was in the ICU recovering from surgery in stable condition, he did so without any spark of satisfaction.

"Thanks for the info," Riley offered, but the way he stalled in the hallway, not making any move toward the exit, made it clear he wasn't finished. "Was there something else, Dr. Hudson?"

"Well . . . yes, actually, ma'am, I also wanted to thank you for your patience with me earlier, Dr. Brighton," he said, his eyes finding the floor. "Sorry for being—"

"We're all a work in progress, Hudson," Riley broke in. "I accept your apology. I believe you thought you were doing the right thing by asking me to wait for your chief to arrive. As a medical student, you were no doubt a victim of the Hippocratic oath. The ancient edict of 'first do no harm' isn't as straightforward as it sounds. I do understand your reluctance about my plans to put in a chest tube without an X-ray—never mind." She cut herself off when she noticed his eyes glaze over with fatigue. "Come with me, Hudson. There's something you should see." She led the way down the hall to the radiology library.

A moment later, they both stood in a darkened room as she pulled out an old chest X-ray from its oversize cardboard envelope in a locked drawer and slipped it onto the lighted viewing box for him to examine. The film had been taken five years earlier on a trauma patient just like the one they had treated that afternoon. A twenty-three-year-old man with a gunshot wound to the abdomen.

"Take your time," Riley said, studying Hudson's face while he, in turn, examined the X-ray. His eyes swept over the film methodically, first from top to bottom and then from left to right, tracing every line. "When you're finished, list everything you see wrong with this picture."

Riley leaned her elbows on the counter. She couldn't wait to get out of her grimy scrubs and go home, but the spark she saw growing in the intern's eyes made the delay worthwhile.

"Well, for one thing, the obvious findings include a metallic fragment in the soft tissue of the upper left chest wall." He turned to her. "It's probably a bullet or bullet fragment. And then, number two, there's a pretty significant pneumothorax—the left lung looks almost eighty percent collapsed. And thirdly, the patient's trachea is deviated significantly from the midline, indicating that this is a tension pneumothorax." He stepped back from the film, seemingly satisfied with his answers. The light from the viewing box reflected off his rectangular glasses, giving him a somewhat robotic appearance as he waited for Riley to confirm his observations.

"You're not wrong, Dr. Hudson," she said, choosing her words carefully, noting he had grasped only the lowest-hanging fruit. "Those are three important findings on this film, and in your words, they *are* 'obvious.' But there's a fourth, more critical issue, that we've missed. And this one might surprise even a seasoned clinician." She waited a moment before adding, "The most significant problem with this X-ray, Dr. Hudson, is the fact that it was taken at all. Tension pneumothorax is a dire emergency, one that will kill a patient in minutes. It should be diagnosed *solely* on physical exam. Unfortunately, in the time it took to obtain a chest X-ray on this young man, he died a painful and unnecessary death."

Before she could finish, the intern was cupping his face in his hand; her message on the hazards of analysis paralysis had seemingly found its mark.

"So, you see, Hudson, 'first do no harm' is not a decree that we, as physicians, shun all potential hazards. When the stakes are highest, we may need to take the biggest risks. And the truth, the hard truth, is we *will* make mistakes. That's the burden we carry along with the awesome privileges we are entrusted with every day."

The intern stood frozen, staring down at her in silence. She wasn't sure, but Riley thought she saw a glimmer of tears building behind his glasses. She'd seen it a thousand times before in medical trainees. In like a lion, out like a lamb.

Teaching was hard. Learning was harder.

"It took courage to question my decisions today in the middle of an emergency. That's an admirable quality in an intern, and one that makes you an ethical patient advocate. Go home now, Dr. Hudson, and get some rest. We've all had a big day."

CHAPTER TEN

By the time Riley made it home from work that evening, she barely had the energy to warm up leftovers for dinner. There hadn't been anyone on her tail on the commute home—as far as she could tell, at least—and she'd seen an LAPD patrol car cruising the neighborhood on her way in, so she felt less concerned about the prospect of a Godzilla-size stalker paying her a visit. But she just couldn't muster the enthusiasm for a walk, let alone a run in her current state. Indio would have to be happy with a few minutes in the backyard.

After a hot shower, she tumbled into bed. It wasn't the way she had intended to spend a Friday night on her weekend off. Normally, she'd join her colleagues from the ER at the taphouse for their customary decompression ritual, but she didn't have it in her this week. For now, she had no regrets. Nothing could beat a hot shower and an early bedtime.

Riley was asleep almost immediately with Artemis crouched next to her on the bed beside her open laptop and Indio in the doorway between her room and the hallway, where he usually stretched out.

It was after midnight when the chime on her laptop, signaling an incoming email, woke her. She rolled over, only bothering to open one eye, intending to close her laptop and go back to sleep, but she noticed the sender was Avenging Allies. A second later, she was clicking open the email from someone called Themis. It was a reply to the Contact Us request she had sent the night before when she'd been searching for information on the Lexi Drake murder case.

The message read, "Meet me at seven tomorrow morning, Abe's Deli in Van Nuys, booth number 18. I'll take the vegan bagel nosh and a black coffee."

*   *   *

The following morning, as instructed, Riley commuted to Abe's and sat in booth number 18, with its shiny green Formica tabletop and faux leather seats. She'd been up before dawn for a run with Indy, and her braid, wet after her morning shower, hung down the front of her jacket, her full-face motorcycle helmet on the bench seat next to her. The waiter approached in his checkered apron to take her order. There was something familiar about him—the deep dimples, the inquisitive eyes.

"What can I get for you, miss? You look hungry today," he said with a wide smile.

"Funny you should mention that," she answered, scanning the already-packed diner over the top of her menu, "I'm famished." Her eyes drifted to the name tag on his apron. "Let's make it two orders of the vegan bagel nosh and a couple of black coffees, shall we, Cedrick?"

"Perfect." He grinned—without the double take Riley had expected—and then headed toward the kitchen.

Ten minutes later, the person calling herself Themis slid into the booth across from her.

She wasn't at all what Riley had been expecting. Themis appeared to be in her early twenties, a petite girl in denim overalls and a Dodgers baseball cap who looked like she'd just hopped off a skateboard. Riley was sure her name wasn't really Themis. She looked more like a Daisy or a Poppy. The girl's strawberry-blonde dreadlocks matched her striking amber eyes and the sprinkle of freckles across her nose. Her alabaster complexion was so light, her eyebrows were almost translucent.

"What's up, Doc?" she said as she pulled her cloth shoulder bag off and set it on the bench seat next to her.

"Well," Riley answered, "I'm hoping you can tell *me*."

"You reached out to me about the Lexi Drake case," Themis said, putting her elbows on the tabletop and resting her chin in her hands. "But that's not the real reason we're here, is it?"

At least the girl is direct, Riley thought, *and informed*.

That simplified things. She had obviously done her research and looked into Riley.

Cedrick arrived with their breakfast then. As he slid a cup of coffee in front of Themis, Riley didn't miss the look that passed between them.

"The reason I contacted you," Riley began, blowing the heat off her coffee and taking a sip, "as it seems you've deduced, is because of the incident on the 101 earlier this week. I happened to come across the scene on my morning commute, and I just can't get the victim out of my mind." She paused, gauging Themis's reaction.

The girl, despite her age, was as stone-faced as a practiced stoic. "I wanted answers once I realized it wasn't an accident. It was all over the news, wasn't it? That it might be related to the Lexi Drake case."

This generated the desired reaction.

Themis's eyes widened just a fraction—a micro-expression that indicated they were both very much on the same page.

"There are too many similarities for it to be a coincidence." Themis picked up the glass cylinder of sugar from the end of the table and poured a long draft of crystals into her coffee. Despite her upbeat tone, there was darkness in the girl's eyes. Something that spoke of loss, of profound disappointment—the same shadow that Riley had seen in her own mother for as far back as she could remember, ever since they had lost her father. "And let me be clear." She shot Riley a sharp glance, her tone at odds with her slight countenance. "It wasn't an 'incident on the 101 Freeway.' It was a cold-blooded murder."

The silence hung between them for a few seconds as Riley read her.

Yes, she'd thought the girl was somehow personally affected by the crime; her tone made that clear now. Riley's mind drifted to the caution she'd received from Detective Roberts about altering her route to work and the man she'd seen sitting outside her home only two nights before. "It's personal for me too now," she said.

"Maybe we can help each other," Themis went on, taking a casual tone as she bit into her bagel. "I'm interested in the man you met at the crime scene. Did he say anything to you?"

"I don't have a whole lot for you on that front. Our exchange was brief. He basically chased me out of the road. In truth, that was a smart suggestion."

"Hmm . . . was he alone?"

"Not sure on that one either. There may have been a passenger in his truck; I didn't really get a look."

"The big black pickup?"

"That's the one." Riley nodded, now more curious about what Themis seemed to know. Evidently, the man she had met at the scene was already on the Avenging Allies' radar. "So who is this character?" she asked, daring to probe. It was only fair that she got in a few of her own questions.

"He could be a psychopathic lone wolf," Themis said, pausing to see how her words had landed. Riley's face gave nothing away. "That's the best-case scenario, though. If he's a foot soldier in the gang we've been looking into, that could be an entirely different nightmare. It's not clear yet. But either way, anyone who could tie him to one of these crime scenes is in danger."

"Really?" Riley knew this already, of course, but she wanted to know why Themis thought this was true too. Perhaps she had more information. "What makes you say that?"

"Well, the giveaway is that he matches the description of someone also spotted near the Lexi Drake murder shortly after her death."

Riley sensed there was more. There was something Themis wasn't telling her. In truth, the girl had already shared more than she'd expected. Riley hadn't provided much in the way of a quid pro quo. She hadn't even given a description of the bald man. So how was Themis sure it was the same person spotted at the Lexi Drake murder scene?

"There's a reason you responded to my message. What is it?" Riley challenged. "What can I do for you? You clearly already know more than I've offered."

Themis sat for a minute, staring at Riley as if she were making a mental calculation.

"Well, I hate to put it this way . . ." She leaned back in the booth, crossing her arms over her chest, and seemed to carefully select each word that followed. "But you're the only one who's actually interacted with this man. Every other witness observed him from a distance, without any exchange of dialogue. And apparently, he left the scene before the highway patrol could intercept him."

Riley thought back to the flashing lights and the blare of sirens, signaling the arrival of the fire department and the CHP just as she was leaving the site that morning. As Detective Roberts had already told her, the man must've left the very minute she had pulled away on her bike. Had her presence been a hinderance to whatever he was up to? After all, he'd been downright intimidating at the scene. A cold chill ran the length of her spine as she remembered Indio's reluctance to leave the house for a run that evening. And now she was wondering if the man hadn't been following her from the time she'd left the scene?

"So, you see," Themis went on gingerly, "if we're going to root him out—"

Riley nearly choked on her coffee. "Jesus, what are you suggesting? I should be the bait in some sort of trap?"

"I don't mean to scare you, but frankly, I have an obligation to warn you. If the man you saw is working for the mobster I had dealings with a few years ago, you're already in danger. I'm talking about a criminal mastermind with a pretty notorious gang wrapped around his little finger." The girl's eyes drifted over Riley's head. She took a long sip of her coffee before she went on. "I was hoping you could offer anything at all that would confirm my suspicions about this guy's connections."

Riley had lost her appetite. She eyed Themis curiously. "You seem to know quite a bit already. His appearance at both crime scenes, the kind of vehicle he drives, and so on—"

"We have our ways, but they have their limitations." Cedrick cut Riley off as he slid into the booth next to Themis, his checkered waiter's apron now replaced by a loose-fitting T-shirt over cargo pants. A solemn demeanor overshadowed his earlier easy smile.

Again, he stirred a glimmer of recognition in Riley. "Have we met?"

Themis interrupted, not skipping a beat, "Avenging Allies is a small organization, Riley. Well connected, but small. And as Cedrick said, we do have our limitations, but at times, we get better help from witnesses than the police do."

"We've been pretty successful in solving hate crimes in the Valley over the last three years," Cedrick added. "Our track record is one hundred percent so far."

Riley didn't dare ask how many cases they'd investigated for fear Cedrick's answer would destroy any credibility. Three years ago, he and Themis would likely have been teenagers.

"I've shared with you as much as I can at this point, I'm afraid. We have an obligation to alert you to the danger you may be facing, but we also must protect our sources." Themis set an elbow on the table, fingers resting on her lips.

"Okay, well, where do we go from here?" Riley tried to appear unfazed, like she hadn't just received a terminal diagnosis. If what Themis was telling her was true, she might already have a target on her back.

"There's a limit to what I can disclose regarding this case and our methods," Themis said, making it clear their chat had come to an end. "We'll be in touch when necessary, and of course, you know how to reach us when—or if—you see the man in the pickup again."

"Breakfast is covered, by the way," Cedrick said as he slid out of the booth ahead of Themis. Riley ignored him, tucking a twenty-dollar bill under the sugar jar as she got up to leave.

On her way out of the deli, she spotted a familiar-looking vehicle parked in the corner of the parking lot under a huge jacaranda tree. It was a Honda wagon with a rainbow bumper sticker.

She put two and two together. Of course, the car belonged to either Cedrick or Themis. The logo on the Avenging Allies website was a rainbow. And Riley was now certain that it was the same vehicle she'd seen cruising by her home on the night she spotted the bald man in his truck watching her.

If she was right, the Avenging Allies had been the ones to call in the fictitious disturbance at her home that evening. No doubt the sudden appearance of a police cruiser and Officers Garcia and Hahn had been what scared off the giant. That much seemed probable, but Riley couldn't figure out the other details. Why wouldn't the Avenging Allies take advantage of spotting their suspect and just stalk the stalker? Why were they asking her questions about him when they surely had had the opportunity to follow him once he'd left her place that night?

The only thing Riley could think of was that Themis and Cedrick had prioritized getting the LAPD involved for her safety over pursuing their suspect. Or perhaps they'd been spotted by the man too. Maybe they'd even followed him, but somehow, he'd cottoned on and dropped them. Whatever had happened that night, it was beginning to look like the Avenging Allies had played a role in scaring off the suspect—and Riley was grateful for that, but she took little comfort in the fact now. It seemed Themis and Cedrick were well intentioned and perhaps even effective, to some degree. How else had they heard of her before she'd even contacted them through their website? They were clearly already interested in her the night she'd seen them cruising by her home.

What wasn't sitting well with Riley was the feeling that the Avenging Allies' so-called organization was probably just the two of them: Themis and Cedrick. And the crazies—the Jaded Justice skull-loving nuts—were apparently a deadly serious gang run by a psychopathic genius.

She wondered what she'd gotten herself into and if the only way out of this mess was to get herself in deeper.

If Themis was right, she was already at risk, a potential target. And Riley wasn't very good at being a victim. Her profession had taught her to take charge whenever things got dangerous. And besides, by their own account, the Avenging Allies had their limitations. And that meant they could probably use the help of someone with Riley's connections at the coroner's office.

CHAPTER ELEVEN

Riley spent most of that Saturday afternoon surfing the internet for any information she could find on the Lexi Drake murder, which had occurred almost three weeks earlier. The more she learned about each case, the more she agreed with Themis's belief that the two cases were unlikely to be a coincidence. There were just too many similarities.

Both victims were young and likely transgender, from what Riley had gathered. Both were essentially blindfolded and reportedly pushed or stumbled, just a few miles apart, into traffic on the same freeway. To add to all that, Themis had revealed that a man and vehicle matching the description Riley had provided to the LAPD were spotted at or near both crime scenes.

Knowing she'd stood right next to him made Riley feel sick. She wondered now, if it hadn't been for the onlookers peering through their car windows, what the man might have done to erase her as a witness to his presence at the scene of the crime.

She scrolled through several other online news feeds. There weren't any posts on the Lexi Drake murder that she hadn't already seen. Then she scrolled through social media posts.

She happened upon a blog on an open LGBTQ forum discussing a celebration of life event scheduled in Santa Monica. The deceased was simply identified as Alexandria. Her life had spanned the years 1999 to 2023. That would have made her twenty-four years old at the time of her death. Riley wondered what the chances were. How many LGBTQ twenty-four-year-olds from Santa Monica with the root name Alexandria had passed away in the prior weeks? The very first news article she'd found two nights previously, in fact, had stated that twenty-four-year-old Lexi worked in Santa Monica as a licensed therapist.

The celebration of life event was scheduled for 2:00 p.m. at the Sixth Street Center for Homeless Youth, just a few blocks from the Santa Monica pier, on Sunday afternoon.

That was tomorrow.

*　　*　　*

Riley turned her motorcycle off Ocean Avenue in Santa Monica and headed inland a few blocks. She found parking on Fifth Street, peeled off her leathers, and stuffed them into her backpack with her boots. She slipped on her sandals, pulled an embroidered smock over her yoga pants, and covered her head and most of her face with a long silk scarf.

It was just a short walk to the youth center, where she could see a crowd gathering in the front yard of a 1950s-style bungalow dwarfed by the surrounding apartment complexes.

A rainbow flag hung above the gatepost to the left, and a large canvas photograph of a petite brunette with sapphire-colored eyes stood on an easel to the right. A wreath of white gardenias had been placed over the frame.

Below the photograph was printed ALEXANDRIA DRAKE, MS. LEXI, JUNE 23, 1999–SEPTEMBER 3, 2023. YOU WERE A BRIGHT LIGHT IN OUR DARKNESS. YOUR YEARS OF SERVICE TO THE SANTA MONICA HOMELESS YOUTH WERE A TRUE LEGACY OF LOVE. MAY YOU REST IN POWER, SWEET ANGEL.

Riley wove her way through the crowd—past dreadlocks, pierced faces, and tattoos—to claim a seat on the stairs of the porch between a young man in a colorful Rastafarian hat and a pregnant teen with a sketch pad in her lap. The air was thick with the pungent odor of incense and the chatter of capiz shells swinging in clusters from fishing line in the eaves above the porch. Folks were making themselves comfortable on the small patch of lawn out front, where bamboo mats and picnic blankets had been spread. The collective mood was somber, as though, despite the stated objective of a life celebration, a referendum on grief had been issued. Most of the crowd had the look of individuals who'd survived adversity through nothing but grit and sheer defiance. All but one seemed to belong.

A young man leaned up against the corner of the house, as though he had just emerged from somewhere behind the structure, and watched the gathering from the shade of the cypress trees separating the small yard from the adjacent apartment complex. His faded jeans, anchored by a large bronze belt buckle, sat high on his hips. His wide-brimmed hat and leather boots spoke of farm labor rather than beach life. His gaze was locked on the pregnant girl sitting next to Riley. When his eyes happened on Riley staring back at him, he dropped his cigarette, ground it into the dirt with the toe of his boot, and disappeared behind the house.

Riley returned her attention to the crowd gathered on the lawn, where someone had begun to strum a guitar. As she studied the group from her perch on the stairs, though she wasn't sure what she was looking for, exactly, Riley heard a familiar voice over her shoulder, just inside the open front door, say, "Be sure to announce that we'll be serving refreshments out back after the service."

Riley turned, keeping her face covered by her scarf, and glanced over her shoulder. The familiar voice belonged to Holly, her new surfing friend from Malibu. She remembered then that during their chat at the coffee shop, Holly had said she was working with homeless youth in Santa Monica. Riley pieced it together. It made sense that Holly might have known Lexi, especially if they had both been working with unhoused teens in the beach communities, a number of whom, statistically speaking, like both Holly and Lexi, would have been transgender.

It was an unfortunate truth that the lives of many young trans people were upended after their families disowned them. Riley had seen the results of that kind of rejection in the ER—the kids who were victimized on the streets after their families had kicked them out. Or those who attempted and often succeeded in ending their own lives rather than face the heartbreak of being shunned by parents who had been trusted to love them no matter what.

The service got underway with music and singing and a few of the young people sitting on the lawn recounting the ways in which Lexi had helped them during their time at the shelter. The pregnant girl next to Riley began to cry softly when a young woman described how Lexi had been the one to talk her out of suicide three months earlier.

"She was an absolute angel. I wouldn't be here today—not without her," the girl mumbled, holding her hands in a prayer position in front of her lips. "She saved my life, and it's just so friggin' wrong that her life ended the way it did. What the hell is wrong with people? What the absolute hell . . ." As soon as the girl took her seat among her friends, who quickly embraced her, a young man in a hoodie and baggy shorts stood.

"Yeah, what happened to Lexi was dred. She helped me and my ol' lady," he said, indicating a dusty blonde sitting on a yoga mat at his feet. "Lexi was like fam to us, man. Helped us get clean, hooked us up with work, and yeah . . . just ain't right, man, what went down. That's all."

The door of the bungalow was open. Riley slipped quietly from her seat on the stairs and made her way inside. Down a long, paneled hallway, she found Holly in the kitchen taking a tray of cookies out of the oven. It was clear she had been crying. She looked confused when she saw Riley in the doorway.

"It's me, Holly," Riley said, pulling the scarf back from her face briefly. "Riley, from the beach."

Holly froze for a moment, holding the tray of cookies as if she wasn't sure where to put it. "What's with the cover-up?" she finally said. Her tone was cool as she slid the tray onto the counter.

"I can explain that later. I take it you knew Lexi well?"

"Yes." Holly at once began to tear up. She stopped to pull a sheet off a roll of paper towels next to the sink and wrapped a section around her forefinger, dabbing it under her eyes, where her mascara had started to run. "I'm heartbroken. I was her mentor over the six years she was with us. I've known her since she was just a scared high school dropout. She was skinny little Levi, bullied mercilessly back in those days. Before she transitioned." Holly wiped her nose with the crumpled towel and stepped forward, looking at Riley as if in a new light. Her tone softened. "I didn't know you knew her too. Small world."

"No. No, I didn't know her, Holly. But it sounds like she was a lovely person. I'm sorry for your loss and for intruding at a time like this. I had no idea you worked here, but—"

The pregnant girl from the porch appeared then. She stopped short, hanging back at the doorway to the kitchen when she saw Riley. "Ms. Holly, the service is wrapping up now. Is it a good time for everyone to go out back?" Her voice was raspy, as though she'd been crying for hours.

"Yes, Sofia. Have them go around the side yard, though," Holly said, her eyes sweeping over Riley's attempt at a disguise. "I don't want them all coming through the house. Ms. Maria has already set most of the food out on the tables. You can take these cookies out, though, if you don't mind, love." Holly stepped over to the back door, pulling the drape away on the small window as if to survey the yard below.

The girl ventured into the kitchen then, her crystalline eyes wide, her pale lips parted in mute curiosity as she sized up Riley. In Riley's estimation, Sofia couldn't have been more than fifteen, though nothing about her seemed youthful. Despite the swell of her belly, she was far too thin for someone carrying a child. Her maternity dress was plainly a thrift store hand-me-down, though Riley recognized her pink suede shoes with their shiny buckles as a handmade designer brand. *Prada*, she thought. *Yes, Prada*. They were in stark contrast to the rest of Sofia's look.

Holly opened the back door for the girl, her gaze roving the yard as though in search of someone, and then she stepped aside, letting Sofia pass.

As the girl exited to the yard below, the platter of cookies held out in front of her like a sacred offering, her delicate ankles in their pink Prada pumps searched cautiously for the stairs below the bulge of her midsection.

"I can explain why I'm here," Riley offered, keeping her voice low. "If you have time, that is. Maybe we could get away when you're done."

"Suuuure." Holly dragged the word out, as if she were weighing the decision. "Let me just check with Maria. If she and Javier will handle cleanup around here, I'll be able to cut out."

*   *   *

"You'll have to forgive me today, Riley. I'm not the best company, I'm afraid." Holly hunched over in her chair on the patio of a trendy bistro on Ocean Boulevard. Her voice was flat in a way that signaled defeat.

It was cooler now that they were near the water. It had been a foggy morning, chilly and damp. The sun battled to gain an advantage in the latter part of the day, shedding a muted glow on the cloud bank still lingering over the Pacific.

"Lexi was an exceptional person. We're all still in shock," Holly said, setting her martini glass back on the table. "She was such an asset to our cause. She raised so many donations for our center over the years she was with us. She's probably the reason we're still afloat. And the way she was murdered . . . ripped from the kids who counted on her to help them find hope. It's just so cruel. It's hard not to lose faith in humanity . . ." Her voice trailed off, as if she were withdrawing into her shell again.

"I try never to lose faith in people, Holly, even with all the crap I see in the ER. There are plenty of good eggs out there. You and everyone who helps the kids at the center are great examples of humanity at its finest."

Holly shot her a dubious look, dabbing her eyes again with her napkin.

"I've come to accept that life is a double-edged sword, Holly. You know, both beautiful and terrifying all at once, an equal measure of yin and yang."

Holly's attention seemed to drift, her dark eyes settling on the olive in her glass.

"It does sound like Lexi left an indelible mark on all the lives she touched," Riley went on, knowing she must have sounded glib but seeing little point in the brutality of truth at that moment. What had happened to Holly's colleague was nothing short of horrific, and there was no platitude or reassurance capable of blunting that.

"You still haven't told me what brings you here, Riley." Holly's eyes snapped back to her. Something between suspicion and curiosity clouded the question. And for the first time in Holly's presence, Riley felt uncomfortable. But she could rationalize Holly's distrust of someone she barely knew in the wake of her friend's unsolved murder.

Riley scooted her chair in closer and brought Holly up to speed, filling her in on the incident she'd been involved in with the pedestrian struck on the 101 Freeway in the prior week. She also shared the details about the bald man in the black pickup she'd met at the scene, who had later stalked her on the night Themis and Cedrick from Avenging Allies scared him out of her neighborhood. As Riley delivered these details, Holly's eyes widened, her guard seeming to drop as her curiosity grew.

"That's truly terrifying, Riley." Holly shook her head, gaze darting back to her, and for a moment, they both seemed to weigh the danger of it all. "What next? How crazy can this get?"

"It really affected me, of course," Riley admitted. "The accident itself was horrific, even though I'm used to seeing trauma and death in the ER. I was caught out of my element to be sure. And now that I know how similar that incident was to your friend Lexi's murder, I have to believe that the crimes are in some way connected."

"And of course, you've been to the police?" Holly asked.

"Oh yes. The detective I spoke with at LAPD was the one who indicated it was a crime and not an accident. But outside of that confession, she didn't tell me much, so I began my own little inquiry, if you know what I mean. That led me to the Avenging Allies—"

"Avenging Allies?" Holly interrupted, as if the monicker had only just registered. "Funny, and is Themis even a real name? Sorry, but Avenging Allies just sounds so hokey. Like a cartoon superhero group or something."

"Yes—just kids, really. I met with them yesterday morning. Amateurs at best, but well intentioned. A couple of citizen sleuths, if you will. They say they've solved several hate crimes in the Valley over the past few years. They're working on Lexi's case now, and I gather they see a pattern between these two events." Riley thought for a minute. "In truth, they're on to something, and I wonder how they're gathering their facts. They seem to have details that aren't public. But for sure, the cases have obvious similarities the media are highlighting."

"What are you saying—we have a serial killer situation here?"

"Well, maybe." Riley sat back, clutching her napkin in her lap. A chill settled over the patio as the sun dropped behind the clouds. "We'll know more, I suppose, when information about the person killed last week is released. For example, if they were also transgender. I sense they were, based on the way the cops were talking, how they kept flip-flopping on pronouns. The autopsy must be done by now. I work on the same campus as the LA medical examiner's office. So I have professional connections. I'm pretty sure I can get some answers from a trusted source. And when I talked with her, Detective Roberts said she assumed the person was homeless. I can find out if anyone has come forward to claim the body. There haven't been any updates on the news, so I don't even think this person has been reported missing yet, and it's been almost a week."

"Yeah, well, that's not unexpected, is it, if they were unhoused?" Holly shook her head. "Shameful but not surprising what some of these kids go through when their families disown them." They both sat quietly in the wake of Holly's comment. Riley was sure Holly was reflecting on her own life traumas. "Even when they're supported, kids sometimes just take off. It happens all the time. Occasionally residents from our shelter go back to the devil they know. They end up back on the streets, selling themselves or trafficked by others. Using. God knows what becomes of them. But it's a sad fact that some end up in the most dangerous place of all—back at home with their victimizers."

The afternoon shadows grew longer, and the temperature continued to dip. It would be dark within the hour, Riley realized, wrapping her scarf around her shoulders as she signaled the waitress for the check.

CHAPTER TWELVE

"Late teens, early twenties, female at birth, but clear signs of body dysmorphia indicating a transgender individual. For example, the breasts were bound firmly to the chest at the time of death, and testosterone levels were abnormally high, suggesting exogenous supplementation for at least several months. You can see here," the medical examiner said, indicating with the end of his pen, "the facial and chest hair is markedly masculine."

Riley stood in the main storage facility of the LA county morgue, a giant refrigerated room that resembled a warehouse, listening to Dr. Joseph Padilla, the chief pathologist, giving a summary on the body of last week's hit-and-run victim. The smell of bleach thinly masked the deeper, mustier odors permeating the facility, which, along with the distant hum of bone saws, stirred a primal instinct in Riley to flee.

The drawer with the still-unidentified body was pulled open, the corpse covered only in a light plastic sheet from the chest down. The victim was petite, smaller than Riley remembered from that morning almost a week ago on the freeway. The torso had evidently sustained massive blunt force trauma that would have immediately disrupted the function of not only the spinal column but also the lungs and heart. No wonder the scene had been bloodless, Riley realized. Death would have been instantaneous.

The head was covered in sandy-blond hair, closely cropped, the chin and upper lip fuzzy with ginger stubble. Swelling and bruising around the eyes made it impossible to judge iris color, but Riley guessed they would have been green or blue. Given her own line of work, she was having difficulty understanding the despair she felt building as Joe described the body's injuries.

"The head was spared from direct trauma, owing to the motorcycle helmet being in place, but as you can see, there had been significant injury in the hours before death."

Riley tried to imagine the face intact, smiling broadly, with animated green eyes that reflected the promise of a long, joyous life. But what she saw in front of her were the remnants of a life cut short, senselessly and brutally wasted.

"From the ligature marks on the wrists, I'd say our victim was bound antemortem—but interestingly, not at the time of death."

"What? To stage the murder as a suicide?"

"That's a possibility, but this is all purely speculation at this point. Incidentally, I saw this same pattern on a similar case last month."

"Involving Lexi Drake?" Riley blurted, and suddenly Joe fell silent, giving her a bewildered stare from behind his clear face shield. Riley did the polite thing and let it go. She had her answer. "Any notion when you might have an ID, Joe?" she asked, changing the subject and checking the time of day on the small pager clipped to the waistband of her scrubs. She'd already overextended her lunch break. The ER would be looking for her by now.

"Working on that, Rye." He smiled patiently. "I'll keep you posted. But please, not a word to anyone about this. The LAPD wouldn't look favorably on me sharing information about an open investigation."

Riley eyed Joe thoughtfully, taking in the depth of his loyalty to her. She could always count on him. He'd been there for her in the wake of her mentor's sudden death during her residency. And a comforting shoulder in the days she'd been unsure she would complete her training. After Marcel's passing, she'd been crushed with grief, paralyzed with anxiety, and haunted by memories from her childhood. It was Joe who had made the connection for her between the loss of her own father years earlier and that of her mentor, Marcel Benoit. She'd never be able to repay Joe for the kindness he had shown her when she needed it most. In truth, she felt slightly guilty for taking advantage of their friendship in the way she just had.

"I appreciate you, Joe, and of course I won't share anything I've learned here. I just feel really connected to this case for obvious reasons. As I explained earlier, when you come across a patient you just can't help, it's haunting. I knew you would understand."

"I do," he said, giving her a longer-than-necessary look that left her cheeks flushed.

"Gotta get back before they send out a search party for me." She smiled, making a beeline for the door. "Thanks a million for your time; I owe you one," she called over her shoulder. He responded then—something about hoping to see her at the next Friday night local taphouse event—but Riley kept moving, pretending not to have heard him.

As she made her way back toward the hospital from the west side of campus, a LifeFlight helicopter whirled overhead. *Incoming*, she acknowledged as she picked up her pace. She knew she had about two and a half minutes before whatever case was in the airship hit the doors of the ER. Her pager had been buzzing ever since she'd left the morgue, and now, she felt the need to run.

"Trauma bay five, Riley. It's you and me again, sister," Sonya yelled, running past her down the ER's main hallway, pushing an incubator. "Obstetrics is on the way, and trauma surgery too. A double whammy—multisystem injuries, pregnant pedestrian versus auto with an anticipated crash C-section."

"Oh, Jesus, OB scares the hell out of me," Riley said, running alongside her. "How long until obstetrics gets here?"

"On the way! Hopefully you're spared." The nurse shoved a plastic apron toward Riley with her free hand.

"Always got my back—Sonya, you're the best," Riley said as she pulled on the apron mid-stride.

The flight crew and the ER staff who had met them on the rooftop heliport swept into trauma bay five amid the chaos of swarming personnel and incoming surgical supplies. Two IV bags were swinging from a single pole at the foot of the stretcher. The blue disposable sheet over the form of a pregnant woman was soaked with blood. A middle-aged paramedic, sweating profusely, was frantically ventilating the intubated woman with a bag device at a rate too fast to be effective. As Riley approached to make an initial assessment of the patient's injuries, pushing aside the crowd of personnel surrounding the stretcher, she cautioned the paramedic.

"Slow it down a little, please, Sam," she said, fixing her eyes on his silver-plated name tag. "We need to drop that ventilation rate to better facilitate oxygen transfer. Take a deep breath for yourself and try to relax. We've got this."

But that was before Riley laid eyes on the patient.

It wasn't the obvious femur fractures or the massive head trauma that caught her eye, nor was it the strip of duct tape over the girl's eyes. It was the pink suede Prada pump on the left foot, now crimson with blood, that knocked the breath right out of Riley's lungs.

*　　*　　*

Riley sat above the ambulance bay, swinging her legs from the windowsill while looking down at the rows of emergency vehicles and LAPD cruisers parked outside the hospital. Local news choppers had been circling for the better part of the afternoon, but now the evening sky was clear.

In the distance, she could see the lights of downtown LA, the City of Angels. The US Bank Tower and the Wilshire Grand, with their twinkling, gold-and-silver lights silhouetted against a black backdrop and the constant stream of red taillights on the freeway overpasses weaving above the darkened alleyways where the homeless staked their camps by night.

The ledge where Riley had perched herself was a favorite place for anyone working on the third floor where the surgical suites were located to sit and watch the traffic in and out of the ER below.

Her shift had ended an hour earlier, but Riley couldn't pull herself away from the hallway outside the operating room, where Sofia was undergoing emergency surgery. She'd seen several blood bank coolers delivered over the past hour, indicating the surgeons were still unable to control the sources of bleeding. And there were many of those, based on the injuries Riley had observed earlier in the ER.

Sofia's baby girl had been delivered via C-section within minutes of LifeFlight's arrival, but no one had expected Sofia to make it into surgery. The chances of her making it out weren't much greater. Riley thought about the massive head trauma the girl had suffered and what kind of a life she would have if she survived. Still, she was in the right place for someone in her condition. If Sofia had any chance of making it, it was here, at City General, where everyone from the orthopedists to the neurosurgeons specialized in trauma.

The baby was in serious condition in the neonatal ICU. The pediatric specialist had estimated her gestational age at thirty-four weeks. She was probably old enough to survive outside the uterus under normal circumstances, but there was nothing normal about being in the womb of a teenager who had been struck by an automobile at high speed.

Riley was torn about contacting the youth center to see if she could find Holly. She felt obligated to do so, but it would have been a patient privacy violation, not to mention what such devastating news might do to Holly. The LAPD and social services would be responsible for alerting contacts. Riley had done her part simply by identifying the girl. Now all she could do was wait for word from the surgeons about Sofia's chances and think about how she would handle Holly when she finally arrived.

It was well after eight when Riley saw the trauma team wheel Sofia out of surgery, heading to the ICU. If the girl survived the night, there would be many more trips to the OR in her future.

Riley checked in with hospital social services, but a shift change had taken place in the last hour, and it was unclear if anyone had been able to reach Holly or any administrator from the Santa Monica shelter. The LAPD had maintained a constant presence at the hospital since Sofia's arrival, but the officers on duty remained tightlipped and more aloof than Riley typically found them.

By now, it was obvious they were dealing with a serial killer. Or at least that was how it looked. Riley still didn't have any details on what had led to Sofia being struck on the same freeway as both Lexi and the victim she'd seen in the morgue earlier that day. But the media had been quick to draw parallels between the first two cases and weren't holding back now. There were reporters out on the hospital's front stairs, and the TV news channels had already raised reasonable questions. Three such incidents in a matter of four weeks on the same stretch of road were a major red flag.

Riley checked the ICU and all the obvious waiting areas in the hospital. There was no sign of Holly or anyone associated with the shelter or Sofia. She regretted not getting contact information from Holly on the two occasions they'd met. She didn't even know her last name. "Holly from Malibu who runs the Santa Monica youth shelter" wasn't exactly helpful. *There was only one way to get answers,* she decided.

*   *   *

Traffic was lighter than usual when Riley left the hospital that night. Instead of heading north toward the Valley, she swung her moto onto the 10 Freeway and headed west to Santa Monica. Nearly forty minutes later, she was cruising past the youth center, where only yesterday she'd attended Lexi's celebration of life service and sat right beside Sofia.

It seemed every light in the bungalow was on, but what caught Riley's eye immediately was the silver Honda station wagon with the rainbow bumper sticker parked across the street. She pulled even with the car, flipped her helmet visor up, and peered inside. It was empty, except for a cloth shoulder bag on the passenger seat. It looked like the bag she'd seen Themis carrying the morning they'd met at Abe's Deli. She rolled her bike slowly forward, slipped her hand out of her glove, and placed it on the hood of the car. The engine was still warm. Holly's dark blue Sprinter van was across the street in the driveway of the center. A chill ran the length of Riley's spine.

When they'd talked yesterday, Holly had given the impression she'd never heard of Themis or Avenging Allies before Riley had mentioned them. She'd been so convincing, even poking fun at the name of the citizen sleuth group. Why on earth would she have lied about that? Especially to somebody like Riley, who was clearly an ally and obviously there to help.

Riley cussed at herself quietly for having ignored her intuition at the time. Holly had been aloof, if not outright cold, when she'd shown up at the shelter. But Riley had rationalized her behavior. She'd been too quick to understand, too quick to excuse. And now she was beginning to regret how much she'd shared with Holly.

Riley cut the engine on her ride and rolled it quietly into the narrow gap between the station wagon and a rusty VW bug parked in front of it. The street was quiet in the way narrow neighborhood roads are at night. She kept her helmet in place and tucked her braid inside her jacket. No need to give herself away, she decided. For obvious reasons, Riley had always taken her wagon to the beach when she was surfing, and because she'd parked a few blocks away from the shelter yesterday, she was sure Holly would have no idea she owned a motorcycle.

She crossed the road cautiously, barely visible in her black leathers and helmet. She slipped through the open gate with its rainbow flag flapping in the breeze and ventured around the side of the bungalow, where she'd seen the young man smoking the day before.

The light from the condo complex next door was enough to navigate the side yard, and in only moments, Riley found herself behind the bungalow, looking up at the windows of the small kitchen where she'd found Holly baking cookies yesterday.

There were voices coming from inside.

She took a moment to survey the patchwork of shadows shrouding the backyard, taking in the lay of the land, looking specifically for any hazards she might stumble into in the dark, should she need to make a hasty exit. Behind the house was a flat area, likely a patch of lawn or perhaps a dipping pool, and beyond that was a small rectangular building with a single window backing to the alleyway. It had probably once been a detached garage—typical for the 1950s-style bungalows that remained in the area. And like most outbuildings in beach communities, where housing was tight, it had undoubtedly been converted to living quarters.

Riley made her way silently along the concrete walkway and ascended the stairs she'd seen Sofia navigating in her pink Prada pumps on the previous afternoon.

Through the lace curtains on the back door window, Riley could see Themis sitting on the kitchen counter, looking as comfortable as if she were in her own home. Holly was leaning with her back against the sink. From their body language, they seemed to know each other quite well. They were evidently in deep discussion, but the conversation was muted. Riley heard only Sofia's name and then the mention of someone named Javier. She had heard the same name yesterday. Holly had said that if Ms. Maria and Javier could manage the cleanup after the celebration of life, she would be able to cut out early.

As she watched Themis and Holly, Riley's stomach dropped. She had to admit she was in over her head. Suddenly, she was acutely aware of how unacceptable her own behavior had been lately. It was one thing to show up to a celebration of life ceremony—wearing a disguise, no less—for a person she'd never met, but it was another to drive forty minutes from home to stalk through someone's private property in the dark of night. Granted, she told herself now, that hadn't been her objective initially. She'd come to tell Holly about Sofia. It wasn't until she'd recognized Themis's car outside that she'd slipped into stealth mode.

And now, here she was, blending in with the night, eavesdropping . . .

Had she lost her mind? *Yes, maybe*, she decided. She had to admit, nothing had been the same since the night Leroy Williams had died. That tragedy had seemed to awaken something in her that she'd battled to keep suppressed for years. And now, she wasn't herself at all. How could she be? Not after everything that had happened recently.

The most daring thing she'd ever done before last week—besides pushing the speed limit—was to borrow the occasional lab coat at work for a few minutes to visit Jackson's office. But here she was, past her bedtime, having forgotten about dinner, trespassing and literally spying.

Even taking all that into account, Riley couldn't let go of the more pressing questions. Who was responsible for what had happened to Sofia? And why was Holly now hugging someone who, only the day before, she'd denied even knowing? There was clearly a connection between the two women that neither one had admitted to Riley, and they both had ties to Lexi—and now, it seemed, to Sofia too. True, Riley acknowledged, Holly owed her nothing. She couldn't be faulted for questioning Riley butting in where she had no business.

She needed time to think, and right now, her head was spinning with more questions than she could process. She was going to have to calculate her next move carefully. Putting her own actions aside, if Riley was purely objective, it looked like Holly had been dishonest with her about knowing Themis and the Avenging Allies. That was disappointing. And now Riley had to consider if perhaps the woman was more than just untrustworthy. Was she, in fact, dangerous? And if she was, Riley had walked right into that one. She'd already told Holly more than she should have about her chat with Detective Roberts, and she had opened herself up by indicating she could access privileged information from the LA medical examiner's office.

Riley stood in the cool darkness trying to lip-read, too afraid to move.

The thought of being caught spying was too disturbing to comprehend. What she was doing came with significant personal risk—and for what? She couldn't even grasp the substance of the conversation between Holly and Themis, let alone details.

Right now, she didn't know who to trust or what to think. Perhaps there was a logical explanation for what she was seeing. Sometimes the best thing to do was nothing at all. Maybe she just needed to go home and sleep on it. It had been an awful day, *an awful week.*

Riley backtracked quietly down the stairs and around the side yard, keeping to the shadows of the cypress trees lining the fence as she headed toward her bike. That was when she saw the soft red glow of his cigarette.

The man was leaning against the open back gate between the darkened alleyway and the bungalow's detached garage. A slow curl of smoke drifted above him as he raised and drew on his cigarette. Riley was sure he was the same man she'd seen leaning up against the corner of the bungalow yesterday. She remembered now how he had been staring at Sofia until he'd spotted her watching him, and then he'd suddenly disappeared.

Fortunately, he now had his back to her, facing the alleyway.

Riley studied the shape of him, the way his jeans were hitched above his hips, and the glint of his belt buckle in the headlights of an approaching vehicle when he turned toward it. She froze where she stood in the shadows, too afraid to breathe, watching as he dropped his cigarette and ground it out with his boot. The vehicle rolled slowly along the alleyway toward him, the gravel crunching under its wheels as it came to a stop. The man stepped toward it, reached out, and opened the passenger door before hopping up into the vehicle.

It was a large black pickup truck with raised bumpers and big wheels.

Riley would have recognized it anywhere by the skull emblem on the back window.

CHAPTER THIRTEEN

It was past eleven when Riley finally sat on the couch at home with a carton of ramen in her lap and a pair of chopsticks. Artemis was giving her the cold shoulder, as she usually did when Riley was home past her curfew, but Indio sat at her feet, watching her every move as though she might suddenly disappear again.

She hadn't been able to catch up on the news all day. So far, she'd only caught sound bites at the hospital from the TVs in the ICU waiting room and the break room outside the suites where Sofia had been undergoing surgery.

Most of what she had suspected about Sofia's ordeal was proving correct. Witnesses reported the girl had either been pushed or had stumbled while struggling with someone outside a vehicle on the shoulder of the freeway in the same area where Lexi had met her end almost a month earlier. The ensuing chaos following an obviously pregnant and blindfolded pedestrian entering traffic lanes on one of the busiest freeways in the world had caused pandemonium. Unfortunately, at the time, no one had thought to pursue the getaway vehicle or snap a picture of the license plate. While accounts from various onlookers were contradictory about whether Sofia had entered the roadway of her own volition, it seemed everyone agreed that a late-model, dark-colored van had been seen speeding away from the scene. Had it been a Sprinter van, like the one Holly drove? It was reported that both the California Highway Patrol and the LAPD were investigating the incident.

After dinner, Riley scrupulously scanned the street outside her house for parked vehicles that didn't belong. When she was confident there wasn't anything to be worried about, she took Indy out for a walk. She was working only a half-day shift tomorrow. Astrid was staying over from nights to pay her back for an exchange they'd made weeks earlier. Riley would be able to take her time getting up in the morning, so she could justify the late excursion. She owed it to Indy. And besides, she couldn't imagine sleep would come easily that night. Not after the disturbing day she'd had. Besides, there was a lot to process, and her own judgement seemed to be leading her down a dark path.

The logical next step was to pay Detective Roberts a second visit. Riley would tell her when and where she'd spotted the black pickup again—though she would have to omit some of the details about how she'd happened upon it the second time, unless she wanted to incriminate herself as a pathologically nosy citizen.

Similarly, she'd have to consider how much to say about Holly and Themis. They hadn't done anything overtly nefarious, as far as Riley could tell. But just dropping their names and perhaps mentioning their associations with both Sofia and Lexi Drake—would be enough. Maybe she'd also casually mention the fact that Holly drove a dark-colored van like the one seen leaving Sofia's accident. Then Detective Roberts could do the rest. She could do the sleuthing, and

Riley would just slip back into her life as it was before she'd been caught up in the drama surrounding the murders.

When she returned from her walk with Indy, instead of jumping straight into the shower, Riley made the mistake of checking her email. There was a message from the Avenging Allies website.

It was from Themis and simply said, "We should talk."

There was also a memo from Jackson's assistant that had been sent earlier in the day asking Riley to plan on meeting with him at four the following afternoon.

Oh hell no, Riley thought as she slapped her laptop closed. *Shit.*

Not even a hot lavender bath and the return of Artemis's affection—who had finally curled up on the bed next to her—helped. Riley lay awake for hours staring at the glowing numbers on her bedside clock, trying to make sense of the past week and of everything that had happened that day, her trip to the morgue to see the still-unidentified murder victim and the gut-wrenching realization that Sofia was unlikely to survive the horrific trauma she and her baby had suffered. And, of course, the last thing Riley wanted to lose sleep over was whatever Jackass was up to now.

*   *   *

It was just before noon when Riley found herself sitting in the office of Detective Roberts, trying to make a preposterous story sound credible. It was proving harder than she'd thought to find a way to express her concerns without bringing attention to the fact that she'd been snooping around.

The door to the detective's office was closed and her partner, Detective Garth—a wiry man with the build of a lightweight boxer—had joined them. Riley had been offered but had declined the customary cup of coffee. She'd already had three mugs at home, which was pushing her limits. Coffee made her chatty. One more drop and she might have trouble sticking to her script.

"So you were just stopping by the shelter to see if your friend Holly had heard the news about Sofia when you saw the pickup truck in the alleyway?" Detective Garth asked again with a deep frown, broadcasting his skepticism.

"That's right," Riley answered, doing her best not to break eye contact. "As I've already said, Detective, I saw a man getting into the passenger side of the truck. I believe he might live in the outbuilding at the shelter," she offered casually, but perhaps not casually enough. The detective's eyes narrowed just slightly. "I don't know what makes me say that," she added in an effort at damage control. "Just a guess."

Detective Garth rubbed his chin, shooting a dubious glance at his partner.

"And did you see who was driving?" Roberts cut in. "Was it the same man you saw on the 101 last week? The same man you told officers Garcia and Hahn had been sitting outside your house the night a disturbance was reported at your residence?"

"I didn't just *say* there was a man sitting outside my house. There *was* a man sitting outside my house that night, Detective. And yes, it was the same man I saw on the freeway." Riley felt a sudden rush of heat in her cheeks. *Coffee wasn't a good idea, but maybe someone would be so kind as to offer a glass of water.*

"And so, when you saw the man and the truck—last night, that is—you alerted your friend Holly at the shelter." It was Garth's turn again. Riley guessed she was caught in a game of bad cop, bad cop.

"No, no. Why would I do that?" She rolled her eyes as if the question were absurd. "The truck was driving away at that point. And besides, seeing him again . . . seeing his truck really shook me, if you know what I mean. How comforting could I be to Holly in that state? It was better to get out of there, to just go home and check in with her later today."

Detective Garth let out a sigh of exasperation and crossed his sinewy arms over his chest.

"I thought Detective Roberts should be the first to hear the news about the truck," Riley added, as if stating the obvious.

Garth's mobile phone rang just then. He looked relieved at the opportunity to step out and answer the call. Riley turned her attention back to Roberts with a cool smile, ready for the next round.

The woman was giving Riley a long, hard look over the top of her glasses, her index finger tapping relentlessly on the edge of the coffee mug she held.

"I'm going to caution you, Dr. Brighton," she said, straightening in her chair and putting her elbows on the desk. "The direction this investigation is beginning to take . . . concerns me. Quite frankly, it scares me. I think the less you have to do with anyone associated with these victims, the better. There are things I can't share with you, for obvious reasons—"

"Of course." Riley was quick to agree, but Roberts was still talking.

"To that end, I'm going to ask you to stay in your own lane, Dr. Brighton. I appreciate your intentions, but please leave the detective work to us."

"It's Riley, just plain Riley, Detective." Riley stood, flipping her coat off the back of the chair. "I hear you, and I will only too gladly let you do your job. Speaking of which," she said, pulling on her jacket, "I need to get to mine."

Riley felt she'd tossed the hot potato back where it belonged. Now Detective Roberts would have no option but to follow up with the man living behind the shelter in Santa Monica and, hopefully, take a good long look at Holly too.

"Thank you for coming in, Riley," Roberts said, softening her tone. Riley nodded as if they'd somehow reached a mutual understanding with her credibility still marginally intact. She realized, however, that she had just been warned—in the gentlest way possible—not to interfere with an ongoing police investigation.

"Cute kid, by the way," she deflected, nodding at the photograph on the detective's desk of a small boy in a bow tie with large inquisitive eyes and dimples. "How old?"

"Oh gosh, I think he was six in that shot," she said, smiling broadly, seemingly taking off her detective hat now that the interview was over. "Lordy, time flies. I can hardly believe he's in his third year of college now." She picked up the framed photo, admiring it in the way a mother would. "He looks so much like his grandpappy Cedrick here."

"Cedrick?" Riley said, barely keeping her surprise in check. "Is that his name too? Cedrick?" She forced a smile. "It suits him."

"Yes, yes it does," the detective said, standing to see Riley out.

*   *   *

As she split traffic lanes at high speed on the 5 Freeway into the city, weaving her motorcycle deftly between the slower-moving vehicles,

Riley mulled over her interview with the detectives. Just when she had resigned herself to staying in her own lane, as Detective Roberts had instructed, she'd been immediately lured back out by learning about Cedrick's connection to the investigation. She recalled how she'd thought Cedrick looked familiar when she'd met him at Abe's. It was those dimples, that smile—he was so much like his mother.

And now it made sense how Themis and the Avenging Allies had details about the crimes that weren't public. Riley was sure Roberts wouldn't have willingly shared confidential information with her son. She seemed to be a by-the-book professional. And with as much concern as she'd shown for Riley's safety in matters surrounding the case, she would no doubt be more troubled if she thought her own son was somehow covertly involved.

Riley mulled over what it might look like if she abided by Detective Roberts's warning. Life would be simpler—and, yes, safer—if she were to shed the burden of trying to discern who in her newest circle of acquaintances might be a cold-blooded serial killer. There was a comforting draw to ordinary life, to which she could so easily return. But in all practicality, Riley conceded, it was a little too late for that. She hadn't been able to get the brutally beaten face she'd seen yesterday in the morgue out of her mind. Someone, somewhere, was getting away with murder.

Riley refused to accept that another nameless soul in the City of Angels would go unclaimed. She couldn't allow a life to be so simply and callously erased. Until the victim was identified, she would never feel free of an obligation. And the visit to the morgue hadn't been the worst part of yesterday. For one thing, Sofia was no longer just a passing acquaintance. Only hours earlier, she and her baby girl had been Riley's patients—and someone had almost killed them in the most heinous way. The girl was fighting for her life in the ICU, and only time would tell if the baby would be all right.

For Riley, tragedy often felt like an invitation—more than that, an edict—to fix what was broken in the world. No doubt the same compulsion had drawn her to a career in emergency medicine, where she fought with a passion to right the social injustices many of her patients faced daily. And all this was why, despite her best intentions, Riley knew she'd never heed the detective's warning.

And now that she realized where Themis and Cedrick were obtaining intelligence, she could see the clear opportunity that created and the leverage it gave her. Themis had emailed her last night, seeking to talk. Riley would meet with the girl again, but this time, it would be with her own agenda.

But that would have to wait. Right now, Riley could only think about her upcoming meeting with Jackson.

*   *   *

"Walk with me, Brighton," Dr. Jackson barked when Riley showed up at four o'clock in his office, as instructed. The man plucked his glasses off his long face, slipped them into the top pocket of his lab coat, and held the door to the hallway open for her.

"Why not?" Riley replied, as if she had any choice. Once they reached the elevator, she finally asked, "Where are we headed?"

"The state medical board has sent a representative to chat with you, my dear."

"Wait . . . What about?"

"Dr. Bach is insisting the Williams case was all yours. He says he only got involved after the cardiac arrest. So it's only natural, you see, that the state needs a little clarification from you."

"What are you talking about?" Riley stopped dead in her tracks, hands balled into fists in the pockets of her coat. "Everyone working that night will tell you differently."

"Well, the medical board is interested in talking to *you* right now, Dr. Brighton," Jackson said, slamming a finger into the elevator down button.

"Wait a minute." Riley felt a flush of panic rising in her chest. The floor seemed to fall out from under her. "In that case, shouldn't I have representation with me?"

"That's my job, Brighton," he said coolly, putting a hand on her shoulder and directing her into the elevator.

*　　　*　　　*

Three people were sitting in the administrative office when Jackson ushered Riley inside. A white-haired stranger caught her eye first. She would soon learn he was a retired surgeon named Karlson. Then there was the puffy-faced Roger Harrison from personnel. And lastly, Riley's eyes fell on the hospital's medical director, and agent of misery, Hilary Stephens. The woman sat at the head of the table, leaning back in her chair, arms firmly crossed over her chest.

"Well, well, well . . ." Dr. Karlson's eyes gave Riley a once-over. He didn't bother to so much as stand or introduce himself, choosing simply to slip his business card with two fingers across the glossy tabletop in her direction. "I didn't realize they were making doctors so pretty these days," he said.

"Perhaps it's time for another visit to the optometrist, sir," Riley said flatly, dropping into an open seat at the table, ignoring his card in front of her. Nothing set her off more than dinosaurs of paternalism, oblivious to their own sense of entitlement and sexist idioms.

"Beautiful *and* witty. Very good, Dr. Brighton, though I'll have you know I've just recently had an eye exam." The man chuckled, clearly missing her rebuke.

The interrogation lasted twenty minutes, during which Riley explained how, from her perspective, things had gone the night little Leroy Williams died.

Her intention had been to stick to the facts. To steer clear of any leaps of logic or allegations that might incriminate anyone, especially as she had no proof to back up her suspicions. Not yet anyway. *But the events should speak for themselves*, she thought, *once all the appropriate information has been gathered*. To say she trusted City's legal team was perhaps a stretch, but she knew they were tenacious, and the truth would finally out. It would be clear from the child's lab results and Bach's actions that night what had happened. Riley just needed to give the process time. It should be an open-and-shut case of negligence—tragic, but indisputable.

Dr. Karlson was taking notes in longhand on a yellow legal pad. Riley heard her own voice as if it were coming from somewhere outside herself. "Leroy Williams was well known to the ER staff. And some of us working that night—myself and two of the nurses—knew him from the first time he was a patient at the hospital. The night of the fire, the night he'd lost his mother."

Riley's mind flashed back to that event the previous year. As she spoke, she tried not to let the words catch in her throat the way they threatened to. When she felt the sting of tears in her eyes, she cautioned herself in just the way her late mentor, Marcel, would have: *Dry eyes, Brighton. Dry eyes.*

"Leroy suffered from asthma ever since the fire," Riley went on. "Most of us in the ER at City General have interacted with him over the past year to manage his breathing difficulties." Riley sat back in her chair, keeping her hands in her pockets. She knew she should make a better effort at holding eye contact with Karlson, but her focus was elsewhere. "On the night he died, he came in by ambulance from his foster home. I was busy in room sixteen with an overdose patient. I don't usually work the night shift anymore. I just happened to be covering for a colleague, Dr. Wolf, who had called off sick."

"When exactly did you become aware the child was in the ER?" Karlson asked, adopting a more serious tone. Harrison and Stephens looked on silently as she provided her detailed testimony, their expressions unreadable.

"Well, I don't know the exact minute. But the charge nurse, Carrie, came into my treatment area and asked if I could help in room eleven with Leroy. Like me, she was familiar with the kid. She knew how he usually responded to his treatments, and she was concerned he wasn't recovering appropriately. She said his nurse was afraid he might go into cardiac arrest. So, of course, as soon as I could, I left my patient with one of the residents and ran to room eleven just as the code blue was called. When I entered the treatment area, I could see that the respiratory therapist and Leroy's nurse, Olivia, were already doing CPR on the little guy."

"And was there anyone else in the room?" Stephens cut in brusquely. Up until that point, she hadn't acknowledged Riley outside of providing her with a flat, two-dimensional stare from across the table.

Riley turned her attention to Stephens. *This* was a question she was ready for.

"Yes, things got hectic once the code was called," she replied. "But naturally, Dr. Bach and his resident were present, of course." And she would leave it at that. She would be careful from there on out to answer only direct questions.

Karlson's brow furrowed. "What happened after that? How were you specifically involved?"

"Well, I immediately set about evaluating the child, checking for a pulse to see if the CPR was effective. Dr. Bach's resident, Dr. Li, had already intubated Leroy, so I listened to both his lungs to make sure the breathing tube was placed correctly."

"And was it?"

"It was in the lungs, but it was in a little too deeply." Riley flinched at having to criticize a trainee's efforts. She knew how stressful it could be to intubate a six-year-old in an emergency. In fact, it could be challenging enough under controlled circumstances. "It's easy, if you're rushed, to put the tube down past the bifurcation and accidentally ventilate only one lung. So I untied the tape securing the tube and pulled it out a few millimeters until I could hear air movement on both sides of the chest, indicating that both lungs were inflating. Then I secured the tube again and asked Carrie to call for a portable chest X-ray to document it was now in the correct position."

"And what was Dr. Bach doing at this time?" It was Stephens again. But before Riley could answer the question, the woman cut her off. "Why did you feel the need to intervene? Dr. Bach has more experience than you do, doesn't he? Wasn't he your program director?"

Riley kept her cool, recognizing she was in the eye of the storm.

"Marcel . . . Dr. Benoit was the director when I was in training . . . before he passed," Riley said, her voice dropping to almost a whisper. Her eyes darted accusingly to Jackson as she went on. "Dr. Bach was appointed residency director just two years ago." She ignored the obvious rebuke Stephens had intended and effectively skirted the question about Bach's competence.

Riley had *wanted* to say that Tobias Bach had been utterly useless during the child's cardiac arrest. He'd stood in the corner, watching her and a second-year resident direct the failed resuscitation, offering no input or help. It had almost been as if he were in a stupor. At the time, Riley had even wondered if he had been somehow impaired. Or perhaps he simply had nothing to offer in the way of saving a six-year-old's life. And in the days that followed, Riley's suspicions had grown about Bach's conduct and what had really transpired before she'd entered room 11 that night.

"But the boy only deteriorated *after* your intervention. Isn't that correct?"

It was Jackson who spoke now. Riley gave him a long, hard look. Something in her chest tightened as she wondered how he could justify asking such a question. Wasn't he supposed to be her representative? Hadn't he said that was what his role would be in the interview?

Of course, she'd known better than to trust Jackass Jackson. Out of sheer curiosity, she had wanted to ask him how he managed to live with himself.

"I wouldn't say he further deteriorated, Dr. Jackson," Riley went on, keeping her tone neutral. She knew if Jackson sensed blood in the water, he would go in for the kill. "The child was in grave condition before I got to his bedside. As a team, we continued resuscitation efforts for over an hour, but Leroy's heart just never responded to any of our interventions."

"And why do you think that was, Dr. Brighton?" Karlson asked. *Just like a surgeon.* Riley almost groaned, deducing the man's former specialty must have been in orthopedics.

"Because he was dead, Dr. Karlson." She did her best not to sound condescending but fell short. "And unfortunately, we still haven't figured out how to reverse that condition." At once, Riley knew she'd crossed a line. But for crying out loud, was Karlson really the best the state had to offer?

The room fell silent then, except for Harrison from personnel. Riley could have sworn she heard him softly snickering behind a closed fist, but she dared not shift her gaze from Karlson.

She stood, pushing her chair back under the conference table calmly. "Now I have an emergency room full of patients to attend to, and my colleagues could no doubt use my help. So I'll be on my way. I suggest you let me know if you have any further questions after you've interviewed everyone else involved. And by everyone, I mean *everyone*," she said, directing her gaze coolly toward Jackson. "Including the inexplicably absent Tobias Bach, our esteemed residency director." She turned to Karlson, softening her tone slightly. "I recommend starting with the nurses, sir. They're generally the most truthful."

She was halfway to the elevator when she realized what she'd done. Her heart was threatening to jump straight out of her chest as she altered her course and slipped instead through the doorway to the stairwell. She expected Jackson to be on her heels, demanding she return to the interview immediately, but she knew he probably couldn't take the stairs two at a time as she observed herself now doing.

Riley's outburst had obviously been in some way cathartic. Either that, or the ER was busier than usual that afternoon. She was able to finish out the rest of her shift that evening without even *thinking* about Jackson. Thankfully, it would be days before she saw him again, but now she found herself obsessing about the absent residency director. *Where the hell was Bach?* He'd seemed to just disappear after the boy's death, which was plausibly, in her view anyway, an admission of guilt. Not even his secretary had answers. His email and voicemail simply stated he was out of the office until further notice.

* * *

Later that evening, after Riley's run-in with the administrators, she sat at home with dinner in her lap, answering emails. She replied to the message she'd received from Themis the day before. At the time, Riley had felt she needed a little reprieve. It had been a tough couple of weeks. Despite her decision to ignore Detective Roberts's warning to stay out of the investigation, she suddenly found herself a little less enthusiastic about delving back into sleuthing. Themis would have to wait a day or two.

Riley responded, "I'm off on Wednesday this week."

The reply came almost instantly: "Thanks, does seven work for you? Breakfast at Abe's?"

There was something about the tone of the response—or perhaps the timing—that registered with Riley. For one thing, it was conciliatory. During their first communication, Themis had simply told Riley when and where they'd meet and even what to order her for breakfast. There had been a shift. Something had changed.

Riley felt she had the upper hand already, even before she disclosed that she was aware of Cedrick's family connection to the lead detective in the freeway investigations. Perhaps Themis was feeling a little overwhelmed since there had now been a third attack, or perhaps she hadn't anticipated a twenty-four-hour delay before Riley's response to her email. Whatever it was, Riley was reassured by the prospect of a more collaborative arrangement with the Avenging Allies.

There was also, much to her regret, an email from Jackson. Riley debated hitting Delete before even opening it. The man would always want the last word; that was Jackass for you. He must have been seething after she'd stormed out of the meeting with Karlson.

Ultimately, raw curiosity urged her to open the email, which read:

> Dr. Brighton,
>
> You are to present the Williams case at the monthly morbidity and mortality grand rounds this Friday morning. The department will be expecting a detailed explanation regarding how the patient's failed resuscitation was handled.
>
> Sincerely,
> Rudolph Jackson, Chairman,
> Department of Emergency Medicine

Riley seethed. She could see his demand for what it was: an opportunity for Jackson to publicly point the finger at her, to link her with the unexpected and still unexplained death of a six-year-old child. If nothing else, it was clear Jackson meant to impugn her on the spot in front of her colleagues.

The morbidity and mortality grand rounds—or M and M, as it was known in academic medicine—was a venue intended to explore and discuss difficult cases, providing the entire audience of medical trainees and their faculty the opportunity to learn from the mistakes of others.

The educational discussions at M and M were privileged information, not accessible to plaintiff's attorneys who might wish to file lawsuits against the institution when patients had been harmed or worse. Often, however, M and M events turned into a trial of sorts—gladiator games, where peers and colleagues pointed fingers, and blame was assigned. While the formal intention of the event was medical education, the unspoken objective was often to humiliate the unlucky presenter into never committing such foolish mistakes again.

Riley realized, guilty or not, she would be the sacrificial lamb at the colosseum that month.

CHAPTER FOURTEEN

Halfway through Tuesday morning at work, Riley received a text message marked as urgent from her contact in the medical examiner's office. It said simply, We need to talk ASAP.

Riley's chest tightened. This wasn't Joe's typical demeanor at work; he was a pretty low-key guy in general, calm and thorough. Patient. She glanced at the clock and was relieved to see it was 10:50 a.m. already, and she could justify taking lunch. "Be there in ten minutes," she replied.

He texted back promptly. Meet me in the lobby.

Sure enough, by the time she'd rushed to the county morgue ten minutes later, Joe Padilla from the medical examiner's office was waiting for her.

"This way," he said, and without another word, he was steering her by the elbow down a dimly lit corridor and into a small specimen library. He pulled the door closed behind them. Either the room itself or Joe smelled like formalin, which, when added to the fact that Riley hadn't eaten yet, made her slightly nauseous.

"What's going on, Joe?" she asked, a little unsettled. "You have an ID on our victim?"

"Soon, I hope, but no, that's not why I messaged you. I wanted to let you know that Jackson and someone from the state medical board were here when I got in this morning. They were asking a lot of questions about the Williams case—the little kid, Leroy, from a couple of weeks ago."

Riley shook her head, at a loss.

Joe took a breath. "Specifically, they were after the toxicology results from the autopsy. After they left my office, I went back and reviewed the medical records from the ER that night, and I saw your name—I mean, *your name* is on the chest X-ray order, Rye." Joe looked at her as if waiting for some reaction. She didn't flinch. "I think Jackson's looking for someone to pin this on. I wanted you to have a heads-up. I might be able to slow roll some of the autopsy lab results, but—"

"I'm not sure what you're getting at, Joe," she interrupted. "I have nothing to hide. You know that, don't you?"

His whole body seemed to relax at her reply. "Well, I'm glad to hear that, because someone ought to go down for this one. The kid's potassium level was through the roof. Twice the lethal level, to be sure. That alone would have stopped his heart immediately." Riley remained silent, watching Joe summarize his findings, her expression giving nothing away. "There's no treatment for asthma I can think of that would increase a potassium level, is there?"

"If anything, you would expect to see a lower-than-normal level in a patient using a beta-agonist inhaler. Low potassium levels are a common side effect of that drug, especially when it's used as frequently as the kid required."

"Okay then, well . . ." He stammered, shaking his head. "That's doubly concerning. I'm stumped. Unless, of course, someone administered potassium to treat a low level in the child and accidentally overdosed him or maybe infused the drug too rapidly. That could easily prove fatal. But the child's electronic chart from that night doesn't reflect any documented blood work or that potassium chloride was ordered or administered. I've already checked with my contact in the ER pharmacy—there's no record of anyone requesting or dispensing potassium that evening."

Riley took a deep breath, weighing what she dared say. She had to throw Joe a bone or two. It was clear he was looking out for her. "Well, I hate to say it, but I'm pretty sure I know what happened that night, Joe," she admitted, watching his expression shift from bewildered to something else that was a little harder to define. His lips parted as if to ask a question, but she beat him to the punch. "I can't prove anything just yet, but I know someone who can. I'm certain that one of the nurses involved that night could solve this mystery." Riley gave him a long look, weighing what she might add without crossing the Rubicon. "The woman just needs the courage to come forward, and that's not easy when the person I suspect is at fault has Jackson's unconditional and, in my opinion, misplaced—no, *corrupt* support."

Joe nodded, staring back at her with tight-lipped understanding. That was all she needed. She'd said enough.

"I don't want to put you in a difficult spot, Joe. If you're called to testify in a lawsuit or a hearing for City, then you will have to disclose our discussion." He leaned in, and she lowered her voice even further. "I've met the representative from the medical board. He's in Jackson's corner, I'm sure. We don't want it to look as if you're trying to cover anyone's ass. As you've pointed out, my name is on the kid's chart. That means I'm already on their short list."

"You're probably right." Joe chewed on his lower lip. "And, of course, everyone knows we're close, so yeah. I don't want it to look like I'm hiding something."

Riley's mouth curled into a tight smile. Joe never stopped trying. He'd always been sweet on her. She regretted it was one-sided. Yes, he was quite attractive. Even Astrid had noticed it, and Riley thought Astrid was generally more interested in softball and trips to Home Depot than in men. But in one of her darker medical examiner jokes, she'd once said Joe was "drop-dead gorgeous," and maybe that was true, but Riley just couldn't wrap her mind around dating someone who spent his days in a giant refrigerator with LA's dead.

"I've known for the last week that Jackson is looking for a scapegoat, Joe. Which means he also suspects what I do—there's something worth hiding. The hospital's legal team will ultimately sort this out, but Jackson's stalling as best he can. I think he's afraid that shining a light on this mess could prove disastrous for the emergency residency program." She cleared her throat. "The medical school is about to be renamed for our biggest private donor, and our own program is set to receive another substantial endowment in the next few weeks." Riley searched Joe's eyes for any inkling he knew about her family's connection to the funding. To her relief, his expression gave no such indication. "Jackson won't want to do anything to jeopardize sponsorship. The department can't handle any bad press right now."

"Yeah, well, I suppose sensationalized malpractice suits do tend to unsettle donors." Joe shrugged.

Riley broke eye contact. She felt awful not sharing more with him about what she knew of the upcoming endowment from the Shira Altman Foundation, but it wasn't the right time for that conversation. Joe was giving her one of his intense looks, the kind that made her flush. She wasn't certain he even found her version of the events surrounding the Williams case convincing. She was beginning to think that nothing she did could change how he felt about her, and that realization strengthened her resolve. She wasn't going to drag him into this any more than she already had.

"I've heard about the renaming; it was in the campus newspaper last month." Joe leaned casually on a bookshelf full of bottled autopsy specimens, some entirely unrecognizable but all equally off-putting to Riley. "Isn't there some big fancy gala planned at the medical school in a couple weeks?"

"So they say." Riley dropped her gaze. "Invitation only, I heard," she added, not wanting to stray into any potential discussion of attending together. Joe seemed to get the message. He shuffled his feet and changed the subject again. Riley had the sense he wanted to keep her chatting.

"I imagine the kid's family will sue."

"There *is* no family, Joe." Perhaps it was the building pressure she'd been facing over the last two weeks, but her eyes were quicker to tear up than usual. "That's just it. Leroy's mother died in the fire a year ago, and as far as I know, there is no extended family. At the time, the PD suspected the mother's death was gang-related. Retribution for snitching or something like that, if I remember correctly. The social workers never got any information out of the kid. Eventually, he was placed into the system. I'm pretty sure he'd been in foster care ever since leaving the burn unit."

Almost at once, her mind was inundated by the unsolicited memory of the terror in Leroy's wide eyes the night of the fire. And his screams, his heartbreaking screams for his mother. Riley remembered how much morphine the child had needed. He'd been in so much physical and emotional pain. And she could feel it now, the raw brutality, the injustice of it all. It stirred something in her that seemed to grow. A darkness that swelled, threatening to smother her.

Dry eyes, Brighton, dry eyes. She heard Marcel's words again, as if he were standing right next to her. She dragged her focus into the present. Her gaze drifted back to the dingy carpeted floor with its old, faded stains. She wondered what had caused them. The smell of formalin seemed to be intensifying as the minutes ticked by. Something about Leroy losing his mother in the fire tugged at her once again, but she shrugged it off.

She looked up at Joe. "That poor kid's life was a living hell." Her voice finally cracked.

"Tragic." Joe's brow knit with concern.

"Not just tragic, Joe—*unforgivable.* Someone's gotta pay for this." Riley's eyes burned. Something inside of her she'd been battling to suppress began to slowly surface. A memory she'd tried to keep buried. She pushed it back defiantly. The injustice of little Leroy's death, the bitterness of how unfair life had been before he died, the tragic loss of his mother. And then it struck her, the parallel she'd been avoiding. The obvious connection she shared with Leroy. The unbearable sorrow of losing her own father in a fire when she was just a little kid.

How had she not seen it sooner? *Jesus,* she thought, was she in that much denial? No wonder she felt as if she was losing her mind. The grief was always there, following her like a shadow. Watching and waiting patiently to surface again. It had caught her once before, nearly derailing her career in the second year of residency after Marcel had died.

She realized suddenly that ever since Leroy's death, she'd felt that darkness again. And now she wondered if it hadn't clouded her thinking in the prior weeks. Some of her decisions had been so risky. *Ridiculously risky.* She'd allowed her emotions to override her common sense, even putting her own safety in jeopardy more than once.

She snapped her attention back to Joe. She couldn't afford to go down that dark road again. Biting her lip, she turned to leave. Joe reached out, placing a hand on her shoulder. She looked up at him then, caught in his gaze. Those hazel eyes. Those thick, long lashes. The perfect angle of his jaw and the irresistible shape of his mouth. Maybe Astrid had a point . . . but looks weren't everything. *Yes,* Riley decided, *it's Joe who smells like formalin.*

"I better get back," she said, stepping away. "Let me know when you get an ID on our freeway victim, would you?"

"You got it," he said, striding ahead to open the door for her. "We're getting close. I think we have a hit through missing persons—I'm just waiting for LAPD to confirm. I'll keep you in the loop."

"Thanks, much appreciated," she said, quickening her step.

"Friday evening?" he called out from behind her as she headed out through the lobby. She turned and waved then, not wanting to ignore his invitation a second time. Joe was a patient man, but then again, he spent his days in the company of the dead, where no one was ever too demanding.

On her way back to the ER, Riley stopped by the cafeteria to grab a to-go lunch box. She'd already used up her lunch break. She could snack between cases, she decided. As she reached the checkout counter, Hudson, the trauma surgery intern, appeared at her side.

"Hello, Dr. Brighton." He beamed, looking down on her. She'd forgotten how tall he was. She was surprised to find him so animated after the way they had last parted. "I just wanted you to know I really appreciated our chat the other night about tension pneumothorax. And I wanted to say thank you and let you know I'm now considering changing my area of interest from general surgery to emergency medicine."

Riley did her best to hide her amusement. She wondered how many times he might change his mind before his year of internship was up. "That's exciting, Dr. Hudson, but keep your options open. You may find yourself both enticed and disillusioned by several areas of specialty. There's no rush. You have plenty of time before you need to make a commitment. But for sure, I understand the draw of the ER. Never a dull moment." And then she noticed the embroidery on the top pocket of his lab coat. *Dr. Hudson, Intern.* She realized then that it was the same lab coat she'd borrowed from a hook outside the OR to visit Jackson's office last week. She remembered the volume of detailed notes filling the pockets and how they had spilled out onto the bloody ER floor the night he had shown up in trauma bay five to help with the gunshot victim. The cornucopia of notations proved Hudson was suitably preoccupied with the specifics of case details—obsessed, even—as only the best medical trainees are. That was when Riley realized he was a perfect candidate for an assignment.

"If you mean what you say, Dr. Hudson," Riley went on, "why don't you come to the ER's M and M grand rounds this Friday. We have a big case to explore, and I've been asked by our department chair to lead the discussion in front of about two hundred of our colleagues from the medical school and residency programs."

The intern's smile broadened.

"Be there or be square, Hudson. Wilcox Hall, the big auditorium on the second floor, oh-seven hundred on Friday." Riley picked up her lunch and turned to leave, but then she added, as if it were merely an afterthought, "But I don't want you to show up unprepared."

"Unprepared?" he echoed, puzzled.

"I'm giving you an opportunity to shine, Dr. Hudson. I know you can handle it." She smiled, raising an eyebrow. "I want you to look up every reason a patient who'd suffered extensive burns in the last year might experience a lethal potassium level—*without* potassium chloride being administered."

The intern's brows knit, as if he were starting his postulations already.

"This is a very interesting and consequential case study. Maybe you can help crack it. I want you to specifically focus on any medications that could cause such a surge in potassium levels. Especially in emergency situations—for example, like the medications used for sedating and intubating an asthmatic who is decompensating."

"Sounds like a challenge, Dr. Brighton. Thanks, I'll be there. You won't be able to miss me," he said, motioning with a hand above his head, referring to his height.

"Top level, back row, okay?" She grinned. "And speak up when called on. I want you to impress your colleagues and classmates."

"See you Friday," he said, pulling out a three-by-five card from his top pocket and jotting down a note.

When Riley got back to the ER, she headed straight to the break room to put her lunch in the refrigerator. Sonya was in the kitchen alone, making a fresh pot of coffee.

"Oh, you're a godsend," Riley said, grabbing a paper cup from the rack above the nurse's head. "Coffee will have to do until I get time to eat."

"It's hazelnut—your favorite." Sonya fanned a hand over the dripping pot. "Mine too."

"I could tell from the hallway!" Riley giggled. As she waited for the last few drops of coffee to finish brewing, she took a bite of her sandwich before putting it back into its box and placing it in the fridge. "Hey, Sonya, how well do you know Olivia on nights?"

"Liv? Oh, gosh, I guess I know her some. Her sister was my roommate in nursing school. Liv was two years behind us. I've been around her occasionally. Why?"

"Well, it's just . . . Oh, never mind." Riley paused, holding her empty cup under her chin. Her brows knit for a moment, then she went on, "I just wondered how open she would be to talking about the Williams case. She was working that night, and I think she might have seen something she's been reluctant to share."

"I've never found her to be particularly talkative." Sonya lifted the coffeepot off the hot plate. "She's a bit of an introvert. The exact opposite of her sister, Tilly, who works in pediatrics. I can never shut that girl up," Sonya giggled, rolling her eyes.

"Do you think you could get Tilly to talk Liv into meeting with me? I hate to ask the favor, but I think Liv needs to disclose what happened that night. It'd probably be a weight off her shoulders."

"I heard about the case, Rye. It sounds just awful," she said, filling Riley's cup and then her own. "That poor little guy. He was such a cutie, and everything he'd been through was just horrific."

"Yeah, what he went through was inexcusable." Riley shook her head. She was thinking more of what had happened that night in the ER than of the suspicious apartment fire the boy had been injured in the year before. "Poor baby."

"Sure, Riley. I'll see what I can do. I can run up to pediatrics on my lunch break or text Tilly to meet me in the cafeteria. I saw her car in the parking lot this morning, so I know she's on today."

"That'd be great, Sonya. Much obliged." Riley headed for the door, raising her coffee cup in a salute of appreciation.

CHAPTER FIFTEEN

That Wednesday, Riley once again seated herself in booth 18 at Abe's. She was early. It was 6:45, and the sky was slowly growing lighter. She couldn't help but notice the place wasn't as busy during the week as it had been during her previous visit on Saturday. Cedrick, in his red-and-white checkered apron, was nowhere to be seen. Maybe it was his day off.

Riley ordered a coffee from a short waitress with pink hair and matching cat-eye glasses. She sat watching the parking lot out the window. The leaves on the trees outside had turned with the fall weather, their muted colors soft in the growing dawn light. There was a definite chill in the air.

She was on her second cup of coffee when Themis finally showed up. This time, she wasn't alone. To Riley's dismay, she saw the girl walking in with Holly. She was even more surprised to see how relaxed Holly looked when she spotted Riley from across the restaurant. Themis and Holly both smiled and waved as though nothing at all was strange about the two of them being together. They stopped at the deli counter to point at something under the glass before making a purchase and heading over to the booth where Riley was waiting.

"They have the best pastries here," Holly crooned a moment later, slipping into the seat across from her. "How are you, my dear?"

Riley wasn't sure how to respond. She sat back in the booth with her arms crossed over her chest, as if observing the scene from a distance.

"I know you two have met," Themis interjected as she pulled off her denim jacket and scooted into the booth next to Holly. "So I'll skip the introductions."

Riley was at a loss. Had she misunderstood what she'd seen a couple of nights ago when she'd been spying on them at the shelter in Santa Monica? Both Themis and Holly were acting as if they had nothing to hide, which was odd as Holly had distinctly given Riley the impression she'd never heard of Themis or the Avenging Allies. But here they were, the two of them together, as if there was nothing to question.

"So, how do you two know each other?" Riley began, not wanting to disclose that she had already discovered they were well acquainted.

"Oh, Bella and I go way back," Holly said, placing an arm around the girl. "We once had a shared passion for saving teens from being trafficked by the gangs in Venice. But more recently, she's been our private sleuth. She's a tremendous help to the shelter, tracking down missing kids and reuniting families where it's been appropriate. Haven't you, Bella?"

"Bella?" Riley questioned.

Holly ripped off a piece of her pastry and popped it into her mouth. "Will you get us some coffee, dear?" she said, catching the eye of the pink-haired waitress as she passed by.

"Well, you didn't think Themis was my real name, did you?" Bella gave Riley a crooked smile. "That's just a holdover from my days as a student of Greek mythology. Citizen sleuths need their anonymity more than most. I thought that would be obvious."

Riley did her best not to look duped.

Holly placed a hand adorned with several rings across her heart. "I'm so sorry, Riley. I had no idea that my Bella was your Themis. We've always been on a real-name basis, and to be honest, if I'd ever heard the term *Avenging Allies* before you mentioned it, I'm sure I would have remembered such a cheesy moniker. Sorry, Bella, but *really?* Avenging Allies is just so cliché," Holly said, putting an arm around the girl again and giving her a squeeze. "I was completely in the dark, Riley. Honestly. Bella filled me in on her meeting with you last Saturday. And, of course, I told her you had been at the service for Lexi and that we're friends."

For some reason, Riley bought every word Holly was saying. Maybe it was just easier, she told herself, to believe the woman she'd thought was her friend had simply miscommunicated than to think Holly could have played any part in a series of brutal, cold-blooded attacks.

"Now that we have *that* out of the way," Bella said, rolling her eyes at Holly. "And by the way, Avenging Allies is a great name, in my opinion. Cedrick, my partner, chose it for us once we started focusing on LGBTQ hate crimes." She puffed her cheeks out in frustration before adding impatiently, "Forget it. Let's get down to business."

"Coffee first," Holly insisted, holding up her empty cup and waving down the waitress again.

"After what happened to Sofia—" Before Bella could go on, her eyes filled with tears. She palmed her sockets, as though trying to stuff the tears back where they came from, and took a moment to compose herself. This surprised Riley. She'd pegged the girl as all business, no emotion, but clearly, she'd misread her.

"I called Bella as soon as the police showed up at the shelter on Monday afternoon," Holly filled in for Bella, passing the girl a handful of napkins from the dispenser at the end of their table. "I was a mess when I heard the news about Sofia. It's just unbelievable. A nightmare. And, of course, the police were asking if I knew of any family, how old she was, how long she'd been at the shelter. I can only assume it was you, Riley, who told them of her link to us."

"It was," Riley confirmed. "Believe it or not, I recognized her shoes from the day before, at Lexi's service. She and the baby were my patients on Monday. So I know what she's going through, and you're right, Holly—it's an absolute nightmare." Riley paused, assessing whether Bella was ready to hear more; judging from her reaction, it seemed she was close to Sofia. "I'm obliged to privacy with my patient's details, of course, but I know I'm not telling you anything you haven't already heard on the news. The only thing I can add is that I had a chance to check on the baby last night after work. She's doing better than I expected. I wish I could say the same for Sofia."

Holly put her hand over Bella's and squeezed it gently. "I knew with Riley's connections at the hospital we'd get the scoop."

Riley had wanted to say more. She'd wanted to tell them it was miraculous Sofia's baby had lived through such trauma. She'd wanted to tell them that after the head injury Sofia had sustained, she would probably never hold her daughter in her arms, and the chances of her ever having a normal life were slim. But more than any of that, Riley wanted to tell them both that if it was the last thing she ever did, she would help bring to justice whoever was responsible for the horrific crime.

"We need a plan." It was Bella who broke the silence in the wake of Riley's update. The despair that only moments ago had colored her tone was replaced by something that sounded like determination. "By now, it's obvious to all of us that these freeway crimes are linked and probably the work of the same person or people. Maybe a gang—"

"First things first," Holly interrupted, turning to Riley. "Do you have any updates from the medical examiner on the victim you came across last week? The press still hasn't released an ID. We need to know how this individual is tied into all of this."

Riley weighed her options. Things were moving fast now. It was clear Bella and Holly expected her cooperation. How accommodating did she need to be, and what exactly was she going to get in return? Only moments ago, their honesty had been in question—and to some degree, it still was. The night she'd eavesdropped on Holly and Bella could have very well been the night they concocted the story about Holly being entirely unaware of the Avenging Allies. How could she *not* have known about the group? But, in fairness, Riley realized that if Holly didn't know Cedrick, perhaps it was possible she hadn't heard of Avenging Allies before Riley mentioned the group.

"Yes, I agree, first things first." Riley placed both hands on the tabletop. "I'm happy to tell you both what I know, but I need some gaps filled in, if you don't mind. Let's start with you, Bella," she said, turning to the girl. "I might be a little rusty on Greek mythology, but I'm slightly sharper in other areas. How are you and Cedrick gaining access to information about this case from Detective Roberts?"

Bella's amber eyes flashed with displeasure. She answered only by chewing on her cheek.

"Oh boy, here we go," Holly sighed, throwing up her hands. "I suggest we order breakfast first, ladies; I have a feeling we're going to be here a while."

Holly was right. Breakfast seemed to make everything better.

Bella clarified her relationship with Cedrick. They had met in a college classroom three years previously at the state university in the Valley. Cedrick was an IT whiz kid, it seemed. Bella didn't outright admit he had been hacking into his mother's work laptop, but that was the revelation Riley took from their discussion. That news prompted Riley to make a mental note that, in the interest of transparency, she needed to disclose to both Bella and Holly that she'd paid Detective Roberts a second visit on the day after Sofia's attack. That tidbit surfacing without her admission wouldn't do much to build mutual trust.

By the end of breakfast, some of the dust had settled. Riley gained clarity on the link between Bella and Holly. They had known each other since Bella, as a runaway, had lived at the shelter in her early teens. They had both known Lexi before she began working at the center. Holly didn't know much about Sofia's past, except that she didn't fit the typical profile of kids who showed up at the shelter. She had apparently come from a life of privilege.

"I can still remember the morning she arrived," Holly said, leaning back in the booth. "She must have been about five months along, so I guess it was almost three months ago now. But she was so thin you would never have known she was pregnant. She was wearing a pleated dress with a bow at the collar and those Prada pumps. She had a small carrying case with her—Gucci, I think. And she looked like she'd just stepped off a bus from Bel Air. She was very naive or maybe just very young. I'm not sure I ever got an answer from her about her age. She didn't have a cell phone or an ID. Of course, I didn't pressure her. Most of these kids share information when and if they feel safe. I figured it would just take a little time, but she never did seem to warm up to me."

"Did she ever get close to anyone at the shelter? Did she develop any friendships?" Riley cut in, remembering the smoking man she'd seen at Lexi's service and how he had seemed so interested in Sofia.

"She was very dependent on Lexi. Excessively so," Holly replied. "I got the sense Sofia was perhaps on the autism spectrum. High functioning, artistically gifted, but in some ways very socially withdrawn. Sometimes that's a reflection of abuse or trauma. I didn't know her well enough to make the distinction. But Lexi had been counseling her." Holly's gaze drifted; it was clear the topic stirred up memories. "It set Sofia back, what happened to Lexi. It set us all back, but I got the sense it really shook Sofia. Poor kid. She seemed even more withdrawn after Lexi's murder. And, of course, that was understandable."

"And that's when I met her," Bella chimed in. "Right after Lexi's murder, when I opened my investigation, Sofia was one of my first interviews. I would agree with Holly—she was very affected by losing Lexi, but more than that. She seemed afraid to be without her. So I started going by every day. It cost me a fortune in gas, but I just had to check on her. I brought her sketchbook paper sometimes; that seemed to cheer her up. I think she began to trust me, but she never talked about her past. Occasionally, I'd get her to take a walk on the beach with me, but she wouldn't go anywhere on her own. She told me once Lexi had warned her never to leave the shelter without an escort."

"What reason would she have to leave the shelter?" Riley leaned back into her seat.

"Well, there were the prenatal checkups, for one," Holly noted. "Once we realized she was pregnant, that is. Lexi didn't want her taking the bus alone. In the beginning, Ms. Maria, our housekeeper, was going with Sofia to the clinic in Venice, but I put a stop to that when I realized it was Javier who was actually escorting her."

"Javier?" Riley raised an eyebrow.

"Ms. Maria's son. He lives on the property with her, out back, just off the alley. He's been with us a few months now—helps with odd jobs and maintenance. I checked him out. He's here legally. I'm very careful about that sort of thing. We can't afford to take any risks with immigration. Seems like a nice enough fellow, but it's my responsibility to keep our kids safe, and I just thought it best not to encourage a relationship there."

"What were things like between Javier and Lexi?"

"Lexi?" Holly's eyes narrowed with curiosity. "Why do you ask?"

"I mean, did they ever interact?" Riley clarified. "Was there any . . . tension there?"

"No," Holly said with confidence. "As far as I know, they had no need for interaction, and besides, Lexi got on well with everyone. She was just so good at reading people. And Javier has never given us any trouble. He keeps to himself mostly; he does his job well. From time to time, he disappears for a day or so, but that's never interfered with any of his responsibilities."

"What can you tell us about the victim in the morgue, Riley?" Bella pressed. "Any updates since we last chatted?"

"Yesterday I was told that identification was imminent. I think there was a hit through missing persons, so the medical examiner is just waiting for confirmation and for the family to be contacted. I'm guessing we'll have an answer by Friday. Early next week at the latest."

She paused for a minute, twirling the end of her braid between two fingers. As soon as the victim's identity was released to the press, so would information on the victim's gender identity—especially given the relevance of that information to recent unsolved cases.

It seemed safe, then, to share what else she'd learned.

Riley leaned in. "What I find most interesting about the victim," she began, eyeing Holly and Bella, "is that, like Lexi, they were transgender."

Holly turned to Bella, her lips parted as if she were about to speak.

But Bella jumped in. "What are the chances?"

"I have an awful feeling that when we get an ID, Riley, we'll find that this victim is somehow tied to Lexi and Sofia." Holly bit down on one of her perfect long fingernails. "Or maybe linked to Lexi somehow through the trans community."

"If we're totally objective," Bella countered, "the only common ground between Lexi and Sofia was the shelter. So it's possible this person was a former resident of the center too, maybe someone previously acquainted with us."

"Agreed. Too much coincidence."

"I don't believe in coincidences, Holly," Bella asserted.

"Nor do I." Riley took the plunge. "I need to let you both know I've learned of another connection that has me concerned. I have reason to suspect that Javier has ties to the man I interacted with on the 101 the morning of the second murder. The man who then staked himself out at my house the night you and Cedrick came by and alerted the LAPD to his presence, Bella."

Bella's mouth formed a perfect O. "How the hell—?"

"*What?*" Holly said, spitting a mouthful of coffee back into her cup. "You've seen them together? When? Where?"

"Suffice it to say, the detectives on this case are aware of my suspicions about Javier," Riley went on, skirting how and when she had gained her insights, "and I imagine they are already looking into him. I don't want any of us getting in the way of their investigation. I think we need to keep a low profile, and, more importantly, we need to be careful not to tip Javier off that he may be under surveillance."

By the time the three of them left Abe's that morning, they had all agreed to use an encrypted app Bella recommended for communications. They shared contact information and agreed to talk again when Riley learned the identity of the victim at the morgue.

In the meantime, Bella would go through Sofia's belongings at the shelter for any clues about her family of origin, and Holly would explore the shelter's records, including Lexi's clinical notes on Sofia's counseling sessions.

An investigation into Sofia's attack would no doubt be underway already. Which meant they had to move quickly before any of those items became the targets of a search warrant. Holly would gently press Ms. Maria for any information she could learn about Javier's activities and connections away from the shelter. And Riley would keep them all updated on the condition of both Sofia and her baby.

CHAPTER SIXTEEN

The following day, Riley took advantage of her morning break from the ER to check on Sofia during the daily trauma surgery rounds. The hallway outside the girl's ICU room was packed with medical specialists and trainees clamoring for tidbits of the report and waiting to be called on for information about her condition. The neurosurgical team was delivering their latest update when Riley threaded her way through the crowd, slipping past the sliding glass door and into the room.

Riley's heart dropped at the sight of her. Sofia was unrecognizable. The skin of her chest and arms was a waxy yellow hue, and her limbs were swollen grotesquely, probably from the sheer volume of intravenous fluid and blood transfusions she'd needed. Below a bulky white head dressing, Sofia's eye sockets looked like two overripe plums. The top sheet of her bed linen was tented where the surgical pins from her broken legs extended into the air like small antennae.

". . . the pupils remain fixed and dilated," the attending neurosurgeon was in the middle of saying. "There are no corneal or brain stem reflexes. It's no surprise that the EEG was flat last night. We'll repeat it today, but, of course, it's looking grim," She rested her chin on her thumb. "A very unfortunate outcome . . ."

The crowd fell silent with that announcement. Only the hiss of Sofia's ventilator filled the air.

"Still no family or visitors, not even a workable ID or accurate age," the social worker, a stout woman with her back to Riley, finally broke in. "So, of course, we can't inquire about the possibility of organ harvest."

"With the massive internal injuries and the number of transfusions she's needed, I just don't see organ donation as an option anyway," Krista, Riley's friend the trauma surgeon, offered. "That, added to a brain death diagnosis, equals a total loss of anything slightly positive coming out of this travesty."

"After we've reviewed the second EEG, we can convene the ethics committee," the intensivist, a bearded man standing next to the ventilator, chimed in. "In the absence of any family, we'll have to make the decision to withdraw life support."

"LAPD was here this morning," a woman said. Riley recognized her as one of the hospital's risk managers. "Still no progress on an ID, but they had a request for a DNA sample, which we facilitated."

"And there was one for the infant too," the social worker added. "The PD was in the neonatal ICU first thing this morning to obtain a specimen."

Riley's pager went off. She extricated herself from the crowd and made her way back down to the ER. She'd check on the baby during her lunch break. For now, she'd heard all she needed to know about Sofia. It was even worse than she'd expected. The girl would no doubt be removed from life support before the day was up.

She paused in the hallway to text Krista, asking to be notified when Sofia was taken off the ventilator.

The response came a few minutes later: Will do ☹

Somehow, it was Krista's confirmation that set Riley off. It was one thing to hear Sofia's status reported on so clinically by a room of professionals, but to hear now, from a friend, that for a fact Sofia would die soon felt so raw.

She swallowed the injustice of it all, pocketing her phone absently.

She mulled over how she might break the news to Holly and Bella. It would be a difficult conversation, to say the least, especially in the wake of losing Lexi. That loss alone had been so upsetting for Bella—she'd learned yesterday—that the girl hadn't been able to force herself to attend Lexi's service.

Hopefully, Bella and Holly had made at least *some* progress in tracking down Sofia's family. Someone would need to take care of the baby, presuming she survived. Riley's thoughts flashed back to the emergency cesarean section performed in her trauma bay earlier that week and Sofia's current condition. It was hard to believe that only four days ago, Riley had seen the girl navigating the back stairs at the shelter with her protruding belly and a tray full of freshly baked cookies. She couldn't imagine what had transpired less than twenty-four hours after that. How had Sofia, who wasn't even comfortable leaving the shelter, ended up miles from Santa Monica, in traffic lanes on the 101 Freeway?

*   *   *

Riley hadn't had a break for the remainder of the day; it had been far too busy. Before she went home for the night, she stopped by the neonatal ICU to see Sofia's baby. Besides being a little jaundiced and still in an incubator, the newborn looked small but healthy. The resident on evening shift, a pencil-thin redhead, told Riley she would be transferred out of the NICU to the nursery in the next day or two if she remained stable.

Riley checked the time on her pager. It was past eight; she needed to get home. She had wanted to catch up with Holly and Bella later, but she couldn't see that happening. She had her big presentation on the Williams case at M and M grand rounds in the morning, and she needed to finish putting her notes and slides together. Delivering an update to her fellow sleuths would have to wait. Besides, she was in no hurry to share the bad news about Sofia's condition.

She took the stairs back down to the ER and headed to the locker room to change before going home. As she passed along the narrow hallway behind the ER and the hospital's laundry, the door to a small, dimly lit supply room cracked open. Riley turned to see Olivia, the nurse she'd seen performing CPR on Leroy Williams the night she'd rushed into room 11 to help, standing in the shadows. The woman poked her head out of the doorway, checked the empty hallway in both directions, then motioned for Riley to join her.

*　　*　　*

Riley stood at the podium in Wilcox Hall with her laptop cracked open in front of her. She connected the cable tethering it to the IT system of the auditorium and checked the sound and overhead slide projector functions. It was 07:03 a.m., and the hall was packed with her colleagues from the ER, some faces she recognized from pediatrics, and a multitude of medical students, interns, and residents from various other clinical specialties. The room was buzzing with chatter as she waited for Dr. Jackson to make his way down the stairs along the auditorium's periphery to introduce her discussion.

In the shadows of the top back row, she saw the towering figure of Doug Hudson, her intern recruit, in his tent-size lab coat. And in the very front row of the auditorium sat Astrid Wolf, whom Riley had been working for on the evening of Leroy Williams's death. Wolf's white curls were almost iridescent under the bright stage lights. They created a stark contrast to her grim expression as she watched Riley preparing to deliver her presentation. Perhaps she was thinking it could just as easily have been her up there at the podium.

A second later, Riley's cell phone pinged, reminding her she needed to make sure it was turned off for her presentation. She pulled the phone out of her pocket and realized the text message was from Astrid—who was sitting right in front of her.

Where the hell is Big Mouth Bach?

That was the name given to Tobias by his peers in the ER. He had a way of getting under people's skin with his constant condescending remarks and self-absorbed bombast. The man had been a disastrous choice for the position of residency director and a very poor replacement for Marcel Benoit, who had been admired and respected by everyone. Riley had adored her mentor, and perhaps that was partly why Bach had been so difficult for her to accept. In fact, he'd been the reason she'd switched from night shift to day shift, even though the most interesting and challenging cases came into the ER at night. Riley made eye contact with Astrid, acknowledging the text message. She shrugged, tilting her head. It was the same question she'd been asking herself for the past two weeks.

Her phone pinged again: Insufferable little prick. Tits on a bull! He should be up there, not you.

Riley shot Astrid a quick response by text before turning her phone off: Right!

The auditorium was at capacity, except for a few spaces in the front row. Riley took a deep breath and concentrated on ignoring her pounding heart and the sea of faces, some already sporting accusatory looks, now staring back at her. She reminded herself that all she had to do was recount the events of that night. She had nothing to hide. And the notes on her laptop would help keep the timeline and facts straight. The truth would out itself. Wouldn't it? Wasn't that how it was supposed to be?

After Jackson's long-winded introduction, which set the stage for the discussion of the "failed resuscitation of a six-year-old boy following cardiac arrest secondary to severe asthma in the ER," Riley finally began her presentation. The first slide showed the boy's height, weight, and medical history, including the eighty percent total body surface area burns he'd sustained a year before his death in the fire that had claimed his mother's life. The slide listed his other medical history, including the fact that he'd been born four weeks prematurely and had suffered from asthma ever since surviving the blaze.

The second slide showed comparison photographs of Leroy before and after his burns. He had been a healthy-looking child, with big bright eyes and a smile full of tiny pearly teeth. After his release from the hospital and his placement in a foster home, Leroy probably hadn't had many photographs taken, but Riley had found a picture among the medical records showing the extent of his burns after his final skin grafting surgery. The image was difficult to view—even for medical professionals—without having a visceral reaction. The child appeared as though his face and body had melted. He'd lost fingers on both hands, and the skin around his neck and armpits was webbed and contorted into folds of tissue punctuated with the classic pockmarked dimples of healed skin grafts. If nothing else, the picture was testimony to the agony and suffering the boy had endured in the year before his death. The auditorium fell silent.

Still devastated by the whole ordeal, Riley tried to focus on the facts and not her feelings and pulled up her third slide, which depicted Leroy's vital signs on arrival to the ER by ambulance. The rapidity of both his heart and breathing rates, coupled with his dangerously low oxygen saturation, demonstrated unambiguously that he had been in severe distress on arrival. "In extremis," as Riley told the audience.

The fourth slide was a direct copy of the chart written up by Olivia, Leroy's nurse that night. The report recounted that Leroy had been evaluated by one of the second-year ER residents assigned to work with Dr. Bach that shift. The child had been given two breathing treatments by the respiratory therapist only minutes apart, neither of which seemed to clear his wheezing or improve his vital signs. On the following slide, Riley had copied and pasted an excerpt from the respiratory therapist's electronic documentation of Leroy's deteriorating condition; the note was marked as being entered four minutes after Liv's charted observations: "Breath sounds severely diminished, ineffective air exchange, oxygen saturation seventy-seven percent."

The notation needed no further explanation. The audience was rapt.

The next slide was from Liv's notes taken a minute later: "Preparations for emergency intubation underway with Dr. Bach."

Riley turned to the audience. "This was the last note taken in real time. All following documentation was completed after the child's failed resuscitation." This was standard practice. Everyone in the audience understood that during emergency situations, a checklist or handwritten notes were often used to keep track of the time and dosage of medications administered to save a life. Typically, after things calmed down and the patient was either stabilized or resuscitation efforts ceased, the documentation of the preceding events was then re-created legibly in the electronic medical record using the timed notes scribbled down during the emergency.

On the next slide, Riley had included the size of the breathing tube used to intubate Leroy and the various pieces of equipment employed to place and secure the tube. These notes came from both the respiratory therapist and the nurse.

Following that, the subsequent slide indicated the medications used to sedate the child for the intubation and their respective doses. Nothing about the listed medications or their doses seemed questionable, given their known actions and Leroy's weight of 17.3 kilograms, which had been listed earlier in the presentation.

Riley kept that slide up on the screen as she swept her eyes over the audience. "Can anyone tell me which drug provides the fastest onset for immobilizing the vocal cords during emergency intubation?"

Immediately, Hudson's hand in the back row flew into the air, as did several hands in the midsection of the auditorium, where the medical trainees were sitting. Riley picked on a young woman seated at the end of the row. She was wearing a short white lab coat, the signature attire of medical students. "Please stand and speak up so we can all hear you," Riley called to her across the crowded hall.

The trainee stood, and, in a shaky voice, she offered, "I believe it's succinylcholine, ma'am," and then quickly took her seat again.

"That's correct," Riley replied. "Nothing has a more rapid onset for the purposes of intubation than succinylcholine. It's historically been the drug of choice in most emergency situations to facilitate rapid control of the airway."

She tapped the keyboard of her laptop, pulling up the next slide, which compared various drugs in a similar class and the rapidity of their onset. Then she turned back to the audience, making brief eye contact with Jackson, who had parked himself up front, next to Astrid. "And can anyone tell me why we typically don't use this drug when intubating children?"

Again, several hands, including that of Hudson in the back row, were raised. Riley called on one of the residents from pediatrics—a tiny Asian woman with enormous glasses and a teal scarf wrapped around her neck. "Succinylcholine, or sux, is generally contraindicated in children because children tend to have higher vagal tone than adults," she answered. "The drug will often dramatically slow the heart rate in pediatric individuals, even causing cardiac arrest on occasion, and therefore it's not the preferred agent for the management of airway in children."

"Exactly," Riley said, resting an elbow on the podium in front of her. "It's not the *preferred* drug, but are there any circumstances in which it could or should be used in the pediatric population?"

Riley pointed to the same woman from pediatrics, who then stood up to expound on her answer. "It's an acceptable drug in a severe emergency—say, for example, in this case, where the rapid intubation of a child to gain control of the airway was clearly indicated.”

“That's correct.” Riley went on. “As sux is the fastest-acting agent, it can make the difference between life and death when intubating a child in a true emergency.”

She let the room fall silent again. In the seconds that followed, she tried to ignore the pounding in her own chest and how the air felt locked in her throat. She could feel Jackson's eyes on her; she could sense that Astrid was holding her own breath. Watching and waiting.

She tried to draw on memories of Marcel and how he might handle the next few minutes. *Breathe*, she told herself. *Just breathe, Brighton.*

“And can anyone tell me why the use of succinylcholine would be contraindicated, catastrophic even, in a patient like little Leroy?”

There it was—the words had been spoken. And perfectly on cue, Hudson's hand was in the air again.

“Yes, you in the back there,” Riley said, raising her chin in his direction. *Perfect*, Riley thought. *I'm counting on you, Hudson.*

Doug Hudson stood in the back row, all six feet ten of him. The crowd shifted, turning in their seats. When he spoke, his voice resonated so clearly throughout the auditorium it was almost as if he was using a microphone.

“Succinylcholine,” he began confidently, “is directly contra-indicated in several preexisting medical conditions, including in patients with a history of severe burns. Administration of that drug would result in a massive release of potassium stores from inside the patient's own cells. Such an excessive surge would quickly raise the serum levels of potassium to a fatal degree, the same way a lethal injection of potassium chloride in inmates sentenced to the death penalty would.”

The room was silent. All heads were turned toward Hudson.

All except one. Jackson's eyes were boring into Riley.

"Go on." Riley nodded in the direction of the intern.

"The heart would stop almost immediately in a patient like Leroy, who had a history of such extensive burns. The administration of succinylcholine for any purpose, including emergency management of the airway, would be an immediate death sentence."

Immediately, Jackson sprang to his feet. He faced the audience, his voice booming over the crowd as he practically shouted, "And *that's* precisely why succinylcholine was *not* administered in this case as Dr. Brighton's earlier slide has already demonstrated!" He turned back to face Riley, his lips pressed tightly. He took his seat again, nostrils flared. It was incredible to witness such a display of bias from Jackson, Riley thought.

But now she could see something darker than bias in his expression.

Astrid raised her brow, tilting her head sideways toward Jackson as she locked eyes with Riley.

"Dr. Jackson is correct," Riley went on, regaining the room's attention. "As the record has already demonstrated, no one documented using succinylcholine to intubate this child. If they had, we would have known immediately what had caused his cardiac arrest, and we might have been able to save him. Perhaps by administering calcium chloride to antagonize the effect of a surge in potassium level."

Jackson shot Riley a look she couldn't quite discern. It was something between an *I dare you, Brighton* and an *Oh shit*. Riley felt her heart rate slowing, a calm settling over her in response to Jackson's obvious jeopardy. The trap had been perfectly laid.

She pulled up the next slide in the presentation. "These two pieces of documentation will at first seem completely unrelated. One will even seem unorthodox in a medical presentation."

The screen displayed two entries of text, one above the other. Both had been copied and pasted from their original sources. The first was the arrival time of the paramedic squad into room 11 at City ER, where Leroy was treated for his asthma attack. The time listed by the lead paramedic was 21:02. The second entry was a record from the ER janitorial service documenting the time that all trash and pharmaceutical waste were removed from the room and replaced by fresh, empty containers. That time was listed as 21:05 on the same evening.

"Keep these two time stamps in mind as we progress through the remainder of this case discussion," Riley teased the crowd.

She tapped her laptop again, pulling up the next slide. It detailed, for a second time, all the medications and their doses that were documented by Dr. Bach in the electronic medical record as having been administered to sedate and intubate Leroy.

Everything looked standard; there was little to question—and no mention of the use of the prohibited drug succinylcholine. The next slide showed that exactly one minute after Leroy was intubated, the record indicated his heart rhythm exhibited a bizarre wide sine wave characteristic of a fatal heart rhythm change. His vital signs rapidly deteriorated from then on.

"Almost immediately after Leroy's cardiac arrest," Riley reported, "I entered ER room eleven and began to direct the resuscitation efforts. Unfortunately, the patient's heart did not respond to any of our standard interventions. The documentation you see on the following slides reflects all the actions taken during the child's cardiac arrest. This includes the code blue response and the eventual recording of his time of death at twenty-two twenty-eight—more than an hour after his demise," Riley said, clicking slowly through the next four slides.

As the close of the presentation drew near, she pulled up a toxicology report from the medical examiner's office. It listed the potassium level in Leroy's blood. The sample had been taken during his autopsy. Even the first-year medical students would have recognized the level as lethal; it was twice the upper limit of normal.

Jackson was on his feet again. "Postmortem potassium levels do not reflect antemortem levels. This is completely misleading information and doesn't in any way reflect that the child's potassium level was lethal or even elevated before his death."

The man was practically foaming at the mouth. Riley had never seen him so animated. The spectacle he was making was satisfyingly self-incriminating. She almost felt sorry for him as the audience sat in stunned silence staring at Jackson.

It didn't take long for that silence to dissipate.

Seconds later, the room was abuzz with whispered discussion. Heads were shaking, brows furrowed. Some trainees and faculty broke out their smartphones and started conducting their own literature reviews while others referred to pocket manuals or turned to their mentors or classmates.

"May I have your attention," Riley interjected loudly, "so we can finish up here?"

The room was, finally, called to order. Riley gestured to her penultimate slide, avoiding the heat of Jackson's glare.

"Let's refresh our memories. The patient arrived in ER room eleven at twenty-one oh-two. Three minutes later, at twenty-one oh-five, the pharmacy waste receptacle in ER room eleven was replaced by janitorial staff with a new empty container. This is verified by the janitor's checklist and by two of the ER nurses, who actually reported complaints to the janitor's supervisor about him making the switch while a patient was still in the room. As you know, these routine janitorial duties are completed between patient visits, not during patient stays." Her eyes swept over the audience, still ignoring Jackson. "The last time listed on the slide—twenty-two twenty-eight—is the time the patient was pronounced dead. I know this, because I was the one who made the pronouncement."

Only when Riley pulled up her last slide did a stunned silence return to the auditorium.

The slide consisted of a single time-stamped photograph taken with a cell phone camera belonging to one of the night nurses. It was a picture of the contents of the pharmacy waste bin eight minutes after Leroy's death at 22:36. It showed the empty containers of the medications used to treat Leroy's asthma attack, the empty vials of medications used to sedate him for intubation, and a myriad of empty resuscitation drug syringes. The contents of the photograph bore testament to the valiant effort undertaken in an attempt to save the child's life.

"Let me draw your attention to the left upper corner of this photograph," Riley said, enlarging the picture and using her laser pointer to indicate the area of the slide to which she was referring. As she faced the screen along with the audience, Riley looked over her shoulder at the crowd. She risked a quick glance at Jackson.

The man was pale as a ghost, but he made no move to leave his seat or interrupt. He sat with one arm over his chest and the other hand across his mouth. Next to him, Astrid was shaking her head in disbelief.

"What is that medication vial we see here, in Leroy's pharmacy waste bin, eight minutes after he was pronounced dead? This vial right here, with the bright-red metal cap?" Riley asked, circling the photo of the drug vial with the light from her laser pointer.

Hudson, in the back of the auditorium, was already on his feet, unable to restrain himself for a moment longer. "There's only one drug manufactured in the US for which the company uses that signature bright-red metal cap as a safety warning. What the photo shows in the child's pharmacy waste bin is a half-empty vial of succinylcholine."

CHAPTER SEVENTEEN

The auditorium at Wilcox Hall was still buzzing with frenetic energy and chatter as Riley and Astrid headed for the exit, Riley with her laptop under her arm and Astrid with both hands in the pockets of her lab coat, head down.

Jackson had disappeared as soon as the auditorium lights had been turned back on.

"Unbelievable" was all Astrid could muster. "Just fucking unbelievable."

"I know, right?" Riley muttered. She was shaky, if not exhausted, the adrenaline having finally subsided. "No wonder we haven't seen Bach for weeks."

"The fact that Jackson passed me over for residency director in favor of that creep makes me sick. Always looked like he belonged behind the wheel of a hearse instead of in a white coat, if you ask me. Let's hope he's under a rock somewhere contemplating a career change."

"Somehow, I doubt that, Astrid. He'd have to have some self-awareness and a conscience for that."

Riley and Astrid crossed the quad between Wilcox Hall and the campus medical library, though neither of them knew exactly where they were headed. Riley just needed to put some distance between herself and the crowd before her shift started. The morning air was cold, but the sky above was clear and bright. She pulled her scarf up around her neck.

Astrid took a deep cleansing breath. "Do we know if it was Bach who used the succinylcholine that night or his trainee?"

"Yes, we know. The nurses did a great job with their documentation. That will all come out. The city's attorneys will make sure of that. He's responsible in any event, I assure you. But does it make a difference?" Riley stopped mid-stride to look at Astrid, the cold push of a breeze chafing her cheeks. "Really? The kid's dead, and Bach is responsible either way, especially for the cover-up."

Astrid stared back at her wordlessly.

"Dr. Brighton?" someone called from the stairs outside of Wilcox Hall. Riley turned to see Hudson bearing down on them, his face beaming.

"Great job, Hudson," Riley offered, turning to face him as he approached on legs as long as ladders. When he was at her side, looking down at her, Riley added, "The trick now is to make sure we examine ourselves as closely as we examine the actions of others. Then we'll be on the right track."

The joy left Hudson's face, a serious expression settling in. "Agreed, ma'am." He pushed his glasses higher on his nose. "I appreciate you trusting me, though."

"Come on, Hudson. We'll buy you breakfast." Riley turned to head away from the quad.

"Breakfast burritos?" Wolf raised her eyebrows. "If it's breakfast burritos, I'm buying."

"You're on," Riley said, throwing her arm around Astrid's shoulder.

*   *   *

On the walk back to the ER after breakfast with Astrid and Hudson, Riley received a text message from Joe. It read Parents of our freeway victim made ID this morning. Mother wants to meet you.

Riley turned to Astrid. "I need a favor, Wolf."

"You name it." The woman was jingling her keys in her pocket. "In light of what you pulled off today, whatever you like."

"I know you're probably exhausted after working all night, but I need you to cover the first hour of my shift this morning. I'll be in as soon as I can."

"I'm pretty sure I owe you at least that much, Brighton," Astrid said, giving her a hug. And on that note, Riley turned and headed in the direction of the medical examiner's office. It was only minutes later that her cell phone pinged again.

It was a message from Krista: Life support on our girl discontinued at 0735. Sorry, Rye.

Of course, Riley had known Sofia's condition was grave, but the tragedy seemed to register more glaringly in the wake of an almost sleepless night and the anxiety of getting through the morning's M and M presentation. Suddenly, her vision began to blur, clouded by an upsurge of tears, which ran down her cheeks unchecked; her mouth curled into a downward twist.

She stood for a moment, staring down at the screen of her phone. The injustice was just so infuriating. Some days, she could barely manage to keep it all in perspective. *Fuck the yin and the yang of it,* she told herself. Realizing she was in no shape to meet the freeway victim's family at that moment, Riley found a sunny spot to sit on the stairs outside the medical examiner's office. She opened the encrypted app that Bella had set up on her phone and texted the group chat comprising Holly, Bella, and Cedrick: Sorry to share this way, but if you don't hear it from me now, you'll probably hear it on the news. Sofia passed away this morning. If you like, we can talk tonight. I'll be home around eight.

The stairs outside the morgue where she now sat were cold slabs of marble. The chill seeped through her scrubs and bled into her legs, making her feel numb, and for a while, she merely sat there, elbows on her knees, head in her hands, trying to collect herself. Her eyes glazed over, her head humming as the morning traffic whizzed by on the freeway overpass above.

"'Sup, Doc?" Riley heard a familiar voice.

She looked up to see Mr. Robinson—Shorty, her patient from the ER a couple of weeks earlier—standing on the sidewalk in front of her. He was accompanied by a tall woman in a knitted purple sweater dress and matching hat with a shopping cart full of bags. *Taller Paula,* Riley assumed.

"Why you cryin', child?" the woman crooned, staring down at Riley.

"Well, she sittin' outside the morgue, ain't she, stupid?" Shorty replied, rolling his eyes.

"Don't you *stupid* me, Shorty. I'll whoop your—"

"It's good to see you, Mr. Robinson," Riley interrupted, hoping to stave off another domestic incident between the two. "I see you got your stitches out, and you're all healed up," she said getting to her feet.

The man's face lit up. His smile lifted Riley's spirits, even with his two front teeth missing.

"I surely am, Doc, thanks to you. This here is my wife, Paula."

"I figured, Mr. Robinson. How are you, ma'am?" Riley extended a hand. "I've heard all about you—"

"You have beautiful eyes, child," the woman muttered, cutting Riley off. "Ain't she got pretty eyes, Shorty? Like the ocean under a winter sky." She sized Riley up, as if discerning a riddle. "The devil's envy, just like my sister, Celia's," she muttered before her gaze drifted, as though she were seeing something no one else could. "Best mind your back, child. The devil done took her, and now I hear her boy, little Leroy's gone too. God rest his soul."

"Wait—what? Leroy? Leroy Williams was your nephew?" Riley stuttered, reaching for the woman's hand, suddenly grasping the implications that the child who had spent the last year of his life in the foster care system had had family after all. But Taller Paula was already moving on, talking to someone no one else could see. She pushed her cart ahead of herself, leaning into the weight of the load, her face turned to the sky, eyes closed.

"S'cuse me, Doc," Shorty said, hurrying after Paula.

Riley stood on the stairs, watching them winding their way down the sidewalk—Shorty in shoes that were obviously too big to be his own and Paula in an alternate reality—until they were both swallowed up by the freeway underpass.

Technically, they were living in the same city, but in that moment, Riley was reminded that they weren't living in the same world at all. An invisible line of circumstance separated their fates as clearly as night and day. A single unfortunate turn of events could do that. A run in with the wrong gang member, or the wrong police officer, or, for that matter, with the wrong doctor. The smallest seemingly inconsequential occurrence could forever change the trajectory of a life. Someone's opportunities, someone's direction. She'd seen it all too often.

She pulled out her cell phone and called the Maple Avenue free mental health clinic where she'd referred Paula for treatment in the prior weeks. She left the contact information of an excellent malpractice attorney with Paula's counselor, Jenna. After all, why did Leroy's only remaining family need to live on the streets when there was undoubtedly a fortune headed their way from a malpractice suit in the case of Leroy's death?

She turned and headed up the stairs to the city medical examiner's office.

"They're in the conference room two doors down on the right," the security guard in the lobby told Riley. "Dr. Padilla said to go right in. Oh, and he said to tell you Detective Roberts is on her way." Riley nodded her thanks before darting into the ladies' room to splash her face with cold water and pat it dry with a paper towel.

Joe was sitting with his back to the door when Riley knocked and entered. The couple sitting across from him in matching armchairs looked like they hadn't slept in days. The woman was in her midfifties, Riley guessed, rail thin with faded ginger hair cropped at the shoulders. The man eyed Riley from behind a pair of thick glasses, his full beard skirting a wide face that looked like it had seen its share of sun.

"I'll wait in the lobby," the man said, standing to leave as soon as Riley entered. The woman watched him go, saying nothing. She held a box of tissues in her lap as if she were cradling an infant.

"This is Dr. Brighton. She's the one who found—" Joe paused before quickly rephrasing the introduction. "She was the first responder on the scene after the accident."

Riley could only deduce Joe's hesitation was a reflection of confusion regarding which pronouns to use for the victim. That made sense. It was also unclear how much he was allowed to reveal before the detectives arrived.

"It's Riley—just plain Riley." She gave the woman a soft smile. "How are you holding up, ma'am?"

"This is Ms. McAllister," Joe clarified. "She's the mother of . . ." Again, Joe seemed unsure of how to proceed.

"Clive," the woman interjected hurriedly, glancing up at Joe as she set the box of tissues on the table. "He wanted to be called Clive."

"I'm terribly sorry for your loss, Ms. McAllister."

"It's Valerie, you can call me Val." She extended both hands to clasp Riley's.

Riley sat next to Joe and across from Val. The woman's face was drawn and pale, she was leaning forward in her chair as if she didn't have the strength to hold herself upright. She rested her elbows on a set of bony knees, dropping her head into her hands as she added, "Ron can't handle this. He hates LA. He just wants to get back to the farm. Forgive him for being so rude."

"That's perfectly all right, Val. We all have our ways of handling grief."

"He doesn't handle much of anything to do with feelings, I'm afraid." She looked up at Riley with red-rimmed eyes. "When Clive transitioned, Ron lost it. He took it personally. He said our baby was gone. Forever erased. He never got used to the new name and the pronouns. Sometimes I slip up too."

"That's understandable."

"But now, none of that matters. Our only child is dead." Val's body shook momentarily. The guttural sound that came out of her was raw, almost animalistic, as she clenched her jaw and slapped the tears from her face violently with the palms of both hands.

Riley locked eyes with Joe. She motioned toward the door with her head, and he took the cue.

"I'll wait in the lobby for Detective Roberts to arrive. That way I can keep Ron company. I'll text you when she gets here, Riley," he added, darting his eyes to the left, indicating that she should exit through the side door when leaving to avoid running into the detective.

Once they were alone, Riley said, "I'm sure you'll have a lot of questions for the police, and I'm sure you're not feeling much like talking right now, so I'll be brief, Val." The woman stared back at Riley as if she was still taking in where she was. "When was the last time you saw Clive?"

"Just over a month ago. He and Ron were always falling out. Clive said he was going to the city to help an old friend. We never heard from him again. I just assumed he was cooling off somewhere."

"You're not from around here?"

"Fresno," she said, wiping her nose. "Ron's family has a farm out there, but Clive had been coming to LA on and off since high school. He had friends in Venice. We just assumed he'd be home for Thanksgiving. I try not to ask . . ." She stopped for a minute, pulling another tissue out of the box on the table. "I tried not to ask too many questions. I didn't want to seem overbearing, but I worried about her. *Him*. I worried about *him*."

"You were worried something might happen to Clive?"

"Yes, he was just . . . so small, you know? Still petite, even though he'd been taking the testosterone for over a year. Something really bad happened to him the first time he came here, when he was still in high school. Someone hurt him, and he was never the same. I can't help but think it was part of the reason he transitioned. I was worried someone might hurt him again—" Val's voice cracked. "A mom never stops worrying."

Riley nodded. She could only assume this was true. She'd heard it enough times from her own mother.

"Clive was such a smart child," Val went on. "He taught himself to read at four years old. Ron was so proud. In those days, he used to say that 'our *baby girl* could grow up to be anything she wanted.' And that's it, see. He just didn't expect his little *Clair-bell* to grow up to be a boy. As I've already said, my husband took it poorly, but it got way worse than that. He went ballistic when Clive legally changed his name." The woman paused for a moment, tears running down her cheeks. She swallowed hard. "But I would tell him, 'Ron, we prayed every day during my pregnancy for that baby. We never once prayed for a boy or a girl; all we wanted was a child that was healthy and happy.' That's what I don't understand about Ron. Why couldn't he just love Clive the same as we did before he was born? Before we knew if he was a boy or girl."

Riley felt her nose tingle in the way it usually did before her eyes filled up.

"I understand," she said, automatically placing a hand over Val's. But the truth was she didn't understand. She couldn't fathom the loss of a child. She forced herself to come clean. "Actually, that's not true," she whispered. "In all honesty, Val, I can't even imagine what you're going through. I'm terribly sorry."

"You don't have children?" Val asked, wiping her face with a fistful of tissues. Riley shook her head, unable to speak. Val passed her a tissue. "You're lucky, Doctor. You have no idea how lucky you are. There is nothing—*nothing*—worse than losing your child. And Ron would argue that we lost ours twice."

Silence funneled in, punctuated solely by Val's sniffling. Riley, again, had no idea what to say—losing a child was completely out of her reference. Yes, she knew how badly grief could cut. She'd learned that lesson early in life, and often. But losing a child? No, she couldn't fathom grief on that scale. All she could feel was sorrow for Val who was plagued by so much regret.

"Maybe one day," Val went on, "Ron will see how he could have loved Clive. How Clive was the same person as his *little Clair*. How our child was always our child—the same heart, the same spirit. The biggest difference honestly after the transition was . . . Clive was so much happier than Clair had ever been."

Riley swallowed the tightness in her throat. "Maybe it's easier for your husband not to see how he missed that opportunity."

"I don't think he's ever going to forgive himself when it hits him." She looked up at Riley, her expression morphing from grief into something darker. "And maybe, *I'll* never forgive him."

"It's time for me to go now, Val." Riley stood as she read the text message on her phone from Joe. "I just wanted you to know Clive didn't suffer—he went fast. I couldn't stop thinking about him . . . ever since that morning. I'm glad I got to connect with you."

She dared not say more; the detectives would be the ones to break the news that Clive's death hadn't been an accident. And for the second time in less than five minutes, Riley realized she'd lied to Val.

Clive *had* suffered. He had suffered terribly before the end.

*   *   *

Twenty minutes later, Riley was back in the throes of the buzzing ER.

An inexplicable weight pressed down on her all morning. There was little comfort in having made her case at M and M. She didn't feel exonerated. She felt used. Jackson had unfairly put her in a position where she'd been forced to expose the disastrous incompetence of a colleague. That wasn't her job. Nothing felt good about that. And she hadn't simply been an instrument of truth—she'd been a hapless pawn in a needless tragedy.

By late afternoon, there was a slight reprieve in the flow of patients. Riley made a fresh pot of coffee, poured herself a cup, and headed up to the nursery to see Sofia's baby. The infant was making good progress according to the charge nurse on duty, who allowed Riley access to the viewing window.

"I hope you don't mind keeping it brief, Dr. Brighton. We have strict orders not to let anyone from the media know the baby is still here. So please keep it under wraps. Social service is looking to find placement if family isn't located soon," the woman said, standing next to Riley with her arms crossed over her chest.

"She's so tiny," Riley commented, her voice barely audible. "Delicate, the way her mother was."

She heard Valerie's words again: *"You don't have children? You're lucky, Doctor. There is nothing—nothing—worse than losing a child."*

Riley felt her throat tightening again.

She thanked the nurse and headed to the elevator, rounding the corner from the nursery and passing by the general surgical ward. A young man in a patient gown was propelling himself with tattooed arms down the hallway in a wheelchair alongside her, perhaps headed to the gift shop or, more likely, to an exit to smoke.

"First floor?" she asked, holding the elevator door for him.

"Yeah," he said, giving her a long look. "Wait, I know you. I know that voice." Riley gave him a double take. She couldn't place him. But that was understandable with all the patients she encountered daily. "It's me—Miguel," he insisted. Riley smiled politely, shaking her head. "You know, from last week? The super-tall dude said you saved my life when I got capped. I remember your voice. You told me I was gonna be okay," he said, a smile spreading over his face. "And you were right. I owe you one, Doc."

Riley couldn't help herself; in a second, she was grinning from ear to ear. "Oh boy, you look great—you look really great, Miguel. I'm so glad to see that."

"I mean it, Doc. You need anything on the streets—*ever*—me and my homies, we got your back."

CHAPTER EIGHTEEN

For the third week in a row, Riley missed the Friday night taphouse outing. She knew most of her colleagues from the ER would be there, talking about the events of the week. Mingling with the surgeons and other specialists they interacted with daily. No doubt the pub would be buzzing with chatter about the smoking gun she'd revealed at her M and M presentation that morning. She wanted no part of that. Joe would be there too, waiting to see her—waiting to hear what Val had said about Clive.

She flipped through the gears on her motorcycle, pushing the limits once the freeway traffic gave way. It was the closest thing to escape she'd felt all week. She leaned into it, relishing every moment of intense focus the speed demanded. She wove her bike between the streams of traffic, absorbed entirely by the extraordinary precision necessary to stay just one microsecond away from disaster. It was the only activity she could think of outside of work that demanded her full and complete focus in a way that prevented rumination of any kind. Only in that singularity was she free, truly free, and strangely at peace.

Later, when she pulled into her driveway and slipped her helmet off, she heard two car doors closing behind her. Bella and Holly had just stepped out of Holly's van, faces drawn with grief. Riley waited for them to cross the street, tilting her head in the direction of her front door. They all walked in together where Indy was waiting eagerly to greet them.

Bella and Holly sat in her living room looking at take-out menus while Riley pulled three beers out of the fridge.

"Is Thai okay, Riley?" Holly called from the couch.

"Perfect. I prefer Golden Elephant over Susie's Thai, though, if no one minds."

Holly placed their order for pickup while Artemis sat on the back of the couch, coldly eyeing Bella, who sat cross-legged on the rug, overindulging Indy with affection.

"I'm exhausted." Riley flopped down into a beanbag with her beer. "Someone else will have to pick up the food." She chuckled before taking a long drink.

"I texted Cedrick. He's picking up for us," Bella said, trying to sit Indio in her lap.

"Cool, we'll have a full house" was all Riley could manage. She was of no mind to protest the takeover of her living room by virtual strangers, especially if it meant she didn't have to lift a finger to have dinner delivered that night. Her phone pinged, and she pulled it out of her pocket. She replied to the text message, surprised to find she was smiling as she did.

"Holly, can you call the Golden Elephant back and add another Pad Thai to our order?" Riley asked, barely lifting her head from the beanbag. "My friend Joe is on his way over."

Bella stopped petting Indy and shot Riley a look of concern. It was going to be their time to talk shop, top secret sleuthing stuff, and no one had even brought up Sofia's death yet.

"Don't worry Bella, it's cool. He's my contact from the medical examiner's office. Not just that, he's a longtime . . . confidant." She grinned. "He's on our side, trust me."

"Excellent. We can use someone like that on our team. Vegan or regular?" Holly asked, peering over the top of the menu.

Riley took another long drink of her beer. "Well, he carves up dead bodies all day long for a living, so I don't think he's that picky."

Within the hour, all five of them were sitting on cushions around Riley's coffee table, scraping the bottoms of cardboard cartons with their chopsticks. Indy, seemingly displeased at the prospect of scoring any leftovers, curled up in Riley's beanbag, pouting.

"Who wants to go first?" Riley asked, crumpling her napkin, and tossing it onto the table.

Holly sighed. "Jeez, where to even begin?"

"You all probably know way more than I do at this point," Cedrick spoke up. "I've been swamped with finals at school this week, so yeah, I'm a little out of the loop."

Riley took the lead. "I suppose we'd better start by coming clean to Joe about the fact that Cedrick here is Detective Roberts's son." She gave him a smirk. "Just so you know, before you say anything disparaging about the woman."

Everyone laughed. It felt good to laugh.

Riley winked at Cedrick, then turned to face Joe. "Bella and Cedrick have been doing their own sleuthing quite successfully over the past few years. How I found them is a long story. I'll get to the important stuff for now. Holly, Bella, Cedrick, and I believe Clive's murder is tied to that of Lexi Drake a few weeks earlier. I know you're familiar with Lexi's case—you alluded to the MO of that crime being similar to Clive's murder that day I visited you in the morgue to go over the autopsy findings."

Joe remained expressionless as he stared straight at her. Riley realized he wasn't about to indict himself for sharing privileged information in a room full of strangers.

"Well, five days ago, as you may have heard on the news, Sofia, a pregnant teen—"

"Riley," Joe interrupted, "the girl's body was brought over to us around noon today. I know the basics—her trauma history, as well as what's on the news—and I had a briefing from Detective Roberts, of course."

"Oh right, that makes sense." Riley suddenly realized she wasn't thinking entirely clearly. She hadn't had much sleep recently, and so much had happened that it felt exhausting to string two basic thoughts together. "I can't imagine the autopsy will tell you much about the events before her trauma and the surgeries, though. Our best hope is finding something to help with ID. Right now, her baby is lying in the nursery, without family even knowing she's been born—"

"Maybe they didn't know Sofia was pregnant," Holly broke in. "She was barely showing when she came to us three months ago."

"Holly runs the homeless shelter in Santa Monica where Sofia was staying," Riley explained to Joe. "She shared an office with Lexi, who was the facilities' licensed therapist."

Joe nodded. "I took a preliminary look at Sofia's body this afternoon. It's clear she had costly dental work; I'd say we're looking for a family of means."

"Agreed," Bella said. "She never talked about her past, but yesterday, I had a chance to go through her belongings and artwork at the shelter. I'd say she definitely came from money."

"So what connects these three individuals?" Joe asked, apparently willing to try his hand at the sleuthing game. "Two of them were transgender. They were all young. Besides the MO of the murders, what else do they have in common? Sofia clearly wasn't trans."

"At least two of the victims, Lexi and Sofia, had ties to the Santa Monica youth shelter," Riley offered.

"But not Clive?" Joe asked.

Holly and Bella glanced at one another.

Holly answered with a shrug. "Never met a Clive."

That gave Riley an idea. She pulled her laptop up off the floor and onto the coffee table, sweeping the empty dinner cartons out of her way. She searched the internet for Google images of Clair McAllister, Fresno. In a moment, she had several hits—mostly high school photos from cheerleading activities. Turning her laptop toward Holly, Riley asked, "Any way you know this face from the shelter?"

Holly's jaw dropped. "Clair?"

"Clair from Venice?" Bella asked, craning her neck over the table.

"Actually, Clive from Fresno," Riley corrected.

"That's Clair, for sure, Bella," Holly said, turning Riley's laptop toward her. "She was staying in Venice at the time she came to us, but she grew up in Fresno. Gosh, it must be at least three years since we've seen her."

"Damn . . . no, not Clair." Bella cupped both hands over her mouth. "Not after everything that kid had been through."

"Sorry. I didn't realize how you'd take the news. Clive transitioned a little over a year ago, according to his mother," Riley filled in.

"Well, that's three for three," Cedrick spoke up. "At least we now have the connection. All the victims are in some way linked to the Santa Monica shelter—or at least to the homeless youth in that area."

The room was silent for a moment.

What that connection suggested was hard to identify, but at least they had a lead.

Cedrick scratched his head. "Bella and I were suspicious that this crime spree was another round of hate crimes by Jaded Justice nuts targeting the LGBTQ community, but with Sofia in the equation, I guess maybe we need to recalibrate."

"Hate crimes are still a logical deduction." Riley leaned back against the couch. "Sofia may have been targeted because, as Bella pointed out, she was close to Lexi. The other possibility is that these *are* hate crimes but against the homeless population rather than the trans community. There just happens to be some overlap in those two groups, as Holly would attest."

"Good thought," Joe added. "We've definitely seen a recent uptick in the number of hate crimes against the unhoused in LA."

"True." Holly wrapped her arms around herself. "And along those lines, someone could just be targeting people associated with our shelter because we serve the homeless. Could that be possible? It's twisted logic, but whoever is committing these murders is a sicko. Which could mean anyone linked to the shelter is at risk—including me."

For a minute, the group was silent, thinking about who could be next on the killer's list and wondering if Holly was right. She did, unfortunately, fit the profile: trans, associated with the shelter, and linked to the unhoused community of LA. But Riley had another hypothesis. She hated to admit it, but she was thinking that the only other clear connection between all three victims was that they were previously known to both Holly and Bella.

Bella let out a long sigh. "The other obvious common thread here is the man in the black pickup truck. Riley ran into him at Clive's murder scene, and the police reports have a description of a similar man and vehicle seen in the vicinity of Lexi's murder only moments after she ended up on the freeway."

"I think it's wise for us all to steer clear of the dude in the pickup," Cedrick insisted, clearing his throat.

"Why would we do that? He's a prime candidate." Riley shot Cedrick a look of surprise. "I've seen that guy twice since the morning he sent me packing from Clive's death scene."

"Twice?" Bella raised her eyebrows.

"Yes . . ." Riley realized she'd opened herself up. "As you know, I saw him the night you and Cedrick spotted him here, across the street, and I once saw him with Javier as I told you at breakfast on Wednesday."

"Where was that?" Bella pressed. "You never told us when that took place or where you'd seen them together."

Riley cleared her throat. She was in no hurry to disclose that she'd witnessed this on the night she'd been spying on Bella and Holly. She recalled that had been the night Sofia was in surgery. She latched on to that time frame and hoped it'd be enough to throw Bella off her trail, at least for the time being. "Suffice it to say it was after Sofia's assault and before her death. I just happened to see them together in Santa Monica. I'm pretty sure of that, but if Cedrick says we forget the pickup dude, does that mean we have to put Javier on the back burner too?"

"That's not exactly what I said, Riley," Cedrick said, parsing his words carefully. "Well, that's not what I *meant*, anyway. Sometimes things aren't as they seem. I'm not taking the pickup guy completely out of the equation, but you'll have to trust my judgment here, since I'm the one with official contacts, so to speak. The last thing we want to do is get in the way of a formal investigation. We don't want to draw attention to ourselves. If this guy in the pickup is being closely watched, and I assume he is, we could end up provoking the PD. As for Javier, I know nothing about him."

Riley noticed immediately that Cedrick's words almost mimicked those Detective Roberts had used on the day she cautioned Riley to stay out of police business. Apparently, Cedrick had gleaned something from his mother's records about the Jaded Justice creep in the pickup that had put him on alert. This raised another question that had been nagging Riley. On her first visit to Detective Roberts, she'd been asked if she could identify the man she'd seen at the scene of Clive's murder, but no one had ever offered her a lineup or even a mugshot of the suspect. She found that odd, now that she thought about it.

"I'm not on board with the okey dokey, Cedrick." Bella shot him a glare of annoyance. "We'll talk about it later."

"For the sake of peace," Joe said, coming to Cedrick's defense, "let's take the man and his pickup truck off the table and focus on what else we have. Cedrick's right—we absolutely don't want to interfere with an active investigation. I, for one, can't afford that professional risk."

This seemed to be something everybody could agree on.

Finally, Joe said, "So what else can we focus on? What other links are there?"

Riley twirled the end of her braid between her fingers. "I hate to point this out, but all three victims were at some time associated with both Holly and Bella."

"True, but also with Lexi," Holly added quickly, without seeming to take Riley's observation personally. "Lexi was very close with Clair when she stayed with us three years ago—or Clive, as we now know him. She was just as close with Sofia. They were inseparable."

"And Lexi was the first one killed," Cedrick noted. "So, yeah, Lexi could be the link here."

"My brain hurts," Riley said, leaning back and stretching. "I got nothin'."

"What about Javier?" Holly added. "You asked me to look into his activities away from the shelter. Why is he on your radar?"

"First, he seemed quite captivated by Sofia the day I attended Lexi's service," Riley explained. "Secondly, since I've seen him with the Jaded Justice guy in the pickup, that makes him doubly interesting. And if Cedrick is saying we must avoid surveilling the pickup guy, Javier makes a good proxy, right?"

Despite what Cedrick had said about the bald man in the black truck, Riley wasn't ready to let go of him. She was convinced he had something to do with the murders, and since she'd seen him with Javier, someone with a close connection to the shelter, they were both prime suspects in her mind. But she wasn't ready to share her thoughts with the others until she tied up a few loose ends.

"I agree with Riley about Javier being interested in Sofia." Holly nodded. "I did my best to put distance between them at the shelter, but that was out of an abundance of caution. I never saw anything aggressive or obsessive about his behavior. I would say he seemed to have a soft spot for her, that's all."

"Okay, so for now, we leave the dude to the cops. Cedrick can keep us posted on any new developments there, and Holly will see what she can find on Javier," Bella summarized, keeping everyone on task. "What other avenues does that leave us with?"

"Any thoughts, Joe?" Riley asked. "You've seen enough of these cases to have an idea on what kind of person we're looking for."

"Looking for?" Joe's eyebrows flew up, so did his voice. "I don't have any objections to the mental chess you all are playing, but this is a brutal, cold-blooded murderer we're talking about. I sure as hell hope you're not 'looking for' anyone like that, Rye."

Riley flinched, remembering just how terrified she'd been the night she'd seen the giant in the pickup spying on her. Nor had she forgotten what Bella had said about the possibility he was a foot soldier working for a psychopathic mobster.

Joe was right, of course, but they were on a roll now. And if there was anything Riley could do to shed light on who had done such awful things, she wouldn't be stopped. She hadn't known Lexi, but she felt a sense of connection to Clive after having talked with his mother earlier that day. And what had happened to Sofia and her baby was profoundly disturbing. Riley knew she was in far too deep to get herself out, even if Joe was making perfect sense.

"Let me rephrase that, Joe. What sort of person do you think the detectives should be looking for?"

"Well, I have no real experience in profiling killers, but I can say we're talking about someone relatively strong—male, most likely. I don't get the sense it's more than one person who's calling the shots. The crimes are just too cookie cutter. This is someone who sticks to the script. Get more than one person involved and the MO usually changes a little as the crimes continue."

"Well, that makes sense," Bella noted. "I'd agree with all of that. Each of the victims was physically small, easily handled by one strong person, and they all met the same bizarre fate."

"Bella, you said you had a chance to go through Sofia's things this week. Any leads there?" Riley probed.

"So, as we've already figured, Sofia comes from money. The few items she had with her were all high-end designer brands. Not the typical homeless teen fare. I came across a small diamond bracelet in her carrying case. I could tell it was real, so I took it to a local appraiser. It's worth almost ten grand. What kid has something like that on her?"

"Who's to say it was hers?" Cedrick frowned. "Couldn't it have been stolen?"

Holly immediately came to Sofia's defense. "She wasn't like that, Cedrick—she was very naive. I don't think she would have had the nerve to steal anything."

"Holly's right. She didn't fit that profile." Bella rested her head on Holly's shoulder, eyes tearing up. "Sofia was just a scared little girl. I went through her artwork too. Now *that's* a different story. Dark—very dark," Bella pulled out her phone. "Fortunately, I was able to get photos of some of her sketches before the detectives showed up yesterday. They impounded everything from her room."

"These are beautiful," Riley said, tilting Bella's phone in her hand and flipping through several photos. Joe peered over her shoulder, observing them as well. "You're right, Bella. These are sad, but the girl had talent. Most of these could make it to galleries."

"That one is disturbing," Joe said, reaching over and touching the screen to enlarge the picture. The sketch on white paper looked like it had been drawn in black pencil. It was Sofia's self-portrait. In the drawing—a close-up of the girl's face—she was crying, and in the reflection of a tear rolling off her lashes was the dark shape of a man with a chain hanging from his hand.

"There were several like that," Bella said, taking her phone from Riley and flipping through a few more of the photos. "Look at this one." She held up a picture of a small girl cowering under a four-poster bed.

"What are you thinking? Sexual abuse?" Riley looked at Bella with a pained expression.

"Well, it sure would explain a lot," Holly interjected. "She got pregnant somehow, and I don't think she had the confidence or maturity to be in a consensual relationship. God knows how old she was—"

"Old enough to have very expensive jewelry," Cedrick interrupted. "Sorry if that sounded cold, but who gives a kid a ten-thousand-dollar bracelet?"

"Well, unless items like that were used as coercion. Maybe something to keep her silent." Bella countered.

Riley turned to Holly. "Anything in Lexi's notes on Sofia indicating abuse?"

"Couldn't find Lexi's notes on Sofia," Holly said, dropping her gaze. "I have no idea what Lexi would have done with those; I went through all her locked files and found nothing from her sessions with Sofia. The detectives were very interested in locating them too. As medical records, they are protected information, so they had to go to the trouble of getting a judge involved, and they weren't too happy this afternoon to come up empty-handed."

Riley noticed the expression on Cedrick's face as he listened to Holly's explanation. His brows knit before he shifted in his seat, subtly bumping Bella's foot with his own under the table. The girl looked at him and raised an eyebrow but said nothing.

"I'll know more about her age and the possibility of sexual abuse once the autopsy is completed," Joe offered pensively. "I'll get to that first thing in the morning."

"We're getting off track here," Bella said. "It sounds like whatever went down with Sofia is a whole other mess. What would her situation have to do with the murder of Clive? Sofia didn't have any connection to him that we know of."

"That's true. We don't want to muddy the waters," Holly offered. "Whatever happened to Sofia before she came to us was no doubt awful. Most kids don't run away from happy homes. But Bella is probably right—let's keep our focus on the murders."

"I say it's too soon to tell if Sofia had any connection to Clive or not," Riley interjected. "We don't even know Sofia's full name. Let's not rule anything out until we get an ID on her."

"That sounds fair," Bella conceded. "Let's hope Joe can make headway in that area."

"I know DNA samples were collected earlier this week on both Sofia and the infant," he added, "so maybe we won't be waiting too long. But am I the only one who finds it concerning that a wealthy teenage girl can just disappear for close to three months, and we've heard nothing about it on the news?" Joe's brows furrowed. "Isn't that how long you said she's been at the shelter, Holly? Something here isn't adding up."

"It happens all the time, Joe." Holly's tone was almost condescending. "It's not just low-income youth who are abused . . . or who run away from home." Of course, Joe would have known this. He was no stranger to kids from all walks of life who met an ill fate on coming to LA looking for a golden opportunity. He held his tongue, but when Riley caught his eye, she could see that Holly's outburst had caught him off guard. It seemed everyone was tired, if not emotionally drained.

"Sofia could also have been from out of state, for all we know," Cedrick suggested, "so maybe someone has been looking for her, just not that we've heard about."

"I'll do a little more searching online tomorrow for out-of-state possibilities," Bella offered, stifling a yawn.

✳ ✳ ✳

It was well after eleven when they called it a night. Joe was the first one to leave. Riley and Indio walked him out.

"I'm glad you could join us," Riley said, standing next to his Porsche. "Thanks for humoring us with your patience; I know you've had a long day too."

"Sure, of course. Thanks for dinner." He looked up at her as he sat in his car.

Riley stood back, keeping a firm grip on Indy's leash. "Did Clive's dad open up to you at all? Val pretty much broke down with me. Told me he didn't take the kid's transition well."

"The guy was wound pretty tight; I think he's the sort that keeps it all in and then one day blows up."

"I could see that." Riley nodded, remembering how he had stormed out when she'd come into the grieving room at the medical examiner's office. "Sounds like the kid left home a few times, so no surprise. Lots of tension in that family."

"The one thing he *did* share," Joe added as he started his car, "was that the kid had had an on-again, off-again relationship with one of the workers from the farm in Fresno. That the guy had moved to LA recently to stay with his mother."

"And that was why Clive came here?" Riley said, piecing it together. She felt a bubble of tension rise in her chest as she thought of Javier living behind the shelter with his mother. "Did he mention the guy's name?"

"Never said."

"Thanks, Joe." Riley wrestled with Indio's leash, trying to stop the dog from jumping into Joe's car. "You've been more help than you can imagine. I really appreciate you—and it looks like Indy has finally forgiven you for Artemis." She laughed. "That cat is still supervising the hell out of him."

Joe squeezed an eye closed. "What was I going to do with a three-legged she-devil like Artemis? There was only one home that would suit her. And since she was in the dumpster behind your favorite restaurant, I took it as an omen."

Riley laughed, shaking her head. "I have a favorite restaurant now, do I?"

Joe grinned, as if hearing her laugh had made his day. "Yeah, you know—the one in Chinatown where they serve that spicy soup."

"The spicy soup that *you* really like?"

"That's the one." He chuckled.

"Give me a call when the autopsy is done," she said, refocusing. "I'll come down and meet you if you like."

"Sounds like a plan." He reached out and petted Indio's head. "In the meantime, don't go chasing cold-blooded killers, Rye. You're making me crazy."

Riley knew Joe meant well, but what was he thinking? If anyone knew of the horrors in the big city, it was someone in her profession.

"I hear you, Joe. Don't give it another thought. I wouldn't do anything dangerous."

He gave her a dubious look, tilting his head toward her motorcycle parked in the driveway.

"We may have different definitions of what constitutes danger," he said, swinging his car door closed and slowly pulling away from the curb.

She watched Joe's taillights disappear into the darkness, absent-mindedly rubbing the tiny blue butterfly tattoo on her wrist. She was sure he had wanted to say more—to tell her it looked as if she were taking too many risks. As if she lived her life like someone burdened with an emotional debt. Like someone who masked her grief as guilt. And if he'd said that, maybe he'd have been right. Because grief was immutable, and guilt felt like something she could fix. Something she could atone for.

Finally, she turned and headed back to her bungalow. The others were just finishing the dinner cleanup.

Holly pulled Riley aside in the front hallway. "I know it's my assignment to see if I can get Maria chatting about Javier without raising any suspicion, but I have to say, I am a little worried about how close to home all this is," she whispered. "I haven't really thought about my own safety until tonight, but now that I have . . . I mean, who's to say I'm not next on the killer's list?"

Riley stepped back, looking at her with concern. She could understand Holly's reluctance to be involved. Common sense suggested they were both in over their heads. Bella and Cedrick might have been comfortable in their sleuthing roles, but Riley didn't disagree with Holly.

She kept her voice down. "If it makes you too anxious to be involved in all this, Holly, I think the others would understand if you bowed out. As I told you on Wednesday, the detectives know I've seen Javier with the pickup truck guy. They'll no doubt be all over him if that's where their investigation takes them."

Holly's eyes filled with relief. "It's not that I don't want to help find whoever has done these terrible things. I'm just feeling a little maxed out. Of course, if the police ask me any questions, I'll tell them everything I know."

Riley put a hand on Holly's arm. "Do whatever you need to do to keep yourself safe. You've lost a close friend. Not to mention a kid you were doing your best to help." Holly hugged her then, holding on a little too tightly.

"Let's stay in touch over the next few days," Bella suggested as she and Cedrick came out of the kitchen.

"Sounds good," Riley agreed. "Until then, I guess you'll keep pursuing an ID on Sofia?"

"Yeah, and I'll help Bella search out-of-state missing teens," Cedrick pulled on his jacket. "I'll drop Bella off, Holly—it's on my route anyway," he called over his shoulder as he and Bella headed for the front door.

CHAPTER NINETEEN

Riley awoke on Saturday morning with Artemis sitting on her pillow, staring into her face. The morning sun was streaming through the bedroom window, highlighting the areas on her bookshelf that hadn't seen a duster in weeks. She rolled over and squinted at the bedside clock. It was past eight o'clock already—hours after she would normally have been up for a run with Indy.

"Beach day," she announced, rolling out of bed and stepping over the dog.

*   *   *

The sky was a cloudless periwinkle blue—a perfect contrast to the navy hue of the Pacific.

Riley dipped her head under a small swell to slick her long hair out of her eyes. The water was cold and fresh in a way that cleared her mind and honed her senses. She was sure she'd just heard the high-pitched squeaks of dolphins nearby. She'd been hoping she'd see them up close that morning, as she often did.

As she paddled out over the surf, she reflected on the previous evening's conversation. When she took the Jaded Justice guy in the pickup truck out of the equation, as Cedrick had insisted, Javier was left front and center.

And yet she struggled to pinpoint what Javier's motive might have been for the murders. If he were a psychopath with opportunity, that could make sense, but these were not opportunistic murders. The crimes had involved planning, kidnapping, and torturing the victims before executing them in the same brutal fashion. An MO like that involves risk and means. She hadn't seen Javier with his own vehicle, and she knew he'd been taking the bus with Sofia to her prenatal visits, so it was unlikely he had the ability to transport the victims. And why bother moving them at all? Why not just kill them in Santa Monica?

Joe had speculated that the killer was working alone. Did that rule out Javier using the bald guy to help transport the victims? And then there was the fact that the vehicle seen leaving Sofia's murder was a van, not a pickup truck. And where would Javier have kept his prey before killing them? Not in a tiny, converted garage that he shared with his mother. Besides, Holly had indicated that Javier seemed mindful of Sofia, that he looked out for the girl. Other than the fact that Riley had seen Javier with the pickup truck man, it was starting to look like he should be crossed off the list of suspects.

As Riley paddled out again, she saw Charlie and some of the older gang he usually surfed with leaving for the morning. It reminded her of their recent argument in the coffee shop over his comments about Holly. Riley found herself wondering if she wasn't ignoring the possibility that Holly was somehow involved in the murders. After all, Holly had known all three victims, and she drove a dark-colored van similar to the one seen leaving Sofia's accident. She also had more of an opportunity to commit the crimes than any other suspect, and she was certainly athletic enough to single-handedly carry them out.

But why? What would her motive have been? *That* was the question.

If Holly was the murderer, Riley felt that Lexi was the common link between the other two victims. A triangle was starting to form in her mind. By all accounts, Lexi was very close to Sofia as well as Clive before he transitioned. So had there been a motive for Holly to kill Lexi, which then resulted in the need to get rid of Clive and Sofia?

Riley started to break her theory into possibilities. Sofia had come from a wealthy background while Clive had come from a farming community of modest means. The obvious things they would have had in common were their shared dependence on Lexi at the shelter, the need or desire to flee their families, and an association with Holly. After meeting Clive's parents, Riley had some idea why he would have wanted to leave home, and she could only guess from Sofia's artwork that she had either fled sexual abuse or her family's reaction to her pregnancy.

What was waving in Riley's face like a red flag, however, was the fact that Lexi's counseling files on Sofia—which should have been securely locked up in her office at the shelter—had disappeared. She wondered who else, besides Holly, would have had access to them. She might see if she could get any information out of Ms. Maria at the shelter, or perhaps Cedrick would have learned something from his mother's investigation about what had happened to the records. She'd check into that later.

As Riley loaded her board into her wagon at the beach, she recognized Holly across the road in the parking lot. She was with a short balding man, and they were both pulling on their wetsuits next to Holly's van. The way in which they interacted with one another was casual and intimate enough to suggest the man was Holly's husband. Riley was sure they hadn't noticed her, so she stayed out of sight until they headed for the water. Then she pulled away from the curb and rolled south on Pacific Coast Highway toward Santa Monica.

She parked a block away from the teen shelter and took the alleyway that ran along behind the condominiums on either side of the center. In the opposite direction, walking toward her, she saw a squat, middle-aged woman laden down with shopping bags approaching the back entry to the center. Riley took a gamble.

"Ms. Maria?" She waved as she closed the distance between them.

"*Sí,*" the woman answered, stopping in her tracks and squinting against the bright sunlight. "Who is it, *mija?*"

"Oh, we haven't met before. I'm Holly's friend Riley. Let me help you with those." She lifted two of the bags from the woman's hands. "I came by looking for Holly, but I guess she's not here today," Riley added, lying so effortlessly it surprised even her.

"Gracías, *mija.* It's the canned goods that are heavy." She huffed as she evened out her load.

"These are for the shelter, yes?" Riley motioned with her head in the direction of the house.

"*Sí,* we go up," Maria said, raising her chin.

"I'll get the door for us," Riley said, heading for the back stairs she had climbed the night she'd been spying on Holly and Bella.

A few minutes later, she was helping Maria unpack the groceries while the woman made a pot of tea for the two of them. She could hear voices coming from the front room, and someone was talking on the phone down the hallway, but none of the teens or staff at the shelter showed themselves.

"How well did you know Ms. Lexi?" Riley asked as Maria pulled up a chair and took a seat at the kitchen table across from her, passing her a cup of tea.

"She was a good girl," the woman said. "So sad what happened to her and to the little *mamacita*, Sofia. *Ay, dios mío . . .*" She made the sign of the cross in front of herself with her thumb.

"Who do you think would do this?" Riley asked.

"*Quién sabe?*" she said, shrugging her shoulders. Just then, the back door opened, and Javier stepped in. He said something breathlessly to his mother in Spanish as his eyes fixed on Riley.

Riley smiled calmly, doing her best to appear unfazed as he lifted his hat off his head and pulled up a seat at the table. She leaned back with her elbow over the top of her chair, watching him. Below a heavy brow, his dark eyes, rimmed with thick lashes, glimmered in the way of someone younger than she had expected. Riley tried to read him; he wasn't nearly as intimidating in the light of day as she'd imagined. Perhaps she even saw a little trepidation in his expression as he took her in.

"You were here at Ms. Lexi's service," he said, running thick fingers through his hair.

"Yes, I was, but I didn't know her. Was she a good person?"

"Everyone liked her," he said, not breaking his gaze.

"Even Sofia?" Riley prodded. His face was unreadable, but she saw the way Ms. Maria looked at him, and she knew right away he was hurting.

"Who are you, lady, and what do you want here? You act like you're the police."

"I'm not the police. I'm a doctor." Riley softened her tone as she leaned forward, placing her elbows on the table. She was relieved to know that Javier had no idea who she was because she knew the bald giant in the pickup she'd seen him with last week knew a whole lot more about her than she was comfortable with. "I took care of Sofia at the hospital, and the baby too."

Javier's chin trembled slightly. "How is the baby? Will she be okay?"

"I think she will. We just need to find her family. Do you know anything about them?"

"The police were here. They asked us about that already."

"And what did you tell them?" Riley leaned forward as Javier leaned back in his chair, holding his hat in his lap. He glanced over at his mother. Maria's head moved ever so slightly before her expression froze.

"I told them I knew nothing about her family, that I barely talked to her."

"Did you mention to them that you'd gone to the clinic in Venice with her for her prenatal checkups?"

Something flashed in Javier's eyes that Riley couldn't read, but she knew she had struck a nerve.

"She needed help. She had no one." He leaned forward, placing an arm on the tabletop between them.

"I thought she was close with Lexi," Riley pushed back.

"Ms. Lexi wanted her to get rid of the baby. But she was scared. She didn't know what to do. Me and my mom, we looked out for her. She was just a kid."

Maria got up from the table to pour Javier a cup of tea.

"She was very young, wasn't she?" Riley turned the screws.

"Fifteen, I think," he said, looking over his shoulder at his mother. He dropped his voice then. "She was the same age as my little sister, Rosaria, when she died."

"*Pandilleros.*" Maria's mouth curled into an unhappy slant as she took her seat again, pushing a cup in front of Javier. "They shoot my baby, Rosy."

"She means gangbangers," Javier interpreted, resting a hand over his mother's. "Rosy was supposed to be helping my dad take care of my little brothers back in Mexico. But she came up here to visit, then she got mixed up with some bad dudes in Ghost Town. That's when I left Fresno to be with my mom."

"Ghost Town?"

"Yeah, Venice."

"I'm so sorry. That's tragic." Riley shifted her gaze back to Maria. The woman said nothing as she stirred a spoonful of sugar slowly into her tea. "What about Clair? Did you know Clair McAllister, Javier?"

"You mean Clive," he corrected her matter-of-factly.

"I guess you did." Riley adjusted her chair, facing him squarely. "Were you close?"

"We were good friends back in Fresno. Either way, nothing changed between us, but I guess now Clive is gone too." His gaze dropped to the table. Riley noticed Maria was watching his expression with the same curiosity that she now was.

She sized Javier up more closely. He couldn't have been twenty years old, but the calluses on his hands and the heaviness in his voice suggested he'd had a rough life.

"This is a lot of death for you to deal with." Riley searched his eyes.

"Things were tough back in Mexico with the drug cartels. We learned to deal with it. My mom thought things would be better in California, after she found work. But trouble came looking for us here too. Rosy showed up without telling my mom she was coming. She wasn't here legally. And my mom didn't want any problem with Ms. Holly. So she told Rosy to go home, but she ended up in Venice." The concern in his voice stirred something in Riley. She couldn't put a finger on it, but Javier wasn't exactly shaping up to be the psychopath she'd imagined. If anything, she was now beginning to wonder if he wasn't also a victim of the man in the black pickup, if he wasn't being used or exploited somehow. And if Rosy had been caught up in it all.

Riley decided to push her luck. "Do you have any thoughts on who might have wanted Clive, Sofia, and Lexi dead?"

Javier and Maria locked eyes for a long moment before Javier finally answered. "The police asked us the same thing. We told them we don't know."

Maria said nothing, but Riley was sure, by the way the woman froze, that she was holding back.

"Who would have had access to Lexi's office? To her work?" Riley pressed. Maria shook her head, perhaps not wanting to say.

"You ask too many questions, lady," Javier said, standing with his hat in hand. "I've got work to do." He leaned over the table, kissing the top of his mother's head before heading for the back door.

Maria watched him go and then stood to clear their teacups from the table. "Ms. Holly, she's your friend?"

"Yes," Riley answered, taking her cue to go. "Is she your friend too?"

Maria kept her face turned and said nothing as she busied herself folding the empty grocery bags and tucking them into a kitchen drawer.

Riley turned to say goodbye. She could see tears were rolling down Maria's face.

The woman cleared her throat. "You want I should tell Miss Holly you come to see her, *mija*?"

"No, no need to do that," Riley said on her way out. "Thanks for the tea, though."

Riley looked down at her watch. It had only been an hour since she'd left the beach. She decided to follow her instincts and headed back to the surf spot where she'd seen Holly and her husband earlier.

Holly's van was still in the parking lot when Riley parked along the beachfront road, under the branches of an enormous sycamore tree. She put up her windshield sunshade, cracked her side windows, and waited. Ten minutes later, she saw the couple approaching the vehicle from the coffee shop across from the beach. They were holding hands. Holly looked relaxed and happy in her sandals and pink sweats—not at all like a cold-blooded killer, Riley admitted. But then again, she'd only met a few of those. Sometimes they were easy to spot when the prison guards brought them from the hospital jail ward for stitches or other injuries sustained in custody. The swastika neck tattoos were a dead giveaway, and occasionally, a black ink teardrop below the eye was also the signature of a killer. But at other times, Riley had been shocked to learn that the clean-cut, baby-faced inmates with quiet dispositions had committed some of the most horrific crimes. The lesson she'd come away with was *you could never tell.*

Riley pulled out into beach traffic slowly, several cars behind Holly and her husband. She kept far enough back to stay out of sight. She wasn't sure what she was hoping to find by following them, but she had already learned that Holly did appear to be married, as she had told Riley on their first meeting, and that was somehow a validation of honesty in Riley's mind.

Riley stayed back, following at a discreet distance as they wove through the weekend traffic toward the Valley. It seemed they weren't going to Malibu, where Holly had said she lived. Several miles and a dozen bends in the road later, Holly's van turned off the canyon and onto the 101 Freeway heading north. Three miles farther down the road, she exited and drove along a surface street where the flow of traffic was reduced to a trickle. Riley was forced to pull over and park next to the curb to avoid being directly behind Holly's vehicle. She watched as the van passed through two green lights and then turned left and into a gated lot full of storage garages and lockers.

Riley swung her car into the grocery store parking lot next door and pulled the hood of her sweatshirt over her head. After putting on a mask that fit snugly just below her sunglasses, she headed out along the sidewalk and into the gated storage lot. She walked behind several rows of sheds, peering around each corner before venturing out. In the fourth row, she saw the van pulled over to the side of the alleyway and one of the storage sheds open. Holly's husband was at the wheel. The back doors of the van sat ajar. Holly was just entering a storage locker, carrying a large file box in front of her—the type used to store documents. Just then, Riley's phone in her sweatshirt pocket began ringing. Holly froze in her tracks, looking in Riley's direction, but Riley was quick to pull back from the corner, crushing her phone in her hand through her pocket to silence it as she retreated to a shed farther away from the idling vehicle.

She waited a few seconds before peering out from her new position. Holly was just exiting the storage garage. She locked it with a padlock, looking in both directions along the alleyway as she did.

Riley's heart was pounding in a way that made it difficult to draw a breath deep enough to calm herself. She scooted behind the building and crouched in the spiderwebs next to an air-conditioning unit on the back of the complex, waiting a full minute after Holly's van had exited the lot before heading back to her car. All the while, she kept her mask and sunglasses in place as she noticed several security cameras on the sheds pointed in her direction.

The phone call Riley had missed was from Joe.

He'd followed up with a text: Done working. Want to meet up?

She knew that was code for he'd just finished Sofia's autopsy.

Riley typed out her response: Headed home from the beach. Need to run with Indy and shower. Can you meet at four? Just say where.

As she pulled out of the grocery store parking lot and headed back toward the freeway on-ramp, Riley saw a large black pickup truck edging out of the driveway across from the storage facility a few cars behind Holly, who had evidently been caught at a red light. She reduced her speed, checked her rearview mirror, and pulled over as if she were about to park, allowing the truck to pull out into traffic ahead of her.

She got caught at the second light, but as the truck turned left and swung onto the freeway heading south, she could easily see the rear window—and its Jaded Justice sticker.

Her heart was in her throat.

What the hell is going on here? she asked herself.

By the time Riley reached the freeway on-ramp, the black truck was long gone. She pushed the speed limit in the fast lane for a few miles but still saw no sign of it. The driver was either speeding excessively or had taken an exit before she'd managed to catch up.

*　　*　　*

When Riley arrived at Tulsi's Grill just after four, the place was almost empty. Joe had secured a booth in the back of the restaurant. He stood as she approached, flashing a wide smile. He cleaned up well. His hair was swept back into a thick, low manbun as he usually wore it at work, and his eyes sparkled from behind full dark lashes.

"How did it go this morning?" She smiled, sitting up straight with both elbows on the table.

"You look great, Rye. Did you get a little sun today?" he asked, evidently not wanting to rush into work details.

Riley felt the heat rising in her face. "I guess I probably did." She placed both palms on her cheeks. "Got in a little surf action this morning."

"Long beach day," he observed, sipping his ice water and eyeing her over the rim of his glass. Riley realized he was piecing together her earlier text saying she was just headed home from the beach. She'd sent that message well into the afternoon.

"You're taking your sleuthing role a little too seriously, Joe." She laughed, trying to deflect, but she was sure he noticed the way she dropped her eyes. It was clear she didn't want to explain where she'd been between her visit to the beach that morning and their early dinner. There were a million plausible reasons outside of suspicious activity, she decided.

The waiter arrived with a round tray of appetizers and set it in the middle of the table before taking their drink orders. Riley was ravenous. Realizing she'd been too busy to bother with lunch, she set about sampling each of the various offerings. Leaning back with one arm over the booth behind him, Joe watched her, seemingly amused.

"I know," she said, stopping to take a breath and looking up. "Right now, you're thinking I'm the human equivalent of a wood chipper."

Joe's smile widened. "I was starting to wonder if it was safe to put my hands on the table."

They both chuckled then, breaking the tension. Riley decided at that point, it might be polite to pace herself and maybe wait until after dinner to ask any questions about Sofia's autopsy. She made small talk about some of the construction changes happening on the medical school campus and asked if Joe had any trips planned over Christmas. He was going to Costa Rica to see his grandparents for the holidays, he said, and asked if she'd ever been. She hadn't, but it was on her bucket list, she admitted, though she immediately regretted giving him an opening.

It was dark outside by the time they finished dinner. The restaurant was starting to fill up. Joe suggested they walk across the street to the coffee shop for dessert. They found a table outside under the heat lamps. It was quieter there. Riley zipped her jacket up and wrapped her scarf around her neck. Rain was coming in the next day or so. Joe leaned back in a wicker chair, tucking his hands into his coat pockets.

"We're still waiting on some results, but it looks like Sofia was probably in her early teens. Cause of death was massive head trauma.

Even without that, though, she'd have had a hard time making it. Her internal injuries were significant."

"Yeah, that was pretty evident," Riley said. "What a tragic waste of a young life." They sat silent for a moment before she added, "I'll check on the baby Monday. I guess we're no closer to locating family?"

"Still no ID yet," Joe offered. His voice was flat. Riley guessed he had the same concerns she did. "We're not likely to get something out of official databases, and now with the new laws in California restricting what we can access from citizen ancestral DNA tests, we could be waiting a while to get a match."

Riley sighed, changing the subject. "So, if Sofia was in her early teens, she couldn't have legally consented to an intimate relationship. Did you get any sense she'd been subject to abuse?"

"There *were* signs," Joe said, clearing his throat. His face clouded. "I won't go into it, but I'd say it's likely."

"What kind of a monster would do such a thing to an innocent child? I know it's a naive question, especially coming from an ER doc, but really?"

Joe gave her a long look, as if weighing his words to spare her. "We both know there are more good people than bad in this world, Rye. Statistically, about five percent of the population is psychopathic. The good news is that means the vast majority are not. Our lines of work can be soul crushing at times . . ." He paused, taking a long sip of his coffee. His voice was heavy as he added, "At least most of the time, *you* can make folks better. Unfortunately, all I can do is help them tell their stories after they've already left this life."

Riley looked over at Joe. He'd always been so analytical when she talked with him at work. Outside his lab, he was a different animal.

"To answer your question, the type of person who could do this to an innocent little girl is the type of person who could do anything."

Riley stared at Joe, his meaning sinking in. "The same type of person who could commit cold-blooded murder," she surmised.

"Maybe, but not all pedophiles are murderers."

"They still rob children of their lives, though arguably in a different way," Riley countered, staring into her coffee.

Joe pulled his collar up around his neck. "I'm just piecing it together. Suppose Sofia was being abused in a home of high social status—which it appears that she was, considering her expensive belongings and the diamond bracelet. Protecting that status would be a compelling motive to commit murder, especially as a pregnancy would provide permanent DNA evidence implicating the perpetrator."

"That's a reasonable guess, Joe. Though we're making some leaps. We have no idea if her abuser was a family member, teacher, or friend, or if anyone even knew she was pregnant. Holly said she didn't look pregnant when she first arrived at the shelter."

"But Sofia felt the need to run away, and that's pretty telling. She wasn't safe at home, or she didn't feel she could share that kind of news. Either way, her family let her down. And unfortunately, as you know, kids are often violated by the people they trust the most. Stranger danger is one thing, but it's the creeps in the inner circle that are the scariest monsters in my opinion."

CHAPTER TWENTY

Riley decided to gamble on Cedrick working at Abe's that Sunday morning. When she peered out her bedroom window, the sky was gray and heavy, threatening rain at any moment. She skipped breakfast, pulled on her running tights and a rain jacket, and took Indio for his run. After a shower, she headed straight to the deli, arriving shortly after it opened. She asked to be seated in booth 18 and waited patiently for her server to show up.

"Well, lookee here. To what do I owe this pleasure, Dr. Brighton?" Cedrick singsonged as he filled her coffee cup. He looked over his shoulder and decided it was safe to slip into the booth across from her for a moment of private conversation.

"I think we need to chat," she said, her eyes sweeping the deli over Cedrick's head. "Just the two of us. When is a good time?"

"This place is about to get hopping. I have a few minutes right now, but let me get your order in first."

When Cedrick returned with Riley's toasted bagel, he sat down with her.

"Why the secrecy?" he asked. "There's nothing you'll ever need to hide from Bella. I could text her and ask her to come by, if you like."

"I'm not worried about Bella." Riley kept her voice low. "But I have to ask . . . What are your thoughts on Holly?"

Cedrick leaned back in the booth, cupping his chin in his hand. "You have suspicions?"

"I do. Or at least I *think* I do. I didn't want to involve Bella—they seem close, and I don't mean to raise any distrust or unnecessary friction until I've got good reason."

Cedrick let out a long sigh. "Why do you think I gave Bella a ride home Friday night instead of letting her get back into Holly's van?"

Riley's eyes widened a fraction. "Ah, so it's not just me then."

"Yeah, I thought Holly's spiel about not being able to find Lexi's notes on Sofia and her being too intimidated to press Maria for details on Javier was a little . . . well, far-fetched. I've only just met Holly, but she doesn't seem like a delicate flower, not the sort of person who'd be intimidated easily, especially by someone like an employee."

"Well, I'm pretty sure she was the only other person who had access to Lexi's counseling files. They were kept in a locked office, as far as I can tell, and yesterday I just happened to have the opportunity to follow her to a storage shed, where she deposited something that looked a lot like a document file box."

Cedrick chewed his bottom lip, frowning. "Sounds like you're onto something. And she didn't see you?"

"No, I'm pretty sure of that, but what's even weirder . . ." Riley hesitated for a moment, remembering Cedrick's warning on Friday night. "I saw the dude in the black pickup again, and I think he was following her."

Cedrick scratched the side of his face, pressing his lips together tightly. "Did he catch sight of you?"

"Nope, I was super stealth."

"You got lucky it seems." He looked over his shoulder again, surveying his section of tables. "Did you notice if Javier was with him?"

"No, Javier wasn't with him. I'd actually just left Javier and his mom minutes before I followed Holly and her husband to the storage facility," Riley confessed, realizing only now, saying all of this out loud, how completely crazy it sounded.

"Wow, you had a busy day, Special Agent Brighton, didn't you?" Cedrick scooted to the edge of the booth. The deli was starting to fill up with the usual weekend crowd. "Ah, I better get to work."

"I'll let you go, but I wanted you to know I think Javier is in the clear. After talking with him yesterday, I don't think he would have hurt Sofia."

"Good to know." Cedrick stood. "Why don't you give Bella an update? She's solid."

"Will do." Riley took her check from him and wrapped her bagel in a napkin to go. "Oh, and one more thing, Cedrick," she said, standing to leave. "See if you can find any mention of counseling records from Clair McAllister's sessions with Lexi in your source's database."

Cedrick nodded slowly, clearly trying to work out what Riley was after. "You think those might help?"

"I'm saying I'd be surprised if LAPD has even sought those. Remember, Clive had a name change a year ago. All his current identification, things like his driver's license and Social Security card, are probably under Clive McAllister. I bet officials are not searching for counseling records from the shelter on *Clair* McAllister. If those are still in Lexi's files and we can get our hands on them before the LAPD wises up and gets the request right, they may shed some light on why Clive was targeted too."

"That sounds like the perfect sleuthing assignment for Bella," Cedrick said, his eyes widening. "Especially as she once lived at the shelter. She's familiar with the facility."

Riley winked at Cedrick as she turned to leave. "Great idea, young man."

*　　*　　*

It was pouring rain by the time Riley got home. She curled up on the couch in her sweats with Artemis and her laptop. Indio settled himself into the beanbag chair across the room, where he was soon snoring.

Riley opened her browser and continued her online search for information about any of the murder victims. She started with Lexi but came up empty. There was nothing informative Riley hadn't already seen on any of the social platforms either. Those seemed to have been taken over by the haters. There were always trolls with nothing better to do than stir discord in the wake of tragedy.

She scrolled through horrid comments like "You've heard about 'he said she said,' now we have he dead, she dead," followed by laughing face emojis. And "Seems like a killer is on a gender bender, good riddance."

Riley cringed, leaving the venue for more mainstream sites.

She moved onto news channel searches for Sofia, using the date of her trauma. There were several hits from media outlets detailing the disaster on the 101 Freeway involving an unidentified pregnant teen and a small article two days later in which one network reported her tragic death but never provided her name.

As Riley read through the report and the spectacle the media were making over Sofia's miracle baby having survived the event, she wondered if perhaps they weren't putting the infant at risk. If Joe was right and someone from Sofia's past was trying to hide the crime of her sexual abuse by eliminating her, then announcing her baby had survived could be perilous. Riley considered whether she and Joe had simply gone down a rabbit hole with that assumption about the motive for Sofia's murder. While their hypothesis was plausible, once Riley factored in the murders of Clive and Lexi, things got murky.

Indio suddenly raised his head from where he was lying on the beanbag chair in the living room. His ears perked up. A second later, someone knocked on the front door, but instead of barking, Indio wagged his tail slowly.

Riley got up and answered the door, holding it ajar as the wind and rain pummeled down from the sky in violent sheets. "Bella! Come on in. I'll make you some hot chocolate."

"That sounds like heaven," the girl replied, shaking her umbrella out and propping it up in the hallway as she entered. Indy was on his feet immediately, recognizing his admirer from Friday night with enthusiastic gyrations as he followed Bella and Riley into the kitchen.

Minutes later, they were all back in the living room. Bella, with her hot chocolate in one hand and the other resting on Indy's head, squeezed into the beanbag with him.

"Did Cedrick share his concerns with you about Holly's story?" Riley asked. Bella nodded but said nothing. "Well, I have to say I agree with him. I'm not convinced she couldn't locate Lexi's files on Sofia. How could they just disappear from a locked office? And why is she too intimidated to ask Ms. Maria any questions about Javier? Something's not adding up."

"Yeah, Cedrick told me he thinks she's hiding something. I can't for a minute believe she's a killer. Honestly, Riley, she has a heart of gold; I've never heard her say an unkind word about anyone. But I'd be the first one to agree she's not being entirely honest with us. It's more likely she's afraid to share something she's learned."

"Sounds like we're all on the same page then," Riley said, bringing Bella up to speed, filling her in on her chat with Javier and Maria, as well as her afternoon adventures tracking Holly and her husband to the storage shelter.

"And you're positive the Jaded Justice guy was following Holly?"

"Without a doubt." Riley frowned. "But when I mentioned it to Cedrick, he didn't seem fazed, even though it sure looked to me like the guy was stalking her. What if Holly's next on the killer's list?"

"Well, that's a scary thought." Bella's amber eyes narrowed. "And a bit of a catch-22. How do we keep Holly safe without letting her know we're onto her? If we don't tell her she's being followed, she could be in danger. And if we let on we know she's being stalked because we've also been following her, we'll probably just alienate her."

"Well, it didn't occur to me until right now, but I say we suddenly become fully transparent about keeping an eye on her."

Bella shot Riley a confused look.

"Hear me out. We admit *you* to the shelter in Santa Monica as a teen runaway with Holly's help. You look young enough to pull it off. We tell Holly the plan is to allow you to keep an eye on Javier from the inside, maybe get a few questions about him answered. In the meantime, you wait for an opportunity to get into the office and search Lexi's files for any notes on *Clair* McAllister."

"That could actually work, believe it or not. I've never met Ms. Maria. She's only been at the shelter the last year or so and I always visited Sofia after hours, so I'll be in the clear there. And if Holly has already removed Lexi's files on Sofia, she'd have no reason to be on guard. She'd never suspect we were after Clive's records. Why would she?"

Riley nodded. "I have a feeling I could persuade Maria to help you gain access to that locked office when Holly goes home. I've got the sense she and Javier have some reservations of their own about Holly."

"It's a brilliant idea." Bella pulled out her rainbow-colored cell phone with its large pink kitty sticker on the back. "I'll see if there are any vacancies at the shelter and if Holly will agree to get me admitted tomorrow."

Riley noticed then how comfortable Bella was with Indy, how the dog gravitated to her. She thought for a moment about all three of the freeway victims. They had each been petite people—roughly the size of Bella—easily subdued by a single assailant.

"Do kids ever show up at the shelter with their pets?"

Bella broke into a broad smile. "Would you really let me take Indy along?"

"Maybe just for a day or two. You shouldn't need to be there any longer than that anyway. He seems crazy about you, and I'd feel a little better knowing you had at least some protection. He's quite a good guard dog; I think he has some Belgian Malinois in him."

"Cool, thanks. But if I'm only staying long enough to get into the files, what explanation do I give Holly when I suddenly decide to leave after only a day or two?"

"That's easy. You tell her you checked into Javier and he has nothing to hide and your time would be better spent elsewhere."

"Perfect." Bella hugged the dog. "What do you think, Seargent Indy? Up for a special ops assignment?"

CHAPTER TWENTY-ONE

It was still drizzling on Monday morning. The gentle hush of moisture was enough to banish all the stubborn late-summer temperatures, plunging the area into something that felt a little more like fall.

Riley left the house an hour earlier than usual to drop Bella and Indio off in the predawn darkness, blocks away from the youth shelter in Santa Monica. They'd both be soaked to the bone by the time they reached the center, but that would only lend credibility to their plight for anyone greeting them on arrival.

The previous evening, Holly had confirmed that the shelter had a vacancy, and she'd agreed to Bella's plan without question. With a couple of phone calls, Holly had arranged with Ms. Maria to meet the shelter's newest arrival first thing in the morning and see to it that she had breakfast and a clean room. Neither Riley nor Bella was sure if that development was encouraging or cause for concern.

Cedrick, however, did little to hide his alarm that the plan was actually being put in motion when they shared the news with him later that evening. He insisted Bella check in with him regularly and activate a location tracker on her smartphone, so he knew where she was at all times.

*　　*　　*

By the time Riley made it to the hospital, she had only a few minutes to run up to the nursery to check on Sofia's baby before her shift started. The charge nurse she'd talked with on her previous visits to the nursery stepped out to greet her. The automatic doors locked behind her with a thud.

The woman kept her voice low and stood just shy of the hallway, out of sight of the security cameras.

"Hey, you should know, the baby's been moved from the general nursery, and we're not allowing any visitors. We're not even supposed to say she's here."

"Seriously?" Riley frowned. "What went down?"

"Dunno. I'm assuming LAPD thinks the kid could be in danger. There are all kinds of nuts coming out of the woodwork since the press made such a spectacle of the 'miracle baby.'"

"Got it," Riley said, nodding. "But she's fine? I mean, she's healthy and all?"

"Yeah, as far as that goes, she's great, but I guess we're keeping her in some sort of protective custody. Sorry."

"Actually, I'm relieved to hear that. And thanks for the heads-up. Do you mind keeping me in the loop if anything changes? If family shows?" Riley pulled out a pen and prescription pad from her pocket and scribbled her number down.

"I'll do my best, but don't press your luck with the rest of the staff here. Administration is taking this seriously."

"No worries. Thanks, Cindy," Riley whispered before stepping back out into the hallway.

The LAPD would have Sofia's autopsy results by now, she realized, and the detectives working on the case would have learned of the medical examiner's suspicions of sexual abuse. A serpent unfurled itself slowly in Riley's gut when she thought about what Joe had said—the baby was undeniable DNA evidence of potential rape or pedophilia, and those were some pretty strong motives for somebody to gain access to Sofia's baby quickly.

As she passed through the general surgery ward, she stopped at the nurses' station where she asked for the room number of her gunshot patient from two weeks ago, Miguel.

Riley knocked lightly before entering. Miguel was seated in a recliner at the bedside, his morning meal spread before him on a rolling tray.

"Breakfast any good?" she asked.

His face lit up at the sight of her. "Not as good as the breakfast burritos in the barrio," he said with a chuckle, "but not bad for a last meal in this place. How goes it, Doc?"

"Cool. You're being discharged then?"

"Unless I end up in the jail ward before I can get out of here." He smirked.

Riley leaned on the windowsill, looking out at the steam rising from the hospital's laundry rooftop below. The rain was still coming down softly. In the distance, she could see the slow stream of lights from the morning commuters grinding along the freeways.

She took a seat on the windowsill, turning to him. "Remember what you said to me the last time we ran into each other, Miguel?" He looked up at her, took a bite of toast, and nodded slowly. "It's a bit of a long shot, but if you can help, I'd be grateful. About three months ago, a fifteen-year-old girl visiting from Mexico got tangled up in Venice with one of the gangs. I don't know much more than that. All I know is her name was Rosaria, and she ended up dead. A shooting victim, apparently."

Miguel shrugged. "Ghost Town, huh? Yeah, Doc, you're right. That's a long shot. And from what I've heard, there are some hardcore homies in that hood. But I'll put my ear to the ground."

"That would be great, thank you."

"I'll get word to you if I find anything." Riley froze, wondering what to say next. She wasn't about to give her phone number to a known gang member. Miguel must have read her mind. A smile spread slowly over his face as he swallowed his toast and added, "Don't worry, Doc. I know where you work."

"I appreciate you having my back, as you put it, Miguel. But do yourself a favor. Have your own back before you have anyone else's." Riley gave him a long look, weighing how she might couch what she would say next. "Rosaria's family came here to escape the dangers of gang violence in their own country. You already have options they didn't. And now you have a second chance, a second chance Rosaria didn't get. You seem like a bright young man." She had his attention. He sat stone-faced, his eyes locked on hers. "Maybe choose a life that doesn't potentially end in prison or the trauma bay at City General. Luck only goes so far."

✳   ✳   ✳

As Riley approached the ER back hallway from the stairwell, she ran into Astrid on her way upstairs.

"Hey, you're still here?" she asked, surprised. "How was nights?"

"Typical Sunday. I think we admitted everyone in LA. Only a handful of treat 'em and street 'em cases. You know, any time it rains, dipshits forget how to drive in this freakin' city."

"Where are you headed? I thought you'd be halfway home by now."

"Jackass wants to see me."

"Why? What's up?"

"Hell if I know." Astrid grunted. "Better be damn good, though. I haven't had breakfast yet, and we all know that's a recipe for a bloodbath." She scowled, pushing past Riley.

"If you need help hiding the body, just give a call. I'll be right up," Riley said with a laugh as she headed to the locker room.

A few minutes later, as Riley pulled on her scrubs, her phone pinged. It was a message from Bella on the encrypted app: Ms. Maria loves me already. I got four pancakes for breakfast here at the shelter. But Indy is the biggest rock star with the residents in this joint. He scored a special treat from the clothing donation box. Bella attached a selfie with Indio in a knit button-up vest with an orange-and-green argyle pattern. The dog's eyes were wide, his mouth hanging open. Bella's grin in the selfie was almost as happy.

Riley answered with a laughing face emoji. I'll come by tonight and we can work our magic on Ms. Maria.

Communication on the encrypted app would be heavy that day. It was midway through a busy morning in the ER when Riley received a message from Cedrick: Looks like LAPD has a hit on Sofia's family. Just now accessing some details. Updates to follow.

Riley's heart raced, her mind flooding with opposing scenarios. Was Joe's theory about Sofia's abuse correct? DNA samples from her baby would have been processed by now. Determining a match for the infant's father would be relatively simple if the perpetrator was someone close to Sofia. Then again, what was the possibility that the girl's family might be entirely innocent? Perhaps they were loving, kind people, facing the devastation of her senseless murder on the heels of her three-month-long disappearance. Whatever the circumstances, how would they react to the news of her baby? Something inside Riley stirred. She couldn't name it, but it didn't sit well.

As the afternoon wore on, Riley found herself watching the clock—something she never did at work. She was anxious for updates from Cedrick, but she was also preoccupied with how things were going for Bella at the shelter. She wondered if Holly was at all suspicious about Bella's purpose for being at the center or if she'd swallowed the line that Bella was there to spy on Javier.

Just before dark, Riley took a short break between patients and headed out to the covered walkway alongside the ambulance entrance to text Cedrick and ask if he could talk. The rain had stopped, but the sky was still heavy with gray clouds, except for a narrow band to the east where the silhouette of the city skyline sat against the backdrop of the San Gabriel Mountains. The wind whipped along the walkway, piercing Riley's back through the light fabric of her scrubs and tugging on the loose strands of her long hair that had escaped her braid.

She answered Cedrick's call on the first ring. Riley shielded the receiver of her phone from the wind with a cupped hand. "What's the news? The suspense is killing me."

"She's from Utah. No wonder we couldn't find any local hits on her," Cedrick replied breathlessly. "Last name is Draper. Stepfather is some higher-up in the banking industry; mother has some political appointment. I don't know anything about her biological father or any siblings. Still working on that. Seems like she did a runner four months ago. Apparently not the first time she'd taken off."

"It's a long way from Utah to Santa Monica," Riley mused, wondering how Sofia had managed the trip and if she'd been alone. "How old was she?" Riley held her breath while she waited for Cedrick to stop sifting through electronic files.

"Holy moly . . . fourteen. If it's her, she was only fourteen."

"Wait, what? You're not sure it's her?"

"I can't be positive; that's just it. I've never seen the girl. I'm just going on what LAPD is reporting. I've been expecting Bella to confirm it's her, but she's not answering my messages. I'm going to text you a picture from the Utah missing person's post. Let me know if you agree it's Sofia."

A moment later, Riley was enlarging a photo on her smartphone of a petite girl with long braids in a plaid school uniform. Her stomach dropped.

"Oh yeah, that's her all right. Jesus, what a tragedy. Fourteen?" Cedrick was quiet on the other end of the line; Riley could hear the clicking of his keyboard as he searched files. "I don't suppose there's any mention that she was pregnant?"

"Pffft, I doubt it," Cedrick scoffed. "I'm not exactly sure a family like hers would be announcing such details, even if they were aware of the pregnancy."

"You're right. Perhaps *especially* if they were aware . . ." Riley's voice trailed off before she thought to share another detail with Cedrick. "By the way, the baby is under lockdown here at the hospital. Some kind of protective custody, so LAPD must either have a need for secrecy, or there is a potential threat to the infant."

"Yeah, I guess that makes sense. Or it could just be a privacy issue if the grandparents are well connected."

"Do we know for sure if the family has identified Sofia yet? How would that happen?"

"Didn't Joe say on Friday that DNA samples had already been taken from both the baby and Sofia? I'm guessing that will be the route they take since the family isn't local. They probably won't be coming in to make a visual ID. But, honestly, I'm not sure how it will be handled in this case. Sounds like you should probably run this one by Joe."

"Okay, I'll text him in a minute and see if he can meet after work. I was planning to swing by the shelter in Santa Monica and distract Ms. Maria while Bella accesses the office where Lexi's files are stored."

"Speaking of Bella—have you heard from her?"

"No, not since early this morning. But I thought you were tracking her movements through her phone. Can't you see what she's been up to? I would imagine she's at least taken Indy out for a walk at the beach."

"Well, I'm not picking up any activity. Maybe it's still raining in Santa Monica, and she's just sitting tight. Or maybe Holly's keeping her under her thumb. Let me know if you hear from her before tonight; otherwise, please call me when you get to the shelter."

"Sure thing, and thanks again for the update."

Riley hung up and immediately texted Joe: Got five minutes after work tonight?

He replied with a sad face emoji and What? Only five minutes?

Joe met Riley in the parking garage on the east side of the medical campus. He'd been off work since six. Riley didn't usually leave until after seven. He'd apparently had time to shower because the first thing she'd noticed was that he didn't smell like the lab. His hair was wet, and his face glowed in a way she'd never noticed before.

"Oh jeez, Joe. I didn't even think about the fact that you're usually home by this time. Sorry, and thanks for agreeing to meet."

"No biggie," he said, grinning. "It gave me a chance to use the campus gym for once, so I should be thanking you for getting me some exercise."

Riley got right down to business, filling him in on what she'd learned from her call with Cedrick.

"Well, that explains it," Joe said, rubbing his chin. "We got word late this afternoon that family is coming for a viewing tomorrow."

"Oh, I guess I'm not surprised, now that I think about it." Riley crossed her arms over her chest. "I figured they would have made and ID by DNA, but I guess because of the baby, they would have to come anyway."

Riley felt something tighten in her chest. Her lips pressed into a pout.

Joe put his hands on her shoulders. "And that concerns you?"

"Yeah, I guess. Strange, right? I know I should be relieved that the baby will be claimed by family, but I'm thinking about what you said the other night." She looked up at him, surprised to find herself not pulling away from his touch. "You said Sofia had either not felt safe at home or hadn't been able to share the news of her pregnancy. Either way, her family let her down."

"Well . . ." Joe stepped back, letting his arms fall to his sides. "We're not going to solve all the world's problems, Dr. Brighton. Parents can be disappointing, but they sometimes learn from past mistakes. Maybe the harshness of losing Sofia in such a brutal way will alter their approach with their granddaughter. We can hope, anyway." He gave her a reassuring smile.

"Yeah, but what if the stepdad is the abuser? Remember Sofia's drawings of the man with the chain and the small girl hiding under the bed? And if he is the perp, then wouldn't that give him plenty of motive to—" Riley realized she was making some big assumptions. "Sorry, am I overthinking this?"

"No, I think you're right on the money. But we have competent, trained professionals charged with making these decisions, and we have to trust they are asking themselves all the same questions we are." He held her gaze. "And I can assure you the LAPD will be looking closely at the possibility she was being abused at home. That baby won't be released until the stepfather and any other possible suspects in the household are cleared. All it will take is a simple DNA swab to accomplish that."

"Providing they consent to the test. It sounds like these folks have money. They could fight a DNA court order, right?"

"You're right, of course, but why would they do that? The end result will be the same, I assume. Granted, I'm no lawyer, but if someone is refusing to be cleared as a suspect in a child sex abuse case, I can't imagine DCFS is going to allow them to take an infant home with them."

"God, I hope you're right. We both know kids slip through the cracks of the system every day."

Just then, Riley's phone rang. She pulled it out of her coat pocket, expecting it was either Cedrick or Bella. Her brows knit in confusion. "What the hell?" She balked, reading the text on the caller ID display: Saint Francis Animal Shelter.

She put the phone up to her ear.

"Hello? Yes? What? Where was that? Venice! How long has he been there?"

Joe's face clouded with concern. Riley held the palm of her hand up to silence him.

"How late are you open? What time in the morning?"

"Shit!" Riley fumed, hanging up. Her chest tightened; she could barely breathe. "Where's your car, Joe? I hope you didn't have any plans for this evening."

CHAPTER TWENTY-TWO

Joe's silver Porsche raced along the 10 Freeway toward Santa Monica. The roads were still wet, and as a result, traffic getting out of downtown had been infuriatingly slow until they neared the coast. Riley sat in the passenger seat beside him, dialing Cedrick for the third time. The call went straight to voicemail again. She'd had no answer when she'd tried Bella's phone from the parking lot at work after hanging up with the animal shelter, and Holly wasn't picking up either.

"Thank God I had him chipped," Riley said, letting out a heavy sigh. "They don't open until nine in the morning. I'm just glad he's safe, and they were able to reach me."

"He'll be fine, Rye. A little overnight stay in the animal shelter won't hurt him. He's probably diggin' the change of scenery."

Riley knew Joe was trying to inject some levity into the situation and distract her from the bigger, more concerning questions, but Indy's safety was only one of her worries. Where was Bella, and why had Indio been found wandering the streets of Venice without her?

By the time Joe and Riley reached the teen center in Santa Monica, Riley had abandoned any pretense of composure. As soon as Joe pulled into the driveway, she was out of the car, leaving the door ajar behind her and taking the stairs to the porch two at a time. She entered through the unlocked front door, jogging down a long, dimly lit hallway under the muted glow of frosted antique light fixtures.

She could hear voices coming from somewhere in the back of the building. She followed the sound, poking her head into a room that appeared to be a salon or library of sorts. A half dozen surprised faces sitting in a circle looked back at her from a deep crimson rug in the middle of the floor. She'd evidently interrupted a group discussion.

"Can I help you?" a young man asked, slowly getting to his feet. Riley recognized him as the man she'd seen at Lexi's service in the Rastafarian hat—the man who had been sitting on the stairs next to her and Sofia.

She beckoned for him to join her in the hallway, apologizing breathlessly to the gathering for the interruption. The young man identified himself as a resident assistant named Delroy. Riley explained that she was a close friend of Bella's who was concerned she hadn't been able to reach her all afternoon. He looked Riley up and down as if weighing the possibility she posed any threat until she pulled out her phone and showed him the selfie Bella had sent her from the shelter earlier that morning with Indy in his orange-and-green knit vest. Riley followed him to the landline on the wall down the hallway. Delroy said he was trying to reach the administrator on call but was getting no answer. He finally gave up and relented, deciding to take Riley to Bella's assigned room.

The girl's belongings were still there. The canvas backpack she'd been carrying when Riley had dropped her off that morning hung from a hook behind the door. The jacket and jeans she'd worn were draped over hangers from the top of the window, perhaps in an attempt to dry them out after her morning walk in the rain. Riley pulled the backpack off its hook and unzipped a small pocket above the main pouch that looked like it might hold a cell phone or a pair of sunglasses. It was empty. Then she opened the main compartment and tipped the contents onto the patchwork quilt over Bella's bed. Delroy watched her, saying nothing, his hands tucked deeply into the pockets of his sweatpants. A small toiletries purse, a pair of sandals, blue jeans rolled into a tight bundle, a Lakers sweatshirt, and two T-shirts were the sum of the contents.

Riley turned to Delroy. "How many residents are here at any given time?"

He was slow to answer, as if weighing both the accuracy of his facts and Riley's need to know. She could see he took his responsibilities seriously.

"I know I'm asking a lot of you, but this is an emergency." Her tone seemed to do the trick.

"We have six rooms; they're all occupied right now. The administrators have a pretty tight vetting process. No drugs, no smoking, and no mental illness." His eyes dropped. "We just don't have the resources for anyone with those types of challenges."

Riley understood the restrictions, but that didn't stop her from trying to imagine any of the homeless people she knew being eligible for admission. She came up empty.

Ten minutes later, Joe and Riley were standing in the kitchen at the shelter with Ms. Maria and Javier, both of whom eyed Riley with overt distrust now. Delroy excused himself, saying his group meeting was just wrapping up for the evening.

Riley was glad to have Joe with her. He was fluent in Spanish, which came in handy when explaining the situation to Maria. Riley understood only snippets of their conversation, but it was evident from Maria's expression that she was distraught that Bella wasn't in the shelter and wasn't answering calls. Javier appeared to be trying to reassure his mother while Joe seemed to be repeating the same questions.

Joe turned from Maria to Riley, explaining that Bella had been at the center all morning, playing chess with some of the other residents and helping Maria dust and vacuum the office Lexi and Holly had shared. She'd taken Indy for a walk in the afternoon around three o'clock, but she'd never returned. No one had seemed alarmed at this behavior; it was nothing out of the ordinary for the typical shelter resident.

"What do we do now?" Riley said, turning to Joe, mind racing. Before he could answer, she was addressing Maria. "Does Holly know Bella didn't come back from her walk?"

"Ms. Holly no come in today," Maria said, her brow heavy with concern. Javier put an arm around his mother. Riley could see they were both replaying Sofia's sudden disappearance and still reeling from how tragically that event had ended. And all that in the wake of losing Rosaria only a few months before.

"Shouldn't we call the police? The detectives?" Riley turned back to Joe. "This thing is completely out of hand. I'm sure Bella would *never* choose to leave Indy. She could be in real danger, Joe."

Joe eyed Riley thoughtfully. She could see he was trying to piece together what they might say to the police.

"Rye, how seriously do you think the PD will take us when we report that a supposedly homeless teen has been missing for five hours?" Joe's tone was patient, the concern in his eyes mirroring her own, but the question—which was, to a degree, rhetorical—needed to be asked.

Riley was quick to counter, "I know all this sounds absurd under ordinary circumstances, but remember, both Lexi and Sofia disappeared from here too. So that should raise alarm bells, shouldn't it? We should probably involve local authorities before involving Detective Roberts. Right? I mean, doesn't that make sense?"

Ms. Maria started to cry softly. Javier sat her down at the kitchen table, straddling a chair next to her. He leaned into her, an arm over her shoulders, talking quietly into her ear as she rolled a string of Rosary beads between her clutched hands. Riley was suddenly flooded with guilt. She'd been the one to suggest Bella pull off this stunt to gain access to Lexi's files. It seemed she'd done nothing but put Bella at risk and upset an already traumatized Maria and Javier, not to mention that she could have lost Indy too. She felt suddenly like she was coming down with a case of the flu. The room seemed to spin.

Her phone rang, startling her. It was Cedrick.

He'd been in a final exam all evening, and he'd only just listened to Riley's messages. Bella's phone was no longer showing up on his tracking app. The last place it had registered was at the shelter in Santa Monica earlier that afternoon.

"It's not like Bella to go offline. I've never known her to turn off her phone. Let me call my mom. I'll get right back to you, but in the meantime, I'd call Santa Monica PD." Just as Riley was about to hang up, Cedrick added, "And the hospitals. Call the hospitals."

"Of course," Riley said. "Naturally, I've already thought of that. Joe's doing that now."

Riley's mind had been racing with possibilities since she'd realized Bella was missing. What if the girl had had some unfortunate event? What if she were lying unconscious in an ER or ICU somewhere, the victim of some random accident? Did the girl have a seizure disorder or some other reason for suddenly losing her faculties? Anything along those lines would be better than the scenarios Riley was left with. There were too many dead girls already.

Riley pulled a chair out from under the kitchen table, slumped into it, and dialed the emergency number for local services. When she got through, the dispatcher sounded less than enthusiastic about sending a unit to take a report on an incident that didn't seem to be a life-or-death issue. She would send someone out when she could.

Joe stood over Riley, looking down at her, his expression grim. She felt awful for involving him in her ridiculous campaign to snoop around in matters better left to professionals. He took the seat next to her, and in a minute, he was calling hospitals in the surrounding area.

As they all waited for the local police to arrive, Riley sat staring at the small rose-colored squares of the linoleum floor, one leg crossed over the other, her foot swinging impatiently. Her eyes came to rest on Indy's food bowl sitting in the corner of the kitchen near the back door. She'd packed it up with his leash and a small bag of his food the night before for Bella. The bowl was full to the brim with dry kibble. Something about that struck Riley as odd, but she quickly dismissed the thought. The dog had probably been spoiled with treats and table scraps by the shelter residents that day. Still, it was unusual he hadn't touched his food.

Riley glanced at Joe as he sat calling the local hospitals. She felt paralyzed and frantic all at once. How would she explain to the police what Bella was doing at the shelter in the first place? Did she even need to reveal those details? Whatever the reason Bella had been there, it didn't change the fact that she was now missing. Riley wondered if she should try calling Holly again. Why hadn't she shown up to work that day? Hadn't Holly arranged to connect with Bella that morning at the shelter?

Joe finished calling the hospitals without any luck. There were no unidentified patients, and no one fitting Bella's description had been brought in unconscious.

Riley pried herself out of her chair, walked over to the corner where Indy's bowl was sitting, and picked it up. *Strange*, she thought. It felt heavier than she'd expected.

"Where's the trash?" she asked. Not wanting to bother Maria, she directed her question to Javier. He indicated a small cupboard door under the kitchen sink. Riley reached down, opened the door, and pulled out the small can below. She'd take the bowl home with her tonight. Hopefully, she could pick Indy up from the animal shelter first thing in the morning. As she tipped the kibble out, Riley heard the thud of something heavy hitting the bottom of the trash can. She looked over her shoulder. Javier and Joe were distracted, chatting in Spanish at the table; Maria sat quietly, head bowed, rolling the beads of her rosary between her fingers.

Riley reached into the trash, her hand sifting through the kibble until it came to rest on the object that had been hidden under the dry dog food in Indio's bowl. As she pulled it out, she recognized it immediately by its rainbow cover and the pink kitty sticker on the back.

It was Bella's cell phone.

Riley slid the phone into her jacket pocket. "Just stretching my legs. Gonna slip out for a breath of fresh air," she said, though it seemed nobody was listening. She stepped out into the hallway, tracing her path back down the dimly lit corridor to the front porch where she could watch for the local police to arrive. She stood in the shadows of the overhang, away from the soft light of the front porch, and pulled out her phone to call Cedrick.

He picked up on the first ring. "Yes?" he huffed. She could hear he was driving.

"I found Bella's phone, Cedrick. She turned it off and hid it someplace where only I would find it. She knew I was coming to the shelter tonight. I can only assume it holds some evidence she wanted to keep safe, and that's why she didn't take it with her. What should I do with it? Santa Monica PD should be here any moment. I don't want to turn it over. We would lose anything she might have stored on it."

"You realize we're tampering with evidence if you don't turn it over, right? I don't think we want to do that. But don't give it to the local PD unless they specifically ask about it. My mom has already called them. She'll want to speak with you too, I'm certain. You can make sure she gets Bella's phone. It makes more sense for her to have it . . ."

Riley could hear the angst in Cedrick's voice. She knew he'd purposely not finished his last sentence. It made the most sense for his mother to have Bella's phone because she was the lead detective on a case in which the other missing individuals from the shelter had all turned up dead on a freeway in her district.

Riley's eyes swept the street in front of the center. There was no movement, no headlights from cars approaching in either direction. She had a little time.

"Should I turn her phone back on?" she asked, pulling it out of her pocket. "She'd obviously turned it off for a reason."

"Yes, no doubt she did that to signal me. She would have known that if I couldn't track her, we'd go to the shelter looking for her. Right now, I'm on my way to Venice. I know some of the areas where she used to hang out. I'll cruise around and see what I can find out. But yes, turn her phone on. Go straight to the encrypted app she shared with us and open it."

Riley set her own phone on the wooden rail of the balcony, keeping Cedrick on speaker while she turned Bella's phone on and waited for the screen to light up. The seconds seemed like minutes. A set of headlights turned the corner onto Sixth Street two blocks from the shelter, advancing slowly in Riley's direction. She suspected it was a police cruiser.

"Oh no, I need a password . . ." Riley swore under her breath, convinced her search was over before it started when Cedrick began speaking over her: "Hashtag thirteen Themis bakes vegan cupcakes," he said. "No spaces, capital letter only for Themis."

Riley's thumbs flew over the keys, unlocking the phone on the first attempt. Her fingertips flipped through the screens. She recognized the colorful logo of the encrypted app a second later and opened it. There were several photographs embedded in text messages that Bella had sent only to herself. Riley enlarged one of them; it was a photograph of counseling notes. She assumed they were Lexi's notes on Clive McAllister.

"Bingo," she said. "She got her hands on what we were after. There are several documents." Just then, a Santa Monica cruiser pulled up in front of the shelter. "The cops are here too; I'll need to hang up in a second."

"You're going to have to delete that app from Bella's phone before turning it over to anyone. The sooner, the better. Nothing on there will be admissible in court anyway, and medical records of that nature could get Bella into serious trouble. Forward the messages to me. We can go through them later. I should be the first name in her contact list on that app."

Cedrick continued talking, but Riley had tuned him out. He was saying something about Holly and a search warrant, but her heart was racing, her thumbs tapping furiously at the keyboard of Bella's phone. She selected all the most recent messages. They each held photos of documents. There were roughly ten pages of notes in all. She hit the forward arrow, then selected Cedrick's name and hit send.

"Gotta go," she said, closing the app before deleting it. She snatched her own phone from the porch railing and stuffed Bella's into her jacket pocket. She turned to head back inside just as the police cruiser cut its engine in front of the shelter. As she reached the door, a shadow slipped quickly past the entryway.

Riley froze mid-stride. Someone had been watching her. She hesitated for a second before deciding to press on. The police would be stepping out of their cruiser by now. She headed down the dimly lit hallway, the hair on the back of her neck standing on edge.

"Santa Monica police are out front," she announced as she thew open the door and fell into the bright light of the kitchen. Maria and Joe were on their feet instantly. Riley reached out, taking Joe by the elbow as Maria hurried past them to greet the police at the front door. "Where's Javier?"

"I think he's just laying low," Joe said, tilting his head to the back stairway. "It sounds like he and his mom have been through hell with his sister's murder and all the recent drama here. No need to involve him, is there?"

"Not as far as I'm concerned, but I'm sure the PD can make those decisions. As you told me earlier tonight, we have trained professionals to handle these things," she said, raising her eyebrows. Joe's lips tightened, the corners of his mouth turning down. "Sorry, that didn't come out the way I meant it," Riley was quick to add. "You were right, of course. I'm just so angry at myself. I've obviously made a colossal screwup of things, haven't I?"

"Well, I wouldn't go that far," Joe said, dropping his gaze. "Bella and Cedrick have more experience than you do in this area. Presumably, they knew what they were getting themselves into. I would even argue that they helped pull *you* into this mess."

To their credit, the two police officers from Santa Monica were more helpful than Joe had predicted. Officer Brooks, a stout blonde woman whose flashlight rivaled Riley's Home Shopping Network version, took a detailed description of Bella. No one at the shelter knew Bella's true age, so Riley felt comfortable omitting the part about her being a citizen sleuth playing the role of a runaway teen. Officer Brooks said they'd put out Bella's description to the local units as well as the LAPD and the LA County Sheriff's Department, both of which covered the Venice area of Los Angeles and its spiraling homeless population.

"Of course, if Bella shows up tonight, you'll let us know," Officer Brooks's partner said as he passed Maria his card on the way out.

The police cruiser pulled out onto the street in front of the shelter just as Holly's van parked along the curb across from the driveway. "What's going on?" she demanded breathlessly as she clip-clopped up the porch stairs in high heels. "I came as soon as I got Delroy's message. Have we found her?"

Holly and Riley joined Joe in the kitchen, where Maria was brewing a pot of coffee.

"You wouldn't believe the day I've had," she said, turning to Riley. "I'll explain later." She sighed. "What do we know about Bella?"

Holly yanked off her jacket and hung it on the back of a kitchen chair. Riley caught her up on what they knew, omitting only the part about finding Bella's cell phone. She hadn't even shared that news with Joe yet.

Maria asked if they still needed her as she set the coffee cups out.

"Not unless you feel you need to be here, Maria," Holly offered. "Try to get some rest. I'll take over for the night, dear."

Joe repeated the phrase in Spanish. Then he was on his feet, taking Maria by the arm. He saw her to the bottom of the back stairwell, where Javier sat smoking in the darkness.

"Poor thing," Holly said as Joe returned and joined them at the table. "I should have been here, and I was the administrator on call for tonight, but I lost my phone this morning and only just got a replacement. Anyway, that's the least of our problems."

Riley looked over at Joe. He'd been a trooper all evening. "Joe, why don't you go home? I've kept you too long. I can't thank you enough for everything you've done. Seriously." For a moment, Joe looked like he might protest, but Riley could see he was spent. "You've got an early morning tomorrow with Sofia's parents coming, and I can always get an Uber back to my car. There's not much more we can do here, anyway. Cedrick is out looking for her, and we have three police departments involved, so . . ."

Joe nodded in resignation, but he was slow to stand and reach for his jacket.

"Besides," Riley added to seal her argument, "if Detective Roberts shows up tonight, it's probably better if you're not here. We don't want to cast any doubt on your official role in these cases."

Riley wasn't looking forward to explaining the whole debacle to Roberts and her prickly partner, Garth. But she would manage that. What she couldn't manage was the anxiety surging through her when she thought about what Bella could be going through—all because Riley had thought to encourage her presence here.

"You working tomorrow?" Joe asked, throwing his jacket over his shoulder.

"No, I'm on this weekend, so I don't go back in until Thursday. Can I check in with you later?" She stood to walk him to the door. "I'll stay a little while with Holly and call Cedrick to see how things are going on his end."

Joe gave her a look that said, *I thought you'd abandoned your detective role*, but what came out of his mouth was "Let me know if anything changes, will you?"

"You know I will," Riley insisted, following him down the hallway to the front door.

When they reached the porch, Joe turned to her, whispering, "Are you comfortable here alone with Holly?" Riley didn't answer. She hadn't told him about her conversations with Cedrick and Bella about Holly's story not adding up. But now she could see, for whatever reason, Joe had his own reservations.

"Why do you say that?" she said, keeping her voice down. "And besides, we're not alone."

"Well, where was she all day? Don't you find it convenient that she didn't show up to work today? And that story about having lost her phone . . . Really?"

"Well, I agree. She's hiding something. Cedrick feels the same way. But Bella's known her the longest and swears she's got a heart of gold." As soon as the words left Riley's lips, she realized how absurd they sounded with Bella now missing.

Joe didn't skip a beat. "I hope for Bella's sake she's right about that," he said, stepping off the porch and heading to his car.

When Riley returned to the kitchen, she found Holly sitting with her head in her hands.

"What a truly horrible day," she said, looking up at Riley. "If I'd been here, none of this would have happened. I would have gone for a walk with Bella myself. For some time now, I've suspected someone was watching this place. It makes sense, doesn't it? Bella is the third person now to have disappeared from here in just a few weeks. Someone has it out for us." Holly's eyes filled with tears. She clutched her hands together as if in prayer, her knuckles hard and white. Riley could see the tension in the angle of her jaw as she bit off her words. "There are *monsters* out there, Riley. Sick bastards who are either targeting our residents because they are the outcasts of society, or they are torturing us because we help them." She wiped a tear from under her eye with her thumb.

When Riley thought about Holly's claim, it really didn't make much sense to her that someone was targeting the shelter's residents because they were outcasts. If someone wanted to single out the homeless in the area, wouldn't it be easier to prey on the growing population living on the streets of Santa Monica? And Bella had apparently disappeared from Venice, not from the center. But even so, perhaps Holly had a point about the shelter being targeted, but she had yet to stumble onto the right reason.

Riley mulled over the possibilities.

The shelter was surrounded by high-rise condominiums, for one thing. The land the center sat on had to be worth a small fortune. She recalled that the area was historically rent controlled. Would ridding the neighborhood of the shelter for another apartment building be a lucrative enough motive for murder? And if so, why murder these specific people? Or was it all random? The MO didn't seem random. It was psychopathic, if anything.

Riley got up and filled her coffee mug from the pot Maria had brewed. She stood at the sink, peering out through the window wondering where the hell Bella could be. It was black outside: moonless, cold, and still. The fog would be rolling in soon, she imagined. She held the pot of coffee up, motioning to Holly, who shook her head, declining. She looked exhausted.

Riley took her seat again at the kitchen table. "I'm really sorry, Holly. I know this has been just awful for you. I can't imagine what you're feeling. I'm scared for Bella too." Riley's voice dropped off to almost a whisper. "Let's check in with Cedrick," she offered, trying to sound hopeful.

"I'm on my way to the shelter now," he said when he picked up. "My mom and her partner are in the car in front of me. We'll be there in a few."

"No sign of Bella, I take it?" Riley knew the answer already.

"Nothing, but I've put the word out on the street. Left my number with at least a half dozen homeless camps between Santa Monica and Venice."

"Good work, Cedrick," Riley heard herself say. She knew, in her gut, that everything they had done today probably wouldn't add up to anything, but she needed to inject something positive into the situation before she hung up.

She was suddenly very tired. It was late, past her usual bedtime. She couldn't imagine dealing with Detective Roberts or Garth at this hour. She still needed to get back to the hospital to retrieve her car so she could pick Indio up in the morning.

Holly shifted in her chair. Riley sensed her anxiety growing as they sat in the stillness, listening to the ticking of the kitchen clock on the wall above them.

After a minute, Riley got up from the table, saying she was headed to the restroom. She made her way along the darkened hallway and into the small green-tiled bathroom with its antique mirror and pedestal sink, where she removed one of the hand towels and wiped Bella's phone down thoroughly. She slipped quietly across the hallway into the room she and Delroy had visited earlier—Bella's room. Using the dim light of her own cell phone, she placed Bella's into the smaller of the two compartments on the girl's backpack and then hung it up behind the door where she'd found it. Her heart was in her throat as she retraced her steps to the kitchen.

As they waited for Cedrick and the detectives to arrive, Holly sat silently, staring down at her empty coffee cup, her fingernail tapping the rim. Riley was at a loss for any words that might comfort her.

Holly looked up suddenly. Shifting her weight in her chair, she cleared her throat. "There's something I should probably tell you, Riley. It's going to come out anyway." Riley felt her stomach drop. She locked eyes with Holly, doing her best not to let her face betray the fact that she suspected Holly had been hiding something. In the seconds she waited for Holly to go on, a vacuum seemed to replace the oxygen in the room. "I got a visit from the LAPD this morning. They had a search warrant for our storage shed in the Valley. They also asked me for my phone." Holly's lower lip trembled as she went on. "They were waiting outside my place as I left to come to work. Talk about humiliating," She reached for a napkin in the middle of the table and blew her nose. "Poor Eli. He's always been so supportive of me, and now he's caught up in this whole ugly mess—"

"Eli? That's your husband, right?" Riley cut in, skirting the bigger questions. She knew Holly would get to those.

"Yes, the man's a saint. Without his support, I would never have been able to make the shelter a possibility. Anyway, I know what the cops are after, and I've been an absolute idiot, so I guess I deserve it." Riley found herself holding her breath as Holly went on. "Honestly, I was only trying to help. I worried Lexi might've been up to something that wouldn't reflect favorably on her. Well, no. I was afraid it wouldn't reflect positively on the shelter."

"What are you talking about?" Riley asked, keeping her voice neutral. Reminding herself that staying calm in a moment of crisis was quite literally part of her job on most days.

"Our anonymous donations increased dramatically after Lexi started working for us. I don't know why I didn't catch on sooner." Holly fell silent for a moment, her eyes glazing over as if she were seeing something from the past. "I became even more suspicious when the donations dropped significantly after Lexi's murder, and then one of our biggest sources dried up completely after Sofia was targeted. I went through Lexi's counseling notes on Sofia—the notes I told you and the others I couldn't find. I just had a feeling there was something going on. It seemed too much of a coincidence that both Lexi and Sofia were targeted by the same killer and that our sources of donation were dwindling. Obviously, it's the same killer, right?" She looked over at Riley, fear growing in her eyes. Riley nodded silently, not wanting to interrupt.

Just then the doorbell chimed.

Holly jumped, then stood to answer it, only for Delroy to poke his head into the kitchen. "I got it, Ms. Holly."

The house had been so quiet, Riley had all but forgotten there were five other residents staying at the shelter. "Where is everyone?" she asked, wondering who had been watching her when she was on the porch earlier.

"Probably where they are every evening: sitting in front of the TV in the library or playing chess. They're all so productive during the day. They work hard on school assignments, job applications, volunteer outreach, and helping with chores around here. But at night, they all turn into TV zombies. Anyway, I'll fill you in later on the rest of the story," Holly whispered.

Detective Roberts was far more patient than Riley had expected, given the hour and the circumstances. Garth, on the other hand, said nothing, but Riley could feel his eyes on her as they sat around the table while she recounted the events of the day. Cedrick leaned against the kitchen counter watching the discussion with his arms crossed over his chest. Riley assumed he had already filled his mother in on their grand plan to seed Bella as a fictitious runaway at the shelter and her role in checking out the residents and employees as potential suspects in the murders. She was grateful not to have those details revealed in Holly's presence.

Holly had little to offer. She stayed aloof, keeping her answers brief, given her recent interactions with the LAPD. Riley pretended to miss the looks that passed between detectives Garth and Roberts as Holly filled in the details about the shelter's residents and staff.

Riley felt heavy and slow as she got to her feet, like she was moving through an undertow in the surf. Her mind raced with things she needed to accomplish, but her body was having none of it. It was rapidly becoming nonnegotiable that she get some rest.

"I'd like to get going if you don't have any further need for me, detectives," she said, and to her surprise, no one objected. She turned to Holly then. "I'd offer to keep you company tonight, but I've got to get my car and pick up Indy in the morning. And I'm totally spent; I skipped dinner, and it's way past my bedtime. I'm having trouble keeping my eyes open at this point."

"You should've said something, Riley. I could make you a snack or order out if you'd like."

"You're very kind, Holly, but at this point, I just want to get home."

"Understood. I'll call you tomorrow, and we can catch up. And if something changes tonight, I'll let you know right away."

"I appreciate that." Riley leaned over, giving Holly a quick, one-armed hug. She felt a little guilty for abandoning her before she'd had time to hear the rest of the story about the search warrant, but who knew how long the interview with the detectives would go. And she was fading fast.

"You have the Uber app?" Holly asked.

Detective Roberts turned to Riley then. "Cedrick will drive you to your car, Dr. Brighton." It was more an order than an offer. Cedrick, who hadn't spoken a word since his arrival, dropped his gaze like a scolded child, crossed the room, and held the kitchen door open for Riley.

Detective Roberts turned her attention back to Holly. "Now, if you don't mind, we'd like to see the room where Bella was staying."

CHAPTER TWENTY-THREE

Riley sat in the passenger seat of Cedrick's 1973 VW bug. The bumblebee rumble of the engine buzzing in her ears was only slightly more grating than the cold air sucked in by the dilapidated window seals. A heavy layer of fog had unfurled itself along the coast like the wet wings of a gargantuan moth leaving its cocoon.

Riley held Cedrick's phone, flipping through the text messages she had forwarded him earlier from the encrypted app on Bella's phone. "So only a couple of these are counseling notes labeled *Clair*. The rest belong to people I've never heard of, but it looks like they were all patients of Lexi's at some point. Other residents from the shelter, I'm guessing."

Riley was quiet for a few minutes as she enlarged the text on the screen and read through several of the records. Cedrick remained quiet; Riley could sense a growing tension.

"The common theme I'm seeing in a few of the notes is the history of sexual abuse, either at home or involving clergy or other figures of authority, teachers, coaches, that sort of thing. But what's weird is that someone has annotated the margins of these records in blue ink."

Cedrick's brows furrowed. "They must have been typed up, right?"

"Yes, exactly. But somebody took the time to annotate them in longhand." Riley consulted the photographed records. "There are phone numbers listed, names of other people—"

"Names?"

"Robert Brooks," Riley began, listing them off. "Phillip Tune, Miguel Franco, Father Milton, Coach McFadden . . . These are all men's names."

Cedrick glanced at her as they both realized what she was saying. His brow knit, hands gripping the steering wheel. "Tell me again what Holly told you about Lexi. What prompted her to search for Lexi's counseling files on Sofia in the first place."

"Well, clearly there was more to the story than I heard. We got interrupted before she could come clean, but she mentioned something about the shelter's anonymous donations suddenly increasing after Lexi came to work for them. But to answer your question, she said she became suspicious that Lexi had been doing something wrong or illegal. Those are not the words she used, but that's the sense I got. Let's see, what she said exactly was. . . . 'Lexi had done something that would reflect poorly on the shelter,' and she was adamant that whatever it was could be the reason both Lexi and Sofia were murdered."

"And I wonder what that 'something' could possibly have been." Cedrick's question, heavy with sarcasm, hung in the air between them, the whine of the engine rising as he downshifted and merged onto the freeway from the coast highway.

"Blackmail?"

"Sure sounds like it," Cedrick said matter-of-factly. "And if Lexi had similar notes on Sofia—notes that named Sofia's abuser as someone in her well-to-do family—that could be quite lucrative."

"Even a plausible motive for murder," Riley added.

Cedrick pieced it together, point by point. "So what probably happened then is Holly suspected Sofia was murdered because of something Lexi had done. She accessed Lexi's notes on Sofia, figured out she was blackmailing someone in the family—let's say the stepfather—and then decided to hide the proof?"

"Yes, essentially, but I think she was doing that to protect the shelter. Maybe even to defend Lexi's legacy. The girl had done a lot of good for the community, from what I learned at her service. I don't think Holly had ill intent. And I don't think she realized she could be hiding key evidence. Evidence that could implicate the murderer—"

"But, unfortunately," Cedrick cut in, "that act now has her in the crosshairs of the LAPD. It makes her look like an accessory, or at least complicit in Lexi's scheme. Especially if the center was benefiting from Lexi's efforts—if the proceeds of blackmail were being donated to the shelter."

"Right. It sounds like Holly made a very poor decision," Riley commented, but as soon as the words left her lips, she felt their sting. She couldn't help but think she was a hypocrite for such a thought. After all, she hadn't been honest with the Santa Monica police about Bella's real purpose for being at the shelter, and she'd even intercepted Bella's phone, broken into it, taken information off it, and deleted an incriminating app before wiping it down and placing it where Detective Roberts was sure to find it.

When she thought of it in light of her own actions, Holly's ethical lapses looked almost innocent.

Riley sat uncomfortably with those truths, mulling over how much she had changed since coming across Clive's body on the freeway that morning almost three weeks ago. A minute later, she realized Cedrick was still talking.

"It's a big leap from blackmail to murder, though, Riley. Even if we're right about the motive for both blackmail and murder, that still doesn't explain Clive. Does it? Lexi and Sofia, yes, but not Clive. I'm not sure where we go from here." Cedrick's words fell flat. He sounded as exhausted as Riley felt. They were both at a loss for explanations about how the three murders were connected. The fact that Bella was now missing overshadowed it all, though.

"Okay, let's try to advance this theory," Riley suggested in an attempt to take their minds off Bella. "How and where does Clive factor into this? He was killed after Lexi but before Sofia, and as far as I can tell, Sofia had no link to him."

"Anything in the counseling notes?"

"Yes, actually." Riley flipped through the documents she had forwarded to Cedrick's phone again until she found Lexi's notes on Clive labeled *Clair*. "The usual teen gripes, political and social view differences with the parents, conflict with the dad specifically, but no mention of sexual abuse at home. But there is a treatment note here . . . Get this. Lexi says 'Clair remains both traumatized and angry over her victimization in Venice. We will work on ways to productively manage her grief at the hands of others.' Maybe Lexi was referring to what happened to Clive in Venice when he was younger. The mom, Val, alluded to something awful happening to him on his first stay in LA. She said she thought it was part of the reason he transitioned. What's interesting, though, is there are no annotations in the margins of his records. So no indication of blackmail in this case, using our current theory."

"We're not going to solve this tonight." Cedrick sighed. "On top of all this, I've got two more final exams tomorrow. I'll be done by three. And then I'll see what else I can figure out by going through those files in detail."

"I'm very sorry about Bella." Riley's voice cracked. Cedrick gave her a sideways glance but said nothing. They sat in silence for the rest of the drive, listening to the whine of the engine, except when Riley had to give directions to the parking garage as they neared the campus. As Cedrick pulled up to Riley's car, his phone rang. Riley looked down at the screen; it read No Caller ID. She passed the phone back to him.

"Yes?" was all he said before putting the phone on speaker so Riley could listen in.

The caller's voice was thick and slow. "Yeah . . . This is Manny from the boardwalk . . . About that girl, the girl with the dog."

Riley and Cedrick could hear the crash of waves in the background and the distant sound of mariachi music, probably from a nearby Mexican restaurant. The reception was broken, spotty at best.

When the caller's voice came back on the line again, he said, " . . . paid twenty bucks to drop the dog off at the shelter." The line went dead for a few seconds before the caller could be heard again. " . . . got into a truck with some dude—"

"A black pickup?" Cedrick interrupted.

"Dunno, man . . . that's all I got . . . Is there a reward?"

"There is if you can tell me where the girl is," Cedrick answered breathlessly.

The caller was silent for a few seconds as if weighing the offer. Then he said, "Screw you, man . . . waste of time . . ." and the line went dead.

CHAPTER TWENTY-FOUR

Riley awoke just as the sun was rising. She felt as if she hadn't slept at all. Her head was thick, her mouth dry. Visions of Bella lying on the freeway covered in blood, her limbs imprinted with skid marks and tire tracks, had kept her awake for hours after she'd gone to bed last night. Then there had been the dreams of Clive, the nightmares. His swollen eyes sealed permanently in death. His bruised and battered body lying in the morgue. His mother, Val, crying over him, and his sullen father still refusing to acknowledge his transition.

Riley blinked her eyes open, trying to focus on her bedside clock. It was 7:13 a.m.

Her gaze roved over the room. Artemis sat on the top of the armchair staring back at her. The cat stood briefly, stretching her creamy white back into a soft arch over her dark legs before curling back up and covering her single front paw with her tail.

Riley rolled out of bed, her gaze landing on the spot in the doorway where Indio would normally be sleeping. She made her way along the narrow hallway and onto the cold tile floor of the kitchen. She hit the start button on her automatic coffee pot and tugged open the freezer door. A moment later, she slipped two frozen waffles into the toaster.

She would call Holly while she was on her way to the animal shelter to pick up Indy and see if there was any news on Bella, and she'd fill her in on the call she and Cedrick had received from Manny last night.

Eating breakfast over the kitchen sink, Riley reflected on the events of the last twenty-four hours. If anything good had come out of yesterday, it was hearing that Bella had paid someone to drop Indy off at the animal shelter. How much stock Riley could put into that account was questionable, but she was hanging on in hopes the report was accurate. That Bella hadn't just suddenly and mysteriously disappeared from Venice, leaving Indy to fend for himself on the streets, suggested that Bella had devised and executed a plan to achieve something.

That something still eluded Riley, but she felt certain the girl was savvy enough not to have made a victim of herself. She'd left her phone where Riley was likely to find it, which meant she'd known she wouldn't be returning to the shelter once she headed out for her walk. That fact was somewhat reassuring, Riley told herself. Some things looked better in the light of a new day.

She checked her messages in the encrypted app, thinking she might have heard from Cedrick, but there were no new texts. He would have told his mother by now about the call from Manny, and no doubt Detective Roberts trand her partner had found Bella's phone in her backpack at the teen shelter, where Riley had stashed it. There were no texts from Joe either. She'd check in with him later to see how things had gone with Sofia's parents.

Riley's mind flashed to Sofia's infant daughter, wrapped up in her little striped blanket, lying in the nursery. She wondered if by day's end she'd have a home—and how the family would receive her and more importantly, if she'd be safe with them.

*　　*　　*

Holly was on her way home from the shelter when Riley reached her by phone. She'd spent the night on the couch in her office at the center, but, like Riley, she'd had little sleep. There had been no sign of Bella and no word from the Santa Monica PD. Delroy had taken over for her at eight that morning. She was hurrying back to Malibu to have breakfast with Eli before he headed off to work for the day. Something about Holly's tone suggested she had damage control to do after the previous day's search warrant fiasco.

"How was Detective Roberts after I left?" Riley ventured.

"She was a little standoffish at first, but I think by the time she and that partner of hers left, they had decided I was suitably cooperative. After all, I didn't have to let them into Bella's room without a warrant, but I did anyway." Holly fell silent, the mention of a search warrant hanging in the air.

Riley took the bait. "So, you were telling me yesterday . . ."

"Yes, what I was saying was . . ." Holly paused. "You don't think they're listening in on my phone, do you?"

"I think that only happens in the movies, Holly." Riley tried to make light of the situation and then added, "And didn't you get a new phone yesterday, anyway?"

"Right." Holly paused again. "Of course, you're right, I'm not thinking straight. But, to be honest, I'd still rather chat about that topic in person."

"Okay, we can change the subject then," Riley offered. "You knew Lexi well. What was her background?" Riley ticked off the questions she wanted to ask while she silently chided herself for having taken the freeway and not Topanga Canyon from the Valley to the coast. The traffic was horrendous at that hour of the morning.

"I'd known her for years. She came to us as a junior in high school. At the time, she was a skinny little whisp of a kid named Levi with absolutely no self-confidence. She hated feeling like she was in the wrong body. She'd been horribly teased at school and not at all supported at home. I think she'd wanted to make her transition much earlier, but that was out of the question in a religious household in a very conservative state. Her father had died a few years earlier, and it sounded like the stepfather was a nasty piece of work. It's a wonder she hadn't fled sooner. Poor thing, to have come all that way by herself. So brave, really."

"What? She wasn't from California?" Riley asked as she pulled her car off the freeway and onto Fourth Street in Santa Monica. She was only a few minutes from Venice and anxious to see Indy after his sleepover at the animal shelter.

She sat impatiently at the intersection, waiting for the car in front of her to realize the light had turned green. Someone behind her laid on the horn, as though on her behalf, and the car in front of them hit the gas. Riley's foot reflexively found the accelerator.

"Oh gosh, no. Lexi was from Utah," Holly went on, snapping Riley back into the present.

"*What?*" Riley almost rear-ended the car in front of her. She pulled out of the flow of traffic and coasted into a parking spot along the curb on the other side of the intersection. "She was from Utah?"

"Yes, but we never really discussed that part of her life. Not in any detail. Naturally, she was anxious to leave it behind. I think she was still grieving her father and hated the fact that she'd been adopted by the stepfather. I know she had a younger sister she was worried about back home. I'd hear her on the phone sometimes when she first came to us. But after she transitioned, it seemed she cut ties with everyone from her past. I'd often hear her telling other residents at the shelter she'd ghosted her entire family."

"Do you recall her name before she transitioned?"

"I think I told you it was Levi, right? Then she changed it to Lexi."

"Right, sorry—I meant her last name," Riley clarified, holding her breath as she waited for Holly to go on.

"If I remember correctly, her previous name—her dead name— was pretty similar to her new name. Drummond . . . Diamond, maybe. Give me a sec." The line went quiet for a minute before Holly returned to say, "Draper. Yes, that's it—Levi Draper was Lexi's dead name."

*　　*　　*

Riley pulled up in front of Holly's Malibu home. It was a beautiful Mediterranean-style villa surrounded by enormous palms. Fuchsia bougainvillea cloaked the front courtyard walls on either side of an archway, which was filled by a massive wooden gate. The sprawling white stucco home sat low in the canyon with an expansive view of the Pacific.

Indy jumped out of the car, seemingly unfazed by his latest misadventures in Venice, and trotted onto a driveway composed of perfectly manicured lawn ribbons and salmon-colored brick framed by two rows of crepe myrtle trees.

Holly was waiting for Riley in the courtyard with her dogs. Ten minutes later, they walked along the beach, the dogs darting ahead, playing at the water's edge.

"Riley, you realize what this means if you're right?"

"I do." Riley looked over at Holly as she brushed a strand of hair out of her face. "I've thought of nothing else since you told me Lexi's dead name."

Holly stopped to empty the sand out of her shoes, stuffing them into the crocheted bag on her shoulder. "Do you think Sofia knew who Lexi was?"

"You said they seemed close, right?"

"Sofia was *very* clingy—overly dependent on Lexi, really—but now we know she was only fourteen and had been through a lot. Perhaps that dependance wasn't so abnormal. Still, I can only imagine Lexi played some role in getting Sofia out here from Utah. There had to be some coordination there, and of course, some trust. But it'd been at least six years since they'd seen one another, as far as I know. Sofia would have been about seven or eight when her brother left Utah. And if she didn't know about the transition, she perhaps wouldn't have recognized Lexi as having once been Levi."

"Agreed. I'm not sure we'll ever know now, though." Riley turned toward the ocean, staring out at the surf line and beyond. The wind was picking up, whitecaps dotting the deep blue waters of the Pacific. The sky was gray under the burden of heavy clouds. It looked like more rain was on the way. "Think about it, Holly. If she was open with Sofia about her transition, why wouldn't Lexi just have Sofia move in with her? Why have her go through the charade of being a runaway at the shelter?"

"Maybe Lexi thought the shelter was a safer place for Sofia. She could keep an eye on her there. After all, she was working long hours, and maybe it was just easier to know that Sofia would never be alone."

"Yeah, that makes sense, I guess."

"What will happen with Sofia's baby? You said her family was coming today. Will they be allowed to take her home?" Holly turned her back to the wind.

"Probably, but I imagine that decision will involve a court order and child protective services." Riley was quiet for a moment, watching the dogs sprinting in and out of the sweeping waterline. She weighed the questions she was curious to ask Holly, wondering if she even wanted to know the answers at this point. She couldn't afford to be complicit in Holly's misconduct. Ironically, she had enough of her own to contend with, she realized.

Finally, she took the plunge. "Holly, what exactly did you see in Lexi's notes on Sofia that prompted you to hide them?"

Holly pulled a tennis ball out of her shoulder bag, whistled to the dogs, then launched the ball in their direction. Then she turned to Riley, her dark eyes seemed pensive in a way that left Riley wondering if the question had crossed a line.

"I first got suspicious that morning Bella found the diamond bracelet in Sofia's belongings. It made me more curious about the girl's past. When I went through Lexi's notes on her counseling sessions with Sofia that afternoon, I found handwritten annotations alongside the transcribed records. At first, I wasn't sure what they meant. There were dates and places written in the margins and a man's name and two out-of-state phone numbers."

Riley stayed quiet, reflecting on how she'd seen similar notations herself on Lexi's counseling records from other shelter residents.

Holly cleared her throat, staring at the horizon. The wind whipped at her dark hair and tugged at the hem of her pale linen dress. "When I called the first of the two numbers, it was a bank in Utah. At the time, it didn't make sense to me. Of course, now it does—now that I know what I do about Lexi and Sofia's past in Utah. The second phone number was a cell phone. I only tried it once, but no one picked up, and the voicemail was generic. Not at all helpful. It was the bank number that bothered me, though. A month after Sofia came to us, we received the largest private donation we've had since the shelter opened from an account at a bank with the same name."

Holly threw the ball again to the dogs, who were swarming around her like gulls around a beach picnic. They jetted off toward the waterline, casting a foamy spray of seawater in their wake as they ripped through the tide.

"I found myself wondering," Holly went on, "what business Lexi could possibly still have with a bank in Utah, especially as she hadn't lived there in years. And why she would make such a note in a client's counseling record in the first place. But after I read through all Lexi's notes on Sofia and learned the girl had been victimized in her own home, I started to put two and two together. That's when it dawned on me."

"That Lexi was blackmailing someone?" Riley guessed, and Holly's eyes lit up. She nodded slowly.

"That Lexi was blackmailing Sofia's abuser—and that it was paying off quite well. I was sure we would be subjected to some kind of audit and that someone would want to know where all that money was coming from." Holly's voice trailed off, as if she were deep in thought, before she added, "and then, when Sofia was murdered in the same brutal way Lexi had been, I knew the records were a liability for us. I had no choice but to hide them. I realized it was wrong. I did it anyway." When she looked back at Riley, the angst in her expression was raw. "Stupid, right? But I couldn't stop thinking about how much good we could do with that money, how many kids we could help . . . How many abused, bullied, and emotionally scarred teens we could save from dreadful futures or suicide."

Holly tried to turn her face, but Riley could see her eyes had filled with tears. She walked away from the waterline and found a dry spot in the deep sand to sit, giving Holly a moment.

Holly's voice was thick with regret when, a moment later, she joined Riley, sitting in the sand beside her. "Hopefully, I haven't screwed things up so much that the shelter gets shut down. Eli and I worked for years to make the center a possibility. It was something I needed to do after what I'd been through in my own teen years, and Eli has always been so supportive."

She sat with her arms wrapped around her long legs, staring out at the water where the dogs were wrestling over the tennis ball. Riley hadn't thought of that aspect, but Holly was right. There was a possibility that her actions, no matter how well intentioned, could jeopardize the center's future.

It was clear from Holly's confession that she hadn't accessed Lexi's records on other shelter residents, the records Bella had photographed and stored in the encrypted app on her phone. If she had, Holly would likely have hidden those in her storage locker too.

Riley didn't mention what she and Cedrick had found in the copies of the records they'd reviewed the previous evening: annotations that also looked very much like they identified and targeted abusers of other victims who'd found their way to the shelter. She wondered just how much money Lexi had procured in her ventures over the years. The other, more important question, however, was how many enemies she had acquired during that same time.

"Last night, you said the anonymous donations to the center started to increase soon after Lexi came to work for you," Riley did her best to keep any hint of accusation out of her voice, but she had to ask. "That was long before Sofia came to stay at the shelter. Did you ever have any way of proving where donations actually came from?"

"Not really," Holly grasped what Riley was intimating. Her mouth dropped open, "Oh, God, are you saying there were others? Before Sofia?"

"So it seems," Riley didn't elaborate.

Holly was quick to explain herself, "when I first questioned the sudden increase in gifts to the shelter, Eli told me that it's not an easy task to trace the source of anonymous donations. I dropped it after that. I guess I was just hopeful that there were so many generous folks out there."

"I can buy that," Riley said, wanting to believe the argument Holly was making.

"I guess it's all out of my hands now. I did what I thought was best at the time. Hopefully, I don't end up in too much hot water for obstructing an investigation or tampering with evidence or whatever else they might call it."

"Let's hope," Riley said, resting a hand gently on Holly's back.

As they walked in the direction of Holly's home from the beach with the dogs in tow, Riley tried to close the gaps between what she suspected about the motives for Lexi and Sofia's murders and how Clive fit into the picture. It made for a welcome distraction from the more pressing question of where Bella was. "Can you think of any reason Clive's association with Lexi would have made him a target of the killer too?"

"I've thought about it a lot, Riley. I can't imagine a connection. If it wasn't for the way he died, I'd never have linked him in any way to recent events. I mean, he and Lexi were close, but no, I don't have any clue how he fits in here."

"What about a connection to Bella? How did Clive and Bella know each other?"

Holly looked down at Riley, her brows knit in concentration. "Venice . . . their connection was Venice. Of course, at the time we knew Clive as Clair. She came to our shelter after she had been staying in Venice with friends. I'm not sure how long she'd been in the area. I know she was having trouble with her parents in Fresno, and I think she'd left home in the middle of her last year of high school. She ended up finishing her GED with us. It might have even been Bella who encouraged her to come to the shelter, if I remember correctly."

"And what was Bella's connection to Venice?" Riley asked, standing in Holly's shadow.

"Oh gosh, she'd done a lot in Venice to get girls away from the gangs. We didn't often get them coming to the shelter. They usually ended up leaving the country, going back to Mexico or South America, but Bella got them funds and a way out of the gang life—out of being trafficked. Her Spanish is excellent, and she's so damn feisty. She fought hard for those kids. But I have to say, I'm glad she's not involved in that anymore. It was so dangerous for her." Holly suddenly froze, turning to Riley, her eyes widened. "I mean, I don't think she's still involved in that shit. But I guess I could be wrong."

"And Clive was somehow involved in this too?"

"I don't have any idea if Clive was involved. I just know since they met in Venice when Bella was pissing off the gangs, it's possible."

"What about a girl named Rosaria? Have you ever heard Bella mention her?"

Holly shook her head. "No, I don't think so. Who is she?"

Riley searched Holly's face for a flicker of recognition. Had Maria really been so afraid of drawing attention to her daughter's immigration status that she'd failed to share the news of Rosaria's visit and subsequent murder with Holly?

"Rosaria was Ms. Maria's daughter," Riley said, dropping her gaze. "Three months ago, right before Sofia showed up at the shelter, Rosaria was a victim of gang violence in Venice." Riley hated being the one to break the news. She found it hard to look Holly in the eye. "I think that's the reason Javier came to stay with Maria. To help her through the grief of losing Rosy."

Holly's face dropped. "Are you serious, Riley? Oh my God, why didn't I know about this?"

Riley had to admit she was asking herself the same question.

CHAPTER TWENTY-FIVE

Riley had just pulled into the driveway at home with Indy when her phone pinged. She pulled it out of her pocket revealing a text from a number she didn't recognize, though it was a local number. It read: FYI, family is supposed to take custody of the miracle baby this afternoon, just thought I'd share. Cleared for discharge by two p.m.

Riley texted back a thumbs-up emoji and Thank you, I'll be there.

She hated the idea of making the commute downtown on her day off, but she'd wanted to talk with Sofia's mother before the baby was discharged, and she knew that Cindy from the nursery had gone out on a limb to share the news with her. When she thought about it, she could justify a visit with Sofia's mother to the hospital's administration. As one of the physicians who'd taken care of the girl, Riley felt she owed it to the family. And besides, she'd never rest until she'd sized up the parents for herself. Had they been vetted by the detectives? Had Sofia's stepfather already been arrested for her rape?

When Riley called Joe, he answered on the first ring. "Let me call you back in five," he said and hung up before she could explain.

A sense of urgency, a familiar dread, rose in her. She felt it seeping all the way down to her bones. Something was very wrong; things were moving too fast. She grabbed her hospital ID, pulled on her leathers, and snatched her helmet from the coat rack at the front door.

She had just started the engine on her bike when Joe called back. She killed the motor and pulled her helmet off, putting the phone to her ear.

Joe was breathless. "You're not going to believe this, Rye, but Sofia's stepfather has suddenly disappeared. He vanished this morning from the Biltmore Hotel downtown, where the family stayed last night. The mother had to come in by herself at noon. Detective Roberts came for the viewing, just to support her. She's beside herself—a total mess, to say the least. LAPD just took her over to the hospital to see the baby. She's planning to take the kid back to Utah tonight." Joe sounded desperate when he added, "Get down here if you can."

Riley sped along the 101 Freeway, transitioned east onto the 134, and then merged onto the southbound 5 toward downtown. She'd been lucky enough to hit the window between the lunch hour rush and the afternoon commute. It was just before two. She hurried from the parking lot to the hospital, barely aware of the buzzing news choppers overhead.

The ambulance bay outside the ER was full. City and county rescue vehicles and several LAPD cruisers jammed the parking lot. She counted herself lucky not to be working that day. If she remembered correctly, she'd seen Bach's name on the schedule. He'd obviously been relegated to the day shift where his actions could be more closely monitored on his return to the workplace. She'd have to catch up with Sonya soon and get the scoop on how that was going.

Riley entered the ER through a side door and darted to the locker room, where she stashed her leathers, snatched someone's lab coat off a hook in the hallway, and headed up to the nursery. As she stuffed her phone into the pocket of the coat, she saw, with a spike of adrenaline, that she'd missed three calls from Joe.

She was pressed for time. It was after two already, and she knew the infant's discharge was scheduled any minute. She'd have to ring Joe back once she'd talked with Sofia's mother.

Riley pressed the buzzer on the intercom outside the locked nursery a moment before the automatic doors swung open, and an orderly, seeing her lab coat and hospital ID, admitted her. She asked to see the charge nurse, and a few minutes later, she and Cindy stood next to a police officer at the door to a private suite, staring at Sofia's mother sitting in a rocker, holding her tiny granddaughter.

Cindy entered first. She squatted down next to the rocker, speaking quietly with the woman whose eyes then drifted to the doorway and to Riley before she nodded. Cindy wheeled a stool out from the corner of the room, placed it next to the rocker, and motioned for Riley to enter. On the way out, she pulled the door closed and waited outside with the police officer standing at the observation window.

As she crossed the room, Riley took in the sight of the woman. She had an avian-esque sort of build: slender bones, sculpted features, observant eyes. Her hair was so fair it was almost opalescent. There was no mistaking she was Sofia's kin. Her eyes, the color of polished tanzanite, locked on Riley with a strange upsurge of hope, as if she expected some announcement that her life hadn't just suddenly been upended.

As Riley took her seat, it hit her. Despite all her despair, the woman didn't yet know the full extent of her loss. But a discussion of the death of Lexi—the person who had once been her son, Levi—would have to wait for another time. Its own time.

"Ms. Draper, my name is Riley Brighton. I'm one of the emergency room physicians here."

The woman broke eye contact with Riley, as if her hope of a miracle had suddenly disappeared. She looked down at the face of her sleeping granddaughter, seemingly hypnotized by the sight of her. Riley could see the woman was hardly functioning. Her slight form barely moved with each breath; her delicate, pale hands gripped the bundle in her lap as if she were holding a fragile treasure. One that might break at any moment.

Riley wanted to tell the woman she'd taken care of Sofia, she'd done everything she could to save her, but unfortunately, the best she'd been able to do was to help the surgeons deliver her baby. But she could see that her words would be meaningless, incapable of breaking the spell the woman was under. Riley sat silently with her for several minutes, just being present. The woman was clearly beside herself with grief; there was not much Riley could offer to counter that.

When she did look up again at Riley, tears streamed from her nose as well as her eyes. She made no move to wipe them away. Riley reached for a tissue box from the windowsill and placed it on the arm of the rocker. She kept her voice low when she stooped down, attempting eye contact. "Is there anyone to help you with the baby?"

"Amelia," the woman whispered, not taking her eyes from the child's face.

Riley looked over her shoulder to where Cindy was peering in through the square frame of the observation window. She gave the nurse a look of desperation, shrugging her shoulders. Cindy held up a finger, indicating she needed a minute.

"My sister, Amelia," the woman finally went on. Her words were slow and thick when she added, "She'll know what to do."

Draper lifted the sleeping baby from her lap and passed her over as if she were battling with a heavy burden. Riley obliged, taking the tiny bundle into her arms. She looked down at the sleeping child, with her peach-colored cheeks and strawberry lips. Dark curly eyelashes shielded her closed eyes from a world Riley was sure she'd never be ready to see. She rose slowly, placed the sleeping baby back into her bassinet, and took her seat again next to the rocker. When Cindy returned, she was in the company of a woman Riley recognized as one of the hospital's social workers.

Riley stepped into the hallway with the nurse, closing the door behind them. "She's practically catatonic. How is she going to manage an infant on top of the news she's had today?"

"Isn't it just awful?" Cindy said, peering back through the window. "How someone deals with this much tragedy is beyond me. Poor thing. The social worker will stay with her until the detectives return. And her sister is supposed to be on the way from the airport right now. That will be a little help, I hope."

"The stepfather didn't show, huh?" Riley asked, knowing full well from Joe's earlier report that he'd suddenly disappeared. "You'd think he'd be here to support her."

"Oh God, I thought you knew!" Cindy gave Riley a puzzled look. "Weren't you working today?"

"No, it's my day off. I only just got here in time, thanks to your text message. Why?"

Cindy's jaw dropped as she reached for Riley's arm. Her fingers closed tightly around Riley's wrist as she leaned in. "It's on every news channel. He jumped from the roof at the Biltmore downtown this morning. The guy's dead."

*　　*　　*

Riley sat in the conference room of the medical examiner's office, waiting for Joe to finish his workday. Since leaving the hospital, she'd wandered around campus, meandered through the medical library, and stopped for a chai at the coffee shop.

In truth, she wasn't sure what to do with herself. Cedrick wasn't answering her text messages or calls, and she didn't have the energy to ring Holly and fill her in on the latest turn of events. With Bella still missing, there was more than enough for any one of them to be concerned about. And besides, it would be all over the news; Holly would be up to speed by this evening.

How would the media characterize the event? "Distraught parent commits suicide after learning of daughter's brutal murder," or maybe, "Utah banker suspected of sexual abuse takes his own life."

As Riley sat with her feet up on the table in the conference room, doing her best not to doze off, she realized she still didn't know Ms. Draper's first name. She pulled out her phone and searched the internet for further details on the events of the day. She came across an NBC affiliate local news brief. The story was vague on details and deep on hyperbole—typical for a still-unfolding incident in which a wealthy businessman from Utah had reportedly jumped to his death—but the article did list the names of Sofia's parents as Fred and Alexandria Draper of Provo, Utah.

Riley searched the internet using Fred's full name, age, and *Utah* for additional information on the man. *Money, Inc.* listed him as one of Utah's ten wealthiest residents. He was the fifty-two-year-old cofounder of a venture capital firm with branches in Utah and Venice, California. He was also on the board of one of Utah's largest banks.

Alexandria was a forty-eight-year-old representative for her district in the Utah State legislature. Riley didn't miss the irony in Lexi having taken her mother's first name when she'd transitioned. She hoped it was an indication that she had loved her mother, that perhaps the woman hadn't been party to her misery at home before she left. That possibility gave Riley hope that Alexandria Draper could be trusted to raise her granddaughter.

Riley's eyes burned with fatigue. She hadn't had a decent night's sleep in days. She needed a vacation, she told herself. Costa Rica sounded nice. She closed her eyes briefly, only seconds before Joe poked his head into the conference room.

"Hey, Rye, I'm just going to hop in the shower and change. I'll be ten minutes."

"Take your time." Riley rolled her head back in her chair. "Wake me up when you get done." What she wanted to say was "Use plenty of soap," but she kept that thought to herself and closed her eyes again. Before she could doze off, however, her phone rang.

It was Holly. "Holy shit, have you heard?"

"Up close and personal," Riley answered. "I'm here on the medical campus right now. I met with Sofia's mother only hours after he jumped. Crazy, right?"

"Karma, for sure. And, of all places, the Biltmore. How ironic."

"How do you mean?"

"Well, you know the history, right? LA's most infamous murder—the Black Dahlia."

"Vaguely."

"Oh God. The Biltmore is notorious for it, even after all these years. Happened in the forties when my granddad was in film. The hotel used to host the Academy Awards back in those days. Anyway, this woman, a starlet of sorts, disappeared from the lobby there a few days before she was found horribly mutilated. Her body had been washed clean and cut into two pieces. It was a super creepy murder, still unsolved. Anyway, folks swear she still haunts the place."

"How awful," Riley said, trying to put the vivid description out of mind.

"I still remember the stories my granddad would tell us about the hotel. Just the name of the place traumatized us as kids. So, yeah, it's poetic justice if you ask me." Holly went on, "I'm assuming his suicide was an admission of guilt?"

"That's a logical conclusion, but why come to LA to take a dive? There are quicker ways of checking out or just disappearing. From what I've read, he had plenty of disposable income. Why not jump on a private jet and just . . . vamoose?"

"Yeah, that's weird. You've got a point there." They were both silent for a minute—thinking, processing. "How was the mother? I can't imagine."

"She's not managing at all well. Almost nonfunctional—of course, that's understandable. Her sister should be here by now. Hopefully she's the type who will take over in a crisis. But I was thinking earlier, the woman doesn't even know about Lexi yet—"

"Oh God, that's right!" Holly gasped. "What a day. Both kids dead and now her husband takes a swan dive on the day she finds out he's responsible for Sofia's rape and probably the pregnancy."

"I don't have those details just yet either. I'm waiting on Joe. He'll have the DNA results on the stepfather and the infant by now, I'm sure. Then it will just be a question of whether this guy was also somehow responsible for Lexi's and Sofia's murders. If he was the abuser, as you say Lexi's counseling notes revealed, he'd have plenty of reason for wanting both of them dead."

"Especially if he knew it was Lexi blackmailing him," Holly added. "Makes you wonder if he ever knew who she really was."

"Unless he was responsible for the murders himself, he would have had to have someone here working for him," Riley theorized, but at this point in the day, her curiosity was blunted by her fatigue. "Obviously, it would be easier to implicate him if we could also prove he was in town at the time of the attacks—"

Joe poked his head in the doorway of the conference room. "Want to grab an early dinner? I'm probably going to have to come back here this evening. Let's get out for a quick bite." He was grinning from ear to ear, his face freshly shaved.

"Absolutely." Riley was on her feet in a second. "I'm famished."

She asked Holly if she could call her later and hung up. She pulled her backpack over her shoulder, and they headed to the exit. On the way to the parking garage, Joe filled her in on the events of the past day.

"While we were looking for Bella last night, this place was hopping. I can assure you Detective Roberts and her partner got less sleep than any of us did."

"Meaning?"

"Meaning they were here until almost midnight with one of my colleagues from forensic pathology and some detective from Santa Monica PD."

Riley shook her head. "So they must have come here after they left the shelter last night. What were they after?"

"Same thing they talked with me about this morning. They were going over my findings on Sofia's and Lexi's autopsy results as well as the DNA results from Sofia and her infant."

"So they know then," Riley said, matter-of-factly. "Good to hear we're all on the same page."

Joe gave her a sideways glance. "They know what?" he asked, testing her.

"That Lexi and Sofia were siblings," Riley said, giving him a wide grin.

"What? How do you do that?"

"Women's intuition, Joe. Never underestimate us." She bumped into his shoulder with her backpack, nudging him off his feet.

Joe stood next to his car, giving her a bewildered look after she filled him in on how she and Holly had figured out the relationship between Lexi and Sofia.

"You're not bad as a detective, Rye. And I suppose you know about the DNA results on the stepdad and the baby too?"

"I'm guessing the threat of voluntarily providing a sample was enough to make the guy jumpy." She winked.

"Funny. Yeah, I think the detectives planned to confront him here, after the viewing. But, of course, it seems at some point he must have realized the jig was up. He disappeared from the hotel room this morning before we could have him provide a sample. Then, four hours later, the guy takes a leap from the roof."

"Desperate times," Riley said, her tone biting. "Where was he in those missing hours? At the hotel bar, building his resolve? What a coward. I just hope the mother had no clue. I can't imagine her keeping that baby safe if she's the type of woman who would let that sort of abuse happen under her own roof."

"If I've learned anything about these situations, it's that creeps like this are very skilled at covering their tracks. Especially the ones with lots to lose. So there's every possibility the mother was clueless."

"I don't know if that's meant to be an endorsement or an indictment, Joe." Riley shot him a critical look. "Either way, both kids were victimized in their own home. That's unforgivable."

"It's not meant to be either," Joe said, stooping to open the car door for her. "This is life. It's what we navigate in the type of work we've chosen. Aren't you the one who's always reminding me of the yin and yang of it all? The good comes with the bad, right? And maybe we're better served when we let go of the compulsion to control it all. We do what we can, within reason, to help and maybe try not to become victims ourselves."

Riley was deep in thought when Joe pulled out of the garage and cruised toward downtown. They wove through the manicured lawns and freshly raked rock paths of the campus before drifting through the huge wrought iron gates separating the pristine grounds of the university from the tangled streets of the city itself. She stared out the window at the homeless camps below the underpass—their blue tarps, dull and frayed from overuse, flapped against the cold autumn breeze. In a concrete jungle, she supposed there wasn't anything to sink a stake into and fewer ways to secure a makeshift home. Some of the campsites were cobbled together with shopping carts, rocks, and debris that had been dug out of the trash or gutters. In one small alcove under the bridge, piles of plastic bags, filled with personal belongings or God knew what, had been stacked alongside an old bicycle. A wheelchair missing a footrest was propped up by a gallon jug of water adjacent to a dumpster that had clearly been liberated from its original station. Beside it, a huddled form, unmoving, lay in a sleeping bag.

What bothered Riley more than any of it was that she and Joe were passing by casually, not stopping to check on the occupant of the bag. Not knowing if that person, that human being, was alive or dead or in critical need of help.

She looked over at Joe as he hit the clutch and downshifted to cruise up to a red light. He glanced at her, pressing his lips into a tight smile.

"You're good company, Joe. I'm grateful for our friendship."

"Yeah, me too," he said quietly, shifting gears.

They stopped at a little café in Chinatown with worn leather booths and low-hanging bamboo lamps. The walls were covered in shiny red paper etched with black velvet stencils of dragons—their mouths menacingly agape, their tails curling below their bodies like serpents.

They ordered a variety of dim sum and Joe's favorite spicy noodle soup. Riley filled him in on her day at the beach with Holly after she'd picked Indio up from the pound. She told him of Holly's confession about trying to hide the proof Lexi had been blackmailing Sofia's abuser. Joe sat in stunned silence, staring at Riley as if he were either in awe of her or incredulous at her level of involvement in what he would no doubt label dangerous if not criminal activity.

"Any word from Cedrick on Bella?" he asked, checking his watch.

"What time do you need to get back to the office?" Riley asked, realizing she'd been talking nonstop since they'd ordered.

"We can head out whenever. No rush."

"To answer your question—no, I haven't heard from Cedrick all day, which I have to say is odd." Riley frowned, checking her phone again. "He told me he'd be finished with his last final by three o'clock, and it's already six-thirty."

"How did he seem last night? I imagine he's pretty upset about Bella's disappearance." Riley filled Joe in on the phone call they'd received from the man calling himself Manny and the news about Bella paying someone to drop Indy off at the animal shelter. "Well, that's somewhat encouraging, if we know she played a part in Indy being taken care of."

"I agree. That gives me hope she's up to something, that she's executing a plan, but the guy also told us Bella had last been seen getting into a pickup. That, of course, was concerning." Riley fell silent for a moment. She scratched the back of her neck. Something wasn't sitting well with her.

"And of course, you let Detective Roberts know that?"

"That's just it, Joe. That's what's bothering me. Cedrick seemed really upset last night by the news that Bella was seen getting into the pickup, but he didn't alert his mom right away as I would have expected. Why do you think that is?"

"Yeah, that doesn't add up. Remember how insistent he was about all of us having to avoid the pickup guy? Told us he couldn't enlighten us, but we needed to keep our distance. And Bella was upset with him over that suggestion. Remember?"

Riley weighed whether to mention her other concerns about Cedrick's puzzling behavior. But that would mean exposing her risky sleuthing activities. She wasn't sure it was a good idea to tell Joe that she'd seen the Jaded Justice guy stalking Holly on the day she followed her and Eli to their storage shed. And that when she'd reported that news to Cedrick, all he'd been concerned about was whether the man had spotted her or not. It hadn't seemed to faze him that Holly was being stalked, even though she fit the same profile as the other victims. Riley pried her gaze away from Joe, thinking better of it. He would only worry needlessly if he knew she'd put herself between Holly and her stalker. And besides, she didn't want to paint Cedrick in a bad light. Maybe there was a perfectly valid reason for his actions. It made sense he was preoccupied with Bella's disappearance above all else.

"Okay," Joe said, nodding as he puzzled it out himself. "Cedrick's keeping something from us."

"Maybe," Riley agreed, absently twirling the end of her long braid between her fingers. "In all honesty, why shouldn't he? So much for my thinking he and Bella were total amateurs. With Cedrick's connections, it's likely they know a whole lot more than we realize. And despite having been down several rabbit holes, I still have no idea how all these pieces fit together. Why Clive was targeted. Or how his murder relates to the murders of Lexi and Sofia." She sipped her tea and added, "and what the hell Bella's up to putting herself in the crosshairs."

Joe's mouth slanted into a scowl. "Yeah, perplexing for sure . . . not to mention extremely dangerous."

CHAPTER TWENTY-SIX

Riley asked Joe to drop her off at the ER on their way back to campus from dinner. Her leathers were still in the locker room.

"Sure" was all he said. He'd seemed unusually quiet ever since they'd left Chinatown. She thanked him for dinner and advised him not to work too late before letting the car door swing closed behind her. She headed for the ambulance entrance, pulling her backpack over her shoulder. When she reached the doors, she turned. Joe was still watching her. He waved slowly and pulled away from the curb.

On her way to the locker room, Riley passed the intake desk. The secretary behind the reinforced glass window flagged her down.

Riley stopped, resting her elbows on the counter. "Hey there, Sylvia, how's it going?"

The woman smiled. "Same old, same old." She reached into a drawer under the desk and pulled out a sealed white envelope. "How come you're in on your day off? I thought I'd be holding on to this till the weekend." She passed the envelope to Riley through a slot in the window. "He didn't leave a name. Just told me you'd know what it was for."

Riley examined the outside of the envelope. It was a business-size letter, sealed and folded in half, without any name, address, or information on it whatsoever. She started to hand it back. "How do we know it's for me?"

"He said it was for the pretty ER doctor with the blue butterfly tattoo. I only know one of those." The woman shrugged, then winked. "Maybe an off-season valentine?"

Riley sat on the bench in the locker room, shaking the envelope around on the slim chance it contained anthrax or some other dangerous equivalent. She half laughed at herself as she tried to recall what she knew about the treatment for anthrax poisoning and came up empty. Finally, she tore open an edge of the envelope and pulled out a folded note. The penmanship was poor, and the message itself was scrawled out in black ink on lined notebook paper:

> Sorry Doc . . .
> Your friend Rosaria met the Devil of Ghost Town
> El Diablo
> Dude's an evil mutha
> Got a long list of dead girlfriends
> Torched one of them and her little kid a while back
> after she burned his stash
> Last chick got creamed in traffic on the 101
> Good luck Doc, remember to have your own back
> first
> A smart lady once told me that luck only goes so far

Riley folded the note back up and slipped it into the pocket of her leather jacket, trying to take it all in. There was no mistaking who it was from. And she realized Miguel would have taken a significant risk to get this information. *Last chick got creamed in traffic on the 101.* She couldn't let go of that line. Sofia, Lexi, and Clive had all met their ends on that freeway. Was Miguel saying that this El Diablo was also responsible for one of their deaths? All of their deaths?

*   *   *

Riley's black moto flashed through the patches of overhead light as she sped from downtown along the 10 Freeway to the 110 toward the coast just after eight p.m. She downshifted and exited onto Fourth Street in Santa Monica, where traffic was moderately heavy until she turned onto the side streets.

Manny, who had called Cedrick last night to report seeing Bella getting into the pickup, said he was calling from the boardwalk. She was guessing this Manny was a creature of habit, if not a victim of circumstance, and she'd find him in the same area any night of the week.

Riley pulled over and checked the map on her phone; she was in the right spot. She found parking in an alley off Washington Boulevard a few blocks from the beach. She locked her helmet to her bike and headed down along the alleyway to the boardwalk on foot. There were only a few streetlights in the area. The ocean air pressed down on her, mingling with the sweet smell of weed, though the pungent odor of human waste in the alleyways overpowered it all. She could hear the muted conversations and the occasional shriek of laughter from people gathered in small clusters around tents or sitting on overturned trash cans. The smoke rising from their lit cigarettes, like so many ghostly snakes, drifted up into the blackness.

She stood tall and lengthened her stride, walking with purpose in the direction of the pier, her backpack over her shoulder. Bars and roll-up shutters shielded most ground-level windows on the graffiti-covered buildings in the neighborhood. As she approached the beach, she could hear the distant trumpets of a mariachi band from a nearby Mexican restaurant. *Bingo*, she thought. As the boardwalk came into view, she could see that only a few homeless campsites dotted the beach, giving testimony that the sheriff's department had indeed cleared most folks out during the pandemic.

As Riley reached the pier, the loose beach sand under her boots ground out her pace on the concrete walkway in a way that made it impossible to be ignored. She headed out toward the end of the jetty without breaking her stride, observing curiously her reckless abandonment of self-preservation.

She reminded herself that only forty minutes previously, she'd been afraid to open an unlabeled envelope, but here she was in Venice, Ghost Town, alone at night, on a mission she hadn't yet defined. But she knew the answers to her questions lay here. The place was the common link between Bella and Clive and now, it seemed, Rosaria and whoever this El Diablo character was.

A handful of stragglers in their windbreakers and hoodies were leaving the jetty with their fishing poles and bait buckets. As she neared the end of the pier, Riley stopped and leaned up against the railing, looking down at the dark churning water below reflecting the overhead lights, as if the ocean were an enormous black oil slick. The air was heavy with the scent of brine rising from the surf below and perhaps the remains of an earlier fisherman's catch. The cloud cover overhead obscured any light there might have been from the moon.

Riley turned, deciding to head back toward the lit areas of the boardwalk, figuring she'd make a few passes along the shuttered shops and stores lining the walkway, looking for anyone who might go by the name Manny.

As she approached the boardwalk along the pier, a wiry man in a stocking cap and baggy pants, fishing alone under one of the lights, turned to watch her pass. Riley pressed on, pretending to ignore the burn of his eyes on her back. She stopped suddenly. Something about him had caught her attention. She turned. He was wearing a button-up hand-knit vest with an orange-and-green argyle pattern. She'd seen one just like it only yesterday morning. It was identical to the vest Indy had been dressed in in the selfie Bella had texted her after breakfast at the teen center.

Before she could think, she was striding toward the man. He stepped back from the railing, eyes fixed on her. The light flooded from the lamp overhead like a spill of bleach, disguising his face in the stark contrast of white light and pitch-black shadow. His hand resting on the rail was wrinkled and cracked, likely the result of years of surviving the sun and the streets. Below him, Riley caught sight of a large knife with a thin blade resting on the lower rail of the pier, just above a grimy bait bucket. She loosened her backpack from her left shoulder and gripped it to her chest, as if placing a barrier between herself and the man, while her right hand dipped into her pocket. The man's eyes were quick to follow her movements.

She gave him the biggest, most disarming smile she could muster. He frowned, his eyes narrowing. A second later, she could see his shoulders relaxing as she pulled her phone out of her pocket. She scrolled to the selfie of Bella and Indio in the vest the man was now wearing and held it out in front of herself like a talisman as she approached him.

He squinted curiously, taking in the photo. Riley half expected him to smile, but what she saw in his eyes was something between humiliation and fury. She stepped closer, sidling up to the rail, looking him straight in the eye and banking on the fact that she was probably three inches taller than he was. Leaning on the rail, she ever so slowly raised her left foot, placing the sole of her boot directly over the blade of the knife on the lower railing. The man was already frozen, his eyes locked on her, seemingly at a loss.

"Where is she?" Riley said, holding the picture on her phone inches from his face. She was as surprised as the man appeared to be at the commanding tone of her own voice. His eyes darted back to the photo of Bella and Indy.

He gripped the pier railing, not taking his eyes off Riley as he ran his fingers along the upper rail. She smiled again, grinding her foot into the blade of the knife on the lower rung. In a moment, he realized his miscalculation.

"I'm not going to ask you nicely again," Riley said, nudging the knife off the railing and into the surf below. The man was silent for a moment as he locked his gaze on her.

His voice was gravelly and low when he spoke. "Only the devil knows." He shrugged then, as if dismissing her. Riley eyed him warily. The man's gaze shifted slowly along the now-deserted pier, as if he were making sure he wasn't being watched. "I did what she asked with the dog." He groaned. "I don't know nothin' else."

"The devil? You mean El Diablo?" Riley pressed. The man's eyes left her face, focusing on the boardwalk behind her as he nodded slowly. The surf below hissed with a surge. "And where would I find El Diablo?"

A toothless smile slowly spread over his face. "You don't find him."

"He finds *you*," a voice from behind Riley broke in.

CHAPTER TWENTY-SEVEN

Riley's breath caught in her throat. The pier seemed to tilt sideways, as though it were about to collapse into the ocean, and for a second, she wondered if the spicy soup she'd had earlier in Chinatown was about to suddenly surge out of her. She found herself leaping clear of the fisherman's reach and turning to see who had spoken from behind her.

"Javier! What the hell—?"

"What the hell are *you* doing *here* is a better question," he retorted, and for a minute, she couldn't read him. He tipped his head toward the boardwalk, signaling for Riley to follow him. "This place is not for you, lady." His voice was almost a growl as he turned away, giving the fisherman a defiant glance over his shoulder. Riley looked back at the man who was now leaning over the railing of the pier—in search of his bait knife, no doubt. Then she followed Javier, feeling breathless and more than a little queasy.

The streetlamps lit up the boardwalk, making her less spooked, but Javier seemed anxious to get out of the light. He motioned for her to follow him into the alleyway before he spoke again.

"You have no idea who you're up against, lady," he hissed. "This guy is not like anything you've ever seen. You don't mess with El Diablo unless you want to end up like my little sister and like Clive." Even in the dim light of the alleyway, Riley could see the anger in his eyes. No, it wasn't anger—it was raw fear.

"You know who killed Clive?" Riley whispered. Javier didn't answer. "And Rosaria?"

"Not here!" was all he said, turning to head up the alleyway. Riley followed, her arms wrapped over her chest, clutching her backpack tightly. Despite her unease, she found herself trusting Javier enough to follow him through the darkness.

A few minutes later, they were standing next to her motorcycle without another word having passed between them.

"You knew I was here? *What?* You followed me?"

"Something like that" was all he answered, waiting for her to get back on her bike. "Like your friend Joe said, lady, you're not a very good detective."

"Really? Joe said that?"

"He's a smart man." Javier left the inference to Riley.

"What do you know about Clive that you haven't told the police?" she asked bluntly.

Javier drew a deep breath and let it out slowly, crossing his arms over his chest. He turned to her, looking her square in the face. "Clive was like you, lady. Wanted to fix everything. He came out here . . . after Rosaria. That was my fault. I never should have told him about my sister's murder." He paused, eyes flashing up to meet hers. "Back when Clive was Clair, they were together, she and El Diablo. She was lucky to get away from him once. Then after the transition, Clive comes back here like an idiot hero—like no one is going to recognize him as having been Clair. That's what happens, lady, when you think you are smarter than you are. You make dangerous decisions. You piss off the devil."

Despite his tone, Javier's voice cracked. Riley felt like a heel. There was no question he had been dealing with a lot since the murders of both his sister and Sofia. And now it was obvious he'd had a deep connection with Clive too. Riley had been oblivious to the magnitude of that loss. It was clearly weighing on him. And tonight, he'd taken a risk for her. To ensure her safety after she'd needlessly put herself in danger. She thought briefly about offering an apology, but she could see she'd already crossed a line with him.

"Be smart, lady. Go home." He stood, waiting for her to leave.

Now anxious to cover the blush of humiliation rising in her cheeks, Riley pulled on her full-face helmet. She started her bike, letting it idle. Then she revved her engine, as if to allow it the last word before she kicked into gear and pulled out onto Washington Boulevard. Across the way, in the alley, something caught her eye.

A large, dark pickup truck edged its way out of the shadows.

The headlights flicked on as soon as she crossed its path.

Why had she seen that pickup twice now when Javier had been in the picture? It made no sense that he'd be with the Jaded Justice creep.

Riley kept an eye on her mirrors for the next few intersections before she finally relaxed. She traveled north, taking the coastal route home. Once she passed Malibu, traffic on the Pacific Coast Highway was sparse.

She headed to Encinal Canyon, choosing the longest, darkest route home. If anyone were following her, she'd see the headlights best out there. She was sure she could outrun any vehicle through the winding foothills where she knew every bend in the road intimately.

The solitude of the canyon in the dead of night was comforting. The full moon poked out between the clouds, lighting the road ahead through the patches of enormous oaks that lined the embankments. She felt the darkness close in around her, like an embrace, a vast cushion, shielding her from the threats she'd faced earlier that evening and the chaos she'd invited.

She focused on the whine of her engine. Clicking through the gears, downshifting for the tighter curves, opening up on the straightaways, pushing her speed right to the limits. The beam from her headlamp like an illuminated tether, pulled her out of the depths of a dark well she had seemingly tumbled carelessly into that night.

CHAPTER TWENTY-EIGHT

The next morning, Riley found herself staring up at the gentle glow of dawn spreading slowly over the ceiling of her bedroom. She realized if Javier had figured out that El Diablo had killed Clive, it was only a matter of time until the detectives knew it too. That was, if they didn't already. She wondered again why she hadn't heard from Cedrick and what Bella was up to in Venice. Riley still couldn't connect all the dots. While Lexi and Sofia had been killed in the same way Clive had, she didn't know of anything tying the two siblings to Clive's nemesis, El Diablo.

Just then, Indy jumped up onto her bed and gave her a look that said it was breakfast time.

She put her hand on his head and peered into the dog's eyes. "How could you just let that scrawny little guy take your beautiful argyle vest?" she said, grabbing him and wrestling him into a hug. "He hardly had any teeth! You should be ashamed of yourself."

The dog licked her face and jumped off the bed, scampering to the kitchen. Artemis, sitting in her usual spot on the back of the armchair, closed her eyes and turned her head from Riley, signaling her disapproval of the far-too-exuberant dialogue.

After her morning run and a hot shower, Riley headed to Westlake Village to meet her mother and the attorneys from the Shira Altman Foundation at a bistro near the lake. It was a beautiful fall day, with clear California skies. The maple trees, fully adorned in their golden splendor, lit up the banks along the water between the constancy of the pale green willows.

There was business to discuss, final touches to be put on the plans for the pending additional endowments to the medical school and the emergency medicine residency grants. Riley had been thinking about a special award in the name of her late mentor, Dr. Benoit, and who she might nominate for the stipend. His widow, Clarissa, was coming to the event, wasn't she?

Riley's family trust had also been funding the free mental health clinic on Maple Avenue for the previous ten years. She'd want to make increases there too. And, of course, now there was the Santa Monica youth center to worry about. Would they soon be out of funding because of Lexi's and Holly's actions? She put those thoughts aside.

Today the focus was her own department at City General. Under normal circumstances, she might have conferred with her department director, perhaps even hospital administration, but Jackson had no idea of Riley's connection to the Shira Altman Foundation and her grandmother's legacy. Riley had always wanted it that way. She'd avoided any chance of special consideration or perception of entitlement. That was why she'd elected to attend medical school in Chicago—where she'd loved the city but hated the weather—rather than her first choice here, at home, in the medical school funded by her own family's foundation. But when it came to residencies, she hadn't compromised. She'd wanted the best—Los Angeles City General. And fortunately, she'd made that match all on her own. She'd been happy to earn her position through the usual challenges of dogged tenacity and hard work.

The grand gala and the renaming of the medical school were only ten days away. Her family would be flying in over the next week: her aunt Naomi and her new husband—number four—and maybe her cousins would make the effort to tear themselves away from their busy lives too. She still hadn't decided what she'd wear. Or if she'd invite a guest. It was almost too late for that now.

She'd spent more than two hours in discussions with her mother and the attorneys after lunch when the alerts on her phone started going off. She glanced down at the screen as she silenced the notifications. Joe was trying to reach her.

Later, when she walked her mother out to her car after the meeting, the screen on her phone lit up once more. She hugged her mom. Anxious to call Joe back, she thanked her for her generosity again and turned to head to her car.

"Rye," her mother said, reaching for her hand. "We'll do the best we can. Don't fret. We can't support every cause, but we can make a financial difference for some, and that will have to do."

"I know, Mum, it's just that—"

"I mean it, sweets. You're just like your father," she said, reaching over and resting a hand on Riley's shoulder. "Constantly chasing ideals. You're on the same path, kiddo. Pace yourself for the long haul. You can't fix it all at once."

"I'll try, Mum," she said, bending to hug her mother again. "I promise I'll try."

"You're still blaming yourself, aren't you? Even after all these years," her mother said, squeezing her hand a little tighter.

"What? What do you mean?"

"It wasn't your fault, the way daddy died. It wasn't anyone's fault. He was a trained professional. More than that, a seasoned firefighter."

"I . . . I know that, Mum. I do. I'm not sure why you're bringing that up again."

She searched her mother's eyes; she could read what the woman had omitted. What she always omitted. That her father had known how much the horses up on Sycamore Ridge had meant to Riley and that that would have colored his decisions that night. That he'd headed into that forest fire for her, he'd taken that risk for her. *And he'd lost everything, just for her.*

"Your head might know it, sweets, but your heart still doesn't get it. You're so much like him, trying to fix everything in the world that's broken. You've got to let go of some of it. Put yourself first occasionally."

Riley stared back at her mother. The familiar darkness had returned. She searched for the words, but they never seemed to come easily.

"Okay, maybe you have a point, Mum. But is that all bad? Taking a risk here and there? Wanting to help where you can?"

"Extending yourself is one thing, Rye. But not at the expense of your own happiness, your own future."

"I'm happy. I'm just fine, Mum."

"Riley. Seriously, you haven't been yourself since Marcel passed. I know he was a great support for you, but it's been two years, kiddo. You work too hard and too many hours. I'm not saying your career isn't important. It's just that I'd like to see you putting your happiness first, for once. You know . . ." She gave Riley a look, bracing herself as she said, "Dating again, having a normal life . . . planning the future you deserve."

Riley forced a smile and gently pulled her hand away from her mother's. She knew exactly what her mother wanted for her, and part of her wanted that for herself, but what Riley always craved was something *more*. Was it that she didn't prioritize herself, or was it that the chance to help others was genuinely more fulfilling than all that?

"Love you too, Mum," she said, wondering why Joe had been trying to reach her.

When Riley reached her car, she called him right away. "What's happening, friend?" she asked, pulling out of the parking lot and onto the boulevard along the lake.

"Hey, Rye, just wanted to share an interesting tidbit about the autopsy on our jumper from Utah."

She hadn't thought about the events of yesterday all morning. But now Riley realized that the autopsy on Sofia and Lexi's stepfather, Fredrick Draper, would have been scheduled almost immediately.

"Go on," she said. "I'm all ears."

"Seems he had a little help finding his way off the roof of the Biltmore. When his body arrived yesterday, his eyes were still blindfolded—get this—with duct tape." Riley's mind flashed back to the morning Sofia had arrived in the trauma bay by helicopter. Despite her horrific injuries, the duct tape over the girl's eyes had been a disturbing enough sight all on its own. And a signature of all three freeway murders. The victims all had their eyes blindfolded: Lexi and Sofia with duct tape and Clive with a motorcycle helmet placed backward on his head.

"Holy shit." Riley's mind was racing. "Okay, so that either explains things—"

"Or raises more questions," Joe said, finishing her sentence. "The obvious inference is that all four of these deaths are linked by the same MO, and as I've said from the beginning, I'd guess a single killer."

"There's always been a missing piece of the puzzle here. I couldn't figure out what all the victims had in common, besides the way they were killed. But over the last couple of days, I've learned a few interesting details that may provide the link. Clive had ties that went back to his days as Clair, before his transition, to a gang leader in Venice who goes by the name El Diablo."

Riley filled Joe in on the note she'd received from Miguel and her discussion with Javier about Clive and the devil of Ghost Town. Naturally, she neglected to tell him that the conversation had taken place in a darkened alleyway in Venice after a brush with a dubious character on the fishing pier last night.

Suddenly, it came to her. Riley pulled out of traffic and into a hotel parking lot just before the freeway on-ramp in Westlake. She rolled up to a shady spot under an enormous ficus tree and turned up the volume on her phone. "Joe, can you access the autopsy records of a murder victim from Venice three months ago?"

"Sure, that's LA County's territory. Who are you talking about?"

"Javier's little sister, Rosaria."

There was silence on the line for a moment. "What are you thinking, Rye? What's the relevance?"

"You'll know right away when you see it—that is, if I'm right about what I suspect."

Neither Joe nor Riley knew Javier and Ms. Maria's last name. That slowed things down. It took Joe several minutes to search through the data online to find any information on Rosaria's murder. He'd used gender and the month and location of the death before gaining a hit.

"Got it," he said. Riley waited as Joe speed-read the electronic report. "And there it is. Single gunshot wound to the head, eyes blindfolded with duct tape." He paused, expelling a heavy sigh before he said, "You're right on the money again. What tipped you off?"

"That's it, Joe—that's the tie. Now we know that whoever killed Rosaria killed all our victims. That individual is the common denominator."

"And I'm guessing that's this El Diablo character?"

"Well, Javier suggested he's the guy who killed both Rosaria and Clive. And so, by your logic, the rest of these victims too. Sofia, Lexi, and now their stepfather, Draper."

"Okay, let's just say you're right. Now the bigger mystery is *why*. What was the motive for all four murders, and how do we make sure this devil guy is apprehended?"

"Not four murders, Joe. *Five*, including Rosaria and Draper. All these deaths are somehow related to gang activity, I'll bet. And now I have a feeling that both Bella and Cedrick have known this all along. Holly told me that Bella and Clive had met in Venice years ago when Bella was saving girls from being trafficked by the gangs."

For a moment, Riley considered the possibilities of how the murders were tied. "I'll bet all this goes back to something that happened in Venice that upset some gang's business operations. Holly said Bella got herself on the wrong side of some of these folks, that she'd been doing dangerous work in those days. And I remember the first time I met Bella, she mentioned some really bad dude she'd had dealings with in Venice—a 'psychopathic genius' she called him. I think we need another team meeting, but with Bella AWOL and

Cedrick ghosting me, it'll just be the three of us. Let me call Holly, get her up to speed, and I'll text you a time and place to meet if you're up for that."

"Wouldn't miss it" was all he said before hanging up.

Riley pulled back out onto the boulevard and accessed the freeway. Instead of heading straight home, she exited the 101 at Kanan Road and took the canyon over to the coast, calling Holly on her way to Malibu.

Later that evening, the three of them sat in Holly's high-ceilinged living room while Eli banged around in their enormous kitchen, preparing a family recipe with an Italian opera streaming through the house. Four of Holly's five dogs sat on the deep-cushioned white couch with Riley, the fifth on Holly's lap.

Riley turned to Joe. "Holly and I talked this afternoon about Bella's time fighting the gangs in Venice, around the time Clive—Clair back then—was staying at the shelter."

"Riley got me thinking back to those days," Holly explained, "and I believe she's right. Clair was a victim of trafficking before Bella brought her to the center. I'd forgotten that detail. I should have remembered when you found those cute school pictures of her online in her cheerleading outfits, Riley, that night we had Thai at your place. She would have been a cash cow for those creeps."

"Do you think that's where Bella is now?" Joe pressed. "Back in Venice trying to explore Clive's prior life there?"

Holly raised her brows. "Oh, I wouldn't put it past her for a minute. She's like a bulldog when she gets an idea. And talk about fearless. That girl's not afraid of anything or anyone . . ." Her expression changed from one of warmth to one hollowed by concern. "And that's what should have us all worried. Some of the girls we got out of those gangs had been through unspeakable—well, you can imagine."

Holly fell silent, and so did the room. Riley's eyes settled on Joe sitting in a large white armchair near the fireplace. He picked up his glass of wine from the side table at his elbow and then set it down again, not taking a sip. "If she'd pissed off the gangs there in the past, why would Bella put herself right back into the mix? Wouldn't that be suicide?"

"Well, she made no friends among the gangs, for sure. But maybe among their victims. Among the girls," Holly said, staring into the fireplace where Eli had built a fire to warm the enormous room before taking on his duties in the kitchen.

"Okay, so for the sake of argument, let's say Bella is now somewhere in Venice doing some deep sleuthing. Cedrick has some idea of what she's up to, and he's decided the rest of us don't need to be included." Joe rested his interlaced fingers on the top of his head. "Who else knows what Bella and Cedrick are doing? Detective Roberts?"

"Hmm, I doubt that. Cedrick's mother looked like a wet hen the last time I saw her in his company. I can't believe she'd sanction his involvement in this case." Riley kicked her sandals off and pulled her bare feet up under her onto the couch, rearranging the dogs as she did so.

"What about Javier? Do you think he's in any way involved in what Bella and Cedrick are doing?"

"I don't think so. Bella had never met him before the day she and Indy went to stay at the shelter. And Cedrick's first time at the teen center was only two nights ago, when he showed up with his mother and Detective Garth." Riley was quiet for a moment before adding, "But I would think Javier is bent on bringing his sister's murderer to justice. I'm just not sure what his link is to the guy with the pickup. I've seen him with that character too many times now. These folks with the Jaded Justice emblems are usually linked to white supremacist gangs. So yeah, I'm totally lost on who he is and his involvement in all this."

"Do you think Javier is playing some kind of inside game? You know, using one gang to fight another?" Holly asked, taking a long sip of her wine.

"I can't see that. What clout does Javier have? He's relatively new in town. I'm not sure how much sway he'd have over well-established gangs or their activities."

"Yeah, but what if he had power with the gangs back home in Mexico, and now he's here to avenge his little sister's murder." Holly's voice faded in a way that said not even she bought her argument.

"I just don't get that sense," Riley maintained. "I really get the feeling Javier is more of a victim here than an aggressor."

"I'd have to say I agree with Riley, especially after my talk with him the other night. I'd say he's not into gang warfare," Joe added. "Besides, he's been in Fresno for the last few years, working as a farmhand. He only came out here to be with his mother after his sister's murder."

The conversation fell silent for a moment, everyone deep in thought.

Eventually, Joe said, "I'm not sure where we go from here. It seems we have a couple loose ends, but without knowing what Cedrick and Bella are up to, we're at an impasse."

"But I think we've made some progress today," Riley added. "At least we seem to have found a common denominator in the murders of Clive and Rosaria, this El Diablo character, and his trafficking operation. Now all we need to do is connect him to the murders of the three family members: Sofia, Lexi, and their stepfather, Draper."

"Well, at this point, it's a foregone conclusion that Lexi was blackmailing Draper about what he'd done to Sofia. And if the man wanted both his blackmailer and his victim silenced, he could have contracted someone local to do the job. This El Diablo guy sounds evil enough to have obliged," Holly said, biting one of her long, polished nails. She looked over at Riley. "I mean, Draper was loaded, right? He had a lot to lose, and wouldn't a hired killer solve all his problems?"

"That makes sense. And I remember reading somewhere that Draper's company had a Venice branch. So a connection to a local gang or mobsters is not entirely unreasonable." Riley sat quietly, running her fingertip over the lip of her wineglass. "What do we do now? We've been warned to stay out of this investigation, but I can't stand the thought of sitting on my hands and waiting for the detectives to catch up—"

"No, we can't do that," Joe cut in. "I think we're obliged to share what we've figured out with Detective Roberts. I could easily do that in my official capacity. I'll send her copies of the autopsies of all five victims. It would be impossible to ignore the common denominator—the killer's signature, the blindfolds. Putting Rosaria's murder on their radar is likely to get them interested in her ties to the gang in Venice, and that move should lead them to this El Diablo character."

"That's a brilliant idea," Holly said.

"Agreed." Riley nodded slowly. "That's probably the most helpful thing we could do at this point." She stared at the fireplace for a minute before adding, "Holly's hypothesis about Draper contracting El Diablo to kill Lexi and Sofia is logical, but why would El Diablo then cut off the hand that's feeding him?"

Joe scratched his chin. "You mean, what did he have to gain by killing Draper as soon as the man got into town?"

"Yeah, what sense does that make if the guy's been paying him a fortune?"

Joe picked up his wine again and twirled the liquid around in the glass, staring at the deep color as if it held the answer to a riddle. "I'm figuring the jig was up, wasn't it? Draper was going to go down for the crime. This case has had so much media exposure with the miracle baby surviving that trauma. The public would be up in arms about a prosecution. If Draper was indicted for Sofia's rape, the only leverage he might have to avoid a maximum prison sentence would be to give up her killer? Right?"

Riley gave Joe a wry smile. "Bingo! And this El Diablo guy is ruthless. He knows Draper is in town with his wife to ID Sofia's body; every news outlet is covering it. And it doesn't take much to figure out why Draper wanted the girl killed in the first place. So El Diablo guesses it's only a matter of time until DNA from the surviving infant pins Draper to Sofia's rape. That's when he decides to neutralize the threat before Draper gets a chance to throw him under the bus for the murder." Riley winced. "Pardon the pun."

"Gotta say, that's the most logical possibility." Joe agreed.

"Dinner's ready," Eli announced as he poked his head into the living room, a broad smile on his face as he raised his own glass of wine.

"Shall we?" Holly stood, motioning to the dining room, where an enormous wooden table had been set under a wrought iron chandelier filled with large white candles.

CHAPTER TWENTY-NINE

The following day in the ER was as busy as usual for Riley. She was in the middle of discharging a postal worker with multiple dog bites when she looked up to see Tobias Bach staring at her from the doorway of the examination room. Riley hadn't seen Bach since his return to work after the Williams case. She tried to keep her expression neutral as she took in the look of him—the dark circles around his eyes, the hollow cheeks. Perhaps the day shift wasn't agreeing with the man, or maybe his conscience was finally eating him alive. Whatever the cause, it was obvious Bach wasn't working on his Southern California tan as he seemed to when he was running the night shift.

She turned her attention back to her patient.

"You can't make this shit up, Doc," the postal worker said, limping from the stretcher to the desk where Riley was writing his prescription. "Who names a chihuahua Cujo?"

"Oh, I believe it." Riley stifled a smile. "Truth is often stranger than fiction around here."

She locked eyes with Bach as she signed the postal worker's prescription. As soon as the patient turned to leave, Tobias approached with both hands tucked deeply into his lab coat pockets.

"There's something I think you need to hear," he said in a low voice, leaning in toward Riley.

"Sure." She didn't blink. "Give me five."

Rumor had it there was now an official suit over little Leroy Williams's death. Riley didn't know who had been named in the litigation. She just knew she was in the clear because she'd heard the news about the lawsuit from the nurses and not from the city's attorneys or Jackson. She wondered if the action had been brought by Taller Paula, Leroy's aunt, after she'd been tipped off by Jenna, the counselor at the Maple Street Center. Riley would look into that later.

Bach nodded. "See you in the library."

Riley grabbed a cup of coffee on the way to meet Tobias. She passed Sonya in the hallway; the nurse held a hand up, stopping her. "Did you see who's here today?" She raised an eyebrow.

"You mean Big Mouth Bach?"

"Aha! And *God*, does he look awful. But then again, vampires aren't well suited to the day shift, are they?"

"I'm on my way to meet with him right now. Can't imagine what he wants to discuss. If I'm not out in five minutes, send reinforcements."

"That's not even funny, Rye. Watch your back. I wouldn't put anything past him. You know he's gotten physical with a couple of the nurses." Sonya hesitated, then she stepped closer and added, "By the way, did you hear what's-her-name dropped out of the residency?"

"Who?"

"Dr. Li, the second-year resident Bach was mentoring on the night shift."

"Really, why?"

"Oh please! She was the one working with him on the Williams case that night the kid died. Jackson and Bach are up to their usual tricks. The evil duo at work again."

Riley immediately thought of the prior residency director, Marcel, and how he'd been squeezed out by the same pair. How Jackson had envied him, hated him even, for being so admired by the residents and how Bach had undermined him at every turn. She felt a fury bubbling up inside her. "That's just plain wrong. I was one of Dr. Li's mentors when she was on the day shift. She's conscientious. And she did her best that night, from what I saw during the code."

"Well, apparently, she's disposable." Sonya made a face of disgust. "You know . . . to Bach, she's just another *Asian* woman. Perfect scapegoat."

"Okay, we agree, the guy's a first-class asshole—but you're saying he's a racist too?"

"Oh come on!" Sonya rolled her eyes, dragging her words out. "You don't think that's why he set Dr. Benoit up?"

"Marcel?" Riley stepped closer, reaching for Sonya's hand. "What are you talking about?"

"Bach used to say Dr. Benoit needed to know his limitations here. That he should go back to Haiti where his people could use someone like him. It used to make me *sick* to hear him talk like that," she said, her eyes finding the floor. "I told Dr. Jackson about it at the time, and not just me. The nurses on night shift had a meeting with him and administration about Bach's racist comments and his behavior in general." Sonya's face grew dark. "But obviously nothing ever came of it. And when the fentanyl vials went missing that time, Bach was the first one to point a finger at Dr. Benoit."

Riley's mind flashed back to that night two years ago—the night the vials had been found in Marcel's locker. She still remembered her mentor trying to explain himself.

Sonya shook her head. "Carrie said she heard Bach directing security to search the men's locker room that evening. And poor Dr. Benoit, he was such a sweetheart. I remember him saying he'd never had a need to put a lock on his locker in all the time he'd been at City General." Sonya's jaw tightened. She leaned in, grasping Riley's wrist. "If Dr. Benoit had any shortcoming, it was that he failed to see the evil in that little fucker."

Riley hadn't known the details of how the drugs had been discovered in Marcel's belongings, but it should have been obvious to anyone who knew the man that the vials had been planted. The damage was done, though. The match had been lit, and Bach and Jackson fanned the flames. They'd always wanted to be rid of him. Shortly after Marcel's arrest, he was cleared of all charges, but the incident had no doubt been humiliating and dehumanizing. Riley believed it was what ultimately cost him his life. In the wake of that fiasco, when Jackson had reassigned the residents Marcel was mentoring to other faculty, the man had seemingly lost his spark. Two months later, he had the first stroke. A week after that, the second one ended him.

Sonya's voice brought Riley back. "As far as Dr. Li goes, I suppose she's plan B. Those cowards couldn't nail you for the Williams case, so I guess she's next in line. But you didn't hear it from me." The nurse snatched her hand away from Riley's then and headed down the hallway, a plastic trauma apron swinging from her clenched fist.

Riley stepped into a storage room in the back hallway and pulled the door closed. She opened her phone directory for the ER and searched for the list of second-year residents, scrolling down to Lilian Li's number and calling it. The call went unanswered. Riley hung up and tried again. After four rings, automated voicemail picked up. She left a message for Lilian to get back to her.

When Riley reached the library, Bach was sitting on the edge of the conference table, his bloodstained shoes resting on the plush cushion of a rolling chair, knees splayed. The midday sunlight streaming through the picture window revealed a jaundice-like hue to his complexion, making the health of his liver a question in her mind. And why was it that his hair was always hanging in his eyes? An involuntary shudder rippled through her. Coupled with the permanent smirk on the man's face, he had the look of a self-obsessed rock star. His elbow rested on his thigh, his hand poised just above his groin as if at any second, he might draw a six-shooter.

"We've got a little problem, Brighton." He shifted his hips back on the tabletop. Riley couldn't imagine who he meant by *we*.

"Really?" she said coolly, placing her cup of coffee on the bookshelf she was leaning on and crossing her arms over her chest.

"I'm not sure the news has trickled down to your little circle, but the department is set to receive a rather juicy endowment when the medical school gets renamed next week." He rubbed his hands together energetically. Riley felt herself recoiling.

She leaned back, picking absently at one of her fingernails. "You don't say."

"I can't figure you out, cupcake." He said this like it genuinely bothered him, his face contorting in irritation. "I used to think you were a simple do-gooder, obsessed with saving every piece-of-shit loser in the city, but now I see there's nothing altruistic about you at all."

Riley raised her brows coolly. "Why is that? Because I refuse to save you?" She laughed.

He seemed to ignore the taunt. Or perhaps he wasn't capable of deviating from the monologue he'd clearly mentally rehearsed for her. "Yeah, you have a real savior complex don't you, Brighton? Well, you're no savior—just a fucking control freak."

"What you think of me is none of my business, Bach," she snapped back, but in truth, that one had hit home.

"This is serious shit, Brighton. That crap you pulled at M and M was so transparent. Your negligence in the Williams case has put the department in serious jeopardy. If we lose any private funding, you might find yourself held personally responsible, and I don't have to tell you the city council is demanding heads roll." Riley stared back at him, her face giving nothing away. "You and that Li woman are going to cost us a fucking fortune over this lawsuit."

"By 'that Li woman,' I'm assuming you mean Dr. Li—the very capable and well-respected resident you were supposed to be mentoring that night?" Riley looked back at him, stone-faced and unblinking.

His expression was bordering on fury. She'd gotten to him. "That fat little piggie needs to go!" He curled his lips in disgust. "Anyone with more chins than a Chinese phone book and zero sense of humor is no loss for the department, believe me."

Riley felt her stomach turn. "I'm just wondering, Dr. Bach, if you have even a trace of self-awareness and if you take any responsibility at all for what went down that night." She gave him a cold, hard stare as she stepped forward. "I mean, I can still see you standing there with your thumb up your ass while the rest of us—including your *trainee*—tried like hell to resuscitate the kid."

He moved so quickly—all she saw was the blur of his white coat and the deep crimson of his face as he launched himself off the table. Riley's head banged hard on the bookshelves as he shoved her up against them; he held her close, his grasp tightening around her airway. "Listen, bitch," he snarled, "that's not what happened." He squeezed her throat tighter. "Do we understand each other?"

Before Riley could think twice, she was tucking her chin and flexing the muscles of her neck, just like she'd learned to do in martial arts as a kid. And then her knee was finding his groin. She slammed it into his crotch with all the pent-up fury she'd felt for him over the previous years. Instantly, he released her throat, doubling over at the waist. In a split second, her thigh jerked up, connecting with his solar plexus like a battering ram. He crumpled to the floor, spluttering and gasping for air.

His expression was that of a crazed maniac when he looked up again, eyes wide behind a veil of black hair and hands grasping at the legs of her scrubs.

She sprang out of his reach, dodging the chair that had rolled away from under his feet as he'd leaped off the table. Though his hands were no longer around her throat, she was fighting for air, her heart thumping wildly, her neck burning from the friction of his grasp.

He lurched back to his feet, drooling from the corners of his mouth, his lips glossing over with spittle. Riley couldn't help but think of a rabid beast when she saw the rage in his eyes.

"You're gonna regret that," he rasped. "Oh yes, you are—"

Riley reached for the mug of coffee she'd placed on the bookshelf, spun around, and threw it in his face. "And *that's* for Marcel, you racist psycho!" She spat the words. The man spluttered and gasped with fury, lunging for her again. This time, she hooked the chair she'd almost tripped over with her foot and shot it in his direction. It hit him in the midsection, throwing him off balance, sending him to the floor in a tangle.

Riley was at the door in a split second. She threw it open, launching herself into the hallway, right into a wall—a wall dressed in a long white lab coat.

"Jeez, you okay, Dr. Brighton?" the wall asked.

She looked up, the rage threatening to erupt from her throat as she choked her emotions back. "Doug . . . Dr. Hudson . . . Yes . . . Fine, I'm just fine," she replied breathlessly, slamming the door shut behind her. "But the library is closed, I'm afraid. Can you come back later?"

The intern gave her a puzzled look, making no move to leave.

She took his arm then, turning him. "There's just a little coffee spill that needs cleaning up. Twenty minutes or so and the janitor will be done."

"No problem, Dr. Brighton." He frowned, looking over his shoulder as she led him down the hallway.

Riley parted ways with Hudson near the locker rooms. She ran cold water in the bathroom sink, washed her face, and checked her neck for proof she'd just been mauled by a psychopath. The welts were already starting to fade as she snapped a picture with her phone. Then she headed for the back stairwell with her head down, blinking back the tears that threatened to spring from her eyes at any moment.

Bach had been accused of physical assault before. But of course, he'd been strategic in his attacks. He'd made sure there were never any witnesses. Riley knew her claim would be billed as a case of he said, she said. Even in the middle of the Me Too era, one needed more than allegations to make an accusation stick. It didn't help that everyone knew there was no love lost between the two of them. And everyone knew how effective Bach's campaign to rid the department of his enemies was. With Jackson always in his corner, there weren't many options.

She took the only logical course of action and made a beeline for Hilary Stephens's office in the administrative block of the hospital.

*　　*　　*

Five hours later, at the end of her shift, Riley headed back to Stephen's office just after the ER night shift came on at seven. The afternoon had been hectic, and she'd been busy with a long trauma case right up until Astrid had relieved her at shift change. She'd wanted to share what had happened earlier with Bach, but the department was too busy to justify taking the time to discuss a problem she was already addressing with the hospital administration. Riley hadn't even mentioned her altercation with Bach to Astrid; she would never have distracted her from patient care that way. Especially as Bach had kept his distance, staying on the other end of the ER. Their paths hadn't crossed for the remainder of the shift. She assumed he must have changed his scrubs and gone about his duties as usual. And maybe he was confident he was going to get away with the assault again. The way he always had.

When Riley let herself into Dr. Stephens's office, she found Lilian Li waiting for her with Stephens and Roger Harrison from the personnel department. The second-year resident stood, crossing the room to meet her. Her eyes and lips were red and swollen; she clutched a tissue in her hand as she wrapped her arms around Riley's shoulders. Riley hugged her back, casting Harrison a curious glance.

"Good that you could stay late," Riley said, addressing the administrators and trying to keep the vitriol out of her voice as she led Lilian back to the conference table. "We've all had a very long day."

"Or an interminable last two years," the resident muttered under her breath as she took her seat next to Riley.

"Dr. Li was just telling us about some of the interactions she'd had with Dr. Bach during her residency," Harrison said as he regarded Lilian, his voice thick with empathy in a way that exaggerated his mouth breathing.

"Let's be honest. These aren't the first complaints you've had about the man, are they?" Riley said, locking eyes with Stephens as she leaned her elbows on the table.

"That would be confidential information." Stephens raised her eyebrows. "But we would like to do what we can to set things right with Dr. Li and have her return to the residency." She paused and turned to Lilian, avoiding Riley's gaze. "Of course, we would have to involve Dr. Jackson in any decisions affecting the department," she explained, pressing the tips of her long fingers together into a rigid steeple.

"As I just told you, I've already been to Dr. Jackson about Dr. Bach's conduct on the night shift." Lilian sounded exactly as exhausted as she looked. She glanced briefly at Riley as if seeking confirmation before turning back to Stephens. "He's been so abusive for so long, even the nurses have given up trying to do something about him."

"I think we're past the point of expecting Dr. Jackson to intervene." Riley leaned forward, her face suddenly flushing with anger. "It's time for the police to be involved. Bach physically attacked me today. Do you not understand that? What will it take for you to *finally* address his behavior?"

Dr. Stephens kept her cool the way a chief of staff would, her words dashing any hope that Riley had her support. "I would urge you to reconsider your timing on this, Dr. Brighton."

Riley could see the wheels spinning. She knew *exactly* where Stephens's priorities lay, and that was on private funding for emergency department trainees and the pending increase from the endowment that had been augmenting the hospital's and medical school's resources for the last few years.

"Really? You think we should put things on hold until we have another incident like the one we had last month with the Williams boy or maybe like the one today?"

Stephens held a finger up to silence Riley. "I'm not conceding his culpability, Dr. Brighton. But he is human, and people make mistakes; I would think you'd understand that."

"Mistakes are one thing. We're not talking about mistakes. We're talking about a loose cannon here. Someone with a pathological level of dishonesty and manipulation to cover up incompetence and perhaps worse. In my eyes, it's clearly predatory. And as far as being *understanding* goes, why would you expect Dr. Li to bear the consequences her mentor should be taking for the Williams case?" Riley said, placing a hand on Lilian's shoulder. She was quiet for a moment, her other hand lifted, her fingertips running over her still-swollen neck. "On top of that, the fact that you are questioning my claim that he assaulted me today is, quite frankly, fucking hard to swallow."

The room fell silent. Harrison froze. He seemed to be holding his breath, his gaze resting on the center of the tabletop. The air felt stagnant, oppressive, as Riley waited for a response. Any response.

Stephens sat back in her chair, rubbing her chin with her thumb.

Riley's eyes turned to Harrison. Was the man ever going to speak up? It was obvious Bach was a liability. Surely Harrison was asking himself why Stephens should want to protect him and why Jackson seemed bent on helping her. Maybe he was thinking that an administrator's concern was the hospital's reputation above all else. The institution couldn't afford the bad press if Bach's behavior was exposed, and Jackson, for whatever reason, was an obstructionist when it came to Bach. Perhaps the man had been a force multiplier for him when it had come to getting rid of Marcel, Riley considered. And Bach had never dispelled the rumors in the department that his own family's fortune was the source of their anonymous funding. The possibility that it was would have made him invaluable in Jackson's eyes, and Riley now deduced that was what was corrupting Stephens too.

But what about Harrison? Why wasn't he taking a stand? Riley asked herself. She was growing frustrated with his silence. "Don't we have a duty to protect? Isn't it that simple? Where is your red line on this man's misconduct?"

"I'll remind you that it's *alleged* misconduct, at this point, Dr. Brighton," Stephens pushed back. The woman's words were like a cold draft down the back of Riley's neck. "I'd advise us all to take a deep breath—"

"And I'll remind *you*," Riley interrupted, "that the only reason this conduct is still 'alleged' is because you haven't previously addressed it. A departmental investigation two years ago would no doubt have substantiated some very disturbing facts."

Harrison was nodding slowly now. Stephens shot him a sideways glance, shaking her head, but he failed to take the cue.

"You're referring to the fentanyl incident with Dr. Benoit?" he asked, his expression resigned. Stephens cleared her throat, her face hard as granite, but this time Harrison outright ignored her.

"I am." Riley's eyes shifted back to Stephens. "And it's appalling that that situation was so poorly handled. If a physical assault on me is not grounds enough for you to act, be warned, it will be a cold day in hell before I allow Bach to get away with another hit job on any of my colleagues." Riley rose from the table. "Fortunately, the Williams debacle is already in the right hands, and I can only hope justice is served. As far as Bach's conduct with his colleagues here on campus goes, you have until tomorrow morning to open an investigation into the allegations against him." Riley knew the nurses on the night shift and Astrid would be only too glad to provide plenty of input on Bach's abusive behavior should they be interviewed.

Riley pushed her chair back under the table. "Let me make myself perfectly clear. This is the order of business. Number one: Bach is placed on administrative leave immediately, pending an investigation. Number two: first thing in the morning the two of you convene a meeting with the offgoing night nurses. After that we tally who will press charges against Bach. I'll be the first person on that list." She shot Stephens a sharp glance. "We all know you can move expeditiously when the mood strikes." The woman remained stone-faced, though Riley thought the color had drained slightly from her cheeks. She let the words sink in before adding, "I'll be contacting the *LA Times* by noon tomorrow if you haven't acted. And I can assure you, the fallout from going public about Bach's verbal and physical assaults on our patients and his colleagues will be far more devastating than a simple investigation."

Stephens and Harrison made no move when Riley and Lilian headed for the door.

Riley parted ways with Lilian in the lobby, where the resident's husband had been waiting for her, and headed back through the ER. She changed into her leathers in the locker room and exited through the employee entrance, making her way toward the parking garage. Her head was racing, her body charged with adrenalin. She breathed in the cool evening air, trying to settle herself. She checked her text and phone messages as she approached her motorcycle, disappointed to find there was still no word from Cedrick or Bella. She thought about calling Joe, filling him in on her altercation with Bach, but worried she'd just upset him, especially as she was still so emotional about the incident herself. Joe knew how ruthless Bach could be. Everyone on campus did. The man's temper tantrums were a regular topic of discussion at the Friday night resident and faculty gatherings. Riley started to imagine how Bach might retaliate when he heard she was preparing to press charges and how Jackson would take the news. She'd have to brace herself for the backlash.

As she approached her motorcycle, Riley slid her phone into the top pocket of her jacket and zipped it closed. She slipped her ID off from around her neck, wrapped her braid around her collar, and reached for her helmet on the back of her bike.

The sudden loud revving of a motor behind her filled her ears like the roar of a jet engine, and she turned to see what was happening—

But it was too late.

The shriek of squealing tires was the last thing she heard as the whole world turned upside down, and her body rolled like a rag doll over skin-shredding concrete. Everything was a blur of color, bright lights, and motion.

And then it all went dark.

CHAPTER THIRTY

Riley was in a cave. A deep, black crevasse that pulsated around her like the belly of a giant prehistoric monster that had swallowed her whole. Far off in the distance, she could hear a faint ringing, which seemed to build slowly until it hummed like a brass gong. A metallic, earthy scent that was vaguely familiar filled her nostrils. She struggled to lift her head, but she found it heavy as an anvil.

Something pressed against her cheek, cold and grainy. It bit into her flesh, as if someone had dragged her face down through gravel. An ache began to pulse in her temples, and a wave of nausea swept over her like a riptide. Now, only the soft rasping of her own breath filled her ears as she lay crumpled in the darkness.

Her fingers were numb. Her shoulders burned with the strain of tension, as if she'd just finished a brutal workout. Only when she tried to reach for the ache in her head did she realize her hands were tied behind her back. She struggled to open her eyelids then, lifting her brows frantically, but there was only the blackness and the tug of something binding. Something was wrapped over her face.

A blindfold.

And with that realization, Riley was wide awake. Fully alert. Her senses suddenly laser focused. Her heart raced, nostrils flaring greedily as she gasped for air. She swallowed hard and tried to slow things down as she knew she must to reduce her consumption of oxygen.

She wasn't sure if minutes or hours had passed since she'd headed to the parking garage after her meeting with the administrators and Lilian Li.

She was cold, despite being dressed in her full set of leathers. She tried moving her legs, relieved to find they seemed to be functioning. She pulled her knees underneath herself and attempted to roll onto her side. The lancing pain in her ribs was enough to make her cry out, but she quickly realized she couldn't. Her mouth had been taped shut.

Over the following minutes, Riley wiggled her way to a sitting position, taking time to overcome the waves of nausea and vertigo that followed. Then she stretched her legs out in front of her, probing her surroundings with her feet in search of a solid surface, which she finally found.

Slowly, she pivoted on her sit bones and scooted herself over toward the object until she was propped in a sitting position against it. Her hands gradually began to regain their feeling as she explored the cold surface with her fingertips. She could feel the distinct outlines of bricks and mortar.

Riley sat propped up against the wall for what seemed an eternity, her hands balled into fists behind her in the darkness, fighting for breath until she thought she'd collapse from exhaustion or terror.

She was suddenly aware of how thirsty she was. Her throat burned like fire. As she tried swallowing, her ears popped, and then she was certain she could hear the faint, distant melody of horns, the rhythm punctuated by the occasional high note.

Mariachi music.

She was back in Ghost Town.

Possibilities about her exact location sprang to mind between the bouts of nausea. It was too quiet for a house. She heard no telltale hum from a refrigerator or sounds of water running through pipes or the distant drone of a TV. A deserted, boarded-up building, maybe. There were probably no basements this close to the ocean in Venice. Perhaps an old storage shed or a detached converted garage, like the one she'd seen behind the teen shelter in Santa Monica.

As she sat in the silence, Riley tried to reconstruct the events of the previous hours. She remembered entering the parking garage at work and tucking her phone into her top pocket—

The phone!

It was probably still in her jacket. She bent her head forward, craning her neck and trying to probe the zippered compartment below her collarbone with her chin. She could almost reach, but the attempt brought back the awful throbbing pain at the base of her skull and the ringing in her ears, like a distant fire alarm—relentless and grating. But she was able to feel the zipper on her chest pocket was closed; she was sure of it, which meant her phone was probably still on her.

In a moment, she realized that dropping her head had been a fatal mistake. Her nostrils filled suddenly with a warm fluid that trickled out, dripping steadily off her chin. She sat still, waiting for the flow to ebb, measuring her breath slowly through thick bubbles, trying not to panic at the prospect that, with her mouth taped closed, she was about to drown in her own blood. And then it occurred to her how many times a Band-Aid in the ER didn't stick when it was wet.

She wiggled her lips desperately, scrunching her face into exaggerated expressions under the tape securing her mouth until she felt the blood dripping from her nose seeping in around her lips. And she worked it and worked it, moving her face, prying her jaw frantically, until the fluid pooled inside the tape, and she was finally able to create a gap between her lips with her tongue. She gasped for air, filling her lungs and retching at the salty, metallic flow seeping into her mouth as the tape pulled away from her face.

Then she sat in the darkness, leaning against the wall, catching her breath, her mind racing. She needed to start planning her escape before another minute passed.

There would be only one chance. One opportunity to get it right. If her captor heard her, it would be all over. Her heart thumped loudly, in perfect synchrony with the throbbing at the base of her skull. She hoped her assailant was somewhere out of earshot or maybe asleep. It was probably late enough for that. She'd listened intently for so long, and there had been no sign of any activity in her immediate surroundings.

Where was he?

What she did next would determine whether she made it out of this place alive. There was only one option, and it didn't involve screaming for help. That was far too risky.

She swallowed the razor blades in the back of her throat, clearing her mind, honing her focus as if her life depended on it. Because she knew now that it did.

Her voice didn't sound like her own when she heard it, but it was clear and more forceful than she'd imagined possible.

"Hey, Siri, call nine-one-one on speaker mode!"

CHAPTER THIRTY-ONE

The distant sounds of mariachi music had faded into silence hours ago. Riley slumped against the cold wall, her numb hands clenched behind her back, listening to the sound of her own breath like the north wind raking through a field of dry wheat.

Her nose had finally stopped bleeding, but she still found it hard to breathe. The muscles between her ribs spasmed viciously with every movement. She considered how much effort it would take to lie down again. And if she did, would that be the end of her? Her head throbbed less if she was upright, and the waves of nausea peaked more slowly now.

The battery on her phone must have finally given up the ghost, she realized.

The last thing she'd heard from the emergency operator was "Ma'am, are you still there? Ma'am, stay with me. Ma'am?"

Riley had feared there was a risk her captor might hear the conversation on the line. With her hands tied, she had no way of turning the volume down or taking the phone off speaker mode without ending the call. If she could just keep the line open, maybe the PD could track her location. Was that how it worked? She was having a hard time making sense of it all.

"Shhh," Riley had responded, "Shhh." She wondered if that would be the last thing she'd ever say to anyone.

She remembered the look of Clive's battered face that day she'd seen him in the morgue, and she imagined what other noises she might utter when her abductor returned. Sounds that could be drawn out of her. That thought sent a cold wave down her spine.

Then she thought of Sofia and of how terrorized she must have been and of what she'd suffered in her last hours of consciousness. Now Riley felt the long, slow journey of a tear that left the corner of her eye, slithering down through a tiny gap in her blindfold, through the patches of dried blood on her face and along the edge of her nose. *Pull it together, Brighton*, she told herself, bending her knees and digging the heels of her boots into the concrete under her, trying to relieve the pressure that had been building in her lower back.

And she waited in the silence, in the darkness.

And for someone who was used to being in control, especially in the most uncertain moments, it was excruciating. It was almost impossible to sit and wait, rather than doing something, *anything*, to improve her situation. But her legs felt like blocks of granite, and the blackness seemed to whirl around her as if she were circling a giant drain.

How much blood had she lost from her head wound?

"Scalp lacerations bleed like stink," she'd told Hudson only last week.

Riley pressed her head gently against the wall, putting a little pressure on the spot that hurt like hell to stem the flow of blood she'd felt trickling down the back of her neck.

In the darkness, she thought about how uncomplicated her life had been only a month ago. And how it seemed she'd brought so much torment, regret, and despair on herself now. So much had changed since the morning she'd stopped to help the victim on the freeway. She could practically hear Bach saying, "It's the Good Samaritan's curse, Brighton: no good deed goes unpunished."

She felt a momentary surge of resentment, but like anger, resentment was so limiting, so blinding. She made a conscious effort to switch from emotion to reasoning, just like Jackson had always chided. That's where her strength had always been. In logic. Even in her current state, there was so much she wanted clarity on, so much to sort through. Bella had been on her mind since she'd disappeared in Venice. Riley imagined she was somehow planning to take El Diablo's trafficking operation down. Maybe with the help of some of his victims or through a rival gang.

Funny, Riley realized. She still thought of Bella as Themis. The girl had seemed to fit the archetype Riley had discovered during an internet search for the character from Greek mythology. The goddess of good counsel and the personification of justice. Riley pictured the images she'd come across. The blindfolded woman in a long robe, holding the scales of justice above her head. And it was the significance of those images that sat with her now.

Was that why El Diablo was blindfolding his victims? Was he using the symbol to call out Themis—Bella—who'd been seeking to take him down since her earlier days in Venice? Maybe it wasn't such a crazy idea that metaphors would be the language of a psychopath, she thought. So then, why the helmet for Clive as opposed to the blindfold? Because the helmet was a sign of a warrior? The sign of a man? Was he so angry at Clive for transitioning? She thought about the other victims. Hadn't Miguel told her in his letter that El Diablo had *torched* one of his girlfriends and her child because she'd *burned his stash* or something along those lines?

And then little Leroy Williams came to mind. Was that what had happened to him and his mother? Had they been El Diablo's victims too? Paula, Shorty's wife, had warned Riley to steer clear of the devil the day they'd met outside the medical examiner's office. That was the word she'd used—*devil*—but she could have meant El Diablo. She'd said the devil had taken her sister, and now, little Leroy was gone too. Suddenly, Riley was overcome with rage. It bubbled up in her chest like hot lava. She gritted her teeth, stifling the impulse to scream at the top of her lungs. To let the fury out. What the fuck was wrong with this monster? *What the absolute fuck!*

In the minutes that followed, Riley sobbed out her fury. When she finally stopped, she felt cold, hard reasoning taking its place. She was going to get this guy. No matter what it took, she'd see to it that he paid for what he'd done to that innocent little boy, to all his victims. The ones she knew about and the ones she'd never heard of.

She found herself trying to deconstruct him, using reason, making him fallible. She'd replace the dread she'd felt only minutes ago with insight. With a plan. Could she do that? Or would the panic return the moment the monster showed himself? She tried to picture him. Was he a gaunt wraith, hollowed out by the shadow of his own evil, trafficking in the misery and torture of young girls? Or was he a fat-cat mobster, with an army of foot soldiers, perversely erudite in the use of allegories and dabbling in particularly sadistic professional hits? Whoever he was, *whatever* he was, Riley wasn't about to give him the satisfaction of terrorizing her too. Handing over that sort of power to pure evil was antithetical to everything she believed.

She'd fought tougher battles at work, she told herself now. That's what she did every day. She looked death in the face.

For some reason, the memory of the first time she'd lost a patient during her training came to mind. Bach had been merciless that evening. "A bit on the emotional side tonight are we, Brighton? Maybe you'd be better off in pediatrics where the patients are a little less . . . How shall I put it? Discerning?" he'd jabbed when she'd just called off the code blue on an elderly cardiac arrest patient. But Marcel had done his best to help her put the incident into perspective. And now, her mentor was leaning on the wall next to her in the ambulance bay, where she'd sought escape after leaving her first failed resuscitation as a resident.

"Every negative experience we have is instructive, Brighton. That is, if you'll let it be."

She'd looked over at him. "What should I have done differently?"

"You'll never know," he'd said, dropping his gaze. "See, that's how it works. You do the best you can, you do all the right things, and shit happens anyway."

"What's the point then? How do I learn anything from that?" she'd snapped.

"The point is that you realize you are merely an instrument in this whole messy symphony of life. And that means you don't get to direct the outcome. That's the lesson, Brighton. Success comes largely from knowing the limitations of your role in any given situation."

That was some of the best advice Marcel had ever offered her. If only she'd taken it these last few weeks. How much trouble she might have saved herself.

Suddenly, she heard Javier's words again: "Clive was like you, lady. He wanted to fix everything."

"I'm going to ask you to stay in your own lane, Dr. Brighton." Now it was Detective Roberts's voice flooding into her mind. Hadn't Joe also tried to warn her of the danger she was straying into? So many times. God, even Bach could see she was putting every sad case she came across ahead of her own interests. And now, it seemed, even her own life. If she didn't make it out of this situation, what would that do to her mother? *A mother never stops worrying.* Hadn't the woman suffered enough? She'd lost so much already.

A groan of exasperation escaped her, the pain in her ribs almost bringing her to tears again. But that helped her stay conscious, she told herself. Though it seemed now she lacked the strength to sit upright. Her shoulders were fatigued, and her head felt so heavy. In the minutes that followed, her spine gradually gave way under the weight of it. She crumpled, slipping down the wall until she found herself curling into a ball. She wondered if this was her end. If this is how she'd leave the world: slowly bleeding to death on a cold concrete floor, face plastered in blood and a band of duct tape dangling from her chin. Would they find her dead smartphone and shake their heads, lamenting that she hadn't taken the time to charge it fully? Suddenly, she realized her survival was impossible. How the hell did she think she had the strength to stay conscious, let alone plan to take down a cold-blooded psychopath?

After some time, her teeth began to chatter, her body shaking violently. It must have been the witching hour. That's what they called it on the night shift—that time around four in the morning when it was most difficult to stay awake, when the body's temperature plummeted to its lowest in the daily cycle. She considered the prospect that she was in shock rather than just very, very cold.

It would be daylight in no time. If she was going to meet the same fate as the others, her captor would be loading her up soon, transporting her to the freeway, just as the Friday morning rush hour got underway. She tried wiggling her wrists loose, but that seemed futile. By this point, she was too weak to resist any assault, even if her hands were free.

Finally, the shivering subsided. It had kept her tethered to her body, and now she bargained with herself just to stay awake as she lay curled on the ground. But that was proving difficult. In the cold stillness, her mind was clouding over again, like a damp fog seeping in at the coastline before dawn, muting the clarity of sound and obscuring detail.

She sank into the growing stillness, and after a while, it seemed somehow soothing.

And then she was drifting, floating outside herself. And somewhere deep in the silence, a distant, muted voice was prodding her to stay vigilant, nagging at her not to let go, pleading with her to stay awake. The sound persisted; it chipped away at her consciousness, penetrating the thickness wrapping around her, and finally, she recognized it as the distant barking of a dog. The world was waking up. El Diablo would be coming for her soon.

And she was right.

Only minutes later, a soft scratching noise woke her. Beach sand grinding under someone's shoes on concrete. It was the same sound her own boots had made the night she'd headed out toward the Venice fishing pier from the boardwalk. And now she was awake, holding her breath. Listening. Then a gentle creaking sound followed, like a rusty weather vane turning in the wind before a storm. Perhaps a door opening. Yes, an open door because now a chilly, briny draft seeped in around her, and she felt her body bracing.

Someone was breathing hard, a ragged harried breath, and then a pause. Silence. And she knew he was watching her, standing only a few feet away. The seconds ticked by with the pounding of her heart filling her ears. She felt her panic growing, the scream trapped in her throat threatening to betray her at any moment.

The door creaked again, and the footsteps drew slowly closer. And with that, Riley felt the remnants of any strength she had left in her body suddenly drain out of her.

"Riley?" she heard someone whisper.

She tried to pretend she was still unconscious, but an involuntary sob escaped her throat, giving her away. She willed herself to draw her legs up and curl into a tighter ball, but that would take strength, and she had none of that.

"Holy shit, it *is* you!"

Riley heard the voice break. Then she felt a hand on her back—someone was kneeling next to her, their breathing almost as frantic as her own. She let out a gasp as she felt fingers on her face and caught a glimpse of light that shocked her eyes when her blindfold was ripped off.

Except for a thin blade of illumination coming from a tiny penlight resting on the concrete floor, it was pitch black. As Riley blinked her eyes, trying to adjust her vision, the outline of the figure kneeling beside her, a tangle of long blonde dreadlocks falling over the shoulders, wavered into view.

"Bella?" Riley whimpered. "Oh, Bella, thank God!"

"Shhh," Bella whispered. "I think he's awake now. There are lights on in the main house."

Bella reached into her jeans and wrestled something out of a pocket that she used to saw through the restraints binding Riley's wrists. As Riley's arms broke free, the pain surged in her shoulders, and she bit down on her tongue, stifling a cry. Seconds later, the agony surged as the circulation finally returned. She curled and flexed her fingers, shaking her hands, willing them to wake up.

Her eyes swept over her immediate surroundings as her vision adjusted. She was in a garage, directly opposite a small doorway, wedged between a brick wall and a dark-colored Sprinter van.

"Do you think you can stand?" The panic in Bella's voice suddenly erased any comfort Riley had felt on seeing the girl.

"I'm not sure," Riley whispered. "I think I've lost a lot of blood."

Bella picked up the penlight and swept its pale beam around the floor where Riley had spent the night. Her voice betrayed her horror. "Oh God," she gasped. "Maybe not a good idea for you to get up just yet."

Suddenly, Riley heard the same sound that had caught her attention earlier. Footsteps grinding over beach sand on concrete.

At once, Bella flipped her penlight off.

Riley's eyes darted to the doorway over the girl's shoulder, just as the door swung open.

And there he was, his hulking form filling the frame, his outline silhouetted by a dim light coming from behind him. His face was a grotesque mosaic of shadows. Deep crevasses filled the space where his eyes should have been, leaving him with the appearance of a vacant skull. His bald head was smooth and threateningly large, just like the Jaded Justice emblem.

Bella was getting to her feet now, but she still had her back to the door. Riley tried to call out a warning, but her throat had pinched itself closed. The man would be on her in a second. Bella was so small; he'd crush her with a single blow.

And then the girl turned to face him. She stood without flinching. *Jesus.* Holly had been right—Bella was absolutely fearless. And then, in a split second, the man rushed at her, her body completely swallowed by the darkness his shadow cast. Riley's hands swept the concrete floor, desperately searching for the instrument Bella had used to cut her loose. One strategically placed blow with the blade and she could save them both. She groped the sticky, blood-slick surface of the concrete floor, her hands searching wildly until they came to rest on the knife's sharp edge. She tried to pick it up, but her fingers were useless tentacles of jelly, her grasp too weak to close around the instrument. The cry that left her throat surprised even her. It was the sound of anguish, of horror that Bella too would now be a victim—and all because the girl had tried to save her.

The man was on them. And now, inexplicably, Bella was turning her penlight on again. Riley could see the outline of his enormous form; he was kneeling at her side, thrusting his arms under her back and her legs. Lifting her as if she were weightless. And the murderous pain in her ribs snatched her breath away, crushing any hope she'd make it out of the situation alive.

And then the darkness returned.

Riley was back in the deep crevasse where she had found herself earlier. And through the fog of fading consciousness, in the cold void of predawn, she could hear a dog barking its warning again. And then a muted cry, thick and distant. And now a sound she struggled to identify. A sound like waves slapping under her surfboard. A commotion she would never have imagined was the stampede of heavy boots on concrete.

Riley wondered how it was that she now found herself out on the swells, her surfboard under her belly, the waves lifting and tossing her, threatening to shake her loose. She tried to tighten her grip on her board, to stop herself from slipping under the water. And strangely, in the distance, far away, over the thundering crash of the waves, she heard someone calling.

"Police! Police!"

She couldn't hold on a minute longer. Her fingers finally gave way with exhaustion and the board slipped suddenly out of her grasp.

And now, she felt herself on her back, drifting, falling weightlessly . . . sinking deeper and deeper down to the very bottom of a dark ocean.

CHAPTER THIRTY-TWO

Riley thought she was dreaming.

She could hear the distant wail of a siren. Flashes of red light shivered through the tears clouding out her vision and webbing her eyelashes. She could feel herself bouncing gently, rolling, as she lay strapped to a long, stiff backboard.

The plastic mask secured to her face flooded her with cool, fresh oxygen. She drew in long, slow breaths and closed her eyes again. It all seemed so clear now, why the black pickup truck had been spotted at two of the murder scenes shortly after the crimes. How she could have been so clueless baffled her. She'd been thrown off by the Jaded Justice decal on the window and perhaps by her own preconceptions. It was so obvious now, she wondered why she'd never considered the possibility before that the bald man in the black pickup had been an undercover police officer—a covert operative. And that, ironically, he would be the one to finally save her from the nightmare he'd warned her to steer clear of from the very beginning.

The first time Riley had seen him that morning on the freeway when she'd come across Clive's body, he'd operated like an off-duty first responder, taking charge of the scene and ushering her out of the road. Those had not been the actions of a cold-blooded killer. And when she'd discovered him parked outside her home that night, he'd been surveilling her, not stalking her. Clearly, Cedrick and Bella had not known his true role at that point either—that was why they had alerted the LAPD about his presence and scared him off. But at some juncture after that, Detective Roberts and Cedrick must have been clued in to the man's true identity. That seemed like the best explanation for why Roberts had never offered Riley a lineup or mugshot to ID the man. Riley was sure now that was why Cedrick had warned them all to steer clear of the pickup truck guy, though he'd never offered an explanation for his caution. And after that, when Bella was back in Venice, the opportunity to work with the same man had presented itself somehow. Riley was certain the girl had purposely sought him out with the aim of helping him infiltrate El Diablo's operation. And now Riley remembered the day she'd seen the guy following Holly and Eli on that afternoon when she'd caught them moving Lexi's files to their storage shed and how, the very next morning, Holly had been hit with a search warrant.

Even Javier's involvement with him now seemed to make sense. They had been working on the murder case of his little sister, Rosaria, together. It all added up. It was ironic how it seemed so clear now, from her current vantage point: half conscious, concussed, and in shock in the back of an ambulance.

CHAPTER THIRTY-THREE

The soft beeping of a pulse oximeter drew Riley out of a deep sleep like some sort of mechanical reverse hypnosis. She tried to open her eyes but could only manage to squint. Her left eye was nearly swollen shut.

Hudson was sitting at her bedside, tall as a marble obelisk in his long, white lab coat. She noticed his eyes were closed behind the rectangular frames of his glasses, his head craned back over the top of the recliner. How long had he been there? How many hours had she been asleep?

A shadow fell across Riley's face as she turned her head gingerly. Joe, sitting on the windowsill, came slowly into focus. His gaze locked on her. He was on his feet in an instant, standing at her side, placing a hand on her bandaged wrist.

"You're one lucky lady." His voice broke in a way that betrayed the hours he'd sat there in silence at her bedside, waiting for her to wake. Riley felt like she was in a tunnel; the world seemed to hum around her, threatening to pull her deeper into the vacuum again. She struggled to remain lucid. "Astrid was still on duty when the ambulance brought you in." Joe gave her arm a gentle squeeze. "So you got the best care possible. Twenty-four stitches in the back of your scalp, but at least your head CT scan was negative."

"Shit" was all Riley could manage. Her mouth was dry, though she could still taste blood.

"Well, yes, you do look like shit; that's true. But luckily, it's temporary." Joe tried to smile but fell short. Riley's eyes threatened to fill with tears at the look of him.

"Sorry, Joe." This time, she heard her own voice break. She let her gaze sweep over the room. She was in the ICU at City General. Did she need to be, or was everyone overreacting just because it was her? "All my teeth?" she rasped. "I still have them?" She tried to smile.

"Most of them." Joe swallowed a chuckle of relief as he wiped his eyes with his sleeve.

Hudson woke up then. The intern blushed three shades of red as he grasped the arms of the recliner and sat bolt upright. "It's okay for me to be here, isn't it, Dr. Brighton? Dr. Wolf said I should stay—"

"Sure," Riley croaked. "She buy you breakfast?"

The intern's hand dropped to his lab coat pocket; he pulled out half a breakfast burrito wrapped in foil and held it up in answer. "She never misses the morning food truck—that's why all the trainees love working with her." He grinned. "She even bought one for the police officer on duty in the hallway."

He tilted his head toward the door of Riley's room. She tried to follow his gaze, but the thick, soft cervical collar around her neck made that impossible, and besides, the pain flooded back into her head whenever she moved. She closed her eyes and swallowed hard, reached for the bed control, and slowly raised the head to an angle that allowed her to feel less like a specimen in Joe's lab and more like a participant in the conversation.

Joe pulled up a rolling stool from the foot of the bed. "I called your mom. Holly picked her up half an hour ago. They'll be here soon."

"You're famous. You're on every news channel!" Astrid boomed with her breathy, larger-than-life presence as she entered carrying a tray full of coffee cups. Hudson jumped to his feet to relieve her, setting the tray on the rolling stand next to Riley's bed. "Jeepers, you've got one hell of a shiner there." She bent over Riley. "You'll be happy to know," Astrid announced, dropping herself into the recliner formerly occupied by Hudson, "that you're going to live, and, more importantly, Krista Lim from trauma and I closed your scalp wounds without having to shave your beautiful locks. You're welcome very much."

"Show-off." Riley offered something between a smile and a grimace.

"Well, I have to up my game, you know, because, as of Monday, Jackson has made me the acting residency director." Astrid grinned. The smile left her face almost as quickly as it had appeared. "But to be honest, I think that jerk is just using me. He hasn't committed to giving me the position full time. Bach may be reinstated if he gets his way. You didn't hear it from me," Astrid leaned in, dropping her voice to a whisper, "but rumor has it our little friend was in rehab for a fentanyl addiction all those weeks he was AWOL."

"Not long enough." Riley held up a bandaged hand to shield the bright light of midmorning that stabbed at her eyes through the enormous window next to her bed. "Congrats," she managed, remembering Astrid had met with Jackson last week. She wanted to know more. And she wanted to fill Astrid in on the altercation she'd had with Bach the day before and the pending investigation into his conduct after she'd met with Stephens and Harrison, but the room was spinning, and her eyelids felt as if they'd been fitted with lead weights.

"I'm surprised you were even aware," Wolf added, sarcastically. "It seems you've been quite busy, living a double life—"

"We'll talk about that in a couple of weeks," Joe interrupted as he got to his feet and pulled the window shade down to shield Riley's eyes. "When the dust settles, you can buy us all a beer and fill us in."

"Deal," Riley mumbled, before her eyes closed again.

*　　*　　*

Joe had left for his office hours before, promising to return in the evening after Riley had had some rest. But there had been an endless stream of visitors between Riley's medical evaluations and a second trip to the CT scanner. In the scheme of things, Riley had come out of the ordeal better off than anyone could have hoped. She had a mild separation of the shoulder, two broken ribs, and a concussion. Krista and a colleague from neurosurgery had visited too and given the green light for Riley to be discharged from the hospital on the following morning if she remained stable.

Holly had spent most of the day at Riley's bedside with Riley's mother. They had left only moments before to beat the rush-hour traffic out of the city and promised to return first thing in the morning. Bella had called earlier; she had Riley's house keys. She'd spent the day with Indio and Artemis at Riley's bungalow and was coordinating with Holly and Joe to take shifts staying with Riley at the hospital until her discharge.

Even Sonya from the ER had popped in during her afternoon break, delivering a cup of Riley's favorite hazelnut coffee, which, despite persistent nausea, Riley had managed to keep down. She'd also told Riley that Bach had been seen being escorted out of the department by LAPD and an administrator first thing in the morning, and Jackson, much to his distaste, had been forced to cover his shift. The nurse had left Riley's bedside only moments before Detective Roberts showed up.

"I won't tell you how lucky you are, Dr. Brighton; I suspect you already know that." The detective leaned back on the windowsill next to Riley's bed. "If it wasn't for the medical examiner's office sending me some autopsy reports yesterday, I think we'd have been less prepared for what happened last night." Riley looked up at her, nodding silently, choosing not to acknowledge what she knew about the autopsy reports. Roberts seemed so intent on filling in the gaps herself. "It didn't hurt either that multiple agencies got involved in this case after we got the call from your colleague."

"Colleague? What do you mean?"

"One of the hospital administrators, Harrison somebody or other, heading home after a late meeting, found your backpack and ID next to a downed motorcycle on the floor of the parking garage. He called it in to the LAPD as a suspicious incident. Campus security worked with the PD in checking cameras in the area for traffic in and out of the garage. A Sprinter van with plates matching those of a suspicious vehicle spotted at the Biltmore on the day Fredrick Draper was murdered was later identified. And then, of course, when your nine-one-one call went through, all the pieces fell into place."

"Just crazy," Riley mumbled. "How's my bike?"

"Pretty smashed up, I'm afraid. I think it took the brunt of the attack. But that probably saved your life."

"I might need you to share that detail with my friend Joe," Riley said, the irony heavy in her voice. She was quiet for a moment. Her eyes returned to the TV mounted across from her bed, where the muted afternoon news broadcast was airing.

"I think I understand his obsession with the blindfolds." Riley shifted herself, splinting her ribs with a bandaged hand, to face the detective, but before Roberts could respond, she added, "But why push the victims into traffic? What a bizarre way to commit murder—"

"Psychopaths often do things for reasons only they understand," Bella interrupted, stepping into the room with a bunch of daisies wrapped in cellophane and tied with a yellow bow. The girl set the flowers on the counter by the sink and took a seat in the recliner next to Riley. She nodded coolly in Detective Roberts's direction, making a point of holding her gaze. "But in this case, I have a feeling I know what El Diablo's motivation was for the way he chose to kill his victims—"

"I think I have at least some of it figured out," Riley interrupted. "The blindfolds on the victims were meant as a symbolic warning to you—a way of calling out Themis. Blind justice, right?"

"I finally realized that," Bella said, resting her chin on her hands, which were wrapped over the side rail of Riley's bed. "I'd been a thorn in his side for years. I bet this was nothing but a sick game for him—one in which I had to decipher his metaphors. The MO of the killings was also meant to be figurative and particularly twisted." She sighed, and Riley could see how exhausted the girl was.

She looked like she'd lost weight and aged five years since the day Riley had dropped her and Indio off near the teen shelter. "Think about it," she said, staring at Riley, waiting for the penny to drop. "My investigation was threatening his trafficking operation. Get it? *Trafficking.* So he literally called me out by subjecting the victims to traffic."

Detective Roberts, sitting on the windowsill, stopped swinging her feet, her face contorted in revulsion. "Lordy, that's crazy, and yes, very twisted."

"Yeah, it's probably best that I spare Riley some of the other details about this guy's operation. I have quite a bit that may be of interest to you," Bella said, locking eyes with the detective. "Some of it will have to be off the record, you understand." Bella smiled impishly before adding, "And naturally, my memory for detail will improve once I hear that any charges my friend Holly might have been facing are dropped."

Roberts rolled her eyes, but it was clear Bella had the upper hand. "We'll chat later," the detective said, her voice low and commanding, as if she were wrestling for just a little power in the discourse.

Riley turned her gaze from the dripping IV above her head to the muted TV on the wall again and followed along with the closed captions on the news broadcast of a local channel. Diego Enrique Herrera, also known as El Diablo de Pueblo Fantasma, the Devil of Ghost Town, was now in custody along with several other gang members. The SWAT team's raid on his property that morning had resulted in the rescue of two underaged girls from his residence next to the garage where Riley had been found by Bella and the undercover officer.

Arraignments were underway, and it sounded like they were numerous.

Riley closed her eyes, put a hand over her ribs, and breathed a deep sigh of relief.

CHAPTER THIRTY-FOUR

The parquet floor of the university's massive dining hall was so polished, it reflected the brilliant lights of the chandeliers on the vaulted ceiling overhead in Steward Hall. Riley lifted her champagne glass from the white linen tabletop to toast the end of the keynote speaker's presentation, unable to contain the smile spreading over her face as the audience applauded.

Joe sat to her right, steeped refreshingly in Old Spice, his hazel eyes sparkling in pure, authentic joy. Even Astrid had pointed out to Riley how well he'd cleaned up. The manbun, the tailored suit. The white flash of his smile and those long, thick eyelashes.

Hudson was seated on Riley's left, next to Sonya and Wolf, and to Astrid's right sat Eli and then Holly in a stunning crimson satin pantsuit. She'd been grinning from ear to ear all evening, no doubt as a result of hearing that Riley had successfully secured a new and entirely legal source of funding for the youth shelter in Santa Monica. As it turned out, Riley's aunt Naomi's new husband—number four—was an exceptionally generous philanthropist with a soft spot for homeless youth.

Jackson, looking more like a turkey vulture than ever in his black tuxedo, had been staring at Riley with curiosity all evening from across the hall. He'd run into her near the bar earlier.

"Funny seeing you here, Brighton," he'd said, looking down on her with his third cocktail in hand. "Not exactly your speed, is it?"

She'd replied with only "Beautiful evening for a medical school renaming, isn't it, Dr. Jackson?"

He had started to probe how she'd secured an invitation to such an auspicious event, but she'd cut him off mid-sentence and headed to the lady's room. She had to make sure her week-old black eye was still concealed by the makeup Sonya had helped her apply earlier and to adjust the sling supporting her left arm.

When Riley returned, Jackson was seated at his table across the hall from hers. He was accompanied by his wife, several administrators, and the dean of the medical school, who had just taken his seat after introducing Talia Altman, the previously anonymous and now primary benefactor of the medical school. Jackson stared at the woman with intrigue and a little trepidation as she took to the podium in the front of the hall. His face flushed slightly as he recalled their earlier interaction at the reception line.

He'd introduced himself, perhaps a little too earnestly, saying he was well acquainted with Tobias and explaining that even the best stumble occasionally, and he was sure Bach's difficulties would soon be behind him. The woman had seemed somewhat confused by his statement. And when he'd pressed on, she'd politely informed Jackson there must have been some kind of mistake, and not only was she not related to anyone named Tobias Bach, she'd never even heard of the man. But she too hoped his difficulties, whatever they were, were soon behind him.

Talia Altman lit up the room as she stood atop the stage. She was a stunningly beautiful silver-haired woman in a sage-colored silk gown and a simple strand of pearls that hung below her modest breast. There was something striking and somewhat familiar to more than a few members in the audience about the color of her violet eyes and the way they contrasted with the glow of her bronze complexion.

"I'm so very honored," Altman started as her gaze swept the room, "to make this endowment to the department of emergency medicine permanent and to have the university rename the medical school in honor of my own mother, the late Shira Altman. I'm very proud of the work you all do every day to help the citizens of our city and train the physicians and health-care providers of tomorrow. Our foundation is privileged to be part of that great work, and my sister Naomi and I thank you all from the bottom of our hearts for allowing us to be part of your future and vision for the school."

Altman's speech was followed by a standing ovation. Riley beamed with pride.

Hilary Stephens, in her black silk suit and office pumps, joined Talia at the microphone. "On behalf of City General and my colleagues from the university, I would like to express our deepest gratitude to Ms. Altman for the generosity of the Shira Altman Foundation." She raised her glass above her head, offering a satisfied smile few in the room had ever seen from her. "The beneficence and vision of this organization will catapult our medical school and training programs in emergency medicine to the next level."

The audience of roughly two hundred people—all dressed in their fine gowns and formal wear—applauded enthusiastically.

"Thank you for your kind words, Dr. Stephens." Altman smiled, taking the microphone at the podium again. Riley's eyes filled with tears of pride and appreciation at the significance of the announcement that would follow. "May I have your attention, please? I do have one final surprise before dinner is served," Altman announced smiling. "Please, take your seats." She waited until the crowd fell silent before she went on. "It is my great pleasure to announce an inaugural special award this year for medical interns in the name of a much-respected and sorely missed professor of emergency medicine."

Riley's gaze darted from the stage to Jackson, unable to deny herself the satisfaction of witnessing his reaction to the announcement. The man was rigid, and when the curiosity left his face, it was replaced with the dark and distinct glower of envy he'd always held for his late colleague.

"But it wouldn't be right for *me* to bestow this award," Talia Altman went on. "I think it only fitting that the person who made the nomination for this year's recipient should have that honor."

The crowd was silent. All eyes were on Altman as she leaned forward again, smiling into the microphone. "I'd like to ask my daughter, Dr. Riley Brighton, to the stage."

A murmur of surprise rippled through the crowd, and heads swiveled as Riley stood and approached the podium. The Shira Altman Foundation had been anonymously funding both the ER residency program and the medical school for over a decade. Now that Riley was through her training and securely in a faculty position she had earned through grit, determination, and long hours, there would be no grounds for anyone to suggest she had gained her status through nepotism. In both her mother's and her own eyes, the time was now appropriate to formally name the medical school for Riley's grandmother, Shira Altman.

Riley didn't bother to cast her gaze in the direction of Jackson or Stephens as she made her way to the podium and hugged her mother. She knew Astrid would be only too eager to fill her in on their expressions of disbelief and shock over dinner later.

"Thank you very much for this opportunity, Mum." Riley beamed as she faced the audience. "I'm delighted to be charged with this honor." She paused a moment, drawing a breath and steadying her voice. "Marcel Benoit was a brilliant physician with a kind heart and a gift for teaching. Not only was his mentorship instrumental in my successful navigation of a challenging residency in emergency medicine here at City General, but he also taught me some of life's more important lessons. Well, at least he tried to," she said with a chuckle.

Riley's eyes settled on Marcel's widow, Clarissa, seated at the head table with Riley's aunt and her cousins. At once, Clarissa rested an open palm to her chest in gratitude as a heartwarming smile spread over her face.

"Dr. Benoit was respected, loved, and appreciated by everyone—*everyone*—fortunate enough to have trained with him or worked by his side over the decades he dedicated to our profession and this institution." Riley's voice shook slightly, and she cleared her throat. "His constant commitment to both the homeless population of LA and his annual missions to hold free clinics in Haiti was an inspiration to all of us who had the privilege of accompanying him on those ventures. It is no stretch to say that losing him as our residency director was a devastating blow to the heart of our organization. On that note, I am very happy to have learned that my dear colleague, Astrid Wolf, has been recently appointed to the post of interim residency director in the department of emergency medicine." Riley motioned to Wolf, who bowed her head and grinned. The crowd applauded enthusiastically. Riley let her eyes sweep over the room while she waited for the audience to settle down. Then she added, "I know all my colleagues in our department join me in the hope that we see her permanently in that position. Dr. Wolf's expertise and dedication have more than earned her that honor."

Riley smiled broadly, indulging in another pointed look at Jackson. The man squirmed, his face flushing, as his wife gently placed a calming hand on his forearm.

Riley returned her attention to the audience. "It gives me great pleasure now to announce that as part of the endowments from my grandmother's foundation, an annual stipend for Intern of the Year will be made in Marcel's honor this year and in the years going forward." She turned her head in the direction of her table, her eyes lit in anticipation as she smiled broadly. "And it gives me even greater pleasure to announce that this year's recipient of the Marcel Benoit Intern of the Year award goes to an inquisitive, tenacious, and delightful young physician, Dr. Douglas Hudson."

The crowd responded with loud applause as Hudson, blushing wildly in a suit two inches too short, lumbered toward the stage on long legs. Riley loved to see he was grinning from ear to ear. Astrid whistled loudly from across the hall. Just past her shoulder, Riley could see Joe beaming with something deeper than admiration for her as he applauded. His face was glowing—and if she was honest, the sight stirred something in her.

After Hudson's brief but gracious acceptance speech, Riley left the stage as dinner was served. She made her way to the table where her aunt and cousins were seated with her mother and Clarissa Benoit. The woman rose to greet her. "You're a gem, Riley. Marcel would be indebted. He always spoke so highly of you. I'm deeply moved by your family's generosity."

"You're too kind, Clarissa. I only hope that others will benefit from his legacy. I want to see to it that every recipient of this award in the years to come knows something of Marcel's brilliance and humanity. Please keep in touch with my mum—we'd love to have you make the annual presentations in the future."

As Riley returned to her seat next to Joe, she could feel Jackson's eyes boring into her. And when she passed Stephens, she couldn't help but notice the flush-faced woman drop her gaze, too craven to meet Riley's eyes.

EPILOGUE

Riley paddled out past the break line. The water here was much warmer than she was accustomed to in California. She gripped the edges of her board, kicked her feet, and turned to face the shore, waiting patiently for the next swell.

On the beach, she spotted Joe with his milk bottle–white legs under a huge red umbrella. He put his book down and waved, giving her a smile she could appreciate even from her distant vantage point. She chuckled. She'd been right about him—he did have the patience of a saint. It was her third day of surfing in a row, and he hadn't once complained.

Costa Rica was every bit as beautiful as Joe had promised. Tomorrow, they would hike near his family's farm and perhaps take a rafting trip before planning the next excursion on their two-week adventure.

As the swell rose behind her, Riley slipped her knees onto the board, standing just in time to catch the crest of a three-footer. She floated along, feeling the power of the ocean driving her forward as she coasted to the shore. The sun was getting low behind her, spilling its warm December light onto the beach in a rosy, golden glow.

When her feet hit the sand, she snatched up her board and tucked it under her arm, reassured that her shoulder and ribs seemed now to be fully recovered.

So this was what prioritizing herself felt like.

It was good. For now, anyway.

www.ingramcontent.com/pod-product-compliance
Lightning Source LLC
Chambersburg PA
CBHW060231100726
47907CB00003B/594